He wa[nted]
to kiss ner...

His eyes moved slowly from her eyes to her mouth, and then back again. "You're about to buy yourself a passel of trouble, sitting here in the dark with a lonesome cowboy." His voice was low, and his lips were very close.

Anne trembled. There was no mistaking the intent of his gaze. Her own eyes did not waver from his. She said, "I'm not afraid of trouble."

His hand moved around to cradle her neck, tilting her face upward. His mouth covered hers. The sensation was paralyzing—heat and moisture and stunning, explosive waves. It was everything she imagined and more. His lips became more demanding, teasing a hunger from within her. The urgency left her blind, the need left her mindless. Josh. That was all she could think. *Josh...*

His breath was uneven, his eyes burning. His mouth left hers. His voice was but a husky whisper. "Tell me to stop now, Anne." And again, "Tell me."

But she didn't.

♥

Also by Leigh Bristol

Scarlet Sunrise
Amber Skies
Hearts of Fire*

Published by
WARNER BOOKS   **forthcoming*

Silver Twilight

Leigh Bristol

WARNER BOOKS

A Warner Communications Company

WARNER BOOKS EDITION

Cover illustration by Elaine Duillo

Warner Books, Inc.
666 Fifth Avenue
New York, N.Y. 10103

 A Warner Communications Company

Printed in the United States of America

First Printing: November, 1987

10 9 8 7 6 5 4 3 2 1

Chapter One

September 1899
Three Hills Ranch, Texas

The young cowboy was a piece of the past, as timeless as the plains he had crossed and the mountains he had left behind. He represented a peculiar paradox as he stood alone in the midst of an abandoned field of churned-up mud and slush. Overhead towered a rough, wooden derrick that supported the remains of a drill pipe and bit; and nearby, other remnants of modern technology—a broken steam boiler, a hydraulic pump, other bits of metal—were already beginning to rust from neglect. Neither the cowboy nor the graphic evidence of man's mistreatment of nature, which formed his backdrop, seemed to belong; they clashed with the still, pastoral scene that swept away on either side almost as much as they did with each other.

He knelt at the foot of the derrick and touched his fingers to the mud, and then, curiously, to his tongue. Immediately he turned his head and spat, cursing as he wiped his fingers on his jeans.

He looked around with contempt. This he had not expected to find, but very little surprised him anymore.

After a moment he turned his back and mounted his horse, riding away from the field and back through the woods. On a hill at the edge of the forest he drew up and leaned forward on the pommel of his saddle, tilting back his hat to survey the land that sprawled before him. A cool, green vista sloped downward from the hillside before rambling up toward a tangled bluff on the other side that was topped with oak and pine.

From his vantage point he could see a length of rusty wire fencing and smoke curling from a line shack and, far distant, the blades of an irrigation windmill turning lazily with an undetectable breeze. The lowing of cattle reached him faintly from the west, but he could not see the pasture. A dirt road bisected the landscape just below him like a scar. It was everything he had expected, and nothing like he had imagined.

He was twenty-two years old and sat the high-blooded roan with the confidence of a man accustomed to turning up the best in life. His clothes were dusty and travel-worn, and he carried with him all he laid claim to in the world: his guns, a Bible, and a change of clothes. He was tall and good looking and bore himself with an innate ease that translated into a sort of reckless charm, but there was none of the soft-faced, pampered swagger about him that was customary in other newcomers to Texas. Beneath the lazy eyes was a frame of coiled steel, the kind of hardness that could only be earned on long trails and rough rivers. He had ridden in from the west, and he had come a long way.

He had left home without destination or purpose, and as the months had passed, sometimes he had found it hard to remember why he had left at all. He was a man accustomed to being in control of his life, and without it for the first time, he felt a strange emptiness. He drifted because he had nothing better to do; he rode because he needed to keep moving. He had never intended to come to this place. Even until the very moment he crossed the border he did not understand why he was doing it. It all seemed so pointless and far away.

But now, looking out over the vast, sprawling vista of Three Hills Ranch, he understood why. He understood everything. And for the first time in months he was at peace.

He straightened up and reached into his vest pocket for a cigarette paper. It was the automatic gesture of a contemplative man, and he had a lot to think about. But just as he raised the cigarette to his lips, something happened to draw a faint frown to his brow. At first, all he heard was the sputtering, chugging sound of a mechanical contrivance, moving slowly down the road toward him. The roan shifted nervously, just as it came puttering into view: shiny black, low and ugly, with skinny rubber wheels, and tubes and spokes and cylinders sticking out at random angles. Lurching and bouncing along it kicked up a stream of dust in its wake that would have choked a drag steer.

But it was not the appearance of the ridiculous-looking vehicle itself—which the young man knew was called a horseless carriage—that caused a slow grin to spread across his lips. It was the driver.

She was perched daintily atop the raised yellow seat of the vehicle, her gloved hands guiding the steering stick, a swatch of delicate chiffon scarves anchoring her wide hat to her head and streaming out behind her in the breeze. She held her head high and pressed her knees modestly together beneath a slim gray skirt as her eyes surveyed the road. She looked for all the world like a queen out for an afternoon ride—completely unaware that her gilded carriage had turned into a pumpkin.

He watched and he chuckled, and the heavy thoughts that had enveloped him for so long disappeared like a spray of fog before the sun. Without warning he was struck by a mischievous impulse, and whipping off his hat, he slapped his horse on the rump. With a leap and a yell he took off down the hill toward the road.

Life was easy on Three Hills: simple, predictable, and undemanding. The hands who worked there liked it that way. Not much more was required of them than that they put up a front of being busy when the foreman was nearby. For room and board and thirty dollars a month, a man could do worse.

Of course, it wasn't the most exciting job around, and boredom, more than anything else, turned the men to what little work they did. When all the stories of the old Chisholm Trail had been told and heard a dozen times, when they were tired of fistfighting and coralling rattlesnakes and most of their wages had already been spent on whores and carnival games in town, there wasn't much else to do but loaf around the camp fire, playing cards against IOU's and practicing rope tricks in a desultory fashion. That was exactly what the men at Line Camp Number Three were doing on that warm September morning when the horseless carriage came clattering around the bend, spraying out dust and pebbles and leaving a bank of smoke in its wake.

They remarked on the progress of the motorcar with little more than a glance and a curse or two. Miss Anne careening around in her new toy was a familiar sight around the ranch and hardly worth working up a good laugh over anymore.

Jess Larch tossed another marker into the pot, while Ribs McCoy folded his hand and Shep Johnson swore as he drew a club. Ladder Aikens, watching the game over Shep's shoulder, scratched his crotch lazily and went to refill his coffee cup. Nobody stirred to conceal their loafing; the lady boss didn't have any idea what their jobs were and wouldn't have been able to stop that contraption long enough to tell them to get back to work even if she did.

And then they saw the big red horse come charging down the hill.

As one, they turned to stare. And it didn't take more than a minute to see what was happening.

The horse hit the road a good five lengths behind the car, a solid piece of western flesh, strong in the flanks and deep in the withers. Its neck was stretched out, ears laid back, legs pushing forward at an effortless, flying gallop. The rider leaned low over the forequarters, cutting down wind resistance, and urged his mount on with the slap of his hat. And that horse was game. Before it rounded the corner, it had closed a length on the automobile.

The men got to their feet, one by one. Somebody let out a rebel yell and tossed his hat high into the air.

"By damn, he's gonna do it!"

"Ain't got a chance!"

"I'll lay you five he'll cut her off at Stirrup Creek!"

"I'll take a piece of that, you son of a bitch!"

For the first time in months there were signs of life at Line Camp Number Three as the men, unwilling to miss the outcome of the race, sprinted for their own horses. The air was filled with yells of encouragement, and the betting grew hot and heavy. It was later agreed that nothing this good had happened since old Doc Middler's daughter had gotten caught screwing Lame Jack in the bushes at Miss Anne's fancy dress ball and the Doc let go a load of rock salt at them both. Come to think of it, this was even better.

Anne was not even aware of the pursuit until the big red horse drew up beside her. It caught her so by surprise that she almost lost control of the vehicle. She exclaimed, "What the bloody—!" just as the automobile lurched over a rock. The horse and rider dropped back, almost as a courtesy, and she had all she could do to keep the vehicle from plowing into a ditch.

Anne had driven into town to have invitations printed for a garden party she was holding later in the month, the last outdoor party of the season. No doubt she could have made the trip just as quickly in a carriage, or even the open landaulet, but the sporty Daimler gave her a freedom that simply wasn't possible beneath the constraints of a team of balky horses, a sense of power that was impossible to duplicate in any other fashion. While certain people might whisper if she took off in a carriage without a groom to escort her, no one could say much about her driving the Daimler alone, since she was the only person, male or female, within a fifty-mile radius who knew how to operate it.

She was duly proud of being the first person in this part of the country to own a hydrocarbon automobile and took it as a compliment when the men of her acquaintance snickered behind her back that nobody but she would have nerve enough to bring such a contraption into cow country. They were right. Anne Edgecomb, Lady Hartley, had as much nerve as it took to get what she wanted. She always had and always would.

On that particular morning she was in a hurry to get back

to the house, and her mind was going in a dozen different directions, ticking off things that needed her attention. She resented both the nature of her worries and the fact that they distracted her from the pleasure of driving her motorcar with the wind on her face and the power of twenty-six horses surging beneath her hands. And then the rider on the roan appeared from out of nowhere.

Once she got the car under control, Anne whipped her head around, but he was no longer there. But when she turned to look behind her, she found him galloping alongside her and to her right, dangerously close to the Daimler's wheels.

She cried, "Are you mad? Move your horse over! You're going to get hurt!"

But either the wind tore her words away or the engine noise swallowed them, for the rider did not even look at her. In fact, he slapped his reins into greater speed, and suddenly Anne understood.

No one would ever say Anne Edgecomb was not a sportswoman. She had ridden to the hounds when she was thirteen and scandalized the county by competing on a polo team during her first season at Court—and had won. For a contest such as this, every competitive instinct in her body rose to the fore with a vicious delight. Now was the time to prove, once and for all, what a progressive woman could do against outmoded notions.

She opened the throttle and gripped the steering column tighter, tension mounting as, for a few yards, the rider kept pace with her. She hardly dared to take her eyes from the road and got little more than a glimpse of a long, rangy body stretched forward over his mount, lean legs gripping the saddle, dark curly hair tousled by the wind. The very audacity of the rider infuriated her, yet his determination evoked her unwilling admiration, and her blood pumped wildly with the excitement of the contest.

When, slowly, he began to drop behind, she gave an exclamation of sheer triumph. She turned her head around to laugh, but he had crossed behind the car and now appeared on the other side of the road—even with the nose of the motorcar and gaining by inches.

Anne leaned forward over the driving stick, as if to urge the vehicle forward physically, and her face grew grim. The wind caught her driving scarves and tossed them over her shoulders but did very little to cool the heat of battle that was flushing her cheeks. "Blast you," she muttered out loud to the little Daimler. "*Go!*"

Then she saw her chance. They were coming to a bend and a narrowing of the road, and the maneuver around that corner was tricky at best. No one knew the roads at Three Hills as she did, and he hadn't a prayer. He would be forced to give way, no matter how fleet his mount, and would become bogged down by the thick brush that grew along the shoulder.

They rounded the bend neck and neck, and dimly Anne became aware of the sound of cheering, excited voices in the background. Just as she had predicted, the horse shied and leapt aside when the road narrowed, and she was left with a clear right-of-way. There was one thing, however, she had not remembered.

A shallow stream crossed the center of the road, generally no deeper than a thimble and hardly wider than the span of a pair of buggy wheels. In dry weather it disappeared completely, leaving only a bothersome rut. In rainy times, like those they had had recently, it swelled to a churned and beaten mud hole that sucked up everything in sight.

Still, on any other day the motorcar would have plowed right through. Anne had crossed that very stream a dozen times—had done so only that morning, in fact. But she had never crossed it at such high speed, never with half her ranch hands looking on, and never with so much at stake. She gripped the steering stick, set her teeth against the jostling, swaying downhill ride, and with never a doubt that she would emerge victorious on the other side, she forged onward.

The automobile careened downward, bounced upward, then slid backward. Mud flew all over Anne's boots and skirts and splattered on her face. The engine sputtered and stalled.

The unknown horseman leapt the stream with the grace of a prime hunter taking a stile, and the splash of the animal's hooves as he went over sent a new shower of mud into Anne's face. She stood up, gasping and wiping her eyes, inarticulate with rage.

The horseman cantered to a stop a few dozen yards before her and turned in the saddle. The cheers and shouts of her own ranch hands were painfully audible. The rider grinned, tipped his hat politely toward her, and then urged his horse at an easy trot on down the road.

Chapter Two

As Anne strode up the steps to the ranch house that noonday, she was far from the picture of aristocratic womanhood she had been bred to be. Her face was dirty, her hat wilted, her skirts spattered with dried mud, and her eyes blazing cold temper. The Daimler was in tow behind a team of pack mules under the supervision of four cowboys who had been hard put to restrain their chuckles until she was out of sight. Anne could not remember a more inauspicious beginning to a day in all the time she had been in Texas.

It was destined to get worse.

She greeted the bug-eyed stare of her maid with a coolly pleasant, "Your apron is wrinkled, Lizabelle. Please change it immediately." She then proceeded at a sedate pace up the stairs while the maid scurried off to the kitchen, no doubt to spread the tale of her mistress's unorthodox appearance as fast as she could chatter.

The lack of properly trained domestic help had been one of Anne's most difficult adjustments to Texas in the beginning, but she had learned to take it all in stride. She sometimes thought she had become more American than the Americans.

In her bedroom Anne stripped down to her chemise and began to scrub off the mud with a vigor that went a long way toward expiating the temper she had not allowed herself to display before her employees. As she scrubbed herself with almost vicious strokes, she thought, That impossible cowboy. Where had he come from, anyway? There should be laws against allowing hell-rakers like that to run about loose. How dare he charge about like that on her own land, threatening life and limb? Her outfit was ruined, and as for the Daimler . . . it might be weeks before she could manage to get all the mud cleaned from its internal workings. Where the bloody hell had he *come* from?

Yet beneath her indignation Anne was honest enough to recognize a thread of excitement—even appreciation—for his nerve. God, what a race while it had lasted! Moments of sheer uninhibited fun were without a doubt too rare for Anne to dismiss them out of hand. She was not a bad loser, but she couldn't help wishing the arrogant challenger— whoever he was—had not chosen to defeat her in front of half her employees. And she surely would have been inclined to view the entire matter in a more sporting light had she not been defeated at all.

Anne Edgecomb was twenty-five years old. At eighteen she had married her third cousin, the heir to the large estate of Hartley, Marc Edgecomb. That was the only thing she had done in twenty-five years of which her family had ever approved.

Marc had been something of an adventurer, which was why she had liked him. Theirs had been neither a marriage of passion, nor of convenience, but one based simply on mutual interests and companionship. Marc had been a splendid businessman, unwilling to rest upon the laurels of past glories, and for that Anne admired him. In many ways he reminded Anne of her grandfather who had first staked a claim in Texas three generations ago, and it seemed only natural that he should follow the lead set by other British consortiums of the day and expand their investments in Texas ranch land. A wealthy young man in his own right, Marc had presented Anne with Three Hills Ranch as a wedding gift.

They spent their honeymoon at Three Hills, and to Anne it was an adventure every bit as delightful as a sojourn in India or an African safari. She was not to realize until much later how much this wild stretch of green Texas countryside meant to her. Six months after Marc carried her over the threshold of the wide-porched, white-columned ranch house, he succumbed to a fever caused by a particularly severe case of German measles. Her brilliant young husband may have been daring in spirit, but he was woefully weak in flesh, and Texas, it was said, separated the willing from the able. Barely three months before her nineteenth birthday, Anne was a widow with some enormously important decisions to make.

She did not return home. Her parents pleaded with her; her in-laws threatened her. But within a few short months Anne had married a husband and buried him, traveled halfway around the world, made a home in a strange new land, and outgrown the grasp of her parents' disapproval. She knew exactly what she wanted, and for the first time in her life she had the means with which to obtain it. What she wanted was independence.

Three Hills was hers. Its peculiar customs, its ill-dressed, skeptical-eyed cowboys, its lazily shifting bovine population, the alien, provincial society that surrounded it ... Marc had given her more than a hundred thousand acres of sprawling ranch land and six months of easy companionship and amusing anecdotes. He had given her an entirely new life. It was the first thing that had ever belonged completely and exclusively to Anne, and she was not about to let it go.

It had been an uphill struggle over the next six years but one to which Anne was more than equal. She had made a place for herself in this society, and a name for herself as an independent businesswoman. Inch by excruciating inch, she had won the acceptance, if not exactly the respect, of the community of men who ruled this part of Texas with an iron fist. That she was jeopardizing it all now in a desperate gamble on the future was a fact of which she was clearly aware, but that was, at the present, the least of her concerns. She would not have gotten as far as she had had she been the type of woman who let opposition muddle her determination.

Anne wound her silver-blond hair into a loose knot atop her head, stepped into a crisp blue skirt, and was just buttoning the cuffs of a white organdy blouse when she heard the hoofbeats coming down the drive. A glance out the window confirmed what she had suspected: not one rider but several, and George Greenley was leading the pack. Anne paused for only a moment, watching their approach, and then she went down the stairs to welcome her visitors.

Reaching the front hall, she turned, went into the library, and took down Marc's rifle. She went on to the porch, holding the rifle casually under her arm with the barrel pointed down, and waited for her guests to arrive.

George Greenley was the head of the local Cattleman's Association. He was a block-faced, loud-voiced man with a shock of thick, dark hair and stern, dark eyes shaded by bushy brows. He was as big as the Texas he wanted to rule, and power emanated from him like a shout with every step he took.

With him were four other ranchers, representing the spreads that bordered Three Hills. George's careful choice of representatives was not lost on Anne; it even brought a faint, dry smile to her face. She had entertained these men in her home, befriended their wives, cooed over their newborns, shared a pew with them at church. In Texas, being a neighbor was much more than a matter of simple geography, and doubtless George meant to remind her of this. Even so, none of these men looked very friendly, with every one of their saddles loaded down with axes, hammers, and wire cutters.

Greenley drew up to the hitching post and started to dismount. Then he noticed the gun Anne held and sat back in his saddle, pushing his hat back a fraction. His smile looked out of place on his coarse face.

"Well, now, Miss Anne," he drawled. "That's not a very hospitable way to say hello to company."

"Mr. Greenley," she responded calmly, "when you come calling for tea, I can promise you the best in hospitality. But when you ride up loaded down with pickaxes and wire cutters, this, I'm afraid"—she made a small gesture with the rifle—"is all you can expect."

The smile faded, but Greenley was careful to keep his expression placid. He folded his hands across the pommel of his saddle and said reasonably, "We didn't come here for tea, Miss Anne, and we didn't come to talk, either. We figured you'd had time to think about what we said, and we're waiting for your answer. We hope it's the right one, but if it's not, we're prepared. That's all."

Anne let her eyes move across the group of men who had

drawn up behind him, lingering with the very faintest of gracious smiles upon each one. Her voice was low and almost musical, her soft British accent oozing old-world charm and inborn sophistication. "Gentlemen," she said, "how very fine you all look. And thirsty, too, after your long ride. Please feel free to water your horses before you start back, and help yourselves to the dipper at the well. Perhaps on a more civilized occasion I can offer you something stronger."

George Greenley drew himself up. "Now, Miss Anne—"

"Mr. Weems," she said, addressing the man just behind and to the right of Greenley. "I do hope your Emily is feeling better. Please tell her I'd like to call later in the week, if she would be up to receiving me."

Weems swallowed so that his Adam's apple bulged, and his hand went automatically to his hat. "Yes, ma'am. She's doing a lot better, thank you kindly, and surely did appreciate that tisane you sent over."

Anne smiled. "Mr. Hamilton, we've missed your daughter around here the past few weeks. That sorrel pony she's so fond of is growing quite fat, I'm afraid, and I may be forced to sell him. I do hope you'll let me know if you're interested."

It was not only Hamilton and Weems who were looking uncomfortable now, but all the men. They shuffled in their saddles and could not quite meet her eyes. Anne turned back to Greenley. They faced each other for a moment, the tall, regal lady and the heavy, brusque man, each secure in their own separate and very different kinds of power. Anne smiled only slightly when she spoke.

"My answer to you remains as it was the last time we met, Mr. Greenley. This is my land and I will do with it as I please. Neither you nor these good gentlemen nor the entire East Texas Cattleman's Association will stop me. If you have further complaints, I suggest you take them up with my attorneys." With that, she turned to go.

"Now you listen to me!" Greenley's voice was sharp, all pretense of politeness gone. Anne turned, the gentle lift of her brows mocking his loss of temper, but Greenley was unimpressed. "This here is cattle country! It was built for cattlemen and it's ruled by cattlemen, and we're not going to stand by while some goddamn foreign contraption poisons our water and dries up our grass. I warned you—"

"Neither your grass nor your streams have been affected by my drilling for oil," Anne returned quietly but firmly. "Until that is the case, I suggest—"

"Your own cows are dropping like flies! It's poison, I tell you, and we won't have it!"

There was a heartbeat's silence in which Greenley's crew began to straighten in their saddles and murmur agreement among themselves. Anne's voice was like ice, and her soft gray eyes swiftly became as hard as steel. "You, sir, are trespassing. Kindly get off my land."

Greenley looked for a moment as though he would stare her down, and Anne could see a shrewd mind working behind the formidable fringe of shaggy eyebrows. He seemed, however, to decide at last upon a different tack, and the muscles in his face relaxed. "We've been friends for a long time, Miss Anne," he said congenially. "We've all come to think mighty highly of you around here, and we don't want to lose your goodwill. Why, Three Hills Ranch is an institution in this part of Texas; we don't like to have to set up against it any more than you like us doing it. So just let me ask you kindly, as one neighbor to another, will you let go this silly idea and take down those drill rigs?''

Anne said simply, ''No.''

They met each other eye to eye for a long moment, and the tension that pulsated between them was palpable enough to make the horses stir. Finally George Greenley gathered up his reins abruptly, turned in the saddle, and barked, ''All right, boys. Let's tear 'em down.''

Anne lifted the rifle and cocked it.

Outright astonishment was reflected on the faces of the riders, and even Greenley slowly turned back to face her. There was nothing in his eyes but quiet amusement, nothing in his manner but patient condescension. ''Now, Miss Anne,'' he said gently, ''you put that thing away. You know you're not going to shoot me.''

Anne's face remained impassive, and her finger rested firmly on the trigger. She did not know whether she would fire or not—she suspected the answer probably was no—but few things had ever given her more satisfaction than she felt when she sighted down that rifle barrel and watched, just for an instant, a shadow of uncertainty cross Greenley's face.

But she was never to know what she would have done, and neither was he, for just as she settled her aim, another voice from behind her spoke out in a low drawl. ''Maybe she won't, but I might.''

Anne saw George's eyes move over her shoulder, and she turned. The lanky, dark-haired cowboy sat astride his big roan, forearm resting casually across the saddle, a .45 Peacemaker leveled directly at George Greenley's chest.

Anne saw the surprise in Greenley's face slowly turn to fury; his hands went tight upon the reins. For a moment he seemed almost ready to chance it, and his hand made a half-formed movement toward his holster. The clicking hammer of the Peacemaker stilled the motion, and the dark-haired cowboy didn't blink an eye.

Greenley looked back at Anne, and one corner of his lips curled into a faint imitation of a smile. Anne thought she had never seen such fury in a man's eyes. "Taking on hired guns, are you, ma'am?" he asked. "Well, now, that does sound serious."

He turned in the saddle. "Well, boys, looks like she means it."

He picked up his reins and tipped his hat to her. "We won't trouble you again, ma'am." He jerked his horse around and rode off, the others following.

Anne focused on the cloud of dust to avoid looking at the man behind her. Her heart was going very fast, but whether that was from surprise, anger, or excitement, she could not be sure. When at last she thought she could address him in a civil tone, she spoke. "I could have handled that myself," she informed him coolly.

"Maybe." He holstered his weapon and swung down from the horse. His voice was pleasant, and he sounded amused. "But where I come from, a man don't let a woman stand down a mob of vigilantes by herself unless he's got two arms in a sling and a couple of hobbled legs."

"I see."

With her peripheral vision Anne saw him give his horse a pat as the animal stretched to drink from the trough, and then he came toward her. He was walking out of the sun, and when Anne at last condescended to look at him, she was startled by the brilliant glare that engulfed him. She blinked in irritation and shaded her eyes. Then he stepped out of the blinding light, and she looked at him fully for the first time.

Anne was not a fanciful woman, but afterward she never would be able to explain adequately what came over her in that moment. It was a heart-stopping instant with no reason or definable cause for being so, something like the flash of sulfur that imprints an image on tin forever. It was only a second, or even less, but it was a fraction of time that left her disoriented and dazed, struck by the sensation that something very important was about to happen. And the first thing she thought was, *I know this man.*

That, of course, was ridiculous. Except for that brief blurred glimpse of him on horseback, she had never seen him before in her life. Yet the sense of familiarity amazed her, and in a determined attempt to regain her balance she tried to analyze it. The second thing she thought was, *He's the best-looking man I've ever seen in my life.*

He was tall, lean, and muscular, and he moved with a fluid grace uncommon to cowboys. His hair beneath the pushed-back hat was thick and dark, and a few loose curls escaped from the back to spill over his collar. His eyes were a pure and brilliant green, his face shadowed by the faintest scrub of beard. He had a broad forehead, a distinctively angular jaw, and a deep cleft in his chin.

But it was his mouth that most held her attention. It was full and cleanly shaped, gentling the remainder of his features while remaining undeniably masculine. There was a faint line near the right corner of his lips that suggested the habit of a cynical smile, yet there was a softness to it that drew a woman's eye, and which, absurdly, made her own lips want to part in response. It was a striking face, an unforgettable face, and Anne couldn't help but wonder where she had seen it before.

And then, from nowhere, the notion struck her. Perhaps she had never seen it before. Perhaps it was simply a face she had been waiting all her life to see. . . .

Embarrassed and impatient with her own foolishness, Anne jerked her thoughts away from such an undisciplined course, and her eyes met his. What she saw made her breath catch momentarily. It was the same sort of surprise and frank approval with which she must have been looking at him.

He stood at the bottom of the steps, his thumbs tucked loosely in his gun belt, his head tilted back, patiently enduring her scrutiny. The faint smile that she had only suspected before now shadowed his lips. "Well, now," he said in a soft drawl, "you're a good-looking woman. Even better than I thought."

Determinedly Anne fought the impulse to jerk her eyes away like a shy and flustered schoolgirl. She stood still as his gaze swept slowly, measuringly, over her. There was nothing ordinary about his regard. Wherever his eyes touched, she felt exposed and naked, and against her will her color began to rise. Incredibly, it was as though he could see right through her—past the prim and sturdy skirt and blouse, beyond the modest underclothing, into her skin and to the very essence of her soul. She felt a sense of indignation prickling to life, but it was stifled by a strange excitement, a titillating curiosity. No one had ever been able to do this to her before.

The muscles of Anne's stomach were tight, as though from anxiety or anticipation. Her heart was beating faster than she would have liked, and it was with the greatest of efforts that she tried to subdue it. Anne met the cowboy's eyes, warm and full with their peculiar knowledge, and her voice was level. "Who are you," she demanded, "and what are you doing on my ranch? Aside, of course, from running me into a ditch and interfering in matters that are none of your concern."

The young man let his smile stretch into a grin. "Well, ma'am," he replied, "you can call me Josh, and I reckon what I'm doing here is looking for the foreman."

"What do you want with my foreman?"

"A job."

Anne looked down at him. "I do all the hiring at Three Hills, and I'm afraid we are fully staffed at the moment. And I might add, sir, that you've a great deal to learn about making a favorable impression upon a prospective employer. Good day."

She turned toward the door, but his low chuckle caused her to stop and look back at him sharply.

"Fully staffed, are you?" He seemed to find that delightful. "Well, I reckon that's one way of putting it. Tell me, ma'am, would you by any chance be from out of town? You've got a little bit of an accent."

Irritation sparked in Anne's eyes, and the spell he had come dangerously close to weaving about her senses dissolved immediately. He was, after all, nothing more than a rude American—a *cowboy*—and no amount of striking looks could overcome that.

Most people thought her accent was enchanting, and she had worked hard to keep its dulcet tones from being corrupted by the Texas drawl. Her tone was neither enchanting nor dulcet, though, as she returned curtly, "The accent is

British, but it is apparent, sir, that you are the one who is from out of town. Otherwise you would know who I am."

He affected an attitude that was properly chastened, though his eyes still sparkled wickedly. He inquired politely, "And who exactly are you, ma'am?"

Anne drew herself up to her full five feet, eight inches. Long ago she had abandoned her courtesy title, but she remained ever aware of how easily Americans seemed to be intimidated by anything connected with nobility. With just the faintest trace of a superior smile, she replied, "I am Anne Edgecomb, Lady Hartley, the sole owner and proprietor of Three Hills Ranch."

Far from being impressed, the impudent young cowboy seemed more amused than ever. His sun-weathered eyes narrowed with surprise as he stared at her. "Is that a fact? Well, if that don't beat all!" With that, the soft, secret chuckles overcame him, and he took off his hat, shaking his head in patent disbelief as he slapped the dust from his jeaned thigh.

Anne said coolly, "I fail to see what is so amusing."

"No, ma'am, I don't reckon you would." He cast his eyes about the rich green lawn, the flower beds lush with their late summer blooms, the graceful willows and the gleaming chipped-granite walkways, as though seeing it all for the first time. He was still chuckling, and when he looked back at her, there was new interest.

The moment Josh had walked up to the steps and looked her full in the face, he had known there was something very special about her. There were some women, like some horses, that set up an instant greed in a man. It wasn't something that could be explained, nor even understood very well, but there it was. For Josh, Anne Edgecomb was just such a woman.

She was not a classical beauty, and no one would ever claim that she was. But there was something about her that had nothing to do with the way her parts were put together, which immediately made the word *beautiful* seem too pale to describe her. Strong, Josh thought, and graceful, but even those adjectives were not quite right. Whatever it was, it was as out of place in this part of Texas as that motorcar of hers.

She was a tall girl, and slender. The high collar, puffed-out shoulders, and nipped-in waist of her blouse made her look as stiff and starched as the material itself, which Josh thought was probably the case. But who knew what kind of figure was concealed beneath the cardboard-straight front of her shirt.

Her skin was as white as cream and her features proud. The pouffed-out halo of her pale hair softened her face, and her silver-colored eyes, Josh imagined, could be quite intriguing when they weren't busy freezing a man. Her light-colored eyebrows and lashes should have made her look washed out, but they were so thick and gracefully arranged that they were quite distinctive instead. Striking, Josh decided at last. She was a striking woman, the kind to turn heads on any street corner. Regal, bold, composed, and about as inviting as an icehouse in January.

He couldn't explain the sense of certainty that came over him the moment he looked at her, nor did he try. He wanted her. It was as simple as that.

He couldn't prevent a small, lazily upward turn of his lips as he moved his eyes back to hers and saw her returning his gaze, stare for stare. He liked that too. "So," he suggested thoughtfully, "you're a Lady, are you?"

Anne favored him with a ghost of a smile. Never had a man aroused her competitive instincts to such a degree, and although he infuriated her beyond all reason, she could not resist the challenge to put him in his place. "That is my Court title, yes," she informed him. "However, it has always been my opinion that ladyhood is more a matter of conduct than title and remains to be proven. I doubt I shall disappoint."

He rolled his weight back on his heels. "Oh, I don't know," he drawled with mock consideration. "That would depend on what a man was expecting. Myself, I've never had too much use for *ladies*."

"A fortunate circumstance for all the ladies of the world, I'm sure."

To her great surprise the blatantly suggestive spark in his eyes blossomed into appreciative laughter, and Anne stiffened against an instinctive urge to respond to it.

He said, regarding her with frank enjoyment, "Of course, now, a lady like you just might change my mind."

Her chin lifted, and she looked down at him haughtily. "What a great relief. And here I've been losing sleep at night wondering why I was put on this earth."

He chuckled, a soft sound of natural pleasure that did its very best to put Anne off her guard. He looked at her with an easy companionship he had no right to claim and said, "Now that we've got the introductions over with, let's get back to that job."

"I told you—"

"Yes, I know. You're fully staffed." With difficulty, he seemed to be keeping a straight face. "And I won't argue with you there. Anytime I ride up to a ranch where the cowhands have time to be playing cards in the middle of the day, I've got to figure that place is fully staffed. Now, it might not be any of my business—"

"You're right." Her voice was clipped. "It's not."

"But," he continued, "when were you planning on bringing your stock down from summer pasture? They've just about cropped those hills dry, ma'am, and somebody should be giving a thought to baling up winter feed before it rots in the field. And it's not that you don't have a right nice place here, but you've got some fences that need mending real bad, and your salt licks are so low that even the deer are making new trails. Of course"—and he made a small, self-deprecating gesture with his wrist—"being fully staffed and all, you've probably got it all under control."

Anne's shoulders squared, and her finger unconsciously caressed the trigger guard of the rifle she held at her side. "On that point, sir, you are exactly right. Now, if you'll excuse me, I have things to do."

She was halfway to the door when he spoke again, mildly and matter-of-factly. "How long have you been losing stock?"

She turned.

"I passed a carcass," he explained with a small shrug. "And the burying hole of a couple of others. I'd estimate it's been going on less than a month, and it's not fever or it would've spread further."

She said carefully, "We know what it's not. What we need now is to know what it is."

He smiled. "Well, now, ma'am, that'd take a fellow some time."

Anne looked at him thoughtfully for a long time. No one

had to tell her he was not an ordinary drifter, and Three Hills got its share of those from time to time. No, there was something odd about this one that flashed like a beacon even as it defied complete definition. That horse of his, for one thing. Seven hands high and bred like a racer, there wasn't another one like it in this part of the country.

Anne placed the rifle on the porch railing and walked down the steps. She passed so close to him that her skirts brushed his boots, and he did not step back. She could feel him watching her, indulgent and amused, as she went to his horse.

"Beautiful animal," she commented, and threaded her fingers through its glossy mane. The stallion nickered and tossed his head in response to the unexpected affection. "He has more than a little Arabian blood, if I'm not mistaken."

Josh lifted an appreciative eyebrow. "You know your horseflesh."

"There's never been an Englishwoman born who didn't." She turned a smile on him that was mild and composed, far too sweet for the implication of her words. "Horses and guns. We are bred to them, you know."

Josh murmured, "I'll remember that."

She turned back to the horse, circling it, running an expert hand over its withers. The saddle was crafted, worn to the shape of his body from long use. It bore none of the silver ornamentation or fancy stitchery that greenhorns liked to sport about, and it was undeniably an expensive piece of work. It was the saddle of a man who knew what saddles were for.

She moved to the horse's flank, and she could feel the sudden wariness in the man who watched her. "If you're planning to make me an offer," he said, and his voice was almost too casual, "I'm afraid I'll have to turn it down. He's not for sale."

"Actually I'm not interested in buying. Your horse has one rather serious flaw, you see." Anne looked up from her examination of the horse's flank, her expression mild and unreadable. "This brand has been blotted."

She saw the muscles in his neck tense, and a sudden stillness came over his eyes. But his tone was of the most careful disinterest as he replied, "Has it?"

"Indeed." She ran her hand over the brand casually. "And not a very good job, either." She met his eyes levelly. "The sort of job one might expect from someone in a hurry, using a hot cinch ring from his own saddle."

Josh lifted an eyebrow. "Well, ma'am, I'm impressed. Who'd expect a lady like you to know so much about hot cinch rings and brand blotting? You wouldn't happen to have a sideline in horse stealing, would you?"

Anne's nostrils flared a little, but her smile was very cool. "No," she said deliberately. "*I* wouldn't."

Josh reached into his pocket and took out the makings for a cigarette, still watching her. A slight breeze caught an escaping strand of her silvery hair as Josh began to tap tobacco into a cigarette paper. "Are you accusing me of stealing that horse?" he inquired after a moment.

Anne replied, "Well, I suppose that depends. Do you have a bill of sale?"

She watched as he brought the cigarette to his mouth, and saw the tip of his tongue extend slowly over its surface, moistening it. Perhaps it was nothing more than the fact that he never took his eyes off her, which caused Anne's chest to tighten, watching him. . . . Finally he replied, "As a matter of fact, I don't believe I do."

Anne came around the horse, and her expression was as composed and as pleasant as his. "Then," she replied, "I suppose that is exactly what I am accusing you of."

He struck a match on the back of his jeans and brought the flame to his cigarette. "Do you check out the brands on every horse that rides up here?"

"No. Only those whose riders look suspicious."

He smiled and tossed the match away. "Then you must stay mighty busy, ma'am."

Anne knew she should dismiss him from her property and go inside the house. She had no idea why she was prolonging this absurd interview.

Or perhaps she did.

She inquired, "Have you references, perhaps? The names of those for whom you've previously worked?"

He appeared to give that some thought. "Well, now," he said at last, drawing thoughtfully on the cigarette, "I could tell you that I've spent the past three years as top hand on the Bar-Four down Amarillo way, and before that drew foreman's wages on one of the biggest spreads in Wyoming. I could tell you I'm a personal friend of the governor of Arizona and rode with the federal marshal out in California. Or. . ." And he smiled. "I could tell you I just broke out of Yuma Prison and have spent the last year or so on the run. Of course, it'd take you a good while to check any of it out, and when you get right down to it, it doesn't really matter, does it? The only thing that's important to you is whether I know my job."

Anne looked him over once again, thoughtfully. No, there was nothing ordinary about him at all. He looked like a cowhand and talked a good game, but there was none of the shuffling, sullen gait Anne had learned to associate with saddle tramps, and he was too well spoken to be an illiterate drifter. His clohtes were dusty and stained with travel, but the gloves that were tucked into his belt were finely stitched kid, and his boots were elaborately decorated with hand-worked embroidery. He could have been any of those things he had implied. Or none of them.

So she brought her eyes back to his and asked him the only question she could. "And do you know your job?"

He brought the cigarette to his lips, inhaled, and breathed out a slow stream of smoke. The grin that slowly insinuated itself across his face was so charming, so lazy and outrageous, that it was almost contagious. It made her skin tingle. "Lady," he assured her without the faintest trace of modesty, "I'm the best."

Anne fought hard against the wry smile that threatened to tighten her lips. "That, sir," she informed him, "is a matter of opinion." And she started up the steps.

Abruptly he was serious. "Listen," he said plainly, and his tone was so unexpected that she had to turn and stare at him. "I know your problems, I know what you're doing about them, and I'm here to tell you there's no excuse for the shape this ranch is in. You've been moving fewer and fewer head to market. You're losing calves. Every year your herd gets smaller and your profits start dipping. So what do you do? You go out and start digging holes in the ground, and you get the whole county up in arms about it. I'm not asking your pardon for saying so, but that's about the stupidest thing I've ever heard of anybody doing, and it's going to get you nothing but trouble."

Anne's eyes widened and she drew a sharp breath, but he did not give her a chance for retort. He continued sternly, "The first thing you need to do is tear down those ugly rigs before somebody gets hurt. This is cattle land, and it'll make you rich if you just let it do its job. The second thing you need to do is find yourself a man who knows how to run a ranch. There's not a thing in the world wrong with this operation that a good cattleman couldn't fix, and you'd be running in the black inside a year with the right management. No more fights with your neighbors, no more worries about oil, no more red ink.''

Anne was so astounded by the firmness in his tone—the utter arrogance with which he assessed the situation and presented his solution—that she almost forgot to be angry. In fact, that was an advantage, for the last thing she wanted to do was to be pushed into a display of outrage with this man. She had a feeling he would enjoy that enormously.

Her expression was tight and her eyes hard as she replied levelly, ''You saw how I handled those other men who tried to tell me how to run my ranch. Be careful you don't blunder in over your depth.''

His grin was slow and easy and, coming on the heels of the stern lecture he had just delivered, totally disconcerting. ''Yes, ma'am.'' He touched his forefinger to his forehead. ''The last thing I want to do is get on your bad side.''

Anne took a breath and in a moment managed politely, ''You seem quite sure of yourself, Mr. . . . Josh. No doubt that's a quality that would recommend you highly to another employer. I wish you luck in finding one.''

Before she could even turn, he spread out his hands in a plaintive, open gesture that managed to look both boyish and endearing. ''Ma'am,'' he said, ''I'm broke and I'm tired and I need a place to light and get a stake. That poor old horse of mine probably couldn't even limp his way to the next ranch, much less the next town, and I'd be might near starved before I made it. Have a little pity on a beat-up cowpoke down on his luck.''

Anne could not quite keep the dimple at bay this time, and she broke into a smile. It was incredible how this man could take her emotions from peak to valley in wild swings in only a matter of moments. Incredible, annoying, disturbing—and, in some incomprehensible way, exhilarating.

''You, sir,'' she accused softly, ''are a pathetic liar.''

He grinned. ''I'll make you a deal. One month, room and board. If you're not satisfied with my work, you don't owe me a cent.''

It was absurd. She did not need any more hands, and even if she did, she wouldn't have taken on the first stray that crossed her path. Most especially she wouldn't have considered *him*, as insolent, arrogant, and presumptive as he was. He had humiliated her in a reckless race and drawn a gun on her neighbors. He was in all likelihood a criminal riding a stolen horse. He was far too full of himself ever to make a productive employee. Besides, he was lying—and about more than the state of his pocketbook and the emptiness of his belly.

Anne stood looking at him a moment longer, and all these very excellent considerations marched logically through her head. Then she said, ''Take your gear to the bunkhouse and find a man called Big Jim. We'll talk again in a month—if you're still here.''

He put his hat back on his head, nothing in his expression suggesting he had ever expected any other response from her. Incredibly he winked at her. ''Oh, I'll still be here,'' he assured her, and he picked up his reins and sauntered away toward the stable.

Chapter Three

Josh had no intention of searching out Big Jim. He had done more than enough for one day, and he figured the lady boss's cows could wait for one more sunrise. He was tired.

He took his horse to the stable, gave it a good rubdown, and scooped up a bucket of oats. "Chow down, fellow," he advised with an affectionate slap on the roan's neck. "You've earned it."

He felt a brief surge of irritation with himself when he caught sight of the blotted Fielding brand, and he swore softly. He should have been more careful. But, hell, he was no cinch-ring artist. And who would ever think a woman like that would be smart enough to check a brand, much less know enough to recognize one that had been altered?

She was some woman, all right, he thought, and a new wash of wonder filtered over him—coupled with admiration. He was certain this wasn't the first surprise she had in store for him, and he looked forward to the others with the anticipatory pleasure with which a hunter stalks a wily prey. Nothing worth having was ever easy, and Anne Edgecomb would make the effort more than worthwhile.

But he did wish he'd been more careful about the brand.

Not that it mattered, he decided with a resurgence of his usual optimism. He had gotten the job, hadn't he? And she wouldn't call the sheriff on him. Josh could not be certain how he knew that, but he did. He was safe.

He shouldered his saddlebags and strolled to the bunkhouse, his eyes lazily sweeping for details as he passed. Three Hills wasn't much like any ranch headquarters he had ever seen, even in East Texas. Of course, he had heard about the main house, with its big white columns and long, lace-curtained windows. An antebellum mansion in the middle of an empty Texas field, it had been an oddity when it was first built fifty years ago. Since, plenty of grander estates had been built by newly rich cattle barons, but Josh couldn't help thinking this house had a certain unique grace that was appropriate to its owner.

What did seem strange were the relatively modern touches— the orderly flower beds and neat mazes of shrubs carefully trimmed to take on the shapes of chess pieces, horse's heads, and some kind of weird crossed-sword design that Josh could only assume to be the family crest. He had never seen anything like it, and he spent a long time staring and shaking his head in amazement.

As he crossed around back, he noticed a stone wall—God only knew how far she'd had to send for that stone, for there was none like it in this part of Texas—that enclosed a large sun-and-shade garden, complete with marble benches, little statues, and trellised rose arbors. There was even a little latticework summerhouse in the middle of it all—a gazebo, he thought it was called. The woman had set up her own little piece of England right here in Texas.

It was all very fine and fancy, but Josh noticed other things as well. The shingling was coming loose off the well house, and climbing vines were beginning to rot the bricks on one of the chimneys. Gophers had started to dig into the foundation of the bunkhouse, and the gate was sagging on the fence that enclosed the vegetable garden. Little things, but the kinds of things no rancher would ever let go unattended.

If Josh was in charge, things would be different. He had a vision of what Three Hills once had been, and what it could be again. He could make sure that vision came true.

What the lady needed, Josh decided, was a man around the house. Fortunately he knew just the man.

Anne Edgecomb. Lady Hartley. Every time he thought about her, he had to grin. Over the past three months and thousand miles he had imagined a lot of things, but none of them even came close to this. Yet it couldn't have been more perfect if he had arranged it himself.

Stepping inside the bunkhouse, he saw that it was much like any other: rows of cots; a couple of tables for playing cards; pegs on the walls for clothes and ropes; and a potbellied stove. It was empty at this time of day but smelled of the stale sweat and smoke of those who made it their home. A small, dry smile touched Josh's lips as he realized that this would be his home, too . . . at least for a while.

He kicked the door closed behind him and found an empty cot near the window. Tossing down his saddlebags, he stretched out, crossed his ankles, and folded his hands behind his head. He was sleeping for the first time in a strange place, and he did not take off his gun or his boots. His pa had taught him better than that.

Pa. The lazy, contented expression on Josh's face faded slowly, and the muscles in his jaw tightened unconsciously.

He still thought of that man as his father. Old habits were hard to break.

One thing he had learned during his months on the road was that anger, bitterness, and pain were all-consuming emotions that could not be sustained for long. Eventually they were absorbed into the business of everyday living, pushed back, even ignored. But they never completely went away. They waited for quiet moments, unexpected moments, and then they surfaced with a brief, sharp clarity.

After a long time, almost as though fighting the impulse, Josh sat up and retrieved his saddlebags. He unbuckled the strap slowly, pushed aside a jacket, a clean shirt, and a bag of pegging strips, until his fingers touched, far at the bottom, what he sought. He withdrew the Bible slowly.

The book was battered and old, marked with age and use. Its leather cover was cracked, and its shape was somewhat warped from a long-ago contact with water. Josh knew by heart the story of how that Bible had gotten wet. The tissue pages were yellow with age and crumbled in one corner where a mouse had gotten to them. Josh did not suppose anything could ever be done to restore that.

A bleakness stole into his eyes as he sat staring at the Bible, absently tracing the faded gilt letters on the cover with his forefinger. It had become something of a ritual with him, taking out this book, holding it before he went to sleep at night or at odd times during the day. It brought him both comfort and pain. But mostly it brought him determination.

He opened the cover and leafed through the first two pages. Four generations of names were recorded there: births, marriages, deaths. The whole of a family's identity, and all the heritage he had in the world. Once it had been accorded a position of honor in a noble household, the keeper of records, the preserver of faith. For the past twenty years it had been hidden away at the bottom of a trunk in a dusty attic, waiting for him to find it, waiting to tear his life apart.

He touched the spidery, faded ink with his fingers. Joshua Edward Fielding, his Grandpa Jed. Born June 1, 1814, married Elizabeth Coleman May 31, 1839. There had been a shipwreck and a man named Hartley who tried to kill him. On that long-ago day in Galveston Harbor, Jed had saved himself, the woman he was to marry, and the Bible—but he had made an enemy for life.

When Jed Fielding first began to gather cattle in these hills, the longhorns had been killers, fierce and mean and smarter than some horses and most men; ranching back then had been only slightly more dangerous than going to war. But he had done it. He had gathered a herd and driven it to New Orleans, and later to Mobile and all the way to Philadelphia. He built a fine, white-columned mansion for his wife in a land that had previously known nothing but shanties and log cabins, and by the time the railhead opened in Kansas, Jed Fielding was already a rich man, on his way to becoming a legend.

Below the names of Jed and Elizabeth Fielding were those of two sons: Daniel Fielding, 1841–1879, and Jake Fielding, 1852–.

But it was the first name upon which Josh's finger lingered, touching it, tracing the letters as though the faded handwriting itself could evoke images, provide answers. Daniel Fielding, of whose existence Josh had not even been aware until three months ago. Daniel Fielding, who had married Jessica Duncan on July 15, 1876. And below their names the last entry, that of their son.

Joshua Coleman Fielding, born June 1, 1877.

Against his will his mind began to retrace the steps that had brought him here.

It had been a lovely June day in the Rockies, his sister Beth's wedding day. The afternoon was perfect: warm and bright but not too hot, with just the faintest of balmy breezes occasionally riffling the festive skirts of the ladies and fluttering the checked tablecloth that lined the long table set up under the trees. The bride was breathtaking in linen and lace; the groom was strong, handsome, and proud.

He had meant to make Beth happy. He had gone to the attic to find a little tintype of her, taken by a cigar-store Indian in Denver when she was three years old. Josh loved his sister, and he wanted her to have something special from him on her wedding day.

Yet in his search he had found the Bible with its family record, hidden at the bottom of an old trunk filled with twenty years of castoffs, and the past had opened up for him like the yawning mouth of a monster.

If only they had told him. It wasn't the truth that had thrown Josh into such turmoil, but their desperation to keep it a secret all these years. What was so shameful about his birth that it had to be hidden away, locked in the past, never even whispered about all this time?

According to the record, Josh's mother had been married to Daniel Fielding and had given birth to one son, Josh. But Josh had grown up thinking Jake Fielding was his father. Who was this Daniel, whom he had never heard of, whom he must now come to think of as his father? What had become of him? Why had Jake married his brother's wife and taken his son as his own—and shrouded it all in such secrecy?

If only they had answered him. When he confronted them, his mother froze with shock, and Jake went livid with anger. If only they had explained it all to him quietly and reasonably, the day might have ended differently. All Josh had asked for was the truth about his father, and the truth was the one thing they had refused to give him.

It had all gotten out of control. His mother pleaded with him, distraught, while Jake issued icy commands. Josh's anger, panic, and confusion mounted, and even now he could not recall what he actually said that caused Jake to strike him. He only remembered lying in the dust with blood trickling from his lip, and before he even knew what was happening, Josh had pulled a gun on the only father he had ever known.

And in that still, frozen moment, everything had changed. He saw the sorrow and disappointment in Jake's eyes and the horror in his mother's face, and knew that nothing would ever be the same. Josh rode away from his home knowing that he might never see it, or the family he once had loved, again.

Three months and a thousand miles had passed since then, and Josh was sitting on a hard bunk in a strange bunkhouse, still wondering how it had happened. For twenty-two years he had lived believing in certain absolutes: autumn was followed by winter; thunder accompanied lightning; dawn followed the night; and his father's name was Jake. Twenty-two years of love and loyalty, of growth and learning . . . what did it mean now? Did any of it matter?

Jake had taught Josh to rope and shoot and hunt for game. He had taught him about cattle and management and bookkeeping and how to survive in the wilderness with nothing but a knife. When Josh was five, Jake had left him in the woods overnight to find his way home with nothing but the faint signs Jake had left as a guide. Josh hadn't been afraid; he knew his father was never farther away than just around the bend and would appear if he needed him. Jake had always been there when Josh needed him.

But Jake wasn't his father, and Josh didn't know what was true or absolute anymore.

Jake had married his brother's wife and raised that man's son as his own. And for years they had kept the secret. Why hadn't they told him? He would have understood if they had told him; he wouldn't have loved them any less. . . .

But Josh had seen the fear in his mother's eyes, and the fury and pain in Jake's. And he knew there was more to it than a simple secret.

But perhaps Josh really didn't want to know. It was a possibility that had occurred to him more than once on the long journey east. But the farther Josh rode, the deeper he had become entangled in the nightmare. He had had a good life back in Colorado. None of it was of his making, but it had happened. Now he was here, the answers within his grasp.

He could still go home. He could ask his mother to forgive him and apologize to his father; he could pick up his old life and pretend none of it had ever happened. It would be the sensible thing to do. Because if Josh stayed here, he would probably find the answers to his questions, and he may not ever want to go back again.

But he was here now, and from the moment he had set foot on Three Hills land he had known more was at stake than a mysterious father and an elusive family secret. This place called to him with its flat fields and rolling hills in a way the rugged majesty of the Rockies had never done. He had felt an instinctive familiarity for Three Hills, as though some long-forgotten childhood memory had been stored against this time, waiting to lead him home. Josh belonged here in some way. So, for better or worse, he knew he was going to stay.

He closed the book with a snap and returned it to the saddlebags. Then, using his saddlebags as a pillow, he stretched out and crossed his ankles, pulling his hat forward to shade his eyes. He stayed like that, still and silent with his own dark thoughts, until the sun sank low in the sky.

Chapter Four

Eddie Baker lounged back in George Greenley's big leather chair and lit a cigar. He was a man who enjoyed the finer things in life—the best brandy, the finest cigars, high-stepping horses, and well-made Stetsons. He had, in his own way, worked hard to be able to afford them.

He wore an immaculately tailored suit of light worsted wool, elaborately tooled Western boots, and a string tie caught with a turquoise buckle. He kept a small derringer in the inside pocket of his jacket, because a gun belt spoiled the look of his suit, and Eddie was meticulous about his appearance. On his small finger was a diamond ring—he told everyone it had belonged to his mother and that he wore it for sentimental reasons. In fact, he had taken it from the pocket of a dead man years ago. He wore it to remind himself of times gone by, and of how far he had come to get to where he was today.

Only, at the moment, he was bored. George Greenley had been ranting about the latest development in his feud with Anne Edgecomb for almost half an hour and had yet to get to the point. Eddie hoped it wouldn't take much longer. He had other things to do.

The two men were meeting in Greenley's office, a large room adjacent to a smaller study in his home. It was from that room that George Greenley conducted all the business pertinent to the Cattleman's Association, which was by way of saying he conducted all the business of the county.

The county had no courthouse, and George Greenley, being a judge as well as a rancher and a community leader, was routinely responsible for all the records and legal documents a citizen might wish to register. Greenley was something of a collector; an historian, he liked to call himself. His walls were lined with accordion folders, books, and ledgers representing three generations of ranching history. There was very little George Greenley did not have on file.

Greenley turned now to one of the shelves, searching along it until he came to a big ledger. He pulled it out.

"Do you know what this is, Eddie?" He set the ledger on the desk at Eddie's elbow with a thud. "That is a complete record of every land transaction that's taken place in these parts since the War for Independence." He smiled a little. "Some interesting reading in there."

He settled his large frame into an easy chair across from Eddie, one hand stretched along its back, a cigar dangling from his fingers. His attitude seemed comfortable and relaxed, but Eddie Baker knew him better. Greenley was as mad as hell.

"See now, Eddie," began Greenley patiently, "you're a newcomer to these parts—relatively speaking, that is—and there's some things you might not know. Myself, well, I like to think of myself as a rancher first, a Texan second, and an American by the grace of God. My folks were some of the first settlers hereabouts, did you know that?" He gave

a low chuckle, gesturing with his cigar toward the book-
and file-lined walls. "Guess that's why I'm so all-fired
interested in the history of the place. Why, my grandpa
knew Jed Fielding personally, and I've got a picture of
Elizabeth Fielding hanging in the front parlor. . . ."

He chuckled again, this time without humor. "Miss
Anne's had her eye on that picture for years now. Sometimes I get almost as much fun out of knowing how bad she
wants it as I get out of having it for myself. My wife made
me buy it when Three Hills went up for auction," he went
on in a comfortable, rambling way, "God rest her soul. It's
worth a pretty penny now, painted by some fancy dude from
back East, but that's not why I keep it. No, sir. I keep it
because it's history. The Fieldings *are* history around these
parts. You know about Jed Fielding, don't you? Now, there
was a man."

His voice fell to ruminating, but Eddie was not fooled.
Greenley had something important to say, and taking the
roundabout way was just his method of catching a man
off-guard. Eddie listened alertly.

"Fielding was a giant in the cattle business," Greenley
continued, sipping his brandy. "Matter of fact, he was one
of the first, and he hung in there when everybody else was
selling their stock for a grub stake back East. Made it pay
too. Built every inch of that house at Three Hills, just him
and his little wife and a couple of hands, out there all by
themselves. Built it into a empire. A goddamn empire."

He fell silent, staring into his glass.

Greenley tossed down the last of the brandy and got up to
refill his glass. "Point is," he said over his shoulder, "that
the time was when Three Hills Ranch meant something
around these parts. And you know why that was, Eddie?

Because it was big.'' He came back over and sat down, nursing a secret smile that Eddie did not quite like. "It was almighty big."

Eddie was getting impatient. "All very interesting, I'm sure," he said in a drawl, "but I don't see what that has to do with—"

"Well, I'm telling you what it has to do with!" It was almost a bark, and Greenley's shaggy brows drew together in the swift explosion of ferocious temper. "It has to do with goddamn everything!"

Greenley gestured sharply toward the ledger on his desk with his cigar, scattering ashes over the green pressboard surface. "Now, you open up that book and you're going to find the records of purchases for every rancher within a hundred square miles of where we're sitting. Water rights, grazing rights, building rights. And I'm willing to bet not a single-man jack of 'em knows what's really written in that book."

He clamped the cigar between his teeth and spent a moment studying Eddie. "Take yourself, for instance. I'll bet you think you bought your little place off old man Jenkins. And sure enough"—he opened the book and flipped through a couple of sheets—"you did. What you don't know is that *he* bought it from a great big foreign company called the Hartley Corporation."

Now, at last, he had Eddie's attention; Eddie, however, was wise enough not to voice his thoughts out loud.

Greenley leaned back, chewing on the cigar. "Same with every other spread around here," he said. "Part of every one, sometimes all, once belonged to the Hartley Corporation."

He gave a careless wave with his cigar, tracing a circle of smoke in the air. "The Hartleys have been playing at buying and selling Texas land since Sam Houston first opened it up. Kind of a rich man's hobby, you might say. But the real trouble started when Jake Fielding sold Three Hills before he left town for good. It was Hartley who bought it all—lock, stock, and barrel. Oh, it went through a proper auction with lots of different bidders, and the way it appeared, Three Hills was divided up and sold to five or six different folks. I don't reckon even Jake Fielding himself, bastard that he was, knew who finally held the deed. It was real slick. I didn't guess myself till I started doing some checking.

"So, Hartley Corporation bought up Three Hills and, with a few other prime lots they already had, started making a quick profit with the turnover. They sold a piece here and there, then that seller sold, and it was all real tidy and discreet. Ranching went on around here like it's always been, and a lot of us got rich. But . . ." And now he paused, fixing Eddie Baker with a steel-hard gaze. "They never sold the mineral rights."

The next words were uttered very softly and very distinctly. "That woman owns the mineral rights on *every spread in this goddamn county.*"

At last Eddie understood. "Well, now," he said softly, "that's mighty interesting."

"Damn right it's interesting," Greenley shot back. "She can bring in her diggers and put up her derricks on my spread, or Henry Adams's, or any other son of a bitch who ever branded a steer, and there's not a damn thing the law can do about it. She can pollute our water holes, dry up our wells, spook our cattle, and damn well drive us out of business, and *that*'s what this is all about!"

Eddie Baker took a long draw of brandy, his mind working quickly. He was trying, as usual, to see an advantage for himself, but so far he was unable to find one. And if there was nothing in it for him, why had George sent for him?

He said after a moment, casually, "So you think she's going to get tired of digging holes in her own ground and start looking for greener pastures." He shrugged. "So let her try. If I know the ranchers around here, she won't get very far."

"Nothing stops that woman! Besides, she has the law on her side. I wouldn't put it beyond her to have the federal marshals down here ordering us off our own land, if that's what she took a notion to do!"

Eddie laughed. "You're getting all worked up over nothing, George. She hasn't even gotten anything out of the wells she's already sunk, and if you want my opinion, she's not going to. It's just another one of her little hobbies, like that toy motorcar of hers. Not a chance in hell."

"Don't make no difference," Greenley said plainly. "If she doesn't strike, all the more reason for her to start digging up other folks' land. That's one all-fired determined woman, our Miss Anne. Like a goddamn bulldog with a notion between her teeth."

Eddie took another swallow of brandy. "There's no oil around here. Everybody knows that Corsicana was just a fluke, and she's not an idiot, I don't care what you say. She can't keep pouring money down a rat hole."

"Well, I agree with you, Eddie. So does every right-thinking man in this county. But she's a woman—and a foreigner, at that. There's no accounting for what she'll do."

George tossed back another gulp of brandy and made a face, as though the taste were bad. "Have you been to

Corsicana lately?'' he demanded. ''You can't walk through
the streets without stepping across derricks, and that's no
goddamn lie. They got wells in their front yards and back
gardens and on their horse lots, and you can't rent a room or
a barn or even a patch of ground to lay your bedroll on for
any kind of price. It's a goddamn jungle, I'm telling you.
You can go deaf from the noise, and the smell will make
you lose your breakfast. Crazy folks from all over flocking
into that little town, bums and derelicts and con artists and
no-accounts hoping to make a little money, flinging up their
shanties and dragging along their whores. . . . Do you want
to see that happen here?''

Eddie lazily swirled the brandy in his glass. ''I can tell
you don't.''

''No, by God, I don't.'' Greenley drained his glass and
set it down on the desk with a thump. ''And you're going to
make sure it doesn't.''

Eddie lifted an eyebrow. ''Now wait just a minute,
George. I've got a lot at stake here.''

George's smile was shrewd. ''More than you know, old
friend.'' He wandered over to the window and pulled back
the drape. He spent a moment looking out over the section
of East Texas that was his, and when he spoke again, his
voice was thoughtful.

''You've done right well here, Eddie. Ten years ago you
didn't have anything but a stolen fortune and a notion to
better yourself, and look at you now—one of the most important businessmen in the county, with everybody looking
up to you, depending on you. Can't help but admire somebody like that. 'Course, that's always been Texas for you—
land of opportunity. Lots of men come here with secrets,
things they'd like to forget. I reckon some of them, like

yourself, left a few bodies along the trail somewheres. I never was one to hold a man's past against him, as long as he was doing his level best to make something of himself."

Now he turned to Eddie, his eyes cool and his expression placid. "I could've blown the whistle when I first found out about you. I think it's fair to say most people in this town wouldn't have been too happy about harboring a cutthroat swindler and murderer. I know of at least three warrants still outstanding on Eddie Baker. But . . ." He shrugged. "But putting you in power gave me the kind of control I needed, and it worked out well for me and the town. Like I said, I don't like to hold the past over a man's head. But I think it's about time we worked out some kind of deal."

Eddie's expression was perfectly calm, almost disinterested. "What if I'm not interested in your deal?"

"Well, then, there's this matter of a sealed letter in a safe-deposit box in San Francisco. It tells all about Eddie Baker, and it will be opened upon my death." He smiled. "A little insurance policy never hurts a man in my position. Of course, the letter could be sent to the sheriff of this town right now. Or it could be given to you, just as soon as you do me this one little favor."

Eddie's expression was pensive. "It would be a shame for that letter to fall into the wrong hands. It could ruin a wonderful career."

George beamed. "Exactly. I don't want to see that happen, any more than you do. I like to see a man reach his goals. And you're mighty close, now, Eddie, to having it all. Mighty close."

Eddie was silent for just another moment. It was impossible to read what was going on behind his eyes. "What do you expect me to do?"

"Simple. Just get those oil wells down. Make sure no more go up. For a man like you, that should be no problem at all."

"I thought you were going to ask me something hard." Eddie carefully tamped out his cigar. "I think I could manage that." He smiled faintly, busy with his own thoughts. "The more I think of it, the more I like the idea, as a matter of fact. It might be best for all concerned."

George brought out the brandy decanter and refilled Eddie's glass, then his own. He lifted his glass in a salute. "I knew you'd see it my way."

After a moment Eddie lifted his own glass and drank.

Stephen Brady was thirty-six years old, a dashing man with a handsome mustache and lively blue eyes. He was well educated for a Westerner, could discuss with ease and aplomb any subject from Plutarch to Sarah Bernhardt, and had a wardrobe that was always at the top of fashion. He was a charming and amusing companion, generally looked upon with favor by men and women alike. As president and general manager of the bank, he exuded confidence and sophistication and was without a doubt the most eligible bachelor in the county.

When Anne and Marc had first come to Texas, Stephen had befriended them both. This was only natural, as he was not only their financial adviser in the States but also the closest thing the community had to offer to a member of their own social class. He had introduced them to their neighbors and helped them adapt to the customs and idiosyncracies of their new environment.

Stephen was the first to admit he was an ambitious man, and being nice to wealthy foreigners was part of his job.

Since Anne had been widowed, his role as a banker had lessened its influence in their relationship, but ambition had not. Stephen Brady intended to marry Anne Edgecomb.

It wasn't avarice that motivated him, but ambition of a different sort. Anne was not a particularly wealthy woman in her own right, and since her family would like nothing more than to see her fail in Texas and come home to them, she could expect no financial backing from the Hartley Corporation. If it was money Stephen wanted, he would not have set his sights on Anne, for she was barely on speaking terms with her wealthy family, and Three Hills was perpetually on the brink of ruin.

What Stephen wanted was Anne—her style, her breeding, her wit, and her intelligence. She was the only woman he had ever met whom he genuinely liked; and she, simply by being Anne Edgecomb, Lady Hartley, opened up a world for him that had hitherto been out of reach. And he wanted Three Hills: the largest, grandest ranch in the county, with its history, its prestige, and its permanence. Anne—and Three Hills—represented for him everything that money could not buy, the achievement of a lifelong goal.

Stephen knew nothing of love, but Anne seemed to be a sensible woman who demanded little passion—another reason they were so perfectly suited for each other. During the past six years he had set everything up so carefully. She had no one else to turn to except Stephen, and he was always sympathetic, helpful, and understanding.

But until this oil business they had always seen eye-to-eye. But now it seemed too many other things were taking her attention away from him, and he was growing impatient.

After he'd been waiting fifteen minutes, Anne came down the stairs to Three Hills's parlor a little out of breath and apologized for her tardiness. It never failed to amaze Stephen how she could hurry without ever appearing rushed. Hers was an inborn elegance that every woman emulated but few ever achieved; it came simply from breeding.

"Stephen, dear, forgive me." She clasped his hands and brushed his cheek with a kiss. "I didn't forget you were due for dinner, I promise, but you wouldn't believe what a dreadful day I've had."

She wore a dinner gown of dusky rose silk, the bodice fichued with pale chiffon and anchored at the tiny waist with a black velvet bow. The long sleeves were tight at the wrist and puffed at the shoulder, just transparent enough to add a blush to the creamy skin of her arms. Her hair was upswept, and around her neck she wore a black velvet band ornamented with a pearl-draped cameo. Even for a casual dinner with an old friend, she was the picture of perfection.

He smiled and squeezed her hands lightly before she withdrew them. "You're always worth waiting for," he assured her.

"Are you starving, or shall we take time for a drink? Don't dare say no; I don't think I can survive another moment without one."

They walked arm in arm into the parlor, and Stephen left her to cross to the bar. "Sherry?"

She gave a soft groan and sank into a chair. "Don't be absurd. Bourbon—and quickly."

He poured a sherry for himself and a bourbon—generously diluted with water—for Anne. Such was the nature of their relationship that he did not have to ask her to unburden her problems to him; he knew she would do so when she was ready.

Anne sipped her drink and made a face. "God, Stephen,

this is horrid. I could have had a drink of water from the well. And if you're worrying about my becoming tipsy, don't. It would undoubtedly be an improvement.''

He replied gallantly, ''I'm sure you would be charming tipsy.'' He settled himself in the petit-point wing chair opposite her but did not offer to bring her another drink.

Anne smiled at him. In fact, she had almost forgotten their dinner, and she blamed that impudent young cowboy named Josh. It wasn't enough that he had humiliated her in public, insulted her business acumen in private, assaulted her senses with his brash, too knowledgeable gaze and bold comments; he had invaded her peace of mind as well.

Even after he had left Anne, the tingling in her skin wouldn't stop, and she found herself repeatedly going over every detail of their encounter, astonished and embarrassed by her own behavior. She felt—why, she felt almost assaulted by his presence, shaken and unguarded and foolishly elated. No one had ever had that effect on her before, and it angered her as much as it intrigued her. She must have been mad to have allowed him to stay on. There could be no other possible explanation.

Yet the thought of him even now in the bunkhouse, mere yards away, was like a jolt to her senses, momentarily scattering her concentration into a quickening of pulses and a spray of heat. Whatever else he did, he made her feel alive. But he also infuriated her.

For that reason, she deliberately squelched all thoughts of him and smiled at Stephen. ''Ah, Stephen, if only you knew how good it was to see a friendly face.'' She was aware, even as she spoke, that she was comparing him to the stranger in her bunkhouse. But it hardly mattered, she assured herself, for Stephen came out ahead.

He grinned. "Even though I don't serve your drink properly?"

"Even though."

She stared into her glass, her smile gradually fading. She said abruptly, "George Greenley came to see me today."

Stephen frowned. "They don't discourage easily, do they?"

She looked at him. "They don't discourage at all." Her smooth white brow knitted with a frown of exasperation. "Oh, Stephen, why are they so incredibly pigheaded?"

"Because they are Texans, my dear," he replied smoothly. "Pigheadedness is a long and gallant tradition with them."

He sipped his sherry and added, "What you've got to understand, Annie, is that the Cattleman's Association has been the only law in ranching country for a long time. And it wasn't necessarily a bad thing—they banded together to protect a common interest, and that common interest was ranching. Don't forget that it wasn't so long ago that the man who was right was the man who had the quickest gun, and a lot of people still think that way. The art of survival isn't something a man can just turn off when it becomes outdated."

Anne masked a mock shudder and gave an exasperated shake of her head. "The barbarism of this country never ceases to amaze me. Why, there are asphalt streets and electric lamps in Forth Worth. Mr. Edison lighted an entire pavilion in Chicago with nothing more than a snippet of wire!" Her eyes grew excited as she continued. "Why, do you realize you can pick up a metal tube and talk to someone three states away just as easily as I'm sitting here talking to you right now? Can you just imagine? And in the midst of all this, a handful of men think they can hold back progress with pickaxes and shovels—why, it's neolithic!"

Stephen chuckled. "I've always said there is nothing more inspiring in this world than a woman with a cause, and you, my dear, are magnificent. Carry Nation could take lessons." He added with a shrug, "George Greenley and his bunch are a little autocratic, I'll admit, but you must give them credit for what they've done. They've kept this community together through a lot of tough times, Anne. But their power is slipping now, as it inevitably must, and they refuse to realize it. They are a group of brave men desperately fighting to hold on to a way of life that's passing away." His tone was grave. "They're playing for high stakes, Annie, and shouldn't be underestimated. Be careful."

She made an impatient gesture with her wrist. "If I were the type of person who could be frightened off that easily, I wouldn't have lasted this long, now would I?"

The frown in his eyes was disturbed, and Anne quickly tried to mitigate it with her enthusiasm. "It's only a matter of time now, Stephen. The refinery at Corsicana can handle all the oil I can ship," she insisted. "The problem is going to be—"

"Finding oil?" suggested Stephen.

"Honestly, Stephen, sometimes you can be such a . . . banker!" And having thus delivered one of the most damning epithets she could bestow, she set down her drink and went over to a small secretary, withdrawing a folded map and returning to him quickly.

"Look," she insisted energetically, unfolding the map on the table between them. "We'll find the oil. How can we miss? Just look." She thumped the map. "Oil is already being pumped here, and here . . . and here. Why, if you want my opinion, this whole section of East Texas is nothing but a field of black gold!"

Stephen laughed softly, his eyes sparkling with muted affection. "Honey, your enthusiasm is hard to resist, and I'm sure your opinion is highly valuable, but you are hardly an expert."

She gave him a look rich with secret confidence. "Don't you worry about experts. I've taken care of that too. All I need do is hold out a little longer," she assured him. "I'll strike. What we've got to concern ourselves with now is laying the pipeline and getting the right-of-way to pump all that oil."

"Oh, is that all?" He let his amusement fade into a small shake of his head, and he added, more seriously, "Anne, I must admit I admire your determination. But I can't help wondering whether the fight you've set yourself up for is worth the cost."

For a moment uncertainty shadowed her eyes, but just as quickly it was replaced with the fire of adamant conviction. "Good heavens, Stephen, you know me better than that. I function at my best under pressure. Besides," she added smartly, "didn't I ever tell you my family motto? 'Great dreams demand great risks.' *I* will not be the Hartley who fails that credo!"

He laughed softly. "You are," he told her, "a wonder. Nothing gets in your way, does it?"

She smiled, a twinkle of mischievousness in her eye. "Not even you barbaric Texans!"

"Bravo!" He stood and held out his hand to her. "Now, as for our being barbarians . . . I would like you to think about something while you take me into supper, for which, I confess, I am famished." He helped Anne to her feet. "Isn't our barbarism one of the main things that attracted you to Texas in the first place?"

It was a rhetorical question that really did not require an answer, but a small frown disturbed Anne's brow as they walked arm in arm into the dining room. And she was to find herself thinking about it a great deal in the days that followed.

Chapter Five

Josh recognized Big Jim immediately, and from more than the size his name implied. Standing around six-four, he was only an inch or so taller than Josh. But the man outweighed Josh by some seventy-five pounds, and what once had been solid, rock-hard muscle had dissipated over the years into flab. What alarmed Josh more, though, was how the man's eyes had narrowed, and how his assessing glance that once might have represented authority and determination now spoke only of suspicion and ill use. Once he had been a big man; now he was just a small-time bully.

Josh had missed chow and was sitting on his bunk, mending a fringe on his jacket, when half a dozen cowhands started filing in. A couple of them looked at him curiously and went on about their business. Big Jim stopped in the center of the room, glaring at him.

"Who the hell are you?"

He was ugly and had a deep, growling voice that came from way back in his throat, hardly seeming to move his lips at all. His face was burned with years of sun and wind and clashed brilliantly with the strands of faded red hair that meshed thinly across his head. His big, flat lips were the color of liver, and his nose looked as if it had been broken more than once. After a brief glance Josh turned back to his mending.

"Name's Josh," he replied. "I'm the new hand."

Big Jim took a menacing step forward. "You are, are you? Says who?"

Josh lay aside the jacket and met his eyes evenly. "A lady by the name of Anne Edgecomb. She seems to think she's the boss."

The challenge hung in the air, still and taut. Big Jim took the intruder's measure and saw a dangerous edge of steel behind his mild gaze. Their animosity sprang up instantly, thickly. But the clatter of spurs and voices broke the moment as another group of cowboys wandered in. Josh picked up his jacket and needle again.

The voices became sporadic and then faded into the expected curious silence. Someone said, "Hey, ain't you the dude on the roan stallion?"

Josh glanced up. "That's right."

There were chuckles and nudges and more hoots of disbelief. "Say, Big Jim, you done messed in your nest if you hired this one on. Do you know what he did to the boss lady this afternoon?"

Jim growled. "I know." He turned away abruptly, stripping off his gun belt and hanging it on a peg above his cot. "It's her mess; let her clean it up."

There was another silence while the men digested this, then they began to drift toward their separate business. A deck of cards was broken out, and someone lit a cigarette. Josh cut off another strip of rawhide and began to thread it into the large-eyed needle.

Someone sat down on the cot next to Josh's. "I don't

think he likes you much," he commented, jerking his head toward Big Jim.

Josh followed his direction. "Nope. Doesn't appear to."

"Name's Dakota," said the other man, thrusting out his hand with a grin. "You just won me five dollars today, and I'm pleased to meet you."

He was a blond young man with an open, likable face and a golden scruff of beard. Josh shook his hand. "You can call me Josh. Glad to be of service."

"Did you really get the boss lady to take you on? Last I saw of her, she was ready to have you lynched."

Josh shrugged. "Reckon she changed her mind. Women have a way of doing that."

Someone from the card table gave a derisive hoot. "Not that woman. You ever try to reason with a bull that's got his horns stuck in a board? That's about how easy it is to get Miss Anne to change her mind." He glanced at Josh slyly. "Must've taken a shine to you."

"Women have a way of doing that too," replied Josh modestly. His comment elicited a couple of grins, but more than a few disgruntled snorts. Big Jim was silent, but Josh could feel his eyes on him, heavy and suspicious.

"I'll tell you one thing," grumbled someone else. "If she don't change her mind about that damn-fool oil scheme o' hers, she's gonna be out one good cowhand."

Dakota laughed and tossed a balled-up shirt at him. "Since when were you a good cowhand?"

The other man caught the shirt with a scowl and pommeled it back, but Josh's attention was caught. He listened alertly.

"I ain't no filthy miner," another man put in. "I come to work cows, and by God, that's what I'm gonna do."

"When you work at all."

Stretching to remove his boots, Dakota said, "Don't make no never mind to me. Way I figure it, the little woman's gotta have something to keep her busy. It's for damn sure she don't know a thing about running a cattle ranch. So let her dig for oil. Keeps her outa my hair."

Suddenly Big Jim spoke up fiercely. "It'll mean something to you the next time you have to push a dead steer in a hole. Pretty soon there won't be nothin' left but corpses, and then where will you be? Out of a job, that's where! We'll all be!"

Dakota grinned, prying off his boot and dropping it with a clatter. "Then I reckon I'll just have to learn to dig holes in the ground, won't I?"

Josh looked up, slightly incredulous. "Are you saying it's oil that's killing the cows?"

Big Jim turned a sharp and threatening gaze on him. "You stay out of this, boy. Ain't none of your business."

"If I'm going to be pushing carcasses in the ground with the rest of you," replied Josh, "I'd better make it my business." There were a few chuckles, and Josh shrugged. "Just doesn't make a lot of sense, that's all, that the lady would go killing off her own stock."

Big Jim's thin, red brows lowered harshly, and he came toward Josh with three deliberate steps. "I don't like your attitude, boy," he said distinctly. He looked him up and down. "Matter of fact, I don't like anything about you at all."

Josh returned his gaze for a moment without much interest, then took another stitch. "Well, now, that's mighty interesting. I've been giving it some thought myself, just sitting here, and I've decided I don't much like you, either."

Big Jim hooked his thumbs into his belt, his sausagelike fingers curling into fists. "You got something you want to do about it?"

Josh didn't even bother to look up. "Oh, I'll be giving that some thought, too, in the next couple of days."

The card game went on, the man across from Josh continued to scrape the muck off his boots, and someone crossed to the stove for a cup of coffee. To all appearances no one was paying much attention to what went on between the two men. But there was an undercurrent of alertness around the room, and Josh was aware that a great deal depended on what happened next.

Big Jim's eyes were hard, and his voice was matter-of-fact and deadly. He said, "You just do that, boy. Because I don't have to give it a damn bit of thought. If I was you, I'd be watching my back, because I'm going to pick the time and the place. And we'll just see what you can do about it."

He turned and strode across the room to his own bunk, and Josh hadn't a doubt that Big Jim would keep his word.

There was an uncomfortable silence, and Josh was aware of more eyes upon him than before, as the activities gradually resumed. Silently he cursed. It wasn't as though he weren't prepared for trouble, but things sure would go a lot smoother if he didn't have to face it.

Dakota leaned forward to strike a match on the back of his jeans, casting Josh a friendly grin as he lit his cigarette. "Don't let old Jim rile you," he advised, keeping his tone low and confidential. "He's just a little crotchety, is all." He shook out the match and let it fall on the floor. "Used to be a big-time rancher, they say, and lost it all in the blizzard of '91. So now he punches cows for some prissy-pants English lady and takes it out on the whole world. Not a good man to cross, but if you stay out of his way, he'll pretty much leave you alone."

He took a drag on the cigarette and narrowed his eyes against the smoke. "As for Miss Anne, well, she's a fancy talker and a high-stepper, but she's got feathers in her brains. Between her and Big Jim, there ain't too much you can't get away with around here, if you just lay low and don't call attention to yourself. Not a bad outfit to work for, all in all."

The man across from Josh looked up from scraping his boots. Suspicion was masked behind a pretense of casual curiosity as he commented, "Nice jacket. Don't see many like it around here."

Josh said, "A Cheyenne woman made it for me."

Someone else remarked, "Good-looking horse too. You ride him far?"

It would have been a breach of bunkhouse protocol to come right out and ask a man who he was and where he was from; too many of those who would have liked to ask had things to hide themselves. But suspicion of strangers was a natural instinct—especially when that stranger rode an expensive horse and sported uncommon gear—and Josh neither held their curiosity against them, nor did he encourage it. He replied only, "He's a stayer, all right."

"Done much punching?"

"Here and there."

Satisfied that they weren't going to get anything more out of him, the cowhands began to drift back to their separate tasks. Dakota, who had been watching and smoking with a mild amusement, said, "They'll give you a hard time for a while, only natural. Hang close to me if you want. I'll be glad to show you the ropes."

Josh's lips twitched in a wry smile. "Appreciate that," he murmured, and took his last stitch. He knotted the rawhide, cut it with his penknife, and began to fold up the jacket.

The door opened, and the jingle of spurs announced a new arrival. The steps halted in the middle of the room, and once again activities ceased for a moment. Then the cowhand strode across the room and stood directly in front of Josh. "Who the hell are you?" he demanded loudly.

The man was small and wiry, with greasy dark hair and a three-day bristle of beard. He had about him the instinctive belligerence that seems to be common to the runt of the litter. His eyes were bloodshot, and the odor of rye whiskey was strong about him. Even more than in the encounter with Big Jim, Josh sensed an excitement go through the room.

Dakota spoke up in his easy, humorous way, making an effort to dissipate the tension. "Hey, Gil, don't you recognize him? This is the *hombre* that chased that motorcar in the ditch this afternoon. You ought to know; you spent the better part of an hour hefting it out."

Gil cast a sharp look at Dakota, and when he looked back at Josh, his eyes were no more friendly. "I don't care who he is, he's sitting on my bunk."

Dakota demanded incredulously, "Since when?"

Someone else said, "God Almighty, Gil, that bunk's been empty since old Sawyer kicked off. What the hell do you want to go picking a fight for?"

Big Jim stood watching silently.

Gil stood before Josh, his fists clenching and unclenching, and Josh regarded him mildly. Then, without warning, Gil made a swipe for Josh's saddlebags.

Josh's gun leapt into his hand in a smooth motion that seemed to have a life of its own. Silence echoed like a slap, and Gil's expression froze in startled disbelief. Chairs began to scrape as men in the line of fire moved out of the way. Josh said quietly, "Drop them."

Gil's fingers loosened on the saddlebags, and they slipped back onto the cot. Then, slowly, he straightened up.

The iron-hard muscles in Josh's neck and shoulders relaxed fractionally; he carefully eased the hammer forward on his six-shooter but kept his thumb in place. A faint and easy smile curved his lips, but his eyes were as hard as glass. He said, his voice casual, "I'm surprised at you Texans. Why, where I come from, a man learns more respect for the property of others."

He leaned back against the wall, bringing up his knee to support his wrist in a casual stance. The gun never wavered. "Now," he continued smoothly, "about this bunk. I can understand you being attached to it; it's a mighty fine bunk, and I've grown pretty fond of it myself. So I'll tell you what I'll do, seeing as how you were here first and I'm a fair man. I'll pay you for the use of it, two bits a week. That sound fair to you, boys?" He addressed the question to the room in general but never took his eyes off Gil. "It's not worth much more than that, 'cause I'm deducting the price of a strong cake of soap to get the fleas out."

There were some chuckles, and Gil's color rose angrily. Josh dug into his pocket with his free hand and brought out a coin, tossing it to Gil. The other man caught it instinctively. "There you go. One week in advance."

Fury blazed in Gil's eyes, and he threw the coin back, bouncing it against the wall. Without another word he turned on his heel and stalked to an empty cot, where he flung himself down and fixed his eyes on the ceiling.

Josh could feel the looks of wariness cast his way, and the conversations that started up again were much more restrained than they had been before. He calmly reholstered his gun and got to his feet. "I think," he decided, "that this might be a good time to go check on my horse."

Dakota ground out his cigarette under his heel, chuckling softly. "I take back my offer," he said. "How about if you teach me the ropes?"

Josh couldn't help returning his grin as he started for the door. When he stepped out into the night air, the events of the day struck him, and he gave a wry shake of his head. Two enemies and one friend, he thought. Not bad for half an hour's work.

They paused in the shadow of a willow tree, and Stephen kissed her.

Anne pushed away from him a little, to look up at him. "It's late, Stephen," she said gently. "I should be going in."

But instead of stepping away, as he usually did, he surprised her by drawing her close again, bringing his face to her hair, and sighing deeply. "Ah, Anne," he whispered, "how much longer must this go on? You know I want to marry you. There's no need for you to face any of this alone. . . ."

Anne felt a tightening of dread in her stomach, and she stepped free of his embrace. "Stephen, please." She tried to soften her words by laying her hands lightly atop his arms and forcing a regretful smile into her eyes. "We've discussed this before. You are such a good friend, you mustn't spoil it—"

But Stephen was not to be so easily dissuaded that night. His eyes held an intense, almost passionate glow, and the clasp of his hands on hers was fervent. "Anne, I know you don't love me—"

"No," she protested, trying gently to withdraw her hands. "I'm dreadfully fond of you, of course—"

"But it doesn't matter." The grip of his hands on hers tightened, so that she could hardly pull them away without making a fuss. "I've always thought that mutual interest and respect for each other, a common outlook on life, are far more important to a marriage than passion. Love will come with time, Anne," he said tenderly, "and I have more than enough patience. Meanwhile we *like* each other and admire each other, and that's all that matters. We are good for each other, Anne."

No, Anne wanted to protest, that's not all that matters. But she did not know what else there could be. After all, she had never really experienced anything else herself. And yet . . . But, no, she had no sound reasoning for any of his arguments, and she could only look at him helplessly, hating the awkwardness, the uncertainty, and herself for being unable to make him see how she felt . . . or did not feel.

"Stephen," she finally said, as firmly as possible. "Please try to understand. I've had one marriage like that. I don't want another." Even as she spoke, she regretted the words that sounded too harsh, even to her own ears. Stephen was her best friend—at the present perhaps her only friend—and she would have given the world not to hurt him.

But she couldn't marry him, either.

"It would be different for us," he insisted, squeezing her

hands. "My God, Anne, you and I—think of it!" His eyes were brilliant with the possibilities, his voice intense. "What you and I together couldn't make of Three Hills—of this whole state! And our children, Anne. Think of them. We'd build a dynasty that would spread halfway across this country!"

Anne jerked her hands away, too surprised to disguise her indignation. "Good lord, Stephen! I am not a brood mare."

Stephen's color rose, and he swallowed hard. He took a quick, apologetic step toward her. "Anne, I didn't mean it to sound—"

Anne pressed her fingers to her temple with a weary sigh, her temper dissipating as quickly as it had come. "I know you didn't, Stephen." She hoped her voice did not sound as impatient as she felt. "It's just that I really don't want to deal with this now."

Stephen reached out and lightly, almost hesitantly, touched her face. "Annie," he said softly, "if it's the . . . physical side of marriage that you object to, that would come in time."

Anne looked at him blankly. How strange it was that for all the comfort of Stephen's embraces, the affection of his kisses, she never thought of the physical side of marriage in connection with him. Perhaps because she had never thought much of the physical side of marriage with Marc, either.

She took his hand and covered it warmly with both of hers, moved by a sudden rush of regret and affection. "You are a dear, sweet man," she said earnestly, "and I don't mean to be unkind. It's just that I am quite content with my life and really don't wish to marry anyone now. You can understand that, can't you?"

His lashes lowered to cover a flash of anger, and Anne's

relief was mitigated by sorrow. She did not want to hurt Stephen.

But when he looked up again, he was smiling, though it seemed an effort. "I won't push you tonight," he said quietly. "But the time has come to make a commitment. And you know me, Anne. I've been patient for a long time, and I'm not giving up this easily."

"Perhaps you should."

He looked at her soberly. "Do you really want me to?"

Anne looked at him with a mixture of helplessness, frustration, and no small amount of confusion. And then she couldn't look at him at all. She sighed. "I don't know," she said softly. "I don't know what I want."

He took her hand and pressed it to his lips. "I'll be back, Anne," he said. He smiled at her and walked away.

Anne released a weary sigh and leaned back against the trunk of a tree, listening to the sound of his retreating footsteps. She was afraid she had handled the whole thing very badly.

God, what was the matter with her? Everything Stephen said was right. They were perfect for each other. They had similar tastes and goals, and they thought alike. They were *comfortable* together. Yet there was a part of her Stephen could never satisfy, she knew instinctively, a part of her so elusive and undefined that she could not even grasp what it was, much less explain it to him.

He had made no secret of his intentions toward her, not since the beginning of their personal relationship. Everything he offered was what she needed. He would be a good manager for Three Hills, a devoted husband for her. Those were the considerations upon which civilized marriages were based.

She should love him. Perhaps she did, in her own way. But it wasn't enough. She was angry with herself for wanting more, and ashamed of herself for allowing Stephen to believe, even inadvertently, that she would settle for less. Marrying Stephen would be the sane, sensible, safe thing to do. And perhaps that was the whole problem. Anne had not come to Texas to play it safe.

Isn't our barbarism the very thing that attracted you to Texas in the first place?

A low chuckle sounded behind her, and Anne whirled with a gasp, her heart leaping to her throat.

"I'll tell you the truth, Duchess. You don't look a bit like a brood mare to me." She saw the red arc of a cigarette spin through the night and land sizzling on the grass. Josh stepped out of the shadows of the gazebo.

Hot color rushed to Anne's face and neck, and her heart was thundering. Her voice was choked with outrage and embarrassment. "How—how long have you been standing there?"

He came forward, an infuriating grin on his lips. "Long enough to hear you leading that poor slob along like a steer with a ring through its nose."

Anne's chest was heaving, and a surge of blinding temper overcame good judgment. "I was not leading him on!"

"Sure you were." He came to a stop only a few feet before her, thumbs casually hooked into his belt. The moonlight kept no secrets, and she could see the tightness of denim around his thigh, the parting of material at his collar, a few wayward curls shadowing his forehead. His voice was easy and made her skin prickle with awareness.

"You've got no more intention of marrying that fellow than I have," he continued. "But he left here counting his offspring and planning an addition to the house. I call that leading a man on."

With every resource at her command, Anne brought herself under control. Or at least she tried. She lifted her chin coolly and replied, "And just what makes you think I won't marry him?"

There was a soft light in his eyes that drew her attention and captured it, making her feel, briefly and absurdly, like a rabbit hypnotized by a snake. He took a step forward, and then another. He was close enough to touch her, and Anne's heart was beating with quick, tight motions that strained against her stays.

He said softly, "Because I know you."

He was looking at her again in that strong, absorbing way, and everything within Anne wanted to run, to snatch the robes of her dignity and her feelings of self-preservation around her and retreat. But she held her ground.

His eyes touched her breasts, and she felt naked. They lingered there, and she felt a swelling and a tingling of her nipples that she was helpless to control. A heat rose in her—of embarrassment or indignation, she could not be sure—but beneath that there was something more, something she would not admit or recognize. Perhaps it was excitement.

He met her eyes again. He said, "You're the kind of woman who faces down a bunch of vigilantes with a hunting rifle and hires a stranger who might be a desperado. You're the kind of woman who would take on the running of one of the biggest spreads in Texas and not even worry that you don't know the first thing about it. You try to outrun a thoroughbred in a mechanical toy and enjoy every minute of it. You don't take life in the ordinary way, Duchess, and your boyfriend there, he's real ordinary.''

His voice had a lazily hypnotic effect on her reason. Sometime during his speech he had moved even closer, and incredibly, she could feel his thighs brushing against her skirts, his body warmth whispering across her skin. Her breath was shallow, and she suddenly realized how secluded they were in the tree-shaded arbor, how terribly close he was and how strong. When he lifted his hand, her heart leapt against her rib cage and she wanted to flinch; deliberately she made herself be still.

The new spark in his eyes might have been admiration, or it might have been mockery. His fingers lightly captured a tendril of her hair that curled against her temple. He caressed its texture lightly while his eyes held hers with lazy, effortless force.

He said huskily, ''You know what I think? I think you're not a lady at all.'' His finger left her curl and trailed slowly, maddeningly, down the side of her face, tracing the shape of her jaw. Every nerve in Anne's body flared and tightened, and she had difficulty catching her breath. ''A lady wouldn't be standing here in the dark with a stranger. A lady would scream maybe, or run away. . . .''

His face was filling up her entire vision now, a dark face with shadowed eyes and lips faintly upturned in the quiet certainty of his power. In a mere fraction of a motion those lips could be covering hers, smothering her cries; another motion and he could be pushing her to the ground. . . .

She was frightened. Her breath was fast, and her veins rushed with awareness, readiness, the swift, powerful elation of senses working at their greatest peak. She had never felt more alive in her life.

His fingers drifted to Anne's throat, and she felt the rapid
flutter of her own blood against his rough-textured touch.
The air between them seemed to throb with electric impulses of anticipation and warning. "You like living on the
edge, Duchess," he said softly, and that finger trailed
upward, across the hollow of her throat, brushing her chin,
moving toward her lips. Her breath stopped. "You like
taking chances; you like doing things the hard way. You like
life quick and surprising and maybe even a little
dangerous. . . ."

Stop this, Anne thought, but it was a distant command
with very little meaning. She knew she should be insulted.
She wanted to deny his words, coldly and firmly, and walk
away. But how could she when her own body was conspiring to betray her, proving everything he said to be nothing
less than the truth?

He was danger, he was excitement. She was terrified and
elated, hovering on the brink of something powerful and
unknown, and she could not for all her life have drawn
away.

Josh's finger traced the shape of her underlip, a feather
touch of textured warmth. The glow in his eyes was like a
magnet. He touched the corner of her mouth, and her lips
parted for breath. Slowly his finger moved along her lips
again, brushing the moist, inner recesses, moving just a
fraction inside. She tasted him, salty and rough. Her thighs
were weak, her stomach tight. Every cell in her body
was a conductor of the spreading fever.

He doubled his knuckles against her cheek, brushing it
lightly. "Your Stephen's a nice enough fellow, but . . ." He
smiled and dropped his hand. "You could do better, Duchess."

Perhaps it was the mention of Stephen's name, perhaps it

was the absence of his touch, but a thread of reason rushed back which felt to Anne like a gust of cool air penetrating a stuffy room. She took a step back to gain more distance between them and was angry because it felt like a retreat. She said sharply, "Someone like you, I suppose."

She knew her mistake immediately and was furious with herself for it. Her impetuous words sounded more like an invitation than an insult, and that was exactly what he wanted. What he expected.

"Oh, yes." He leaned his weight back, his thumb going to his belt again, the far too confident gleam in his eyes relaxing. "I, for example, would never make any promises about 'the physical side of marriage.' "

Anne no longer made any pretense at controlling herself. She drew herself up, her lungs expanding with an outraged breath, and reason rushed back with an explosion of indignation and fury. "You vile, insulting, filthy swine! How dare you insinuate—! How dare you lurk in the bushes and *spy* on me! Who the bloody hell do you think you are?"

His eyes were gleaming softly, sweeping her stiff figure with thorough enjoyment. "Me?" he inquired, a maddening undertone of laughter to his voice. "Why, I'm just the man who's going to make you the happiest woman in the world."

Anne's only regret was that she was too well bred to hit him. She gathered up her skirts, her nostrils flaring, her eyes blazing. "You, sir," she informed him in a low, steady voice, "are dismissed. Kindly be off my property before morning."

She swept past him and stalked toward the house.

Josh stood still, chuckling softly. He wondered at how she could set his blood afire quicker than any woman he had

ever known. It didn't matter whether she was cold with
contempt, or hot with anger, or still and eager for a man's
touch, as she had been a moment ago. . . . She was magnificent.

He rolled a cigarette at leisure, enjoying the cool night air
and the visions of Anne that lingered in his head. Anne
Edgecomb. Proud, strong, powerful. Sharp-eyed and dazzling, soft and cutting, as full of surprises as a twisting
canyon road on the edge of spring. Life with her would
never be dull.

She needed a man, all right, and in more ways than one.
But the best part about it was that she didn't even know it
yet. She was like a winter flower frozen under layers of
earth, waiting for the touch of the sun to bring her to life. It
would be a careful process that couldn't be rushed, but once
she was touched, her awakening would be like nothing that
had ever gone before. And Josh was looking forward to
taking his time.

He smiled at the prospect, and his eyes wandered toward
the house. His smile deepened. "God, lady," he said softly,
"you take it too damn easy."

Still chuckling to himself, he started back toward the
bunkhouse.

Chapter Six

Anne slept remarkably well, as was her custom. No long-limbed, laughing-eyed cowboys, angry cattlemen, or pleading suitors invaded her dreams. Marc used to tease that the soundness of her sleep was the sign of a woman with absolutely no conscience. Anne's own explanation was much more practical. Day by day, as life's problems came along, she handled them with efficiency and dispatch; she saw no reason to allow unpleasantness to disturb her sleep as well. And because even her subconscious mind dared not challenge Anne's will, she awoke each morning rested and refreshed, with no remnants from the previous night lingering to haunt her.

Anne's method of dealing with unpleasantness was quite simple and very effective: She simply ignored it. Remembering the encounter in the garden with Josh would have shocked and disturbed her, taken her concentration away from the business of the day, and caused her considerable embarrassment. So she chose not to remember it at all. He had been dismissed; he was off her property and out of her life; and that was the end of that.

Or so she thought, until she came down for breakfast the

following morning and found him sitting at the dining room table. His hat was on the sideboard; the plate before him testified to the remnants of an enormous meal of ham and eggs. He was leaning back in the chair, one leg flung casually over the armrest, eating a biscuit and drinking a cup of steaming coffee. There were small scars on the gleaming, waxed surface of her floor, which Anne realized had been left by spurs.

Anne paused in the center of the room, and he said cheerfully, "Good morning."

His clothes had been brushed clean of dust and travel stains. His face was closely shaved, and he looked remarkably fresh and well groomed. His vest was a soft, crinkled leather, and his forest-green shirt picked up the emerald color of his eyes. The soft curls that teased the back of his neck and shadowed his forehead looked freshly brushed, crisp and springy and provocative to the touch.

She looked at Josh, and every detail of the evening before blossomed clearly and sharply in her mind. Heat began to creep out of her collar and her cuffs, but that was not the worst of it. The worst was the way her heart gave a little lurch and a warmth that felt absurdly like pleasure began low in her abdomen.

Quickly Anne snatched back the wayward emotions. She was even proud of the tone of quiet deliberation she managed to give her voice when she demanded, "What are you doing here?"

"Well, ma'am, I've always thought it was a downright sin to let a lady eat breakfast alone." He gestured obligingly with his coffee cup. "I'm happy to be of service."

She refused to become angry so early in the morning. Besides, it wasn't anger she was feeling at all. It was that new and sharp alertness that seemed to afflict her whenever he was around. Poised for challenge, and eager for it, Anne could feel every fiber of her being opening in readiness for adventure that seemed to be just around the corner. There was nothing unpleasant about the sensations. Nothing at all.

She said calmly, "I thought I had dismissed you, sir."

He grinned, popped the remainder of a biscuit into his mouth, and licked his fingers. "You can't fire me, Duchess. I'm not on the payroll."

Anne inclined her head graciously. "I see." She came toward the table.

His eyes followed her as he said, "What's that outfit you have on?"

Anne stopped in the process of pulling out her chair and stared at him. That day she intended to visit the drilling sites, and she had dressed accordingly in a cotton shirt and a split-legged riding skirt that fell only a few inches below the tops of her boots. The trouser skirt was an innovation of the bicyclists back East and still met with a great deal of disapproval in Texas, but Anne had never before felt self-conscious about wearing it.

She said sharply, "I fail to see why that should be of any interest to you."

She pulled out her chair, sat down, and unfolded her napkin with a snap. Josh watched her with a slowly spreading grin and a rapidly growing swell of pleasure. Every move she made was an exercise in grace.

Her breasts were high and round beneath the soft shape of her tailored shirt. The short pant skirt she wore was a little shocking—almost indecent—but it had its advantages too. The material outlined her thighs and drew flat across her belly, and the way it was divided between her legs was nothing short of suggestive. One had to admire a woman who could wear something like that and still hold her head up.

Anne picked up a little silver bell near her plate and rang it. Josh sipped his coffee, and Anne deliberately avoided looking at him. But she could feel his eyes on her just as surely as if they were his hands instead, and when she could stand it no longer, she shot a glance at him. Indeed, he was studying her, and looking as though he enjoyed it immensely.

She jerked her eyes away, brought her hand up to touch her throat, felt foolish, and folded her hands in her lap again.

Josh smiled. "Do I make you nervous?"

Anne looked back at him. "Frankly, yes. Your staring is quite rude and makes me uncomfortable."

The smile deepened at one corner. "Good. I never want you to be comfortable around me."

A small black maid in a dark uniform and a crisp white apron hurried in, and Anne had rarely been so grateful for prompt service. She requested in her gently rounded, perfectly British voice, "Tea and toast, please."

The maid bobbed a curtsy and turned to go, but Josh held out his coffee cup with a beguiling smile. "How about bringing the pot, sweetheart?"

The maid flashed him a smile, glanced quickly at her mistress, and hurried out. Josh looked back at Anne with a lifted eyebrow. "Tea and toast? No wonder you're so skinny."

Anne inquired evenly, "Do you have a last name?"

"There's plenty of ham and eggs left. I had them make up a big batch."

Anne kept her faintly condescending smile frozen in place. "Your name?" she repeated.

"Why do you want to know?"

"So that I can put you on the payroll and dismiss you properly, of course."

He laughed.

Anne watched him thoughtfully. The vibrancy of his presence was an intrusion into her elegant dining room, a challenge to her mastery. Masculine laughter and lazy, sensual glances were as out of place as spurs and dusty hats, yet in some strange way all of him seemed to belong. She, in fact, became the intruder. It was an uncomfortable feeling but an intriguing one.

Of course, what she should have done was to order him out of her house and off her property, calling an armed escort if necessary. And, of course, she had no intention of doing any such thing.

She said thoughtfully, "I could make your life very uncomfortable, too, you know."

His eyes glinted and he murmured, "Oh, please do."

Anne casually straightened a corner of her napkin on her lap. "I could, for example, ask the sheriff to look into you and your fine horse with its mysterious brand."

He smiled at her over the rim of his cup. "Seems like an awful lot of trouble to me. All you have to do is be nice to me and I'll tell you anything you want to know."

Anne couldn't help noticing the long, dark fingers that cradled the cup and what a contrast they made with her delicate china. She couldn't help remembering their touch and their taste. She thought he was remembering too. From the soft gleam in his eyes she was almost certain.

But she would not be intimidated. Not by his smile, not

by the shape of his hands nor the images they evoked. She merely returned a polite smile and suggested, "Why don't you start with your name?"

Josh sipped the last of his coffee, his rich, green eyes half shaded by a fringe of lashes, a sober expression drawn on his face. "I'm not one to point out other people's mistakes, ma'am, but you being new to these parts and all, I guess you don't realize that's not exactly a polite thing to ask."

The maid came in with a tray and set a plate of toast and a pot of tea before Anne. Anne poured with the wrist, from the silver pot her elbow at her side. Josh cocked his head, watching her. "As it happens," she responded evenly, "you are far newer to these parts than I am, and if there is one person at this table whose manners are in question, it most certainly is not I. However, just for the sake of argument, perhaps you would be good enough to tell me why it is impolite to ask an employee his last name?"

"Plenty of reasons, ma'am," he explained. The maid refilled his coffee cup and set the pot before him, and he winked at her. He turned back to Anne, his expression deadpan. "You see, the West is where a lot of folks come to escape from something, and it's just not a good idea to poke around too much in a man's background. You might brush up against something he'd rather keep to himself and you don't really want to know."

She inclined her head, stirring cream into her tea with not even the slightest rattle of her cup. "Such as?"

"Oh, I don't know." He leaned back, sipping his coffee. Anne noticed the way the material of his shirt rose and fell against his chest when he moved, faintly outlining the shape of a breast muscle and the line of his arm. His chest would be lean, she suspected, firm but not bulky, and his arms would be very strong.

"He might have a wife he's trying to get away from," Josh continued, "or a jealous husband, for that matter. Might have a flock of bad men on his trail, or a reputation he's trying to outlive. Or he might be—"

"Running from the law?" Anne inquired.

Josh met her gaze with a spark of admiration and a faint curve to his lips, which admitted nothing. He agreed mildly. "Maybe." He sipped his coffee. "Amazing what they can do with the telegraph these days," he mused. "Why, with a man's full name or even a halfway decent description of him, a wire can go out over half a dozen different states in a matter of minutes. An outlaw hardly even has a chance anymore."

Anne lifted her cup, commenting, "So, of course, a man of dubious status with the authorities would be quite foolish to give out his real name."

"He sure would." Josh smiled. "Mine's Coleman, by the way. Josh Coleman."

She gazed at him over her cup. "Is that the truth?"

He grinned. "Do I look like a fool, Duchess?"

She sipped her tea, regarding him with absolutely no expression at all for a time. Josh broke open another biscuit, slathered it lavishly with butter, and sat back to eat. Anne set her cup silently on its saucer and reached for the butter.

"This is what you look like to me, Mr. Coleman," she said, buttering her toast with smooth, neat movements. "You look like a young man who's had his own way far too long. An indulgent mother or doting grandparents might be responsible, but at any rate, you've grown up spoiled and pampered and quite convinced that the world would spin upon the tip of your finger should you so desire. Of course, being so good-looking hasn't helped matters much, for it is an unfortunate fact of life that physical beauty and charm open far too many doors for those so endowed. In many ways, Mr. Coleman, you are little more than a spoiled child with a great deal of growing up to do.''

The arrested attention in his eyes was gratifying, though he seemed more intrigued than insulted. Anne placed her toast on her plate and set down the knife, addressing him directly. "You also," she added, "have a great many secrets. Whether they are as important as you seem to think they are remains to be seen, but I intend to find out, have no doubt of that. You seem to think a great deal of yourself, but that, too, remains to be proven. Overconfidence can be quite dangerous, Mr. Coleman. You should be careful you don't take on more than you can handle."

Josh leaned back in his chair, an appreciative spark coming into his eyes that was not at all what Anne had expected. "You know something, Duchess?" he said, and Anne inclined her head in question. "I really like you."

Anne smiled. "But am I right?"

He grinned and lifted his cup to her in a small salute. "I think I'll let that be one of my secrets."

Anne tore off a corner of her toast. "Why have you come here, Mr. Coleman?" she asked. Her question sounded careless, almost rhetorical. She bit into the toast, chewed, and swallowed, watching him all the while. "What do you want?"

He finished off his biscuit and drained his coffee cup. There was a relaxed and speculative gleam in his eye that both infuriated and intrigued Anne. "Well, now," he drawled, "you're a smart lady. It ought to be obvious. I've come here to swindle you out of your fortune and take your virtue."

She met his eyes without a flicker of expression in her own. "That might not be so easy to do as it sounds, Mr. Coleman."

Behind the half-playful light in his eyes Anne sensed something quite serious, something she was too wise to ignore.

He said softly, "Or it might be even easier."

For just an instant Anne was unsettled, and she was reminded of how little she knew of him. This man with the sultry eyes and tousled curls could be dangerous; there was power in his lanky form and purpose behind his lazy drawl. He brought adventure into her formal dining room with its gleaming mahogany furnishings and tastefully subdued hangings; he brought a taste of the wild into this place that had been too civilized for too long. Everything about him appealed to her sense of drama and the unknown, and she could no more have turned her back on the challenge he offered than she could have bowed under to George Greenley the day before. Certain things were simply impossible to resist.

She sipped her tea and studied him for a moment over the rim of the cup. "You always get what you want, don't you, Mr. Coleman?"

He replied without hesitation. "Yes."

She smiled and looked back at him. "Well, I do hope you are prepared to face disappointment, because there is one thing you are not going to get."

Josh lifted a questioning eyebrow, and Anne folded her hands before her, looking him over in a frank and leisurely assessment. "You are a very attractive young man," she informed him graciously. "Earthy and masterful and even rather entertaining in a somewhat unpolished way. I suppose all those things have a certain appeal, for some women."

He inclined his head in modest agreement, and Anne smiled at him indulgently. "However," she added, "if you don't mind a bit of well-meant advice..."

"By all means, Duchess. I'm here to learn."

"First of all, I am not a duchess, and I would appreciate it if you did not continue to call me that. Secondly," she added, "please don't expend any more of your considerable charm on me. Save it for someone who will appreciate it, for I'm afraid you're simply wasting your time here."

For a single breath he was silent and appeared to consider her words with all due seriousness. Then his mouth slanted upward in an easy grin. He said, "Don't you worry, Duchess. I'm not wasting my time at all." Then he shrugged and added lightly, "Of course, like you said, that all remains to be seen." He refilled his coffee cup. "What I came here for today was this."

He reached into his pocket and tossed a handful of weeds atop her snowy white tablecloth.

Anne made an expression of annoyance at the clumps of dirt that spilled across her breakfast table. "Are you mad? What—"

"Ragwort," he explained, and leaned back again, engulfing her delicate china cup in both his hands. "That's what's been killing your cattle."

She stared at the weeds and then at him. "How can you be sure?"

He shrugged. "The pickin's have got so lean in the summer pasture that your stock has started wandering across the creek. That's where you've been losing most of them, isn't it? That field's just full of ragwort. Any good cattleman can recognize it.''

"My foreman said the cattle were dying from polluted water, because of the oil."

He brought the coffee cup to his lips. "It'd take a fool not to know ragwort poisoning when he saw it. I knew what it was yesterday, but I thought I'd better bring back the evidence for you to check out for yourself."

"Are you implying that my foreman is a fool?"

"No, ma'am," Josh replied. "I'm not implying any such thing. I'm saying it flat out."

Anne stood up, taking the little bundle of weeds with her. Her head was reeling with anger at Jim's incompetence, mixed with an overwhelming relief that she was not, after all, to blame. She walked away from the table, turning the weeds over in her hand, her thoughts coming with rapid, demanding precision. She said at last, carefully, "You realize, of course, that you are implying a conspiracy—that all my ranch hands knew of this and determined between them to keep it from me."

"There you go with the 'implying' again." There was a trace of impatience in his tone. "What I'm *saying* is that your hands don't know or care. Why should they? Big Jim makes it easy for them if they do what he says. And I reckon he's got his own reasons for wanting you to think it was oil that was killing your cattle."

She turned sharply to look at him, her expression probing. "Do you think he knew what was killing the stock and lied to me?"

"I don't know," Josh replied. "I wouldn't put it past him. But Big Jim is a lazy kind of fellow, and I figure he'd

just jump to the first explanation that came his way—
especially if it was the one he wanted, anyway."

"I see."

Anne held an attitude toward her employees that Marc,
who was of an intellectual bent, had referred to as "disgustingly
classist and terribly, terribly British." She relied upon her
hirelings completely, yet she did not trust them out of her
sight. When they did not do their jobs, she took it as a
personal affront.

"This is intolerable, of course," she decided, and she
tossed the weeds onto the sideboard without ceremony. "I
can't have a foreman who doesn't know his job. I shall take
this up with him immediately."

Josh seemed surprised. "You're going to fire him?"

Her raised eyebrows mocked his interference. "You have
an objection?"

His reply was quick and adamant. "Well, now that you
ask, I do. It takes more than cash and cattle to run a ranch.
There's a little thing called loyalty. And you can't expect it
from your hands if you don't give it to them."

His audacity never ceased to amaze her. She stared at
him. "I hardly see—"

He didn't even acknowledge the interruption. "You run a
real fine house, ma'am," he continued plainly. "Everything's shined and polished and running like clockwork, and
I'm sure your *staff*"—he emphasized the word slightly
—"is the finest in the business. But what you don't know
about running a ranch could fill a book."

She drew herself up for an indignant reply, but he gave
her no chance. "It all filters down from the top, Duchess.
Maybe it's different where you come from, but in America
the boss has got better things to do than sit around in a

fancy house flipping through magazines and planning socials. He's out there riding the range with the rest of the hands every day, throwing steers, lifting a branding iron, shaking out a loop. You show me a cattleman with clean hands and I'll show you a fool or a shyster. You only get back what you put in, and if you don't know your business, you can't expect someone else to know it for you."

"I'll have you know I've been running this ranch quite successfully for six years—"

"Is that a fact? And when was the last time you rode a roundup? How many steers did you pull out of the brush yesterday? Done any good fence work lately?"

Her eyes glittered, and she did not even bother with a reply.

Josh opened one hand palm-up on the table, a gesture of conciliation. "Look," he said patiently, "all I'm saying is that you're a little quick on the draw when it comes to blame casting, and plainly speaking, you can't afford to be. None of this would have happened if you'd paid attention to what you're responsible for—your land and your cattle."

He shrugged. "You want to fire your foreman? I can't stop you. But it's going to stir up a lot of hard feelings, and if you think you've got troubles now, wait till half your hands ride off and you're trying to replace them in the middle of the season."

Anne looked at him sharply. "It was you who told me Big Jim was a fool. Now you're defending his job."

"I've got nothing against the man personally. Matter of fact, I feel kinda sorry for him." He smiled a little, but it was an absent smile, rather sad, devoid of his usual deliberate charm. Anne's attention quickened.

"You've got to know his type," Josh said. "A hard man,

yes, but this country was made by hard men. And now it's outgrown them, wants to push them aside. Where's a fellow like Big Jim going to go nowadays? What's he going to do? All he knows is horses and cattle. So maybe he's gotten a little lazy. I can't like that, but I've got to understand it. A man with nothing to fight for grows soft. A man with nothing to look forward to stops caring. Big Jim is just a lonely man who'll die alone with nobody to even miss him when he's gone. Yeah, I feel sorry for him.''

Something had changed about Josh during the speech, and Anne caught a glimpse of something surprisingly genuine. His voice had softened, and his gaze was absent, as though he were speaking to himself. Anne knew he was thinking of more than just Big Jim and his fate.

Anne said softly, ''And you? Will anyone miss you when you're gone?''

He looked at her, but the smile that traced his lips was still rather sad and faraway. ''Maybe.''

Anne probed carefully. ''A woman?''

She knew then she had struck a nerve. Something crossed his eyes, a flicker of pain that was repressed in only the next instant. But Anne felt something hollow form in her stomach when she saw it. Perhaps it was a woman he missed . . . and loved.

And then his old smile was back, the relaxed twinkle in his eye, and he admitted slowly, ''Yeah. A woman. Three of them, as a matter of fact.''

Anne's eyes widened.

''My sisters.'' He grinned. ''The ones that spoiled me so. I reckon they'd miss me some—enough to lay out for a decent-sized marker, anyway.''

Her relief was silly, her fascination inexplicable. The

strange sense of delight she felt was no more than having been able to put, at last, some sort of label on him. The man had sisters, he displayed unwarranted compassion for a foreman he hardly knew, and when he talked about the land and the ranch, his eyes glowed with a fierce, protective pride. . . . He had become three-dimensional to her in the past half hour, real and solid and singular. And he was more of an enigma than ever.

Anne found herself wanting to pursue the conversation, to slip through the slightly opened door that seemed to lead to his inner self and discover more. But she knew the moment had passed, and she would be foolish to try to prolong it.

Instead she said, "I must say, Mr. Coleman, it seems strangely out of character for you to show such concern for my foreman. A man you hardly know and whom, I've heard it said, isn't easy to like."

He grinned. "Well, to tell the truth, maybe I did have a little self-interest at heart. Big Jim didn't take much of a shine to me, and if you fire him now—especially with me finding the ragwort and all—who do you think he's going to blame? I've got enough folks gunning for me as it is."

"Indeed? Who?"

He grinned. "You, for one."

Anne murmured a dry, "Quite," and felt he had scored properly. One could not expect honesty from an outlaw, after all. "Well, I wouldn't want to inconvenience you, of course. Nor would I want to stir up discontent among the remainder of my employees. Perhaps you have a suggestion?"

He pretended to ponder the question. As much as she loathed asking him for advice, that was how much he enjoyed it. "Well, if this was my ranch . . ." He seemed to like the way that sounded and repeated it. "If this was my ranch, I reckon I'd take years of loyal service under consideration and find Big Jim another job on the place, where he couldn't do any harm. And let him keep his pride. Make him think he's doing you a favor. A cultured lady like you shouldn't have any problem making a man feel like a hero while you're kicking him in the teeth, now should you?''

Once again irritation flared, and a hasty retort was on her lips when she turned. She swallowed it the moment she saw the laughter in Josh's eyes. ''I will certainly take your suggestion under advisement,'' she responded rather stiffly.

Josh pushed up from the table. ''Meantime, what you need to do,'' he advised, ''is start pushing those cows down out of the hills, before they all starve to death.'' He retrieved his hat from the sideboard and clapped it on his head.

''Yes, of course,'' she murmured distractedly. ''And . . .'' She looked up at him. The next words were very difficult. ''I suppose . . . you'd better stay on for a while, after all.''

He grinned at her. ''Why, that's just what I was planning to do, Duchess.''

Anne wrestled back another stab of annoyance. Just when she thought she was beginning to reach an understanding with him, he did something to provoke her again—and with so little effort or forethought on his part that it was doubly frustrating.

''You are a very peculiar man, Mr. Coleman,'' she said. ''And perhaps not so easy to catalog as I first supposed. But I will continue to try,'' she assured him firmly. ''Upon that you may depend.''

''And I wish you all the luck in the world, Duchess,'' he replied, but the merriment in his eyes warned her that better women than she had failed.

Anne's lips tightened as he turned and started down the front hall, his spurs gouging tufts of wool from her carpet. Of course he would leave by the front door. The man was insufferable.

"Mr. Coleman," she called sharply, and he turned. "The next time you enter this house," she informed him, "you will kindly remove your spurs."

He winked at her, touched his forefinger to his hat, and opened the door. He was whistling as he left, and the tune was "The Yellow Rose of Texas."

Chapter Seven

Josh hadn't realized how much he missed the range until that morning, when he had ridden out to look over the land. The challenge of all that was waiting for him swelled in his blood and sent his mind down busy trails. He was filled with pride as he looked around the ranch yard and toward the rolling hills beyond. Nothing had ever felt so right or so perfect. Already it felt like coming home.

Josh spoke to the roan, gave him a lump of sugar he had filched from Anne's breakfast table, and unwound the reins from the hitching post. He was preparing to mount when he noticed two riders coming down the drive. One was an odd-looking character dressed up in a white shirt and string tie but sporting a seedy scrub of beard, and riding a pack animal loaded down with camping gear. He looked like a prospector in from the hills for a funeral. Josh's curious expression widened into a grin as he recognized the second rider.

He leaned his shoulder against the roan as he measured the competition for the first time in the light of day. Stephen Brady was almost as tall as Josh, not bad looking and obviously well-to-do. He had the look of a man who had been over the trail a few times and knew the taste of power.

All of this was enough reason for Josh to dislike him, but there was more. Something about Stephen Brady was too smooth, too rehearsed, as though he had spent a lot of time learning what people expected from him and giving them just that. Whoever he was, he was definitely not the man for a passionate woman like Anne.

"Well, good morning," Josh said in greeting as they rode up. "We weren't expecting you back this soon."

Stephen dismounted, hiding his surprise with a polite, if somewhat abrupt, "Good morning. We're here to see Lady Hartley. Is she in?"

Josh watched him carefully, and he could not read Stephen's eyes. He had long ago learned not to trust a man who masked his eyes. Absently patting the roan's neck, he kept his own expression amiable. "Kind of early to be calling, isn't it?" he asked. "Anne and I just got up from the breakfast table."

Stephen's gaze sharpened, but what he might have said next Josh was never to know because Anne had come out just in time to hear that last remark. She came quickly down the steps, and her color, thought Josh, was even more attractive than it had been in the hallway. If she was flustered, she did not show it, but her eyes were glittering. Josh liked that.

"Stephen," she said warmly, "how pleasant." She darted a quick glance at Josh, and her voice was tight. "Didn't you say something about moving the stock?"

Josh remained where he was, looking Stephen over with a negligence that easily could be misconstrued as friendliness. "Are you going to introduce me to company, Duchess?"

Anne's jaw tightened, but the disturbed curiosity in Stephen's eyes left her little choice. "Stephen," she said briefly, "this is Josh Coleman, the new *hired hand*.'' She put particular emphasis on the last two words, but Josh cast her an amused look that completely negated their effectiveness.

Josh tipped his hat. ''Pleased to meet you, Steve. Anne and I were talking about you just last night.''

There was a half second's pause, and Anne could feel the latent hostility between the two men. It didn't surprise her—Josh seemed to have that effect on everyone, and he certainly had been going out of his way to annoy Stephen. But Stephen kept his expression smooth and, acting the better man, chose to ignore Josh. Anne was not at all certain she admired Stephen for that.

Stephen turned back to her.

''Anne, this is quite irregular, I know, and I hope you'll forgive me for barging in at this hour, but . . .'' He glanced somewhat guardedly at the bedraggled-looking character on the packhorse. ''This—er—gentleman was asking in town for directions to Three Hills. He said you were expecting him. I thought I had better ride along and show him the way.'' He lowered his voice a fraction with the last, and what he really meant was that he was offering his services as a protector.

The man on the mule tipped his hat. ''Amos Wright, ma'am, at your service.''

Anne *was* flustered, and it took every ounce of poise she had to keep from showing it. She had hoped to keep this part of her venture from Stephen, at least for a while, for she still valued his judgment and didn't wish to provoke him into a senseless argument. Valiantly she tried to make the best of it.

''Stephen,'' she said airily, ''I completely forgot to mention this. Amos Wright is the expert we've been looking for—the famous creekologist." She turned quickly to Mr. Wright. "I'm so happy you could make it. You're as good as your word. We've corresponded for quite some time," Anne added to Stephen. "And I'm convinced of Mr. Wright's credentials as the foremost creekologist in the country."

Stephen, still somewhat preoccupied with Josh's outrageous behavior, seemed to require a moment for this to register. He looked at the man on the horse, and then his eyebrows drew together in puzzlement. He turned back to Anne. "What?"

"He's a creekologist," Anne explained. Enthusiasm was mitigating both her dismay at this unplanned meeting and her pique over Josh. "That's something of a cross between a geologist and—well, I don't know what, exactly. He studies the way the creeks run, and the way the land is formed and"—she finished triumphantly—"he finds oil."

Stephen could only stare, but Josh put forth with every pretense of interest, "Oh, I get it. Like dowsing for water, huh?"

Anne shot him a damning look, but Amos Wright spoke up lazily, squinting at the sun. "Well, now, not exactly, young feller. It's a little more scientific than that. It ain't like it was one hundred percent guesswork, you know. Oil leaves signs on the land, just like a rattler crossing the desert or a bear drinking in a stream. All you got to know is how to read the signs. 'Course, when you get down to it, there's a lot of plain old intuition involved, but about the only thing I really got in common with a dowser is that if I don't find oil, I don't get paid."

Josh nodded soberly. "Sounds like you've done some dowsing in your time."

Wright scratched carelessly behind his ear. "A mite," he admitted.

The expression on Stephen's face went from bafflement to patent disbelief, and he turned to Anne.

Anne said quickly, "Now, Stephen, I know how it sounds, but . . ."

Stephen's brow lowered. "You can't possibly know how it sounds!" he protested in a careful undertone.

Josh gathered up his reins, working hard to keep a straight face. "Well, ma'am, with all this going for you, I can sure see why you're not too worried about the ranching business. Just in case it doesn't work, though . . ." He swung into the saddle and looked down at her, fighting a grin. "I think I'll go mind your cattle." He wheeled his horse, and he was chuckling as he rode away.

Anne did not know whether she was more annoyed with Josh's laughter or with Stephen's incredulity. She definitely knew that she was embarrassed and rather annoyed with Stephen. She brought all her emotions under control, however, and managed a polite smile at the man who called himself a creekologist. "Mr. Wright, would you excuse me for a moment?"

She took Stephen's arm, and guided him a few steps away.

"Stephen, I know what you're going to say—"

He matched her low tone, although his outrage was hardly disguised. "Then why in the world would you ever do such a thing?"

"Now, Stephen, don't you think you're being a little close-minded about this?"

Stephen chose his words carefully. "I certainly always try to keep an open mind, and please believe that I'm appreciative of the trouble you must have gone to in order to find this—er—gentleman, but . . . Anne, be reasonable! Only last night you were talking of the troubles you're having, financial and otherwise, and do you really think any of them can be solved by this sort of superstition? I'm surprised at you. After all, this is 1899. We're living in the age of science, and I'm not at all sure how much room there is in the oil business for . . . water dowsers."

Anne's mouth formed a smile that was half impatience and half indulgence, though she was working hard to keep her temper under control. "Don't be silly, dear, you know I wouldn't have brought him here if I didn't have reason to believe in his professionalism. Naturally people are skeptical of what they don't understand, but Mr. Wright has an unsurpassed record of success. The oil industry is a relatively new field," she continued earnestly. "Who is to say what will work and what won't? Isn't the whole idea behind exploration to make discoveries? With Mr. Wright we'll be pioneering in more ways than one."

Stephen glanced back at Amos Wright, who was leaning on the pommel of his saddle, complacently picking his teeth. "Perhaps," he murmured, and his tone was unconvinced.

Anne touched his elbow. "Don't be difficult, Stephen. The least I can do is give him a chance. What have I got to lose? As he said, I don't owe him anything until I strike."

Stephen was obstinate. "I don't like it. Not one bit."

Anne fought to hold on to patience, but she hardly thought it was worth the battle. Her voice went very cool. "I hardly need your permission, Stephen."

"But, Anne—to bring in a man like that without even

consulting me! Who knows what kind of character he might be?"

So that was it, Anne thought with a mixture of frustration and amusement. Stephen's feelings were hurt because she hadn't asked his advice before taking action. She was certain his proprietary interest in her affairs was quite sweet and much to be appreciated, but it could get irritating at times. Why did men always fly into a panic when it looked as though a woman might be able to manage her life on her own? She had thought Stephen had more respect for her than that.

"I'm sorry I didn't consult with you first," Anne said, making a concentrated effort to disguise her annoyance. "But really, Stephen, all that's important is that he find oil, isn't it? You know I'm running out of time. This could be the breakthrough I've been waiting for."

He looked far from convinced, and Anne could tell he had a great deal more to say on the subject. In the nick of time he thought better of it, however, and Anne was reminded of why she was so fond of him. Eventually Stephen always followed his better thoughts.

He released a sigh and looked at her frankly. "There's no chance of talking you out of this, is there?"

Anne smiled. "None at all."

He gave a small shake of his head. "Very well." But his attempt at a smile was rather strained. "I suppose your stubbornness is only one of your more appealing traits."

"So you've always said," she returned brightly.

"I rue the day," he murmured, and half turned for his horse. But then he stopped and looked back at Anne.

"I really should show Mr. Wright around," Anne said quickly, but Stephen lifted a restraining hand.

"Just one more thing?" he requested.

His expression was cloudy, and Anne knew before he spoke what was on his mind. She tensed for it.

"Anne," he said carefully, "that man who was here before . . . that cowboy. You didn't really have breakfast with him, did you?"

If he had phrased it any other way, Anne would have laughed and reassured him. But he sounded—and looked—so much like a disapproving father that she was instinctively rankled and she only lifted an eyebrow. "It was business, Stephen."

"Now, there's no need to get on your high horse," he said, but he still sounded a bit too condescending for Anne's liking. "It's just that I really don't think it's wise for you to be giving him the run of the house. You know how these drifters are, and there's something about that one I don't like. With you living here all alone—"

She laughed. "Good heavens! You make him sound like one of those mustached villains in a vaudeville farce, and me the innocent maiden ripe to be ravished. What is he going to do, storm the house and bend me to his wicked will? With over two dozen ranch hands and half a dozen house servants to look over me, I hardly think that's likely, don't you?"

But Stephen was not amused. "There's something suspicious about him," he insisted. "Maybe even dangerous."

Anne lifted her eyebrows, a delighted smile on her lips. "Dangerous, is he? I shall have to remember to lock up the silver." But something prickled at her defensive instincts, and she was much more annoyed with Stephen than she cared to let him know. It was one thing to have her own suspicions about Josh Coleman but quite another to hear her thoughts put into words. When Stephen spoke the obvious out loud, she felt foolish.

Stephen frowned sharply. "That's not a bit funny, Anne. No decent man would stand here and make the kind of insinuations he made to me, and it isn't at all like you to tolerate them. Or him. I wonder if you're not losing your perspective on this entire situation."

That stung, and only a blatant truth could do that to Anne. What *was* the matter with her? The man rode a stolen horse, lied about his name, refused to tell her who he was and where he was from, and she defended him as though he were the answer to her prayers. Anne was usually more sensible than that. She was usually *smarter* than that.

But for the moment all she could do was look Stephen straight in the eye and reply coolly, "I appreciate your concern, Stephen, but I assure you I have matters quite under control. Now, if you'll excuse me..."

As she walked back over to Mr. Wright, Anne was ashamed of the lie. In her heart she knew matters had never been further from being under control.

The drilling crew that Anne had brought in from Pennsylvania was one of the best in the business—and one of the most expensive. They had arrived at the beginning of the summer and had already sunk three wells. The first, after innumerable delays caused by quicksand and the thick, miry gumbo that had proven to be a deterrent to any well drilled in Texas, was pumping nothing more than water. The second, after a gas explosion that knocked down the derrick and caused yet more delays, had seemed more promising, but after another month of accidents and bad luck, Anne had been persuaded to abandon that site and drill again. So far the third endeavor showed no more promise than the first two.

It was late in the afternoon by the time Anne rode out to the third well. The crew boss was named Chance—appropriately, Anne thought—and he was working on the boiler when Anne rode up. She noticed that the drill did not appear to be operating at all.

As she approached, Chance left his tools and crossed the muddy field to meet her. Anne knew that Chance considered her visits an unwelcome intrusion by a woman into a man's territory, and he was never very comfortable in her presence. However, Anne paid his salary, and he always made an effort—however pained—to be cooperative.

Chance removed his grimy hat and squinted up at her. He was covered from hip to toe in gumbo, and his face was visible only where sweat had streaked through the mud. One thing Anne knew for certain—these men worked for their money, which was more, she was learning, than she could say for her cowhands.

"Ma'am," he said in greeting as Anne reined in her horse. "I was just thinking about coming up to the house to talk to you."

Anne hardly needed to question. Dread had formed in the pit of her stomach the moment she rode up. She nodded toward the rig. "Is the drill broken again?"

"Well, ma'am, the fact of the matter is, we've hit bedrock. There's no point in trying to cut through it with the equipment we have here. We've already busted one pipe."

Anne took a breath, trying to keep her expression composed. It would never do to let the hired help know how important this really was. Every day the drill was down cost her money she could not afford; everything she had or ever hoped to have was sunk into this last desperate hope. When she thought about it, the sick, gnawing fear inside caused her breath to catch. She couldn't afford to lose. Not this time. Not now.

She crossed her gloved hands on the pommel and eased her weight forward a bit, absently tapping her riding crop against her boot. She inquired, "How long will the rig be down?"

"Well, that depends. If we send off for a new pipe and another drill, it shouldn't take more'n a month."

"I suppose that's dreadfully expensive." Anne's voice sounded calm, almost nonchalant.

"Yes'm. It is."

Anne looked toward the derrick without really seeing it. The afternoon was hot, and her hat, though shading her face from the fierce Texas sun, was heavy on her head, pressing into her scalp and causing rivulets of perspiration to form on the nape of her neck where her hair was bound with a ribbon. She tried not to think about how much was at stake for her. Not just one woman's grand vision for the future but *everything*. Three Hills. All in the world she could call her own. She couldn't let her financial reserves go much lower or Three Hills would be lost to her. This *had* to work.

The horse shifted restlessly beneath her, its tail switching a fly, and Anne courageously fought off despair. God, she thought, can anyone's bad luck last forever?

She looked back at Chance. "What is your other alternative?"

Chance turned his hat in his hand. When he looked back up at her, his eyes were steady and frank. "Ma'am," he said simply, "I don't want to lose your business, but I've got to tell you, things don't look so good right now. I've been an oilman for nigh on to twenty years, and I've seen a strike come within days after sinking the first well—yes, I have—and I've also seen it take years. What I'm trying to say, ma'am, is that this is just the beginning. This wildcatting business is for poker players, them that's got nothing to do with their money but lose it, because this is a blamed expensive game you're playing here."

Anne looked down at him calmly. "Are you telling me, Mr. Chance, that in your considered opinion there is no oil to be found on Three Hills?"

"No, ma'am. I'm not saying that at all. What I am saying is that in my considered opinion this bedrock could lie under most of this side of the valley, and it's going to take one hell—that is, a fierce amount—of digging to get through it. That means a lot of time and a lot of money. Now, you've got a nice ranch here. Why," he asked her reasonably, "do you want to keep digging it up for a well that might not even be there, when everybody knows there's no way a Texas oil field can compete with the ones back East?"

Anne knew that Chance meant her no offense and was genuinely trying to be helpful. But one man too many had told her how to run her life that day, and her patience was at an end. She returned curtly, "Thank you, Mr. Chance, but kindly confine your advice to matters concerning oil. That, after all, is what I'm paying you for. Now," she continued briskly, "would it be less expensive to abandon this site and dig on the other side of the valley?"

"It's be less expensive, yes, but I'm not guaranteeing any better results than we've had at any of the other three."

"No one is asking you for guarantees," she retorted. "Just follow my orders and give your opinion when it's asked for." As further testament to the desperation of her situation, Anne found herself hoping Mr. Wright would be able to choose a location for the new well soon. She had tried everything else.

If there was any resentment on Chance's part, he hid it well. His constant tolerance and politeness never failed to irritate Anne. He replied, "Yes, ma'am. I'll start looking over new sites first thing in the morning." He put his hat back on and turned to go, and then they both heard the distant rumbling in the hills.

At first Anne thought it was thunder, but the sky was cloudless and the sound was too low and slow and insistent to be natural. Then she saw the cloud of dust growing on top of the hill just distant, and heard the faint sound of men's voices and whistles raised over the rumble. Chance turned back to her as the first group of steers broke through the brush at the top of the hill.

"I didn't know you was running cattle on this side of the hill."

Anne replied faintly, "I didn't, either." And she stared.

A drover appeared, and then another, waving their hats and calling to the cattle. The lead steer started ambling down the hill, the others trailing.

Chance said disbelievingly, "It looks like they're going to drive them right through the valley."

Work had ceased on the rig, and everyone stopped to stare. A few wise men were hastily gathering up equipment. And then chaos broke loose on top of the hill. The lead steer stumbled and started to run. The others, spooked, picked up the pace. The drovers, with their wild yells and waving about, only complicated the situation.

In an instant the size of the herd seemed to double and triple, cutting a swath that looked at least half a mile wide across the hill. The rumbling rose to a roar as trampling hooves and swinging horns raised a cloud of dust that blurred the landscape. The air was thick with lowing cattle, and the ground shook with their approach.

Anne exclaimed, "That *fool*!" And Chance ran toward the rig, shouting to his men to secure the equipment. The herd spilled down the hill at a wild and driven pace, cowboys breaking off and cutting in and emitting wild, exhilarated shrieks. They were headed straight for the derrick.

Anne's blood was thrumming in a blind fury so intense she could actually feel it swell and pound in her vessels. Through the haze of dust and her own paralyzing horror she saw the diggers scramble for shelter only steps ahead of the charging herd. And she didn't hesitate, didn't think about it for a minute. She whipped off her hat and slapped her horse into a leap, racing directly toward the surge of the onrushing stampede.

Like floodwaters rushing downhill they came, tearing up turf, crushing the campsite, and scattering equipment. Anne whipped her horse onward, yelling and waving her hat, and before she knew it, she was in the midst of them.

It was like riding into a fog bank. Immediately her vision was blanketed by a thick, choking screen of dust as the roaring, clamoring grunts of cattle deafened her ears. Chaos surrounded her, complete and uncontrollable; she couldn't see or hear, and she could barely breathe.

Immediately she knew her mistake. The earth vibrated with the thud of hooves, and her terrified horse jerked at the bit. She felt the large bovine bodies moving around her, brushing against her, bruising and shoving her. Her mount was bred for jumping and hunting and knew nothing of the nightmare into which his mistress had plunged him. He began to scream wildly and tried to turn and rear, and every move he made pushed Anne against a thundering body.

She fought panic as she fought her horse, and it was all she could do to control either. She knew that if she were thrown, she would be crushed, ground into the dirt by a thousand trampling hooves. That possibility became more inevitable by the moment, and she felt trapped in a nightmare without sight or sound. Every breath she took was exhaled in a choking, strangulated cough.

Suddenly the reins were jerked from her hands, her feet from the stirrups. A strong band clamped around her waist and swept her away, and she was in another saddle, plowing through the throng. Dimly she heard a voice shouting above the roar of the cattle, clearing a path, and then she was galloping free.

She saw her riderless horse plunge and make a break for freedom, scampering through the milling herd and to the safety of the hillside. Coughing and wiping her streaming eyes, she watched as the wood scaffolding of the derrick creaked and swayed at a dangerous angle. The herd parted around the steam boiler, but heavy hooves kicked over fuel and crushed tubing. She gave an involuntary cry of despair.

And then, as abruptly as it had begun, it was over.

The herd had flailed into the gumbo surrounding the rig, churning it so that some of them went up to their necks; others stumbled and sank on their knees and then, helpless and stupid, stayed there, lowing pitifully. The stampede halted in confusion, since there was nowhere left to go, with half the herd trying to fight its way out of the mud and the other half looking for a leader. It would have been ludicrous had it not been so tragic.

A voice roared in her ear, "What the hell did you think you were doing?"

It came as absolutely no surprise to Anne to find that Josh Coleman had swept her off her saddle and onto his. Her legs were thrown over one of his thighs, the pommel was digging painfully into her hip, and his arm was still crushing her ribs. When she twisted to face him, his face was dark with fury.

"Your job!" she shouted back at him. "*That*'s what I was doing! Look at that!" She gestured so frenetically that she almost lost her seating, and he jerked her upright painfully. "They're tearing down my derrick! Do something! Stop them!"

But he hardly seemed to hear her. Incredulity colored the anger in his voice as he returned, "Lady, are you out of your mind? What did you think you were going to do—turn the herd single-handedly?"

"Somebody had to!" Residual panic had translated into fury and pumped a rushing stream of energy through her veins. "I hold you personally responsible for this! This—this is deliberate sabotage, and *you* were in charge!"

His eyes went so sharp with anger that Anne was momentarily startled out of her own rage. "You don't think I'd do this on purpose?"

"Do you deny that you were in charge of this drive?" she shouted back.

His horse shifted restlessly, and Josh's arm tightened around her waist as he steadied it. He thrust his face very close to hers. "No, dammit, I don't deny it. My job was to get those cows out of the hills, and there was only one way out of that pasture—something *you* should have known! My job was *not* to teach that sorry bunch of saddle tramps you call drovers how to move a herd. None of this," he said, jerking his head back toward the leaning derrick and the stranded cattle, "would have happened if you'd spent more time looking after your ranch and less time trying to dig to China!"

Anne stared at him, for a moment speechless with indignation. But even her own outrage offered little defense against his righteous anger, and she was aware of the weakness in her argument as she returned loudly, "You have no right to raise your voice to me, sir! You've destroyed my property and—"

"You'd better get your facts straight, Duchess, before you start charging at me with both guns blazing!" He released the bridle with a lurch, and Anne knew then that however great was her own fury, his far overshadowed it.

"You can accuse me of a lot of things; letting a herd get out of my control is not one of them. Look at this goddamn mess!" He swept his eyes in full circle, his tone taut and his face twisted with disgust. When his eyes stabbed back at her, the fury was so potent that she actually shrank back from it. "And who do you think is going to be pulling cows out of the mud from now to sunset?" he challenged tightly. "You?"

His eyes narrowed. "Let me tell you something, Duchess. I'm not a bit sorry for your *property*." He spat the word out like an oath. "If you ask me, someone should have pulled it down a long time ago and gotten it out of the way, and by God, if I'd thought of it, I would have done it! But I would *not* have driven a herd of cattle into a mud hole just to prove a point, and if you think I would, then you've got something bad wrong in your head! Don't you realize we're going to lose stock out of this day's work?"

Anne stared at him, startled as much by his outburst as she was by the realization that she had absolutely no defense against it. And suddenly she realized something else that was an even greater shock—the incredible intimacy of their position.

He had pulled her sideways onto the saddle so that her back was supported by one arm, her torso pinioned by the other. His hand was spread so that his fingers cupped one breast and his thumb rested against her cleavage. She could feel the heat of his pelvis against her hip, and the hardness of his thigh beneath her own. Those arms, she realized irrelevantly, were just as strong as she had suspected they would be, and his chest beneath her shoulder was as hard as rock. She could smell his masculine scent of perspiration and leather, and his face was so close to hers that his breath fanned her cheek.

Anne quickly realized that she had more important concerns than how close his hand was to her breast and how hard his thighs were. She squirmed against him, a dozen unworthy emotions combining to sharpen her tone. "Put me down!"

And as was his custom, he seemed to read her thoughts the moment she had formed them. The anger that darkened his eyes became underscored with a gentle—though much more alarming—gleam of amusement, and mere frustration took the place of the sharp disgust on his face.

"I don't think so." He loosened the reins in his hand and brought his other arm around her, low on her abdomen, forcing her to turn even closer to him, making any thought of escape possible. "I'm not finished with you yet."

Anne's nostrils flared with an indignant breath. "I am quite finished with you! Let me go!"

She pushed against him but succeeded in doing nothing more than unsettling his horse and almost losing her balance again. Impatiently he righted her. "You beat everything, you know that?" he demanded. "Riding a thoroughbred horse right into a stampede—what were you trying to prove, anyway? If you were trying to impress me, I could think of a dozen better ways to do it."

"Impress you!" If she could have freed her hands, she would have struck him then. Her chest was heaving, and her skin was afire.

He was so close, she could see the tiny pores on his face and feel the slow, steady beat of his heart against her arm. "You are the most arrogant, conceited ass it has ever been my misfortune to know! None of this would have happened if it weren't for you. Now set me down immediately, before I—"

And suddenly his eyes sparked with a delicious and irrelevant knowledge. "You're afraid of me, aren't you?" he declared softly.

Anne went still, her eyes widening with an instinctive and unpreventable acknowledgment, then swiftly narrowing again. "Not of you or any man alive! *Set me down!*"

But there was gentle, wondering enjoyment in his eyes, laughter in his tone. "Oh, yes, the brave lady duchess in her snappy little riding pants charging a stampeding herd hell for leather—nothing scares you, does it?"

She said tightly, "Take your hands off me this minute!"

His eyes were dancing. "Is that any way to talk to the man who just saved your life? Maybe I'd better take my reward now." And before she knew what he was about, or had even imagined it, his mouth covered hers.

It was swift and hard and shocking, hardly a kiss at all,

and it was over almost before she realized it had begun. In the very next moment she felt her feet hit the ground so hard that she almost fell backward, and he was cantering off.

She stood there with her head reeling and her mouth still heavy from the force of his kiss until he returned, her own horse in tow. His expression was implacable, his tone mild, as he tossed the reins to her. "From now on," he advised, "stay in the house where you belong."

It was automatic instinct that caused her to catch the reins and, in a moment, swing into the saddle. He had already turned his horse and was riding away when she regained full control of her senses again, and she stood in the stirrups to call angrily after him, "You just keep those cattle out of my oil fields from now on!"

He turned in the saddle. "You keep your oil away from my cattle!" he shouted back, and rode off.

Anne drew a sharp breath and released it impotently. He was too far away to hear anything she might shout at him. With a silent oath she jerked the reins and turned her horse toward home.

Chapter Eight

No one had to tell Josh he was not the most popular man on the ranch. It was an unusual situation for him, but not one that was impossible to understand. Texans were a clannish lot, and he was an outsider. He took charge when no one else was willing to do so, which naturally stirred up resentment. Worse than that, he was an outsider who took charge and was *right*, and that was not an easy thing to overlook. But perhaps the single most despicable thing Josh Coleman had done since arriving at Three Hills was to put the men to work. That was one thing the bunkhouse crew simply could not forgive.

He had been at Three Hills a week, and things were starting to take shape. Josh avoided run-ins with Big Jim by simply avoiding the man himself, although the murderous look Josh saw in the foreman's eyes every night at the bunkhouse didn't make it hard to guess what was going on in Big Jim's mind. Josh knew that Big Jim suspected him of usurping his authority, and he also knew that a showdown was coming, but he did not spend a lot of time worrying about it. He had his hands full just doing his job.

He had asked casual questions about the Fieldings, but

none of the hands was very interested in ancient history, and he wasn't on friendly enough terms with any of them to push it. Nobody at Three Hills knew who he was, and he wanted to keep it that way. He certainly wasn't in any hurry right now. Josh had waited twenty-two years to get this far; he didn't mind waiting a little longer.

Josh had seen very little of Anne the past week, and that was hard on him. He had known from the first possible moment that he wanted her, but he had never expected to become so *attached* to her—the flashing of her eyes; the way she tightened her lips when she couldn't decide whether to laugh or be angry; the way she glided across a room with just the barest swish of her skirts; and the sound of her voice with its soft, low timbre and funny little accent. Missing Anne was as much as a surprise as it was a discomfort, and Josh thought there might even be something dangerous in it. For that very reason he went out of his way to avoid crossing her path; it gave him some time to get the situation back under control. Besides, there was the very distinct possibility that by now she was missing him too.

Today was Saturday, a slow day on any ranch because it was payday, and the men were looking forward to going into town that night. Josh was riding fence with Dakota who, from what Josh could tell, seemed to be the only worthwhile hand on the place. Of course he, like the rest of them, had rather sit in the sun and think about catching cows than actually get on a horse and do it, but for all of his joking complaints, he took orders when they were given and could be counted on to do a job right once he got down to it. And Dakota was an easy man to ride with. With all the hostility that surrounded Josh from other quarters, that counted for a lot.

They had finished up their section of the fence sooner than expected and circled toward home. Josh was absently scanning the fence line as they rode, wondering what Anne would be doing tonight, calling up images of her in an absent, sun-drowsy way. Suddenly he noticed something unusual. He drew up, frowning.

"Who was riding this section?" Josh was looking at a gap in the wire more than five feet wide. A fallen tree had pulled the wire away from its post, and scrub brush was already beginning to grow through it.

"I don't know. Gil and some of the boys were supposed to be riding ahead of us, weren't they?"

"Wonder why they didn't spot that."

"Maybe they didn't get this far yet." Dakota's voice was hopeful. He had told Josh he had a girl waiting for him in town.

Josh shook his head, pointing at the tracks on the ground. "At least three of them rode right by. Didn't even slow down."

Dakota took off his hat, ran his fingers through his hair, and leaned forward on the pommel. His tone was reluctant. "You want us to fix it now?"

Josh hesitated, studying the tracks. "No," he decided thoughtfully. "Something might've happened to them. We'd better see if we can catch up."

The two men followed the tracks for half an hour, moving steadily away from the fence line and in the general direction of the bunkhouse. It didn't take a very smart man to see that Josh was getting angrier by the minute. He didn't say anything, and that was the first sign.

They spotted the horses tethered by a branch on the north side of the far pasture. By that time Dakota wasn't feeling too friendly himself. No one liked to know that he had been working up a sweat all day for the boss when he could have been sitting in the shade spinning yarns for the same pay.

And that's exactly what six of the Three Hills cowhands were doing. Josh could tell that three of them had just drifted in on their way back to the bunkhouse and stopped to pass the time of day. Two were still mounted. Someone had corraled a couple of terrapins, and the men were lackadaisically betting on the outcome of a very slow race. The man called Gil was sitting with his back against the trunk of a huge spreading oak, a bottle of whiskey between his knees.

Josh drew up and pushed back his hat. "Howdy, gents."

One of the men looked up from his solemn study of a motionless terrapin. "You want my advice," he said, "you'll put your money on that yallar-backed critter. This green 'n' don't seem to have much spunk." And he poked the closed shell with a stick.

"I think he's dead," commented someone else.

One of the men on horseback gave a hoot. "If that ain't just like old Cal! Betting on a dead horse!"

Josh joined in the laughter companionably and swung down from the saddle. "Looks to me like you'd all be better off to shoot both them animals and save your pay for some real action." He looked around casually. "Which one of you hardworking boys was supposed to be riding the east section today?"

Humor evaporated, and some uncomfortable looks went around. The man with the yellow terrapin straightened up. "You playing ramrod today?"

"Just curious." And all the while Josh's eyes fastened on Gil; the other man returned his gaze sullenly.

Gil spoke up. "Me and Johnson was. What's it to you?"

"You missed a couple of spots," Josh pointed out mildly. "Just thought you might be interested."

"Well, I ain't." Gil lifted the bottle to his lips and took a swig. His mean black eyes were watery with drink but still sober enough to boil resentment. "And I don't need no wet-behind-the-ears pup shadowing my back trail, either."

Josh's expression remained mild, his stance casual, but the little knot of men began to separate cautiously. Gil had never gotten over that business about the bunk, and they all knew it. He had been waiting for a chance like this, and he was just drunk enough to push it.

Josh inquired offhandedly, "Does Miss Anne allow drinking on the job?"

Deliberately Gil raised the bottle again. His eyes were contemptuous and hostile. "She allows," he replied lowly, "whatever I take a notion to do."

Josh nodded, considering that. "Well," he agreed, "I guess she hasn't been in the cattle business long enough to know any better. Dangerous thing, mixing longhorns and whiskey. Accidents can happen. Seen a man get gored once when an old curly-horn got in an argument with a cowhand over his bottle. It was a terrible sight. That old steer dragged him ten miles, tromped on him once or twice, rolled him into the creek bottom, then broke open the bottle and drank his fill. Mighty greedy critters, them longhorns."

Some chuckles broke out, and Gil's face went tight.

Josh said thoughtfully, "I tell you what I'm going to do. I like you, Gil, so I'm going to save you from a life of drink and a horrible death." And before anyone knew what was on his mind, Josh reached down, scooped up Gil's bottle, and poured its contents on the ground.

Gil lurched to his feet, disbelief overshadowing his anger

for a moment. "You crazy son of a bitch! What the hell do you think you're doing? That whiskey cost me two dollars a bottle!"

"Too bad." Josh shook out the last drop and tossed the bottle away. "Maybe if you worked a little harder for your money, you wouldn't be so quick to go throwing it away."

Gil's face went red, and then black. "Why, you low-down chickenhearted—"

He lunged for Josh, but fury and drink impaired his judgment. Josh let him swing, ducked easily, and came up in a swift, unexpected motion, catching the front of Gil's shirt collar with a grip so tight that it half lifted the smaller man off his feet and completely bound the motion of his arms.

Josh jerked him close and held him there. "You're in no shape to take me on, Gil," he said quietly. It sounded more like gentle advice than a warning, but not a muscle moved in his face and his eyes were hard. "Now, you just back off and think it over, and when you sober up a little, you think about something else. You got a boss up at the big house doling out your pay every month, and she ain't doing it to watch you rest your saddle sores. I figure it's a man's beholdin' duty to help a lady out whenever he gets the chance, and it'd really make me proud if you'd start helping out once in a while. We wouldn't want to put the little lady to all the trouble of looking up your replacement, would we?"

Gil was trapped and immobile; he couldn't swing, he couldn't break loose, he couldn't reach for his gun. Fury and humiliation churned in his eyes like a hungry animal, and his face twisted into an ugly sneer. "The little lady, is it?" A deliberate, nasty gleam came into his eyes, and for a man whose throat was just inches away from the grip of an iron fist, he held himself straight. "Now, don't you go worrying your head about that little she-cat, boy," he said in a drawl. "I know just how to handle her. She might dress herself up and prance around like a two-dollar whore, but she's too busy flashin' her hind leg to care much what goes on out on the range. 'Course," he suggested, prodding, "you been sniffin' mighty close to her since you got here. Maybe she's already givin' it to you for free. Is that how come you're so all-fired interested in making a good show?"

For a long moment Josh did not move. He didn't even seem to breathe. And then he smiled and slowly released Gil's shirt collar. He turned to walk away.

Josh spun on his heel, and his fist connected with Gil's jaw with a force that cracked the air and sent Gil sprawling into the dirt. He lay there, stunned, and Josh advanced on him in a single stride, jerked him to his feet, and swung again. Gil's head rolled, and blood spurted from his mouth. He tried to get his fists up, and Josh threw two vicious blows to his belly. Gil doubled over, and Josh brought him upright again with an uppercut to the jaw. Teeth cracked.

Distantly Josh heard the murmurs of the gathered cowhands turn to shouts, and he couldn't tell whether they were shouts of encouragement, excitement, or objection. It was all a blur to Josh. He heard the sound of blood thrumming in his head. He felt the grim and hateful satisfaction of his fists connecting with flesh, the blinding surge of power that fed on itself and redoubled with every blow. All he saw was a black wall of hatred and the jagged red edges of rage, and he forgot who he was hitting and why, only that he needed to keep on hitting and that it felt good. . . .

And then someone's hands were tearing at his shoulders,

and someone's voice shouting in his ear, "Enough, damm it! He's had enough!"

Josh spun around, shoving the man who was pulling at him, and just before he swung, he saw that it was Dakota. Then he realized Gil was on the ground, his face a pulpy mass of blood, his knees drawn up to protect his belly, and his arms covering his head. He was a weak and pitiful sight, and Josh felt no sympathy whatsover.

While Gil struggled to sit up, Josh flexed his bruised fists. He was breathing hard. "You get your gear and be off this ranch by sunset," he said curtly. "And if you can't ride, get somebody to carry you. I don't want to have to tell you again."

The reaction of the onlookers, after their initial shock, was mixed. They all knew Gil was a drunk and not good for much, and any man who would let a gutful whiskey persuade him to take on a man twice his size deserved what he got. No one could argue Josh's right to defend a woman's good name, or deny that Gil had asked for it. To a point one could even say that Josh had handled himself admirably.

On the other hand, Gil was one of their own, and Josh had more than stepped over the line. He had leveled Gil with the first blow and kept on coming. Nobody would hold with beating a man after he was down, but it was very likely the tale would have been told much differently had not Josh issued that last ultimatum. Coleman was an interloper, and that was an insult to all of them.

Someone took an angry step forward; another man said harshly, "You don't go firing anybody on this ranch, mister! Who the hell do you think you are?"

"You've got no call to come riding in here throwing out orders—"

"There's going to be hell to pay when Big Jim hears about this, Coleman! We ain't puttin' up with no two-bit tinhorn pushing us around—"

And even Dakota looked at him warily. "Man, are you crazy? What do you want to go starting trouble for? Back off."

"Who died and left you the goddamn boss?"

Josh looked them over for a long minute, regaining his breath, easing his muscles. And then he said quietly, but firmly enough so that there was no doubt of his meaning, "I ride for the brand, and any man that don't has got no place on this ranch." Calmly he started for his horse. "You pass that along, boys. I don't like to repeat myself."

He retrieved his reins from the limb over which he had looped them, then mounted up. He rode off without looking back.

Chapter Nine

Big Jim had been top hand on Three Hills for five years. Though he had owned a good spread of his own once, he had been through a lot since then, and by the time he drifted into Texas, he was just looking for a place to rest. He found it at Three Hills, and he had been content there. Until Josh Coleman arrived.

No one would ever accuse Big Jim of being an easygoing man, but neither was he known for making enemies as long as people left him alone and didn't cause him any trouble. The truth was, Big Jim didn't care much about anything and liked it that way, and he resented getting mad almost as much as he did the reason behind it.

He would have taken care of Coleman himself—and he might end up doing it yet—except for two things. First, he had a feeling the only thing that was going to stop a young smartass like Coleman was the business end of a Colt .45, and Big Jim hadn't forgotten the way Josh had handled his own gun that first night in the bunkhouse. Besides, knowing how Miss Anne felt about gunplay on the ranch, and given the fact that his own position with her was none too steady right now, Big Jim had too much lose. The second reason he hadn't taken matters into his own hand before now was that he firmly believed that given enough rope, Josh Coleman would hang himself and Big Jim wouldn't have to lift a finger. He thought Josh was swinging pretty close to the noose right now.

"It was one of the worst beatings I ever heard tell of," Jim was relating to Anne now. The concern in his voice was genuine and had the added advantage of masking a grim satisfaction. "There's a difference between a fair fight and just plain out tearing into a man. A savage throat-cuttin' redskin would've given poor Gil more of a chance. He laid him out and kept on going at him, long after Gil couldn't fight back. If some of the boys hadn't pulled him off, ma'am, I think he would've killed Gil with bare fists, and that's the truth."

Anne looked alarmed. "Is he all right?"

"Some of the boys took him into the doc. He's gonna be laid up for quite a while. Might not ever see straight out of that one eye again, and it's for sure he won't be in any shape to sit a saddle anytime soon."

"Oh, how terrible." Anne's voice was faint and greatly preoccupied. She crossed the room and sat down behind the desk, the better to organize her madly rushing thoughts.

Big Jim followed, to stand before the desk. He was obviously restraining himself with an effort. "The only reason I come to you, ma'am, is because after he got done beating Gil to a bloody pulp, he fired him. Told him to get off the ranch before sundown. Now, what I want to know is whether he had the word from you to do something like that. Because if he didn't, he's got a peck of trouble on his hands, and somebody needs to let him know it."

Anne hid her surprise with an effort. That information put

an entirely knew light on the matter, and she hardly knew what to say—or to think.

Her heart was beating fast, and part of it, she knew, was from shock. The other part, she was very much afraid, had to do with nothing more than hearing Josh Coleman's name.

She wrinkled her brow a little, trying to recall the man Gil. She was ashamed to realize she could not. She looked up at Jim. "What started the fight?"

Jim shifted his weight on his feet. "Well, I wasn't there when it happened, so I can't rightly say. But you can be sure of one thing—Coleman started it."

Anne lifted her eyebrows mildly. "What makes you say that?"

"He's a troublemaker, ma'am," Big Jim pronounced adamantly. "A hotheaded loudmouth and a brawler. I've seen his like before; they ain't happy unless they're stirring something up. He's been stirrin' since the day he rode in, and there's not a man on this place that's happy about it, either. And I'll tell you something else." He took a breath and paused meaningfully. His flat eyes held Anne's. "He's mighty handy with that gun of his, ma'am. A little too handy, if you know what I mean."

Anne appeared to think this over for a long moment. "I see," she murmured at last. She glanced down at her hands, which were folded calmly on the desk, and then looked back to Jim. "It couldn't be, could it, Jim," she suggested mildly, "that you are perhaps a bit prejudiced against Mr. Coleman?"

Jim's florid face flushed with an even deeper color, and his eyes flared briefly. He remembered too well the last time he had stood before this desk, listening to the lady boss give *him* instructions on how to run a ranch. That was only part of the reason he was back here now. "If you're talking about the ragwort business," he said curtly, "I already explained about that. He just got lucky, is all. Another day and I would've found it for myself, or one of the boys would've. The only thing he did by coming to you was try to make me look bad, and it was a low-down, sidewinding thing to do. No, I don't like him if that's what you're asking. I wouldn't trust a man who'd go behind his foreman's back any further than I could throw him, and you shouldn't, either, ma'am, if you'll pardon my saying so. I've been up and down the trail a few times, and I can tell you now, that man is up to no good."

"Yes, of course." Anne cleared her throat softly, her tone reasonable and her expression unperturbed. "Still, that isn't the point now, is it? I may not know a great deal about the behavior of cowboys, but it doesn't take a genius to realize one man does not try to kill the other with his bare hands for no reason at all. What could have happened to provoke such an incident? There must be an explanation."

Big Jim insisted stubbornly. "No, there don't. You know what he's like."

Anne was thoughtful. One thing she knew was that the simplest explanation would rarely apply to a man like Josh Coleman, so she was very careful about forming a judgment.

She said after a moment, consideringly, "Yes. I do know what he's like. He's hot-tempered, presumptive, overconfident, and very easy to dislike. He is also a good cowhand, and . . ." She looked at Big Jim meaningfully. "I can use every one of those I can get right now."

She got to her feet with decision. "I think the only thing to do is to hear his side of the story before we go any further. Where is he?"

Big Jim looked startled. "Why, he's back at the bunk-house. Sprucing up to go into town like nothing ever happened, if you can believe that."

Anne hid the corner of a dry smile by turning toward the door. She could believe it.

"Good," she said briskly. "I'll speak with him right now."

She paused at the door, then turned back thoughtfully. "As a matter of fact, Jim, this entire incident serves to illustrate a point that has been on my mind for some time now, and I'm glad for the opportunity to discuss it with you."

He looked at her curiously.

"It occurs to me," she continued easily, "that I have been guilty of mismanagement, and it's past time I corrected that oversight. These bothersome little personnel details shouldn't be your responsibility; your talents are far too valuable to me for that. Gathering strays and organizing daily crews—those are menial tasks hardly suited to some-one of your experience."

He said cautiously, "That's what a foreman does, ma'am."

She smiled graciously. "Not on Three Hills Ranch. This is the ranch of the future, and I've every intention that you be a part of that future. Therefore, as of today, I'm making some changes. You will be my supervisor in charge of co-ordinating the two operations of Three Hills—cattle and oil. The first order of business is to make certain that the disaster of last week won't be repeated. I'll need strong fences built around all my drilling sites to keep the cattle away. I suggest you take three or four of the most experienced hands and set to it right away." She added considerately, "Naturally, since you will be working so far from the ranch house, you'll want to move into one of the line shacks closer to your work.''

His face was tight. ''You want me to move out of the bunkhouse?''

''You and your crew. It's only a matter of convenience.''

The choleric tint of Big Jim's face seemed to grow mottled, and his eyes were dark. ''Ma'am,'' he inquired lowly, ''are you demotin' me?''

Anne's eyes widened with gentle astonishment. ''Good heavens, no! I'm reassigning you. Naturally, the pay will remain the same.'' And then, ''You will do it, won't you, Jim?''

His hand clamped down harder on his hat, his jaw set. ''Yes, ma'am. You're the boss.''

Anne smiled. ''Very good. I knew I could rely upon you.''

She left him standing there as she opened the door and started toward the bunkhouse.

Anne had not seen Josh since that afternoon at the oil field, but he was never off her mind. She kept expecting to look up and find him leaning against a wall or strolling in to pull out a chair at her supper table; she spent more time on horseback than she usually did and found herself scanning the landscape for a glimpse of a lanky figure on a big roan; she even guided her evening walks to take her closer to the perimeter of the bunkhouse, but he never appeared. After creating such havoc with her life the first two days he had been here, his sudden absence now was somewhat like waiting for the other shoe to drop.

At odd times during the day she would find her fingers straying to her lips, and the power of that brief, forceful kiss would heat her skin and rush through her veins again. He had *kissed* her. He had all but assaulted her in a public place where anyone might see, and then he had dumped her on the ground like a piece of luggage. But that wasn't the worst of it. The worst was that that was only the beginning.

Because it hadn't been a kiss at all, only a suggestion of one, and now what had only been a suggestion of a fantasy in the back of her mind had blossomed into a full-grown daydream. At night, or in the private moments of her day, she would wonder what it would be like should he really kiss her, should he take her into his arms like a lover and kiss her thoroughly, deeply, and for a long time, the way a man should kiss a woman. That man would know how it should be done. She wondered what his skin would feel like, and the texture of his hair, and how he would taste. Wondering filled her with a restlessness, an anticipation, a tightness of excitement in her chest and stomach that felt like a promise.

Of course, they were only fantasies, pleasurable, but harmless, and they had little to do with the reality of Anne's day-to-day life. Josh Coleman was like a desert storm: wild and dangerous and maddeningly exhilarating, but only a fool would deliberately stand in the midst of its destructive force. But that did not explain in the least why she felt alive again for the first time in a week when Big Jim mentioned his name.

Anne was not at all certain she had done the right thing. Instinct told her she should have fired Big Jim a week ago; logic told her that Josh was probably right about the trouble it would cause. But the only reason she had waited this long to take any action was precisely because she hated to admit Josh was right about anything.

She was disturbed by the report about the fight, of course, but not nearly as concerned as she was curious. And she wasn't a fraction as upset with Josh as she was irritated with Big Jim. She was beginning to realize that she didn't like the man; perhaps she never had, but the ragwort incident had seriously begun to erode her trust in him. His motives in coming to her now were patently transparent, and he fell another notch in her esteem. A man should be able to fight his own battles, and she could have little respect for anyone who chose the easy way out.

Josh Coleman could certainly never be accused of doing that.

Anne had never been to the bunkhouse before—she simply had had no reason to do so. Amusingly enough, her striding, determined approach toward this sanctuary of men produced as much shock and openmouthed incredulity as though she had made her entrance in a flying machine.

The door was open, but Anne did not go in. Several of the men were outside, using the natural light to shave before mirrors tacked onto the wall, polishing their boots on the porch rail, brushing off their hats, and buffing their gun belts. There was laughter and high-spirited conversation, which may or may not have been ribald—Anne could not tell, because absolute silence fell the moment she came into sight.

A couple of men who were shaving had their shirts off. They immediately made a scramble for them, their faces growing scarlet underneath patches of lather and overturning washbasins and shaving mugs in their haste. Someone else came stamping out of the bunkhouse in his long johns, loudly demanding if anybody knew how to fix the newfangled zipper on his pants. He saw Anne and scrambled back inside like a scared rabbit. Had Anne been in a more congenial mood, she would have laughed out loud at the chaos a single woman could create in a man's domain.

One of the braver of the bunch finally recovered himself enough to ask, "Ma'am? Is something wrong?"

Anne swept the group. "I'm looking for Josh Coleman."

"Well, he's out back." The cowboy gestured uncertainly toward the side of the bunkhouse, where a blanket had been rigged up between the wall and a tree. "You want I should—"

"Thank you." Anne said, and marched toward the partition.

She caught a glimpse of several shocked, horrified looks, and someone called, "Ma'am you can't—"

She flung back the blanket partition and found Josh Coleman sitting in a wooden washtub, placidly soaping his arms and chest. His hair and part of his face were covered with frothy lather, and the expression in his eyes when he looked up was outright disbelief.

Vaguely Anne was aware of a sense of triumph, and later she would savor it. Soap was dripping into his eyes, his knees were sticking up out of the water in a most undignified way, and she could not have found a better circumstance for this interview had she arranged it beforehand. But at the moment she had more pressing things on her mind than his discomfiture, and she pronounced without preamble, "I want to talk to you."

A bubble of stinging soap in his eyes startled Josh out of his paralysis, and he ducked his head under water, coming up gasping and pushing back his streaming hair. "Lady, have you lost your mind?" he demanded, and then he realized that more important considerations were in order. He grabbed for his hat, which was hanging on the post of a broken ladder-back chair nearby, and decided against ruining a perfectly good hat for the sake of modesty. He then made a swipe for his pants and missed.

Josh could feel a dozen laughing eyes on him. After the events of the afternoon he was far from seeing the humor in the situation. He sank down deeper in the water. "What are you doing here?"

Anne seemed completely oblivious to his discomfort. She said calmly, "I understand you fired one of my employees this afternoon."

Josh spotted a towel trailing from the seat of the chair and grabbed it. He watched her cautiously while he pulled the towel into the water with him. "That's right."

Imperviously Anne laced her hands in front of her, her voice controlled and pleasant. "Before I have you thrown off the ranch, I would like to hear your side of the story."

"Well, that's real kind of you. . . ." Josh managed to get the towel around his waist and felt marginally more comfortable. "But couldn't it wait until I get some pants on?"

"That won't be necessary. I just want to know what happened."

Josh tried to shift his legs into a more modest position, but that was impossible. The towel floated upward, and he pushed it down hastily. "I don't approve of drinking on the job," he answered, for there was obviously no other way to get rid of her except to tell the story, and as quickly as possible. "Gil was drunk the day those cattle scattered over the oil field, and he had a bottle with him again today. I figured something needed to be done before it got worse."

Anne lifted an eyebrow. "So you decided to do it?"

Josh made an effort to relax in the tub. Other people were coming out of the bunkhouse now, and all of them made it a point to stroll close to the blanket partition. "Actually," Josh responded, "all I did was pour out his whiskey. He didn't take it too kindly."

"And then you decided to settle the argument with your fists."

Josh hesitated. "Not exactly."

"What, exactly?" There was an edge to her tone.

Josh tucked the sodden towel more securely between his legs, shifting uncomfortably, "Are you sure you wouldn't rather talk about this later?"

Now Anne's eyes snapped with impatience. "I'm quite sure," she returned curtly. "I am here to find out what, if any, justification you have for attacking a man with your bare hands and beating him so severely that he had to be carried in a wagon to the doctor. And I must say, Mr. Coleman, so far you are not presenting a very convincing defense."

Josh murmured wryly, "I'm doing my best, ma'am, under the circumstances."

But her eyes were icy and her lips were tight, and he saw no alternative but to forge ahead. "I told you he was drunk. He was looking for a fight."

"So you gave it to him. I expect more self-control from my employees than that, Mr. Coleman."

Now he was impatient. "No, blast it, I didn't lay into him for that. I don't go around beating up every drunk I stumble across."

Her eyes swept over him coolly, taking in his bare shoulders, his lean arms, the pattern of dark, wet hair on his chest, and his protruding knees. She commented archly, "You seem remarkably unscathed for one who has engaged in anything like a fair fight. Your bathwater must be getting cold, Mr. Coleman, and unless you intend to stay there all night, I suggest you stop evading my questions and tell me exactly why you decided to assault and dismiss one of my most long-term employees.''

He said sharply, ''His mouth got too big for him, that's why. I don't hold with any man talking about a lady like that, and he deserved what he got. And you're right: This water is damn cold. Are you finished?''

A surprised, then speculative, look replaced the anger and disapproval in Anne's eyes. ''A lady? Need I ask who this lady was?''

He met her gaze obstinately. ''No. You don't.''

''I see.'' Anne regarded him thoughtfully, hoping the slow sense of proud pleasure she felt did not show on her face. She knew it was unladylike to approve of brawling, and wicked to derive satisfaction from the knowledge that she had been the cause of it, but there was an undeniable thrill in the realization that Josh Coleman had leapt to the defense of her good name with his fists. Primitive, undignified, and unforgivable—but thrilling nonetheless.

And she was unaccountably glad to know that this time, at least, she had been wrong about him.

Still, she was taking no chances, and she fixed him with a sharp look. ''And that is the absolute truth?''

With a gesture of resignation, Josh released a breath, leaned back in the tub, and rested his arms on either side of the rim. ''Lady,'' he said, putting it to her simply, ''would a naked man lie to you?''

Anne fought the smile that attacked her lips and subdued it to a mere twitch. A lightness went through her, a sense of victory and delight that was as satisfying as anything she had ever known. Behind the wheel of the Daimler she felt free; confronting George Greenley on the front porch of her house with a shotgun, she had known power and control; sinking wells into the ground with the hopes of discovering the future fulfilled her need for reckless adventure and gave her an indescribable thrill of satisfaction. But nothing had ever given her such wicked enjoyment as confronting Josh Coleman naked in his bath and having him, for once, completely at her mercy. The fact that he was innocent only compounded her pleasure, and she could not resist the opportunity to prolong her appreciation—and his discomfort—to its fullest extent.

She let her eyes wander over him with clinical detachment and thoroughness. This was a sight she wanted to remember for a long time. His knuckles were bruised and raw, and there was a scratch on his arm that might or might not have been a result of the fight. He had a wonderfully intriguing chest—lean and tight, with muscles like rawhide, and covered with a light pattern of dark hair. Marc had had no hair on his chest at all.

Gooseflesh was beginning to rise on his arms, and a faint flush began to stain his cheeks as Anne's eyes wandered lower. The strategically placed towel and the high rim of the tub prevented any effort on her part to embarrass him further, however, and at last she looked back at him. She deliberately kept all hints of expression from her face and her tone.

"You did quite right, of course," she commented nonchalantly. "I do hope in the future, however, that you will discuss any possible changes in personnel with me before you take matters into your own hands."

She started to go, but his irritated voice stopped her.

Chapter Ten

Popular wisdom suggested that had it not been for the cowboys needing someplace to go on Saturday night, no town ever would have developed west of the Mississippi. Redemption, Texas, was in many ways proof of that theory.

It had begun in 1845 as a trading post that fed off the profits of Three Hills Ranch. Thirty years before it had gotten its own telegraph station, followed shortly by a rail spur that transported mail and Three Hills cattle. Now it numbered among its permanent residents some four hundred citizens, a number that doubled on Saturday nights. It had a general store, a small jail, a resident doctor, and a Baptist church. There were eight saloons, six brothels, and two lodging houses that rented beds by the hour or the night to cowboys too drunk to make it home.

By the standards of Forth Worth, Redemption was a primitive little town, even backward. Most of its buildings were false-fronted; the saloon floors were covered with sawdust; and boardwalks had only been installed on the east side residential area, where the two-story houses and picket-fenced gardens of the preacher and the doctor formed the core of society. But the railroad tracks divided the town right down the middle, and this social segregation resulted in few complaints. Prostitutes could roam the west side from sundown to sunup, as long as they were inconspicuous and caused no trouble for decent women. Cowboys might come into town shooting off their guns and letting off steam as long as they paid for the property they damaged and did not intrude into the east side or disturb the peace of proper citizens. Redemption was a town that had learned how to serve its own purpose, and compromise kept it peaceful.

By ten thirty the town was going hot and heavy; with only ten hours in which to make up for a week's hard work, there was plenty to do. Outside the Poor Man Saloon there was a shooting contest with tin pie plates for targets, and across the street a sideshow where for a time a man could take a look at a two-headed snake and kiss the bearded lady. Some of the cowboys had already taken their girls upstairs; others drank themselves into a raucous stupor or cheerfully parted with their week's wages on a hand of cards. A group gathered to watch the evangelist on the corner, who was warming them up for all the sins they'd be repenting tomorrow morning. That evangelist put on the best show in town and, wise man that he was, knew enough to pass the plate on Saturday night while the cowhands still had money.

Most of the men in Redemption that night wandered from one place to another—spending their money, making noise, looking for fun. But one of them had a notion to spend his time more wisely.

Two men sat in a small back room of the Lone Star Restaurant. One, dressed in the clean jeans, polished spurs, and freshly brushed hat that comprised a cowboy's town dress, sat counting a stack of bills. A slow and appreciative smile was making its way across his face. The other, wearing a big expensive Stetson and a diamond on his small finger, smoked a two-dollar cigar and watched him complacently. A flat candle on the table between them sputtered out a low, swaying flame, but each man kept well to the shadows.

"You understand," said Eddie Baker, "that this is just for starters. You get the rest when she pulls down that last oil rig and sends those Yankee diggers home."

The cowboy carefully tucked the bills into his pocket. Except for the faint, somehow unsettling smile, his face was expressionless. "How come you picked me?"

Eddie shrugged. "For one thing, I need somebody on the ranch. For another..." And he fixed the other man with a shrewd, level gaze. "I know who you are. And there aren't so many like you around that I could afford to pass up a man with your—er—considerable skills."

No surprise registered on the cowboy's face. In certain circles a man's reputation traveled ahead of him, and though he hadn't intended to advertise the fact, some things just weren't easy to keep secret.

Though he did not realize it, the young cowboy was the last of a dying breed. Born and bred in the west, he made his own laws and lived by them. He knew cows and guns and was good with both. He had made a name for himself in Wyoming with the Johnson County cattle war, and like others who had hired out their guns for a cause or a profit, he knew the price men paid for their ideals. There would always be men like the slick dude across from him, willing to pay others to do their dirty work, and there would always be men like himself willing to take the job. But even he had his standards.

"I don't like to walk into anything blind," the cowboy

said after a moment. "You mind telling me just what's in this for you?"

Eddie frowned sharply. "Yes, I mind. You just do what you're getting paid for and keep your mouth shut."

The cowboy fingered the money in his pocket. "You got any particular rules about how you want this job done?"

Eddie Baker's eyes were cold and hard. The answer was there before he spoke. "No," he said flatly. "Not a one."

The cowboy nodded and got to his feet. "Whatever you say," he responded mildly, "all I need to know is if anybody'll be fighting back."

"No one will be fighting back. And another thing," he said sharply as the cowboy reached for the door. "If you get yourself caught, you're on your own. Mention my name and I'll deny it before God, and we both know who they'll believe. *I*'ll be the one holding the rope they're going to swing you by, so you'd better be damn careful."

The cowboy grinned and opened the door. "Don't you worry," he assured him. "I'm *real* good at not getting caught."

Chapter Eleven

Saturday night was Anne's favorite time of the week. Stephen had supper in town on Saturday, the ranch hands were away, she sent the servants to bed early, and she had the place all to herself. The peace and the stillness was a thing of magnificence to her.

Tomorrow morning she would play the lady of the manor again. She would drive into town for services—in the carriage, with a proper groom, have Sunday dinner with Stephen, tea in the afternoon with one of the ladies from the Social League, and take a leisurely drive home, stopping at neighboring ranches for lemonade and idle chat and to make the Hartley presence known. These things Anne did for her family, because she had been bred to be gracious, and nothing less was expected of her. Tonight, alone, was for herself, to sit in the dark and listen to the silence and remember why she had come to this wild and wonderful land.

No one had ever told Anne that it was improper for a lady to drink alone, much less to drink hard liquor—possibly because they were too busy telling her of all the other things she did that were improper, and possibly because that advice, like all others, would have been met with a careless laugh and utter disregard. So, as the hour approached midnight and the house grew still, Anne put away her account books and her troubles, poured herself a large bourbon, and went out into the night.

The air was pleasantly cool, and she drew a light shawl over her long, full dressing gown. As she moved through the back garden, the damp grass tickled her bare feet, and the evening breeze threaded playfully through her loosened hair. She felt delightfully wicked and daring, alone beneath the night sky in her state of undress—wanton and adventuresome and free, master of her own destiny.

In the center of the garden she paused and tilted her face to the brilliantly starlit sky, experiencing a rush of intoxication at the sheer vastness and richness of it. Safe in her own garden, yet free beneath all of nature's splendor, she was for a brief moment all that she was meant to be—bold and unfettered, expanding with the joy of being alive. *This* was why she had come to Texas. These were the chords this rough and untamed land had stirred within her the first time she'd seen it.

This was a land new and poised with promise, where surprise awoke with every sun, and wits and strength were tested every day. More than adventure called Anne to this place; more than challenge made her stay. She felt possibilities grow from the soil here, infusing the very air she breathed. Here a woman might rule an empire, build a dynasty, open up the future. Here a woman might walk beneath the night sky in her nightdress, feel the dew on her bare feet, drink straight bourbon if she pleased, and no one could tell her otherwise.

On an impulse she lifted her glass in a salute to the sky.

She laughed out loud in a rush of sheer exhilaration, twirling around until the stars spun dizzily and the damp hem of her nightdress tangled around her ankles. Bourbon spilled on her lace cuff, and she laughed at that too. How wonderful it was to laugh, softly and all alone, from nothing but enjoyment of oneself and one's surroundings.

This was the Anne few people suspected existed, and fewer even knew. But this was the deepest part of her, a wild and restless and questing Anne Edgecomb, an Anne she kept wholly for herself. Marc had caught glimpses of that side of her. Stephen suspected it. And Josh Coleman came closer to understanding it than anyone else.

That last thought sobered her a little, even disturbed her. She tried to put it out of her mind as she inhaled, deeply and appreciatively, the cool night air. But the night tasted of things feral and earthy, of tangy surprises and elemental richness—strong scents, manly things . . . like Josh. The way he might smell, were she close enough—of dust and labor and masculinity. The way he might taste . . .

The gazebo was Anne's private retreat. It was a piece of the familiar past to which she could return when being a brave and adventuresome woman became a bit too much for her. She thought upon the fact that neither Marc nor Stephen had ever come here with her as she followed the starlit flagstone path to it now, instinctively seeking seclusion for the night's most secret thoughts, those revolving around Josh Coleman.

She sat down upon one of the wide, cushioned benches and drew her knees up to her chest, sipping the bourbon. A smile played across her lips. She was remembering the look on Josh's face when she had surprised him in the bath this afternoon. A warmth tantalized her skin—though that may have been from nothing more than the bourbon—when she called to mind the way he had looked, unclothed and unguarded. The wet, dark hair that clung to his chest and his forearms shadowed his armpits like an intimate secret; and his nipples were hard and brown, intriguingly puckered from the cold like a woman's. She remembered the swell of his tight breast muscles and the slim plane of his waist and the pattern of hair, which narrowed just before it dipped beneath the water, and she studied these memories with a naughty fascination that felt very much like excitement.

Anne did not blush when she thought of Josh this way. These were her secret moments, her exclusive fantasies, and no one would ever know. The next day, when she saw him again, she might remember and blush. But that night, alone in the dark, she had no secrets from herself. And no shame.

Sound carried clearly on a night such as this, and Anne heard the muffled thud of hooves leaving the road and approaching the stable from the back entrance. With a sudden leap of her pulse she wondered if it might be him.

Immediately she quelled the notion. The older men sometimes came in early on Saturday night, but the young ones—especially, she thought for no defined reason, a man like Josh—would be sure to take full advantage of all the attractions town had to offer. Yet she listened, almost straining to listen, to the creak of the corral gate, the greeting whinnies of other horses, and the jingle of bridle and bit as gear was stowed in the tack room. And she waited.

There was a magic about the Texas night that seemed to epitomize all she loved about the place. She looked at the endless sky with its uncounted stars suspended in three-dimensional brilliance in the vacuum of space, and the whispering shadows and still, moonswept dips and curves in the ever-changing landscape. The very air seemed to tremble with speculation, as though on the verge of a promise too outrageous to be guessed. She heard the wail of a coyote, the whisk of an Indian arrow, the explosion of musket fire, the thunderous stampede of great longhorn steers. . . . Here the past and present bloomed and merged, and surprise took on a new meaning in light of the richness of possibilites. Wild, unpredictable, elemental, even a little dangerous . . . much like Josh Coleman.

Just then Anne caught a trace of cigarette smoke on the clean night air. Her heart speeded, but not with surprise, as a long shadow fell over her.

"Well, well, Duchess. So we meet again."

Anne tilted up her face to look at him. He was little more than a silhouette with the moon at his back, lean and lanky with one foot propped on the lower step to the gazebo, the red tip of a cigarette trailing from his fingers. He is a pleasure simply to look at, she thought, and she smiled again. Her voice was low and smooth. "So we do, Mr. Coleman."

Josh grinned. "Considering the last time we met, don't you think you know me well enough to call me Josh?"

"Perhaps. But I'm not at all certain that would be proper . . . Josh."

Josh went up the three small steps to the gazebo. He felt *compelled* up the steps, drawn by the huskily amused tone in her voice, the glint of moonlight on her hair and the intimacy that radiated from the shadows in which she sat like an intoxicating perfume. Something was different about her, he knew instinctively, only it wasn't really different at all . . . it was right.

She sat in a latticework of silvery light and violet shadows, the long, full skirts of her white dressing gown cascading over her drawn-up knees. A heavy froth of lace brushed the floor and dripped from her wrists, from the pale lavender shawl looped around her elbows. Her hair, as fine as gossamer and silvery pale, caressed her shoulders. Josh felt a faint catch in his chest as he looked at her. This surprised him, for he had seen beautiful women before. But this was more than a beautiful woman. This was Anne Edgecomb, and he was alone with her in a patchwork of moonlight and soft evening breezes, and *enchantment* was the word that came to his mind.

He gestured with the tip of his cigarette, a slow and irresistible grin of delight coming to his lips. "Drinking alone, Lady Hartley? I'm shocked."

Anne chuckled, surprised to experience no sense of invasion now that he had entered her private place. In fact, what she felt was just the opposite—inevitability. This was almost an extension of her fantasy. Hadn't she guessed that with him, and no one else, there would be no reason to hide her secret self?

She looked up at him. "Shall I shock you again?"

He tilted his head inquiringly, and she extended her fingers. "A gentleman would offer a lady a cigarette."

He made a soft *tsk*ing sound back in his throat as his eyes danced. " 'Who can find a virtuous woman?' " he said, quoting, " 'for her price is far above rubies . . . .' "

"Mine is merely the price of a cigarette."

" 'Favour is deceitful, and beauty is vain, but a woman that feareth the Lord, she shall be praised.' "

Anne choked on laughter even as he passed the cigarette to her fingers. "Scripture, sir? Surely you'll not have me believe you've spent the evening in church!"

Josh grinned and settled his long frame beside her on the bench. The lace from her skirt folded up against his thigh. "Not exactly. My mother used to make me memorize verses when I was bad. Skipping chores was two verses, putting frogs in the teapot was eight, cussing was a whole chapter. By the time I was twelve, I knew the entire Old Testament by heart."

The sound of her laughter was low and throaty, and it drew Josh's attention to the creamy arch of her neck as she tilted her head to regard him speculatively. "And now?"

"I can outquote any preacher in the business," he admitted modestly.

Anne chuckled again and brought the cigarette to her lips. It was still wet from his mouth, and she savored the taste, just as she savored the way his eyes were watching her. There was a pleasant tension in her stomach that went all the way up to her chest, echoing anticipation and forbidden delights. The taste of bourbon and sharp cigarette smoke combined with the shadows of the gazebo and made her feel as if they were two naughty children sharing a secret. For now, for just a little while longer, Lady Hartley could be pushed far in the background and there was only Anne, enjoying the moment.

Josh took the glass from her unprotesting fingers and sipped its contents. There was amusement in his tone. "You wouldn't by any chance be drunk, would you?"

"Don't be absurd." She took a final draw on the cigarette and passed it back to him. "Why do men persist in assuming that every time a lady has a drink, tipsiness must inevitably follow?"

"My mistake." He returned the glass to her, and she drained its contents.

"So." She looked at him, putting the glass aside. "Now that we've established you didn't spend the evening in church . . . what did you do in town?"

He drew on the cigarette and passed it back to her companionably. "What do cowboys usually do in town?"

"Not being a cowboy, I'm sure I can't imagine."

"Well, now." He pretended thoughtfulness. "Some cowboys go to get drunk, I suppose, or play cards. Others watch the dogfights, and there's usually a crowd around the tonsorial parlor. Of course"—and his glance was askance—"most of them end up sooner or later paying a little call on the ladies' establishments at the far end of town."

Anne blew a very precise stream of smoke into the air and returned the cigarette. "And you?"

"Well," he declaimed modestly, "I don't drink much and can't afford to lose a whole lot at poker, and as for the ladies . . . I didn't see any that struck my fancy."

Anne lifted an eyebrow. "You must be a man of very exacting taste."

"It's important to know what you like," Josh agreed, and brought the cigarette to his lips. His gaze was dark and steady on her, waiting.

"And what is it that you like?" Anne invited. This was insanity, and she didn't care.

He seemed to consider that, studying the cigarette, his eyes narrowing fractionally. "Generally," he said at leisure, "I kind of lean toward the tall, skinny blondes. You know the type." He tossed the cigarette away with a lazy gesture, and it sizzled on the grass. She could feel his gaze on her skin like a caress, moving slowly up and down, lingering to explore, traveling again. "Their noses are usually just a little bit up in the air, their mouths prissed up, their shoulders as square as a chopping block.''

Anne lowered her legs so that she sat with one ankle folded beneath her and fussily arranged her skirts. Irritation sparked her eyes, and her tone was testy. "I must say you have very peculiar preferences.''

He leaned back and folded his arms across his chest, and Anne could see the laughter that played with his eyes. She then heard it in his tone. "Now, that all depends on what you call peculiar. The woman I have in mind has hair like spun silk, and eyes that could freeze a man to ice or set him on fire with a look.''

His voice dropped a fraction, became husky, tenuous. His eyes were shining still, but there was no amusement in them now, and when they rested upon her lips, Anne's breath caught. "That mouth, even when it's stern, can make a man ache from wondering how it would taste. And when she moves . . .'' His eyes wandered lower, to her throat, and her breasts, and even lower, until she could feel the center of her stomach grow hot from the touch of his gaze. "When she moves, just watching her can make a man think about all sort of things he should never think about a lady.''

He's going to kiss me Anne thought, and a pulse beat wildly, drying her throat. *He's going to kiss me, and I'm going to . . . I'm going to let him.* She knew it suddenly and without a doubt. In a moment he would reach forward and touch her hair or her cheek. Only a shifting of his weight, a lifting of his arm, and his rough hand would cup her face, his fragrant breath blend with hers, and she would know the feel of his lips, his strong cowboy's arms. . . . Nothing more than an instant separated them, the smallest of movements.

But he simply sat there, arms folded across his chest,

looking at her with eyes that scorched her skin and thinned her breath. Maddeningly to Anne, he did not move.

"The kind of woman I've got in mind," he said lowly, "puts me in mind of a high-bred filly. She'll bite and she'll kick and she'll buck, but she wants to be ridden. And in the end that's just what I'm going to do."

Heat flamed in Anne's cheeks, and she jerked her eyes away. "You are vulgar and disgusting," she said shortly. "Little wonder you find yourself alone tonight."

His laughter was soft and melodious, as full of promise as the night air around them and just as sweet. "Oh, I'm not exactly alone, Duchess." And then, unexpectedly, "How did you get to be a duchess, anyway? Were you born to it, or did you marry it?"

"I told you, I'm not a duchess. Actually, I'm a viscountess. I married my third cousin, who was heir to the title."

"So you were always a Hartley."

"Indeed. In fact, it was my grandfather who first came to this land over fifty years ago." And she cast him a look bright with interest. "Do you know the story of the Hartleys and the Fieldings? Of course not, how could you? It's really quite fascinating."

Josh's gaze quickened with alertness, but his voice was a mild drawl. "Is that right?"

She nodded, flicking a strand of hair over her shoulders. "My grandfather originally owned this entire corner of Texas—all of Three Hills and most of the surrounding area. A man named Jed Fielding won the entire lot of it in a game of poker—the story is that he cheated, but if I know Grandfather, he cheated too. He was the most delightfully wicked man; scandal chased him from England, and he had a reputation even before the encounter with Mr. Fielding."

Josh lifted an eyebrow. "Sounds like you're mighty proud of him."

She shrugged carelessly. "I think it's rather dashing to have a villain in one's ancestry, don't you? Besides, it was all so long ago. It hardly matters except to tell the story."

"Are you sure you didn't inherit your grandfather's wickedness?" he said teasingly, half trying to stray her from the subject. She was moving close to dangerous ground.

"One does not inherit wickedness," she informed him archly. "One acquires it. At any rate, Grandpa was quite put out by Mr. Fielding's action—and his losses—and declared a vendetta against him. Unfortunately, however, things did not work out the way he planned. Jed Fielding shot Grandfather and left him in an unmarked grave somewhere along the Sabine."

Josh's heart was beating fast. Now was the time. Was he going to tell her?

He said carefully, "I reckon you've got a pretty big grudge against the Fieldings, with all that behind you."

She laughed lightly. Her eyes sparkled with moonbeams. He wanted to kiss her. And he wanted to hear what she had to say.

"Well, it was a long time ago, after all. Of course, we were grievously wronged, but now we have Three Hills back, almost as though by divine ordinance. That's really all that matters."

Josh studied her in the moonlight, seeing more now than a beautiful woman from whom he wanted more with each passing moment. How easily she dismissed the past with all its complexities and mysteries; she seemed to care little about it. He had come here with an obsession for the past, and she saw history as nothing more than an entertaining tale. Would he be able to accept whatever he discovered about his own past as carelessly as Anne accepted hers? Would she care more if she knew what he had come here for?

Was he going to tell her?

But that, at least, was one question whose answer Josh knew. He was not a complete fool.

He changed the subject. "And your Lord Hartley. Was he as dashing and as wicked as your grandfather?"

She laughed. "Hardly."

With one arm still crossed on his chest, he brought a forefinger to his mouth and looked at her thoughtfully. "Let me guess. It was a very civilized arrangement, I'm sure. Mama and Papa set their sights, snared the game, and the poor fellow never had a chance. A *very* proper gentleman, I'm sure. A few years older, stiff upper lip, bit of a paunch, all that. Balanced your accounts, bought you pretty frocks, bowed from the waist, drank claret. He was polite, generous, patient, and about as exciting as a bedbug on a cold night. Am I right?"

Anne slanted a look at him, torn between amusement and a vague, annoying suggestion that she should be insulted. Amusement won out and dimpled faintly in the corner of her lips. "Hardly close. In fact, Marc was quit slim and my own age."

Josh's further assessment of Marc's character had been uncomfortably accurate, however, so she ignored it, and added, "Actually, my parents had nothing whatever to do with the match and were quite shocked. We eloped, you see. I don't believe they ever quite forgave me for that."

Josh listened to the sound of her voice, as sweet as music with its soft, rounded vowels and unexpectedly placed lilts.

He watched the motion of her head and the changing expressions in her eyes. All of it was a fascination for him. He could now see the shape of one bare foot, slim and long and drenched in lace, and he found the image inexplicably exciting. Being here alone with Anne in the moonlight was like being captured in a web of sticky-sweet delight; it was dazzling, provocative, and promising.

He was going to kiss her. The anticipation brought a tingling to his mouth, a tightening to his muscles, and a warm fullness to his loins. He was going to kiss her . . . but not just yet. He wanted to listen to the sound of her voice, watch the gentle rise and fall of her breasts as she spoke, see the lights that played in her eyes, and let himself experience her, fully and wonderfully, for a while longer. He wanted to savor this moment.

"Why did you marry him?" Josh asked.

What might have seemed to her an odd question was perfectly natural when coming from Josh. "Because I wanted to," Anne answered him directly. And then, with a small lift of her shoulders, "It seemed the thing to do at the time. Marc and I had always gotten along famously—I suppose eventually we might have married, after all, for there was no one else I particularly preferred. But Marc had just inherited the ranch and was going to Texas, and I wanted to come. So I more or less ran away with him, and we were married on the high seas. It was all rather impulsive, I suppose."

As she was speaking, Josh had turned slightly toward her, resting his arm across the back of the bench so that his fingers draped only inches away from her shoulder. His lips were soft with an indulgent half-smile, and when Anne glanced up at him, he playfully brushed a strand of her hair away from her temple. "You should be careful of those rash impulses," he said, teasing her gently. His eyes were deep and softly lit as they moved slowly from her own eyes to her mouth, and then back again. "See what it's gotten you? Sitting here in the dark with a lonesome cowboy..." His voice was low and slumberous, and his eyes, his lips, were very close. "And about to buy yourself a passel of trouble."

Anne's breath trembled in her chest, and she struggled with pulses of uncertain anticipation. There was no mistaking the intent in his gaze now. No doubt of the promise. Her own eyes were wide and still and did not waver from his. She said, "I'm not afraid of trouble."

His hand moved around to cradle her neck, tilting her face upward. He moved closer, and his eyes filled hers, as green and glowing as living jewels. His mouth covered hers.

The sensation was almost paralyzing. His lips were soft on hers, pressing, exploring; and his hand firmly held the back on her neck. His chest brushed her breasts. Anne saw nothing but a gray scene studded with pinpoints of light, and she could not feel herself breathe, she couldn't feel the thundering of her heart, she couldn't feel anything except his lips on hers and the floods of mind-consuming sensation. It was everything she had imagined, and more. So much more that for the longest time she couldn't even move or draw a breath or think of what was happening. She could only drown in the sensation.

Josh's fingers tightened fractionally on her neck, and she could feel him inhale. She thought he was going to pull away and let a small, high, ultimately greedy sound escape from her throat. He responded by slipping his other arm around her waist and pulling her close.

His kiss became more demanding, teasing a hunger within her that infused her with instinctive response. Her hand lifted weakly and folded against his shoulder. Her lips parted, and he turned his mouth against hers, tasting her. Slowly, inexorably, he thrust his tongue inside.

It was shock that caused Anne to pull away—shock and a rush of sensation so intense that it was blinding. There was no more thought, no more reason, only instinct, and instinct warned her, just for a moment. But before that moment could be captured, he had banished it, cupping her face with both his hands, raining light and gentle kisses across her brow, her cheekbones, her eyes.

"Anne," he whispered huskily. "Lovely lady..." His forefinger lightly traced the curve of her eyebrows, from the tip of one to the tip of the other, and her eyes fluttered open.

Through a haze she saw his smile, a wonderful, welcoming smile, and his eyes, bright with delight and deep with secrets she could not even imagine. All she could see was his face. The dark shadow of his jaw, the lush curls that tumbled toward his forehead, the gentle curve of his lips. And his eyes, so brilliant, so alive, eyes that seemed to draw her in and swallow her whole.

His lips touched hers again lightly, and a strangulated breath died in her throat. "Darling Anne," he murmured. "So little pleasure in your life...so many mysteries. Let me give you the pleasure. Let me show you the mysteries..."

His mouth took hers again, and there was no thought of resistance or surrender; there was no thought at all. His tongue was a slow and thorough invasion, a sensuous echo of the mating ritual. She tasted him. A part of him filled her and became a part of her, and she opened to him helplessly, willingly.

Anne was trembling. Inside her, something was spinning

and tightening; she could feel it from the hardened tips of her nipples to the center of her abdomen. Her limbs were weak, yet they had the strength to clutch at his back, to feel the straining muscles and the heat of his skin that burned through the fabric. Inside her head there was nothing but wave after wave of intensity: color, light, and shadow, sheer sensation. There was no need to ask how this could have happened to her. There was no point in questioning its essence, for what did she know of passion? It had begun from curiosity and daring and was spiraling into something dark and dangerous and wildly promising. It was completely out of her control. It frightened her, it thrilled her, it swept her up and out of herself and left her dizzy and aware of nothing but Josh and what he was making her feel.

His lips touched her throat, causing her to arch backward to receive his kisses. His breath fanned her heated skin and redoubled the flame. She touched his hair—and it was not crisp and springy as she had always imagined but soft and satiny. His fingers lightly touched the pulse in her throat, caressing, and then drifted lower, to the satin ties of her bodice.

From somewhere far away, a dim reason filtered through to Anne. She formed words, but by the time she uttered them, the first tie had already fallen away and they no longer seemed important. "No," she whispered. "We mustn't . . ."

Yet her voice sounded faint, heard through a tunnel filled with the roaring of her own blood, and the only thing that was clear to her was Josh's eyes, soft-dark, sleepy, and brilliant; his face, flushed and hazed with passion; his smile, slow and tender and all-enveloping. He said softly, "I told you to be careful. . . ."

The last ribbon fell away, and it didn't matter.

She felt his lips upon her naked breasts, his half-whispered words of adoration and wonder, the silky-rough texture of his tongue touching, teasing, adoring. It was madness. She felt the fire within her veins, the ache that spiraled and receded and spiraled again, and the dizziness that made her cry out in helplessness and wonder. And the driving, desperate, mind-blotting need.

She whispered, "Please..." and thought she meant to plead with him to stop, for she could not take this intensity of pleasure and wanting any longer. But she never finished the sentence. Anne only thrust her fingers in Josh's hair and held him closer, squeezing her eyes closed against the helpless sensation that was building in her. She had never known it would be like this.

Dimly Josh knew that he had not wanted it to be like this. He had not planned it; he had not expected it. Yet it had begun, was beyond his control, and was right. He could feel the shape of her, the sensation of her, the need within her wrapped around him and seeping inside him until he could hardly tell where she began and he ended. This was madness. It was Anne, and there had never been anything like this.

He could not get close enough or touch enough of her. He traced her shape, slim and lithe, from waist to hips. His hands were trembling. All of him was trembling from the force of his thundering heart. He kissed her and thought, *This much I knew...I knew it would be like this with us....* And then he could think nothing but *Anne....* For she filled all of him.

He moved until she was lying back on the bench, her legs on either side of him, her muscles were straining for him, cradling him. Josh stretched his arm and touched her bare ankle. The gossamerlike cotton fabric fell away in waves with the upward motion of his hand as he traced the shape of her leg beneath her skirt, cupping her knee, exploring the tender flesh of her thigh. He whispered her name out loud, and it was a celebration.

Anne thought incoherently, This can't be happening. This mustn't be happening. . . . And yet her skin was aflame, her head spinning, and somehow she was lying back with his warm length covering her. The night air teased her naked legs, legs that pressed against his hips and cupped him to her, straining against him. Distantly she was frightened and disbelieving, but those emotions were lost in the collage of sensations that assaulted her. His fingers caressed her bare skin, and his mouth was upon hers, hungry, greedy. The need she felt left her mindless. Josh. That was all she could think of. . . .

His mouth drew deeply on hers and then left her. His hand moved between their bodies, working the buttons on his trousers. A flash of panic, clear and fleeting, opened Anne's eyes, and she saw Josh's face, damp and heated and intent. His breath was uneven, and his eyes burned into hers. His voice was but a husky whisper. "Tell me to stop now, Anne." And again, "Tell me."

Anne knew she should answer and that she should stop him, before it was too late. They could not do this thing. *She* could not. She wanted to stop him. She *should* stop him.

But her arms were winding around his shoulders, her mouth was seeking his, and the only sound that came from her throat was a small, muffled cry. . . . Not of protest but of welcome. She felt him poised against her, and her own body was straining to open for him. Even until the moment he slid into her she knew she should stop him.

But she didn't.

Chapter Twelve

It was a clear autumn morning as Josh crossed the dewy grass from the bunkhouse to the main house. The faint hint of coolness in the air was invigorating, reminding him of home and about how Anne would look in the firelight with her hair loose about her shoulders and the warm colors playing on her face and sparkling in her eyes. Anne. The entire world seemed freshly washed and born anew in her presence.

Josh knew that a certain amount of lightheartedness, even tenderness, toward one's partner was to be expected after making love, and it was a feeling that could last hours or even days. Sometimes, if one was very lucky, it never completely went away. But what Josh was feeling now had nothing to do with the ordinary emotions that followed lying with a woman. What he was feeling now was so sure and so powerful that he could barely comprehend it, and in many ways he was as dazed as he had been the previous night when he'd left her.

Visions of her played through his head, and each memory provoked a swelling of awareness and wonder within him. From the beginning he had known it was inevitable and right. His mother would say this was destiny. He had looked at Anne and known, but he had not expected it to be like this. Nothing in his poor imagination had prepared him.

Josh climbed the steps and put his hand on the door. He hesitated. With a smile he bent down and removed his spurs before going inside.

The house was cool and morning-lonely; the sun had not yet touched the front windows, and the servants were occupied in the back part of the house. He smelled the faint aroma of breakfast and heard distant sounds of domestic stirring, but otherwise everything was very still.

Josh paused in the parlor, caught by the atmosphere of this room that was so distinctly Anne's. There was nothing about this place to suggest it had ever belonged to a rancher, or even to an American. Dusky roses climbed the paper on the walls; spindly-legged chairs and small, plump sofas were upholstered in striped silk. Heavy rose draperies swathed the windows, and delicate fripperies in porcelain and glass filled every available space. The tables were covered with lace and chintz, and even the legs of the piano were modestly skirted. Josh had to grin when he saw that.

There was a gramophone in one corner that intrigued him; he had seen a picture of one in the newspaper once but couldn't imagine what earthly use it could have. Next to it was a stereopticon—this he had seen in Denver once and knew exactly what it was for. He picked it up and looked through the viewer, but the picture inside was a pastoral scene, probably of England, and he put it down again. The pictures in Denver had been of a much more titillating nature.

A week ago, even a day ago, he would have looked upon this room, with its overdone furnishings and its absurd

mechanical playthings, with disdain, even resentment. Today the whole of it struck him with an indulgent delight,
because it was Anne. With all her idiosyncracies and incon-
sistencies, she left her unique brand on everything she
touched. He would not have it any other way.

He heard a footstep in the hallway and went to the door.
The maid gasped and almost dropped the heavy tray she was
carrying when she saw him.

"Is that Miss Anne's breakfast?"

The maid stared at him as he relieved her of the tray.
"Yassuh, but—"

"You go on and have yourself something to eat. I'll take
it up."

The girl's eyes went round with horror. "Law, suh, I
cain't let you do that! No gemp'um's allowed upstairs; we
all knows that! Miss Anne, she'd have my hide, an' you'rn
too! Please, suh, doan go up dem stairs!"

Josh was already on the second step, and he paused to
wink at her. "Rest your mind, Lizabelle," he assured her
cheerfully. "I can take care of my own hide."

He left her staring after him and took the stairs two at a
time.

Anne sat at the dressing table, brushing her hair with
clumsy, tugging strokes, staring blankly into the mirror. The
woman who stared back looked ill and pasty—her eyes
bruised with mauve pockets, her expression distant and
lifeless.

For perhaps the first time in her life Anne had not slept at
all. She had no memory of leaving the gazebo, only a dim
impression of lingering kisses and trailing caresses and
whispered words. A lightness, a separation, had carried her

beyond time and place, as though the woman who had left the gazebo and the woman whose reflection was now caught in the mirror were two different beings entirely, neither recognizable to the other. Only when she had reached her room and lit a lantern and glimpsed that rumpled, flushed, and starry-eyed creature in the mirror had reality descended. And it was a reality almost too shocking for her to bear.

The ivory-handled brush slipped from her heavy fingers and clattered to the floor, striking the dressing table and knocking over a bottle of toilet water in the process. Anne barely noticed. She gripped the edge of the table in a heroic effort to hold her memories at bay, but to no avail. The hot-and-cold shock was sweeping over her again, and there was no way to escape or deny it, try as she might.

Dear God in heaven, what had she done? Visions of herself flashed through her head—writhing in the dark beneath the body of a cowboy, her skirts pushed aside, wanton sounds of urgency and greed coming from her throat. His hands touching and stroking her most private flesh, his mouth opening and exploring hers, his body invading hers in the most unspeakable act of intimacy. . . . Fever assaulted her, quick and harsh and draining. No, it could not be. It could not be Anne Edgecomb who had done such a thing.

It had been a fantasy, no more. A harmless curiosity, a secret daydream. But it had somehow gotten out of control. She had never intended it to go that far. How could she imagine it would go that far?

Marriage had left Anne with fading memories of a few quick, embarrassing fumblings under the sheets, connubial duties that were not particularly pleasant but nonetheless necessary. How could she have imagined it would ever be like this? How could she have even known enough to be wary of it, much less long for it? Not even with her own husband had she felt such things, done such things, as she had known last night. And the worst was . . . the most horrifying part was . . . she had enjoyed it. Perhaps it was shock at what she was capable of, as much as at what she had done, which caused her to feel so hot and ill that morning.

Anne stood up and began to pace the room as she had been doing most of the night, the hem of her dressing gown fluttering about her ankles and kicking out before her with each step. The low terror inside her began to struggle and swell into panic when she saw the edges of morning sun peeking through the folds of the draperies and realized that the worst of it was not over. Oh, no, it had just begun.

What had happened last night with a stranger in the gazebo had not ended with the last moist kiss, the lingering caress, the subtle rearranging of clothing. It was something that she, Lady Hartley of Three Hills Ranch, would have to live with the rest of her life. She would have to face it in the mirror and carry the shocking secret of it with her to bed at night, but more than that, she would have to meet it in his eyes.

She had lain with Josh Coleman. She had coupled with him with no more forethought or discretion than a common trollop, and every time she looked at him she would remember. *He* would remember. Even now, just thinking of him, her heart began to speed, and a rush of heat engulfed her that made her light-headed. Dear God, how could such a thing have happened? How could she have let it get so out of hand?

And then, hovering on the edge of flyaway panic, Anne

caught herself. She stood still, took a deep breath, and released it slowly. She said out loud to herself, quietly and firmly, "*Stop it.*"

She took another breath and deliberately unclenched her fists. It didn't matter how it had happened or why, only that it had happened. Nothing could change it now. But she would *not* let herself be reduced to tatters over it. She could deal with this. She was Anne Edgecomb, Lady Hartley, and she had never in her life failed to rise to whatever was expected of her. She could handle this.

A cheerful voice sounded behind her. "Good morning, Duchess. Breakfast is served."

She whirled, and he was standing there.

All of Anne's newfound courage and resolve evaporated in a rush the moment she looked at him. The fever started again, swift and enveloping and as unpreventable as the rising of the sun. For an endless moment all she could do was look at him.

She saw his sleepy smile, the gentle light in his eyes, and something inside her seemed to melt and be drawn to him. The familarity in those eyes beckoned to her like a warm embrace, and she could no more understand it than she could fight against it.

It was the power of his familiarity that spun her so off-guard, just as it had the first moment she had laid eyes upon him. The knowledge, the intimacy, the feeling of possession . . . and she thought, *I do know him now, and he belongs to me. All of him—his lean, rangy shape, the curve of his ear, the curls that nestle against his collar, the dip of his throat, his hands . . . ah, his hands.*

She looked at his long brown fingers, and the tightening started in her stomach, a dryness in her throat that seemed to catch her very breath. She remembered the tautness of his waist beneath her hands, the strength of his back when she wrapped her arms around him. She remembered the salty, feral taste of his skin and his private masculine scent.

And in the instant her breath was suspended and she could not draw her eyes away, she was flooded with the memory of deep, drawing rhythms of intensely escalating sensations unlike any she had ever known before. Nothing more than the memory, swift and brief and sharp, caused an instinctive and shameful flood of heat to her private regions.

It was shock that gave her strength, shock and humiliation at her own weakness and the awful light of intimacy in his eyes. There were no secrets anymore. He knew all of her. And that she could not bear.

She squared her shoulders; she closed her fists. And she demanded, very quietly, "How dare you enter my bedroom without knocking. What are you doing here?"

For a moment he looked surprised, and then a rueful chuckle softened his face. "That's what I love about you, Duchess. You're so predictable." He set he tray on the bedside table and came toward her, a spark of indulgent teasing in his eyes. "Nothing changes you, does it?"

Anne stiffened her muscles with each step he took, and she lifted her chin. Her voice was cool, her face composed. "Why should it?"

"Well, after last night I did at least expect a friendly 'good morning.'" He was close now, and something inside her swayed and weakened with his nearness. She could feel the beating of her heart in her throat as he reached out playfully and captured a strand of her hair. "Nothing fancy, mind you. Just a little smile would do."

Anne jerked her head away. "I've no idea what you're talking about."

He slipped an arm around her shoulders; his lips nibbled playfully at her ear. There was an undertone of amused forbearance in his voice as he murmured, "Then let me refresh your memory."

Anne's heart slammed against her ribs with his first touch, and the pores of her skin seemed to open with eager welcome. She dragged in a breath with sheer force of will and flung herself away. Her heart was pounding with alarm. She whirled on him. "Keep your hands off me, you vile creature!" Her voice was shaking, and she had to draw another breath to steady it. Her eyes narrowed and her fists bunched tighter. "Nothing happened last night, do you understand me?" And then, with low and desperate ferocity, "Nothing happened."

Josh stared at her, and his first impulse was to laugh. How could he feel anything else? Everything he had ever known about women and their feelings, and himself and his feelings, had been tossed to the winds on the bizarre whim of Anne Edgecomb, and in shock, self-defense, and sheer incredulity he wanted to laugh.

Then he saw her eyes. There was anger there, but it was only a manufactured cover for something even worse. Fear. Fear of him, fear of herself, fear of what they had shared. And shame. A horrible, soul-staining shame that made Josh feel tainted even to look at it. And he understood.

She was serious. This was a woman who covered the legs on her piano, for chrissake. The memory of having slept with him filled her with such disgust that she couldn't even admit out loud that it had happened. She was ashamed of him. What had, for Josh, been the singular most stirring experience of his life filled her with nothing but repulsion. And Josh, understanding this, felt sickened and empty.

And then he was angry. More than angry. He was cold with fury and humiliation. He had come to her that morning ready to bare his soul; he had left her last night believing they had only touched the beginning of something vast and beautiful and—yes, damn it—permanent. And she stood there now, looking at him as though he were no more than a particularly distasteful clump of refuse staining her carpet.

He looked at her, and she saw each and every one of those passing emotions on his face. He took a small step backward—not much, but enough to make it seem as though an ocean separated them now. Enough for Anne to see the contempt in his eyes, which went through her like a knife.

Then he said, very quietly, "Yeah, I guess you're right." He never took cold eyes off her. "Nothing happened."

His face was very stiff. "But just for my information, would you mind telling me who that was I was with in the gazebo last night? I'd like to give her my thanks."

Anne drew herself up as though slapped. The air left her lungs and, for a moment, left her speechless. When she recovered, it was with a rush of blind fury that blurted out words even before her mind could form them. "You conceited fool! You surely don't think that *I* would ever consent to—consort with a common, crude—*cowboy* like you! Not—" And she drew in a swift shaking breath. "Unless you forced me against my will!"

His eyes narrowed and his face went so dark that Anne instinctively stepped back. His voice was low and icy with fury. "Now you listen to me, Duchess. I guess you've gotten so used to throwing out orders and having the whole world bow and scrape that you think there's nothing you can't change just by saying so. But I'm here to tell you that you can't change me, and you damn sure can't rewrite history to please yourself. It happened. And you enjoyed every minute of it. You tell yourself whatever pretty lies you please, but it's not going to change a goddamn thing. Do you understand that?"

Anne felt some of the color drain from her face, and her breath went shallow in her chest. Never had she seen such raw anger in a man's eyes. The power of it frightened her, shamed her, made her feel small and defenseless. And with every ounce of strength that made her Anne Edgecomb, she held his gaze.

"If you ever," she said steadily, "breathe a word of this to anyone, or even imply it, I shall have you horsewhipped within an inch of your life and thrown off this ranch."

There was a flash of something in his eyes—could it have been indignation? Or even hurt? But whatever it was, it was quickly erased by a smooth, hard gleam of sarcasm. "Why, Duchess," he said in a drawl, "I sure do wish you'd said something sooner. I had them old boys back at the bunkhouse up half the night telling about what I'd just finished doing with the lady boss. I didn't miss a detail, either. You couldn't really expect a common, crude cowpoke like me to keep a secret like *that*, now could you?"

Anne recognized the taunt for what it was and hated herself for having pushed him into it. For the first time in her life Anne wished she were the type of woman who could faint or cry. Didn't he understand? How could she *expect* him to understand? She was Lady Hartley, leader of society, dictator of fashion, figure of authority and propriety. . . . *Why couldn't he understand?*

"I don't even know your real name!" she cried, and it was wrenched from her without forethought or warning. "I don't know who you are or where you're from or what you might be—you're a stranger to me, a hired hand, a drifter! Don't you see this is impossible?"

For a moment there might have been a softening in his face, a thread of uncertainty or hesitation, and it almost seemed that he took a step toward her. In that moment, if he had come to her, if he had taken her hands and looked into her eyes and let all the barriers fall away, if he had said even one of those things she was so hungry to hear, it all might have been different.

But the moment of hesitation was there, and it was gone, and nothing was in his eyes except a cool, sardonic gleam. "If it will make you feel better," he drawled softly, "I always intended to marry you."

The pain congealed in Anne's chest like a muffled blow, and she thought that, after all, it was for the best. Easier to despise him than to want him. Easier to hate than to hope.

She lifted her chin, looked at him coldly and deliberately. "You are a good worker, Mr. Coleman," she said. "And, no doubt, you will make a good foreman. I think we will deal very well together as long as you remember who is in charge and keep your place. Now..." She made a smooth, graceful gesture toward the door. "Kindly leave me to my breakfast."

She saw a tiny muscle twitch near his eyes, and for a moment the fear fluttered again. But all he said, very politely, was, "With pleasure."

At the door he turned back. "You know, Duchess," he said, "I really feel sorry for you." A slow and mirthless smile curved his lips. "You don't have the faintest notion what you just turned down."

The door closed with a soft and final click behind him, and Anne wrapped her arms around herself against a sudden severe chill. She walked over to the window and leaned her forehead against the frame, staring out bleakly, feeling drained and empty inside. She stayed like that for a long time.

Chapter Thirteen

Josh's first impulse was to mount up and ride off without looking back. In the blindness of throbbing temper, that was most probably exactly what he would have done, except for the fact that when he got to the corral, he was not alone.

The other men had finished breakfast and were preparing for their day off. Some were still saddling up; others were leaning against the boards or standing around with their reins in their hands talking in a desultory fashion. All of them looked around at Josh when he walked up, giving him brief, wary, curious glances.

It seemed that years, instead of hours, separated the events of the previous day from that morning, and a feeling of weary surprise came over Josh when he remembered that he was now foreman of Three Hills Ranch. That was what he'd wanted, wasn't it? But today it was the furthest thing from his mind, and of the least possible importance.

Once before, he had allowed thoughtless impulse to push him into action—a small thing that had gotten out of control and ended with him pulling a gun on the man he knew as his father and turning his back on his home and family for a two-thousand-mile quest that had led, at last, nowhere.

There had been no reason for it, no excuse for it. It had just gotten out of control. He wouldn't ride off in anger this time, he promised himself.

The men were looking at him with uncertainty, and for that moment at least, Josh didn't see that he had much choice. He said, "Johnson, did you get that section of fence you and Gil were supposed to be mending yesterday finished up?"

Johnson muttered, "Not quite."

"Take Ribs with you and get it done." He led out the roan, speaking over his shoulder. "Shep, take three men and get started on the winter sheds in the North Spring pasture. Most of them are falling down with dry rot. And use hewn logs this time, not planks. Cut them yourself."

The men were staring at him. "It's Sunday!"

Josh threw his saddle on the roan's back. "I know what day it is."

"Even God took a day off now and again!"

"If He hadn't, He might've done a better job." Josh tightened the cinch and then straightened up, resting his arm on the saddle. "Look, boys, I don't like this any better than you do, but if we're going to get this place back in shape, we're going to have to work Sundays, and that's just the way it is. If you don't like it, I'll settle up with you right now."

He waited, but nobody made a move. Josh gathered up his reins, tossing over his shoulder, "The rest of you scout for strays. I saw a couple of calves locked up in the brush south of the low hill yesterday; pretty soon their mamas'll be following. Dakota, you ride with me."

And so it was of necessity, not desire, that Josh began his first day as foreman of Three Hills.

It was perhaps mid-morning when Josh remembered an incident when he was twelve. Jake had caught Josh and another boy fighting; Josh couldn't even remember what it was about now, but he had been as angry as hell. When Jake pulled the boys apart, Josh was still swinging, and at that point he was angrier at his father for stopping the fight than he had been over whatever started it in the first place. Josh's mother would have had him memorizing scripture until his next birthday for that incident, but Jake had just caught him by the collar, dragged him over to the wood pile, and Josh was certain he was about to get the whipping of his life.

Instead Jake put an ax in his hand. "You want to hit something?" he advised. "Have at it."

Josh had split logs until his muscles knotted and his hands bled and the stack of firewood almost overflowed the shed. And by the time the sun went down that night, he was no longer angry.

It was much like that today. With a grimness born of nothing more than the need to be moving, Josh started to patch fence, and when he ran out of broken fence, he began replacing posts whether they needed it or not. Dakota, sweating and tired after the first hour, gave him peculiar looks but kept his comments to himself, and after a while Josh wasn't angry anymore.

He didn't exactly know what he was feeling when the anger went away, but it wasn't happy—that was for sure. After the grand euphoria of the morning this emptiness was like a bruise in the pit of his stomach, and no amount of hard work or loud cussing over stubborn stumps and tangled brush would make that go away.

He felt like a fool, for one thing. Josh had not grown to know as much about women as he did without getting his face slapped a few times, and he should have expected this from Anne. She was more than just a lady. She was a British lady, and all she knew in the world was how to point her nose in the air and snap out orders. Somebody could have written a book about what she didn't know about passion between men and women—a book she promptly would have burned. Josh knew all that, and he should have anticipated her reaction that morning. But he hadn't, and he felt like a fool.

Before, Josh had always known what he could expect from women. Adoration, admiration, temptation, manipulation . . . never rejection. And maybe it was the shock more than anything else that had set his blood to boiling that morning. She had stood there as cool as frosted glass and pretended like *nothing had happened*. As though he were nothing more than an annoying insect buzzing around her face. That had never happened before, not to him. And it was the last thing he had been prepared for from her.

From far away a little voice mocked, *Surprised you, didn't she? She couldn't be too much for you to handle, could she?*

He jerked the reins of his horse with more force than necessary to turn him up a hill, and he answered himself grimly, *Maybe more than I want to handle.*

Of course, the worst of it was that she was right. She had no idea who Josh really was, not that it would have mattered after this. There were women, and there were women. A man might steal a kiss from a blushing town girl behind the draperies at a box social; he might, if he were very lucky and willing to put up with her tears afterward, fumble beneath the blouse of a bolder country girl out back of the barn. Of course, there were always the dance-hall girls and the saloon girls and the good-time girls, like the Montgomerys back home, who didn't care what you did as long as their brothers didn't find out. But a lady like Anne Edgecomb you didn't even smile at unless you had marrying on your mind.

Those were the rules. Josh had been raised with them and taught to respect them and, with a few unnoteworthy exceptions, had always abided by them. He didn't know what had come over him the previous night, except that he couldn't have stopped it had he tried. And no matter how much he knew that he should feel otherwise, he could not be ashamed of it.

Because, damn it, it *wasn't* just another tumble in the grass for him. Did she really think he had pushed up her skirts last night just so he could laugh and walk away this morning? And that's when he got angry all over again. Because she *did* think that, and it made Josh feel as low and dirty as she had accused him of being.

More than once during the morning Josh wondered bitterly what the hell he was doing there, tearing up his hands on her fences, straining his back on her tree stumps, worrying about her cattle, and setting himself up for nothing but more humiliation. And the answer was always the same: *Because, lady, you're not going to get away with this. Because I can be just as all-fired stubborn and ornery as you can, and it's about damn time somebody showed you what's what.*

It wasn't a very good reason, but it was, for the moment, all that he had.

They stopped and made a small fire for coffee at noon, dug out some sandwiches, and heated a can of beans. Josh was mostly silent, eating in a desultory fashion, and Dakota let him have his peace.

After sitting in the sun for a while, feeling the fatigue in his muscles and looking out over the landscape with its dotting of orange-red ground cover and surprising flashes of goldenrod and wild aster, Josh began to feel a little better. It was always like that with him and the land. Out-of-doors, in the midst of all that was perfect and right, it was difficult to think about the things that weren't perfect—like people.

"It's a shame," Josh said thoughtfully after a while, leaning back on one elbow to sip his coffee.

Dakota looked surprised, for that was the first idle thing he had said all day. "What is?"

"This." Josh made a small gesture with his cup, indicating the land that surrounded them. "I was just thinking how it must've looked twenty years ago, or even before that, when the first man settled here. It's rich land, good cattle-growing land. And she's letting it go to hell."

If there was a slight bitterness to the last statement, Dakota was smart enough to pretend not to notice. He began to toss dirt onto the fire. "Well, you can't put too much blame on her for that. After all, she's just a woman."

Josh gave a small, mirthless laugh. "I've seen many a woman put a man to shame when it comes to running a ranch. A man gets himself hurt or killed, and who's to take over but his wife—or sometimes his daughter. Some of the finest-looking outfits you'd ever want to see west of the Missouri are headed by women. And there's not a thing wrong with your boss that she couldn't do it if she put her mind to it."

Dakota glanced at him. "My boss? Seems to me she was your boss, too—last I heard."

Josh tossed the remainder of his coffee toward the fire, getting abruptly to his feet. His face was impassive but his reply was brief. "I guess." He didn't speak again until they were mounted up.

"You been here long?" Josh asked when they had ridden a half mile or so.

Dakota edged his horse around a spill of broken rocks. "Just since last winter. Drifted in from El Paso." And he grinned. "This is the farthest east I've ever been—or hope to be. Heard the lady needed hands, and knew a good thing when I saw it. I've done worse, believe me."

A corner of Josh's lips turned down dryly. "Haven't we all?" He gestured toward the stream, where a lump of rocky earth had tumbled down and was impeding the flow of water. As one, they dismounted and went to clear it. They worked in silence for a while, tossing aside the larger rocks, kicking in the debris with their heels. "We'd be missing this water come dry season," commented Josh. "She overgrazes this land something fierce. You can't run this many head without being prepared for trouble."

"Sounds like you're used to working for big outfits."

"Here and there." Josh braced his legs and dug his fingers under the mud to lift a particularly well-settled stone. Dakota contributed his weight, and they rolled it up into the bank.

"That ought to do it." Josh wiped his hands on his jeans with satisfaction. "We keep an eye on it, and she'll pool up just fine down in at Crooked Rock. That way, when dry times come, we know where to water the stock." And even as he spoke, he wondered whether he would still be there when the dry season came. What the hell was he worried about any of it for?

They started back toward their horses, and Josh stopped,

his attention caught by something on the ground. He stooped to pick it up. "Well, I'll be damned," he said softly.

He straightened up slowly, and Dakota peered at the small, round piece of lead he held between his fingers. "What is it?"

"A shot from an old ball-and-cap pistol," Josh replied absently. "The kind that Sam Houston gave the first Texas Rangers, back in '36. A Colt-Patterson five-shot. First revolving pistol made."

"Is that a fact?" Dakota seemed impressed. "Must've been buried under one of those rocks, who knows how long." Josh was distant and preoccupied, rolling the ball of lead between his fingers, thinking about a gunfight sixty years ago on this very piece of land—his grandfather's land. Had the owner of that five-shot taken cover behind that big boulder over there while his enemies attacked—renegade Indians? greedy white men?—knowing he might die and willing to die, fighting to protect his own? Josh would have done so. He would have taken cover behind the rock and bought time until he could work his way down the trail and toward the back side of the cabin. . . .

Dakota's voice broke into his thoughts, as though from far away. "How come you know so much about it?" he asked curiously. "You a gun expert or something?"

"No." Josh answered slowly, without even thinking about it, still staring at the ancient souvenir of forgotten times in his hand. "My pa has a gun like this."

And then Josh realized that his thoughts had been turning toward home and family quite a bit today. He didn't bother to wonder why, or to make the connection between what had happened with Anne and feeling homesick, because he suddenly realized something else.

He had been thinking about Jake, and there was no anger. He had thought about his mother, and there was no hurt. The bitterness that had been coiled inside him like a hard cancer ready to spread was dissolving, dispersing, being absorbed into the greater stream of life and washed away. It had happened so subtly that he was hardly even aware of it, yet the cognizance now was powerful and unsettling. What had caused it?

Anne?

He slipped the shot into his pocket and was very thoughtful as he walked back to his horse. Like a talisman, the presence of that small remnant of times gone by gripped him, absorbing his attention, spurring his imagination, and taking him, for a brief time, outside himself. He felt distantly excited, as though on the verge of a discovery. He was ready to continue the search into his past.

Dakota was his last possible source of information at Three Hills, since he certainly wouldn't risk asking Anne.

"You know about the folks that used to own this place?" he said after a while.

"The Fieldings?" Dakota shrugged. "Some."

"Yeah, even where I come from we've heard about Jed Fielding." Josh's voice was contemplative, thinking out loud, working it through. "There was some kind of man. Rode with Sam Houston at San Jacinto, lived with the Cherokee, made this ranch out of the wilderness. He was one of the first to raise cattle for profit and drive them north—even before the railheads. Some folks even say if it wasn't for Fielding, there wouldn't be a cattle industry in Texas." His eyes moved over the land thoughtfully, and he spoke slowly. "A man like that . . . a place like this. What do you suppose made them just pack up and leave?"

Dakota clucked to his horse and guided the reins, sitting back easy in the saddle. His voice was lazy and disinterested. "Well, the story I heard was that his seed turned out bad. One of his sons—Jake—killed a sheriff somewheres and went on the outlaw trail. You still hear stories about him now and then, the last of the big-time bad men, a real legend hereabouts, I guess. . . ."

Josh felt something icy grip the back of his neck and travel on slow, prickling fingers down the center of his spine. Dakota's words began to blur and fade out, and he had to concentrate to hear the rest.

". . . finally ended up in a shoot-out with his brother, the senator—"

"His brother?" It was Josh's voice, hoarse and faraway, and he wasn't even aware of forming the words. "Daniel?"

"Yeah, I think that was his name. Anyway, the senator ended up dead, and old Jake ran away with his brother's wife. That was the last anybody heard of the Fieldings around here."

Josh's head was roaring. The movement of his horse, the in-and-out expansion of his lungs, even the workings of his vocal cords were all on automatic, none of them guided by his own will. He didn't intend to speak. He did not know how he made the words come. "Jake Fielding . . . killed his own brother?"

Dakota shrugged, slapping at an insect buzzing near his face. "Seems that way. Elsewise, why would he and the woman have lit out the way they did? Like I said, I'm not from these parts. Only know what I hear. Guess some of the old-timers would remember. Anyway, he was some rough character, I reckon."

Then, bored with the subject, Dakota turned in the

saddle. "You wanna ride out and scout for strays"—he grinned—"or you got some more fence posts you want to kill?"

Josh replied absently, "Yeah. Sure." And he didn't even see the puzzled look Dakota gave him as he nudged his horse ahead.

Anne spent the morning in her office. It was a small, utilitarian room, its shelves lined with ledgers, its walls studded with ranch maps. One big window looked out over the lawn and flooded the room with light, and a coal stove kept it warm. It was a safe retreat from the rest of the house, for no one bothered Anne when she was working.

Most of the ranchers around remembered the time the Fieldings ruled Three Hills, and when Anne took over, they were reminded of another woman who had sat in this very office and had run the ranch. Many of the comparisons were unfavorable, Anne knew, but she didn't mind. There was comfort in knowing that a woman had gone before her and succeeded in what she was attempting—and against much greater odds.

It was for that reason that Anne had made no changes in the room since she had moved to Three Hills. She could sit here and take courage from the presence of Jessica Fielding, which still seemed to linger between the four walls, as well as in the small, neat handwriting that filled some of the old ledgers and in the square marks and crosses that dotted the yellowed maps.

There was a woman, she thought, who could survive anything. She wasn't afraid of ridicule or risks or adversity, and she had what it took to stand up in a man's world and make her own rules. Whether what she had done was right or wrong was not for Anne to judge, for the fact remained that she had *survived*. If only women today had that kind of courage.

But times had changed. The rules were more binding, and the last thing Anne was feeling today was courageous.

She was appalled by the way she had behaved that morning. Twice in less than twenty-four hours she had been faced with a part of herself she had never before suspected existed, and she was sickened by the recognition. She remembered the look in Josh's eyes—his shock, disbelief, and anger. And worst of all, his pity.

Oh, God, she hadn't meant to do that. She hadn't meant to hurt him. The last thing she had wanted to do was make him hate her.

She drew her shawl more tightly around her shoulders against a sudden chill, though the room was quite warm. The flood of weakening memories came over her again, and she had to close her eyes against them, drawing a deep breath. It didn't help.

She had *lain* with him. What had begun as an adventure, a delightfully wicked taste of the forbidden, had culminated in an act of unspeakable intimacy, and no amount of wishing or pretending could take it back. She had engaged with him in the most private act of human nature; he had touched her nakedness, he had been inside her, a part of her. He had made her feel things that were so shattering that even now she could not think about them, and nothing would ever be the same again. She would never be the same again.

Anne opened her eyes and looked bleakly around the room. And what was she supposed to do now? How was she supposed to feel? There had never been a woman in her life to advise her on such matters. Anne's mother would have

died of mortification had Anne even broached the subject of
connubial obligations—which, of course, it never occurred
to Anne to do—and her girlfriends giggled and blushed over
their various bits of misinformation. Anne had gone to her
marriage bed in ignorance and had emerged sanguine and
unimpressed, understanding why no one ever spoke of it. It
was simply too vulgar and boring.

No one had ever told her about the madness of fever, the
blindness of desire, the explosive joining. No one had ever
suggested sensations so sweet that they brought tears to the
eyes, nor feelings so powerful that they could blot out
reason and wisdom and the world. No one had ever told her
how she was supposed to feel afterward.

So she hugged her shawl to her shoulders and whispered
out loud, "What would you do, Jessica Fielding? You
always knew what to do. You ran this ranch and defied
public opinion with every breath you took. . . . What would
you do now?"

But the words fell hollow in the empty room, and it didn't
matter. She was not Jessica Fielding, which, perhaps, was
fortunate. Anne knew the stories her neighbors told of how
Jessica Fielding had taken her son and run off with her dead
husband's outlaw brother after a dubious shoot-out between
the two men. But it was Jessica and Jake's flight that
enabled the Hartleys to buy back Three Hills, after all. She
had always felt certain that Jessica Fielding harbored her
own, equally engrossing, version of that tale to tell.

Anne snapped herself back into awareness. She definitely
was not Jessica Fielding. She was Anne Edgecomb, she had
made a mistake, and she was terrified.

You should have fired him, Anne thought quite clearly.

Why didn't you fire him this morning while you had the chance? God knows you've done it for less. . . .

Perhaps he would leave, anyway. She had a flash of the anger in his eyes, and she thought, *Why would he stay? He'll go, and I'll never have to see him again, and all my problems will be solved.*

Oh, God, she did not want him to leave.

But what could she do? Seek him out, apologize, beg him to stay? It was unthinkable.

Mr. Coleman, I just wanted you to know I'm sorry for my behavior of this morning and would like you to be my lover again. I hope there are no hard feelings. She went hot with the imagining, and then cold with misery.

What would Jessica Fielding do? She would survive, that's what. She would do the best she could with what she had, and she would hold her head up high and go on living. That was the kind of determination it had taken to tame a wild land, to live in a world harsher and more unforgiving than this, when every day was a challenge and the next sunrise was a gift, not a promise. That was the kind of strength that was inbred into this place, the very thing that had drawn Anne to Texas and made her love it. The women of the past had done what they had to do.

And Anne Edgecomb could do just as well.

She went back to her desk and sat down, firming her shoulders, then pulling in her chair. Before her was a thick book that listed by description and drawing the brand of every rancher from here to California. Next to it was a sketch she had made from memory of the brand on Josh's horse.

She hesitated, hating what she was doing and ashamed of

herself for it. But damn it, she had to know. And then, determindedly, she opened the book.

The brand she had sketched was of four interlocking circles, double eights crisscrossed over one another. It could have been anything. A Circle Eight, a Double Three, A Flying Ring . . . She was appalled by the sheer number of brands listed, none of which or all of which could have represented the original brand on Josh's horse. And if she found it, what then? What would it prove? What would she do if she could prove anything?

But after turning no more than ten pages Anne began to realize, with something akin to a weary sort of relief, that the questions were academic. The chances of finding the original brand with nothing more than a poor sketch of the altered one to go on were astronomical. And that, perhaps, was what Josh had relied on. It would take someone far more expert than she.

Then go to the sheriff, a treacherous little voice whispered. *That's his job, after all.*

But she knew she wasn't going to do that. Not now. Not yet. Perhaps not ever . . .

"Excuse me. Ma'am?"

The voice caused her to jump and slam the book closed guiltily, and when she whirled in her chair, Chance was standing at the door, hat in hand. "I knocked," he explained. "I guess you didn't hear. Sorry if I scared you."

Anne cleared her throat; she grasped for her composure. "That's quite all right, Chance. I didn't expect to see you, that's all. I left orders I wasn't to be disturbed."

"Yes'm. That little black gal of yours told me. But we've had a bit of trouble, and I thought you'd want to know about it."

Dear God, Anne thought. No more. No more today. But nothing in her expression gave a hint of the bony fingers that were closing around her heart, and she replied only, "Quite right, of course. And what is the trouble today?"

"Well, ma'am, we were getting ready to test out a new site, like you said, and I went to the shed to get some equipment—meters and gauges and such that we'd be needing. It'd been ransacked, Miz Edgecomb. Padlock broken. We've got some expensive tools in there and always keep it locked, you know—but they didn't just steal. They wrecked it. Everything that could be smashed was smashed, and what wasn't was twisted or filled with grease—just plain vandalized, ma'am."

Anne released a long and ultimately steady breath. Her ability to do that surprised her. "How serious were your losses?"

"Serious enough," he replied grimly. "But that ain't all."

To her inquiring look, his eyes were somber. "This was more than just meanness, ma'am, and that's what I thought you ought to know. Somebody took a piece of charcoal and wrote all over the door, 'Yankee go home.' A warning, like."

Anne closed her eyes in a rush of fury and anguish. How dare they! Hadn't she enough to worry about without arrogant outsiders firing their opinions on her, threatening her livelihood? Didn't they realize this was her *life*? How dare they!

Everything was closing in around her; all her hopes and plans and desperate schemes were falling apart. How much more could she take?

She said softly, tensely, "Dammit."

If Chance was startled to hear the lady swear, he did not show it. He took a step farther into the room, and his tone was simple and frank. "Listen, ma'am, like I told you before, I don't want to lose your business. But I think you ought to know what you're getting into here. I've seen this happen before—wildcatters going up against the oil companies, mostly, or sometimes the other way around. Starts out little, just trying to scare off the competition, but it can get right nasty. Me and my boys ain't drawing fighting wages, you know. We're just here to dig."

Anne looked up at him, drawing up all her resolve and trying to make it penetrate her voice. "There will be no fighting, Chance, I can assure you of that. There has been some . . . discontent, yes, but it's nothing I can't handle."

She took another breath, thinking of the look in Big Jim's eyes the previous evening when she had told him he was being retired to the oil fields. "More than likely it's one of my own employees, or even"—she thought of George Greenley—"a neighbor expressing his opinion on the way I choose to run my ranch. You needn't worry. I'll get to the bottom of it and make certain you are promptly reimbursed."

But Chance was shaking his head slowly, thoughtfully. "No, ma'am. I don't think it was anything like that. Your own hands have sort of got used to having us around, and if they wanted to do anything about it, they would've done it before now, don't you think? It could've been one of your neighbors, of course. It'd be a far piece to ride just to throw around some equipment and write on the door, but it could have been."

He looked at her curiously, hesitantly. "Ma'am, you haven't noticed any strangers hanging around lately, have you? And the only reason I say it is because sometimes it starts with a hired gun. Rich men don't like to get involved in the dirty work, you know, and they don't want anything falling on them if it should go wrong. So they bring somebody in from the outside." He shrugged. "Just a thought, ma'am. You might want to keep an eye out for suspicious characters."

Anne stood up, smiling stiffly, and walked him to the door. She must have said something reassuring and authoritative, because he was thanking her when he left. And when she was alone finally, Anne leaned against the closed door, the fingers that had closed around her heart squeezing so tightly now that it hurt. *You haven't seen any strangers hanging around lately, have you?*

And Stephen's voice: *Who is he? Where did he come from?*

Josh, sitting at her breakfast table, looking contemplative and enigmatic: *An outlaw hardly even has a chance anymore. . . .*

No. It was ridiculous. She pushed away from the door, annoyed and embarrassed. This was nothing more than a spot of mischief, a child's temper tantrum to get even. Big Jim was the most likely culprit, but she wouldn't put it beyond George Greenley to send one of his hands over to wreak a little havoc with the lady rancher's plans.

Confronting either of them would advance her nothing and only give them the satisfaction of knowing they had achieved their goal and upset her. Of course, she would report it to the sheriff at the first opportunity, but there was little he could do that she could not do for herself. And the best thing to do was to forget it. It was a prank, over and done with, and the only way it could lead to trouble was if she started trouble herself.

Sometimes it starts with a hired gun....
Who is he, Anne? Where did he come from?

Anne walked back over to the desk and touched the brand book hesitantly. For a long time conscience warred with instinct, common sense with better judgment. In the end she did not know what caused her to pick up her sketch of the blotted brand, crumple it, and thrust it into the stove. She just did.

She left the office and closed the door firmly behind her. The brand book, with its twenty-year-old Clover Three brand stamped into the leather cover, lay facedown on her desk, and it stayed that way, ignored and forgotten, for many weeks to come.

High in the mountains a man could walk for miles, following a trail in the snow and thinking his feet were making firm contact with the ground. And then a small sound, a sudden wind or a loose stone, would set the earth in motion; he would look back to see the whole side of the mountain collapse into an avalanche behind him and realize, with a sort of sick astonishment, that what he had trusted to be solid rock was nothing more than thirty feet of loosely packed snow.

Josh had that same sort of sick, amazed feeling now as he looked back and saw the bedrock of his life collapse into an avalanche of drifting, amorphous lies. He was disoriented, stunned, and a little snow-blind.

He left Dakota scouting for strays, spent a few hours helping to shore up the winter shelters, and worked his way homeward, clearing out streams and pulling strays from the brush. As it happened, he arrived at the bunkhouse a few minutes earlier than the others, and he was glad.

A weary sense of distant amusement fell over him as he crossed the dusty bunkhouse floor and sat down heavily on his cot. He sat there for a moment, looking at nothing, his face tired and his shoulders slumped. It had been a hell of a day.

He smiled a little bleakly when he remembered how clear it had all been the first day he'd ridden up here. A hundred thousand acres of verdant cattle land, a county on the verge of war, a vulnerable woman, and a bunch of shiftless, lazy cowhands . . . The perfect setup for a man who knew how to take advantage of an opportunity. He had never expected it all to get this complicated. But then, maybe that was his problem. He never expected anything to get out of hand.

He had come for answers he wasn't even sure he wanted to know, and he had found more than he bargained for. Much more.

Now he knew. Jake Fielding, an outlaw. His mother, an adultress. Daniel Fielding, his father, a senator and a statesman, dead at the hand of his own brother in a lustful triangle over a woman. He knew the secret. And it was more horrible than anything he could have imagined.

He touched the names traced in the Bible, and the dried and faded ink seemed to be tinged with a malevolent power that made him shudder. Jake Fielding. Jessica Duncan. The only two people he had loved exclusively, unquestioningly, for all his life. Two people he had never known.

It wasn't just the man who had pretended to be his father, but his mother . . . his mother, who had run off with a murderer. Who had possibly collaborated in the murder. Corruption seemed to ooze from his pores; depravity crouched in the corners of his mind and clawed at him with tentacled fingers. His chest was tight, crushed down by a nameless weight. His belly felt empty, hollow, and nausea roiled in his throat.

All his life he had been taught pride in his family, in the name: *You're a Fielding, son. Act like one. Don't ever forget you're a Fielding.* Being a Fielding meant something. Being a Fielding meant you held your head up high and said your name loud and clear and defended what was yours with honor and dignity. And all he had ever known about who he was and what that meant was nothing but a squirming ball of ugly lies.

His mother. So pious. So devout. So perfect. All her sanctity, all her serenity, was nothing but a blasphemous act. If she had been a party to this, there was nothing she was not capable of. He had never known her.

He was lost and alone wihout a compass. He no longer knew who he was or what he was supposed to be. He felt shattered and empty inside—and old. Older than he had ever expected to feel.

Absently he weighed the lead shot in the palm of his hand. He remembered the first time he had been allowed to hold the gun from which this shot had almost certainly come. Josh couldn't have been more than nine, and the weight of the gun was almost more than he could support in his two hands. Jake had taken it down from its wooden case over the fireplace and put it in Josh's hands and told him how the great Sam Houston had given this gun to Josh's grandfather and how it would be his someday. And Josh had been so filled with awe, so swelled up with pride, that he thought he would burst. There was something of that same sense of awe in him now, holding the lead ball in his hand, but it was shot through with remorse and, yes, shame.

Josh was glad Jed Fielding hadn't lived to see this day.

That he would never know what had become of all he had built and given his life to, that he had never known the day when his own son would betray his legacy.

And what was Josh to do now? He had gotten what he had come for. He knew the answer. There was nothing left for him here. The past was finished; the future was a bleak and empty landscape. And Anne...Anne, who did not want him.

It didn't make sense to Josh. Was this the truth his parents had needed to hide from him so desperately? He felt he could never go back to Colorado, to the people who had been his family. All he wanted to do was forget.

Abruptly he closed the Bible and shoved it back into his saddlebag, dropping the lead shot into his pocket. A bleak certainty crept into his face as he slowly secured the flap on the saddlebag and stood up. Everything he owned was packed away already into those saddlebags, and perhaps it would always be that way.

His face was set and his eyes were empty as he flung the saddlebags over his shoulder. It was over, then. He didn't know where he would go, or what he would do, but he knew there was no point in staying here. Maybe someday, someplace, if he kept moving long enough, he would find something he could call his own. A woman, a piece of ground, maybe even a family. It might be out there somewhere if he kept moving.

Or he could ride forever and never have anything of his own but the tracks he left behind.

He was at the door, looking out at the late-afternoon landscape, when a sorrow stole over him that was even stronger than the pain that drove him away. His feet refused to take him any farther. He couldn't rightly leave this place now.

There was Anne, and Three Hills, each a part of the other and both of them twined about his soul. He could ride forever and never get away from that. "Destiny," Anne had said. And he thought now, slowly, Yes. . . .

Daniel had died, but Three Hills remained. Jake had walked away, but Three Hills remained. Josh could leave, but Three Hills would still be here, the blood and tears of Fielding men and women imbedded in its soil, their sweat and toil and sacrifices a monument to greatness. The brand of this place was stamped upon his soul, and it would always be waiting for him, belonging to him, calling him back. . . .

He could not change the past, but he could try to understand it in order to build the future.

Slowly he crossed the room and hung the saddlebags on the post above his bunk. It was perhaps the hardest thing he had ever done, but he must have known all along he couldn't leave. Not now. Not yet.

A Fielding never walked away from a fight. It was up to Josh to redeem what was lost when Jake and Jessica fled Texas. Josh touched the lead ball in his pocket, feeling its pitted texture, its weight, its power. "I owe you this one, Grandpa," he whispered out loud.

Slowly his face began to harden and his eyes lost their emptiness. His fingers closed around the lead ball. "It's worth fighting for," Josh said slowly. His fist tightened. "It's worth everything."

Chapter Fourteen

Josh spent the next morning working around the ranch house: repairing the gate latch, replacing shingles, reinforcing the weakening foundations of some of the outbuildings. It was work that needed to be done, of course, but Josh was aware that there was more than one reason he had decided to take care of it personally—and today.

With each nail he struck, each carefully trimmed edge and tightly set bracket, Josh was putting his own brand on this place. The work he did that day would still be here a year from now, five years, and so would he. He needed, after the crisis and decision just past, to set down some physical evidence of that promise.

And he wanted Anne to know it too.

Since mid-morning she had been watching him. He would look up and see a shadow at the window that moved quickly away, a curtain falling back in place; he would hear a step on the front porch and turned in time to see the door closing. And he smiled.

He was repairing a leak in the barn loft when she came to him. He heard her footsteps on the old straw beneath him, the soft clearing of her throat, but even before that he was alerted to her presence by a more visceral awareness. There seemed to be a change in the atmosphere—a small, almost undetectable, charge in the air like a gritty smell of thunder an hour before a storm, only sweeter and more pervasive. As the fabric of his skin tautened and the small hairs at the back of his neck began to prickle, he looked, and she was there. That was how attuned he was to her.

Disguised in the shadows as he was, Josh had a perfect view of Anne, but she could not see him. She stood below in the center of the vaulted barn, caught by crisscrossed beams of dusty light that filtered through the old boards. She was wearing a simple gray dress with cotton lace at the collar and cuffs, nipped in tight at the waist and firmly outlining her bosom. The halo of her piled-up hair seemed almost translucent, and her pale skin looked fragile and delicate. Standing all alone in the great barn so far below him, she looked both small and imperious, courageous and vulnerable.

She looked around uncertainly for a minute, sensing his presence but unable to find him. And then she called out loudly, "Mr. Coleman, I'd like to speak with you for a moment, please."

Josh picked up the hammer and calmly drove the last nail just before he climbed down from the loft. "So," he said, ignoring the last three steps and springing lightly to the floor before her, "we're back to Mr. Coleman again."

He jumped into sight less than three feet in front of her, and Anne caught her breath. She was taken by surprise by a distant, frantic pulse that surged through her.

In Anne's imaginings she had thought the worst of her remorse and guilt over the impulsive act she had committed with Josh Coleman was behind her. She never imagined that it could begin all over again. . . .

The red shirt he wore was molded to his chest by dark patches of perspiration, starting beneath the taut rise of breast muscles going down the sides toward his waist. Between his knotted bandanna and the first button of his shirt she could see his throat and the gentle beginning of the pattern of dark hair that covered his chest. Dusty denim caressed his hip and thigh, molded the shape of one slightly thrust-forward leg, and cupped his sex. He need do nothing more than appear, and Anne's nerves were alive with sensory impact; she was as trapped by his presence as a fly in amber.

She had not been prepared for the tight, anticipatory eagerness that was winding itself around the core of her stomach. She hadn't expected knowledge, welcome, and desire to flare between them like sparks of heat lightning on a summer day, awakening old memories, generating new needs. She hadn't expected to still want him.

That faint, familiar smile was on his lips, full of knowledge and rich with speculation. The subtle light in his eyes was more of a suggestion than a gleam, effortlessly seeing through her and gathering from her all her secrets. It's not over, she thought helplessly. It will never be over.

Anne pressed her hands tightly together before her, as though physically to stem the tide that was swelling and pressing inside her. She said precisely what she had come here to say. "One of the storage sheds on the oil lot was broken into yesterday." The words came out in a rush, not with the cool detachment she had intended. "I wonder if you know anything about it."

His slightly lifted eyebrow expressed an eloquent disinterest. "Should I?"

"You are the foreman, after all."

He half turned to place the hammer and a handful of nails on an upturned packing crate nearby. He answered, "Last I heard, the oil fields were Big Jim's department. Unless, of course . . ." And he glanced at her, his head half bent as he turned. His expression was smooth, eyes slanted toward her and hiding secret amusement—or perhaps just secrets. "You think I had something to do with it?"

Anne's heart caught on a half beat and doubled its rhythm for almost a full breath before slowing again. Guilt tingled in her palms and warmed her face. There was no hiding from him. None at all.

But still she was persuaded to try. She clamped her hands tightly together, digging her nails into her own flesh, and took a steady breath. Her eyes did not waver from his, and she let him read there what he pleased. "It was an act of deliberate sabotage," she said coolly. "Childish and vengeful, and except for the obvious malicious intent, completely beneath contempt. I would hate to think that you—or anyone in my employ, for that matter—would stoop so low."

"Well, you're right." He leaned against the crate with his weight on his palms, his pelvis thrust forward, his shoulders relaxed. A lazy smile touched his lips. "I wouldn't. But seeing as how I'm foreman and you seem to be upset, I'll look into it for you if you want."

His voice was low and easy, and his words were casual. To any disinterested observer they were nothing more than employee and employer discussing amiable matters of business. Anne knew differently. It registered in the beat of her heart, in the slow stretching and coiling of her smooth inner muscles, and in the helpless way the screen of her eyes was imprinted with the shape of his chest as it moved for breath.

She felt naked when he looked at her. She thought suddenly, *He knows what I'm thinking and what I'm feeling because he feels it, too . . . has felt it all along*. She couldn't break away from his eyes.

He said, "Was there something else?"

The sound of his voice was low and sonorous, dangerously soothing to her already saturated senses. She had to fight against its power, just as she fought against the mesmerizing effect of his eyes.

"No," she said briefly. Then, "Yes." Her hands, clasped as tightly together as they were, began to ache, and she made a conscious effort to loosen them. It took courage to stand still and meet his eyes. She drew a breath and said, "I'm surprised you're still here."

The corner of Josh's smile deepened into a bitter curve. The glint in his eyes might have been self-mockery, or it might have been wry surprise, and he made a soft sound of amusement in the back of his throat. "You know," he admitted, "I am too."

And now it was here. The moment of truth, the moment of courage. She stood very tall. "I'm glad." She had to swallow. "I'm glad you decided to stay. I need you."

He answered gently, "I know."

Her nerves clenched into themselves as though stung by a hot probe, and she jerked her chin up. "I meant, of course, that the ranch needs you."

"Of course."

She took another breath, holding firm. "After all that has

happened, I'm sure I wouldn't blame you if you decided to leave without notice.''

There escaped from his lips what might have been the beginings of a rueful chuckle, though his gaze was very quiet and steady, with a deep, unreadable meaning. "I've tried to ride away from this place," he admitted quietly, "but I couldn't.''

He pushed slowly away from the crate, his eyes holding hers, and whatever amusement there might ever have been in his face was completely gone. He added quietly, "And you know why, don't you?''

The barn was very warm, fragrant with a hundred mixed and muted scents—crushed straw, oiled leather, animals, and seasoned wood—the resonance of a half a century rich with memories. Sunlight and motes of chaff drifted slowly over them, turning and glistening on unfelt breezes, suspending them in a moment that was still and quiet. They looked at each other, and the air between them was alive.

He came toward her. Anne stood still. She thought, Don't . . . but it was a shout no one could hear, nor would obey—not even herself. Her heart was a heavy, pulsing mechanism, squeezing out breath by the spoonful until he stood directly before her.

He was so close, his thighs brushed her skirts and his heavy leather belt touched her abdomen. His shadow enveloped her, and her very pores were infused with the sun-baked masculine scent of him. But he didn't touch her.

He said softly, "Don't you?''

Anne thought frantically, Don't do this. Let me go. . . . Which was absurd, because he wasn't holding her. Nothing was holding her that she could see—or fight against.

With a force of will that felt like tearing flesh, Anne

jerked her eyes away from the quiet demand of his gaze. "No." If her voice sounded unsteady, it was only because she could not hear it over the shuddering rhythm of her heart. "I don't know what you're talking about."

The soft light in his eyes mocked her, and then he did touch her. He reached down and took her tightly clasped hands in his rough, warm ones, prying them apart. Foolishly and instinctively she resisted, and she felt the strength of his fingers overcoming her will, opening her defenses until she was as exposed and as vulnerable as was the small hand he held so firmly in his.

"This is why," he said roughly, and he dragged her hand to his chest. She felt muscle and heat beneath the material, firm flesh and the strong, rapid beating of his heart. Her fingers tried to clench and draw away, but he held them steady. His eyes were alight with a deep and steady blaze, and so close that they seemed to sear her skin.

"And this." His voice fell to a lower, huskier timbre, and his other hand pressed beneath her left breast, embracing the frantic, tumbling thunder of her own heart.

"Stop it!" What was meant to be a shout was less than a hiss, a choked-off whisper that ripped away the last of her breath. She tried to twist away, but he did not seem to notice her feeble effort.

His face filled her vision now, intense with emotion and fierce with demand. His breath heated her face. All Anne had to offer in her own defense was the panic that rose in her eyes and lips, which parted for a plea that was never spoken.

His chest expanded against her fingers with a breath; he murmured, "And this." And his mouth covered hers.

Anne did not fight against his kiss. She did not cry out

against the pressure of his lips, the strength of his arms, the raw, demanding power of a man's desire for a woman. What she fought was the molten fire that rushed through her veins. A quickening, blinding throb of raw sensation took her in its grasp and stripped her bare. She fought against the helplessness and the twisting need and the drowning, suffocating sweetness. She knew that if she succumbed now, she would never again break free.

With a surge of superhuman will and a cry that seemed to be wrenched from her very soul, Anne tore her mouth away from his. In the same motion, and without her even being aware of what she was doing, her arm swung back and she slapped him hard across the face.

The sound of blow was like a gunshot in the still, sun-drowsy barn, its echo a sickening reverberation of flesh against flesh. Anne fell back, her chest heaving, her palm stinging, awash in horror over what she had done. Josh stood still, looking at her.

She could see the red imprint of her palm on his face, the dark immobility of his eyes. The singing rush of passion that had swelled her veins a moment ago twisted and spiraled into a queasy disbelief, leaving her clammy and dizzy.

She uttered a strangulated gasp, and her hand shot out to him as though to take back the deed, then fluttered helplessly back to her lips.

Josh's face was very tight, his eyes like emeralds in the dark; hard and banked with a low, dangerous flame. He said quietly, "Does that settle it, then?"

Anne was trembling so violently all over that she feared her legs would not support her. She took a stumbling step backward, and her hand met the cool, smooth surface of a support beam. She braced herself against it, staring at him through the veil of emotions that misted her vision. Her voice was hoarse. "I—I'm sorry—"

"Do you really think it's that easy?" He took two steps toward her and stopped. She could see the elongated tendon in his neck and an angrily pulsing vein at the side of his throat. His eyes were churning, but his tone was quiet and controlled.

"It was real, Anne," he said low. "What happened between us wasn't just a fantasy that got out of hand, or a dream you'd like to forget." He spoke slowly, with deliberate emphasis on each word, as though the force of his voice could somehow push the truth into her head. "*It was real*. And you know it, because you can feel it. You didn't come out here today to talk about break-ins or oil wells; you came because I was here and you could *feel* it. Couldn't you?"

Anne pressed her palms against the post, shaking her head. Before the angry demand in his eyes she was helpless. And her only defense was a truth of her own.

"Why can't you understand?" she cried. "It doesn't matter what happened—it doesn't matter what I feel or what you feel—it can't be!"

Her arms and her legs were trembling, and her voice rang with a wild note of desperation. The remnants of passion-induced perspiration dried on her face and left her chilled. Yet deep within she felt an anger of her own rising, perhaps nothing more than a by-product of panic. "What do you think can come of it?" she demanded. "You're my employee, for God's sake, nothing more than a drifting cowhand and a *stranger*. Do you really think I'm going to sport you about as my lover? Shall we marry and fill the nursery with children whose surnames are nothing but a figment of your imagination? What happened between us was wrong! I can't change it, I can't repent of it, but I can forget it—and I can make damn sure it doesn't happen again! Why can't you understand that?"

The sun-drenched motes of chaff that once had hung so benevolently between them now looked like the still, dead smoke that lingers after a disaster. The sweet fragrances of autumn were cloying and suffocating, trapping their anger and pain. And for a long time nothing but the echo of Anne's words filled the space between them.

His eyes flickered over her, taking in her panic-streaked face, her tousled hair, and her heaving chest. When he met her eyes again, something had changed within his—a new kind of knowledge that was no more comforting than the last. "Oh, I understand," he said softly. There was an edge of mockery in his voice, but worse, a shadow of pity in his eyes. "It's just fine and dandy for you to wheel about the country in your short skirts and your motorcar; you don't give a damn about what people say about you then. The grand Lady Hartley, strong enough to run one of the biggest spreads in Texas, brave enough to face down a band of vigilantes with a rifle and charge a herd of stampeding cattle—but inside you're just a scared little girl."

He came toward her, placing his hands lightly but firmly on her shoulders. The strength of his presence pinned her, not his touch, and his face was a profile of will that dwarfed even her own. "How long, Anne?" he insisted fiercely. "How long are you going to keep running from what you don't even understand?"

Anne hitched in a breath, closing her eyes against a sudden wave of exhaustion and defeat. "Damn you," she said shakily, but she did not try to move away from him. There was no point.

She opened her eyes, pressing her head back against the support post to look at him. All her muscles stiffened against him, and she made her voice steady. "I have done," she said clearly, "everything I know how to do. I have fired you, I've ordered you off my property, I've rejected your advances, and now I've even . . . struck you. What will it take . . ." A note of pleading came into her voice that she hated but could not control. "To make you leave me alone? Why won't you—please, just go away?"

He smiled, a slow and mirthless smile that was neither mocking nor threatening, merely certain and somehow pitying. "All right," he said softly. "I'll leave. I'll get on my horse and ride away and you'll never see me again, but that won't be the end of it."

His hands slipped upward, cupping her face, his fingers threading through her hair. If ever she had wanted to run, it was then. But she couldn't.

"You can kick me off this place," he said, "you can throw me in jail, you can bury me under six feet of dirt and put a curse on my bones, but that won't be the end of me." His fingers tightened on her scalp like a caress, and his face was so close, his breath scorched her skin.

"Go ahead," he said, gently mocking. "Fire me. Stand at the end of the road and watch me disappear, post the guards so I can never come back, lock yourself in your big fine house and feel safe . . . but you won't be safe. Because I'll still be here.

"I'll be the hand that touches your hair when no one is there," he said huskily. "I'll be the air you breathe and the sun on your face and the ache you feel in the dark when you're all alone. I'll be the name you cry out in the middle of the night when nobody answers. I'll be the fever in your blood, the hunger you can't fill. I'll haunt you, Anne Edgecomb, every minute of every day and night for the rest of your life. You'll never be rid of me.''

Anne stood there, captured by his hands and his eyes and his voice, without breath or heartbeat or living will for an endless moment. And then, with a rush of consciousness and a surge of strength that felt like terror, she broke away.

And she ran.

Chapter Fifteen

The two men met again briefly the next Saturday night in the Six Shot Saloon. The crowd was heavy, and no one noticed what appeared to be a chance meeting, or cared.

Eddie Baker spoke under the cover of raucous noise, looking at the mirror over the bar opposite him. "So far you haven't done a hell of a lot for your money."

The cowboy casually lifted his finger for another beer. He did not look at the man next to him. "I thought you wanted it done professional."

"I want it *over*," the other man ground out, and his fist tightened reflexively around his glass.

The cowboy grinned and accepted his beer. "Up the ante a bit, huh?"

"She's more determined than ever. I want something done."

The cowboy sipped his beer thoughtfully. "Tonight soon enough?"

The other man did not answer.

The cowboy finished his beer in leisure, paid, and left the saloon. Eddie Baker lingered, glowering into his whiskey, until an old acquaintance came up and slapped him on the back and he accepted an invitation to join a game of cards.

Anne found herself pacing again, walking back and forth between the fireplace and the window, always pausing to peer out the window although there was no possible way she could see the bunkhouse from there. The cowhands had ridden into town before sunset; it was now almost completely dark. Had all of them gone, or was one still here, waiting . . . ? If she stepped outside, would she find him standing in the garden, the tip of his cigarette a tiny beacon in the shadows? If she stayed inside, counting the ticks of the clock, would there be a step on the front porch, a soft knock on the door—

And would she open it?

It had been two days since her volatile encounter with Josh in the barn, and every hour had been taut with expectation, dread, and remorse. Anne had not so much as caught a glimpse of him since then. The waiting had been as nerve-wringing as the oppressive nighttime silence that now bore down on her, all alone in the empty house.

There was no point in asking herself what she was afraid of. She knew. It wasn't Josh.

Anne halted in the center of the room, laced her hands behind her back, and took a deep, steadying breath. This was quite ridiculous, of course. She was not going to spend an entire evening as a prisoner in her own house, torturing herself with memories and jumping at shadows. Nor was she going to sit here like a crippled bird and wait for the inevitable to happen—for him to come to her . . . or for her to go to him.

Anne had lived alone for the past six years, and in all that time she had never been nervous at night, or even lonely. Never before had she had to face temptation.

But to Anne the best method for resisting temptation was simple and direct: One simply stepped out of temptation's way. She wasn't going to stay in the house that night at all.

On the wings of that decision, she started up stairs for her gloves and wrap. And then, on the bottom stair, she stopped.

Where would she go? Stephen was the logical choice, but the very thought of running from Josh to him—of facing Stephen after—She went hot with shame and then repressed a shudder of sheer misery. She would have to face Stephen soon enough. She couldn't go to him tonight.

She turned slowly back into the parlor, faint, surprised puzzlement shadowing her face. Then where? She thought of all the people she considered her friends: the neighboring ranchers, the townspeople. Any one of whom would be greatly alarmed to see Miss Anne driving up after dark unannounced. Oh, after they recovered their shock they would be hospitable enough and make every effort to make her welcome, but the room would be filled with awkward silences and uncomfortable looks, and the peculiar visit would be the gossip of the county for weeks to come.

How very strange it was, Anne reflected with a pinpoint of pathos, that after all this time she had no real friends in this country. And then she thought back and wondered whether she had ever had a real friend. Someone on whom she could call for no particular reason, someone with whom she could simply sit in silence and understanding, answering no questions because none were asked; someone who was never surprised to see her but always glad.

And the answer was quite simple. *No one but Josh*.

Almost against her will, Anne lifted the curtain and rested

her head against the window frame, looking out. There were few stars visible, and the half-moon was an in-and-out shadow behind drifting clouds. The shrubbery, the lawn, and the barn roof composed a still life in gray and blue.

Last Saturday the sky had been brilliant and the garden alive with mystery. She had needed, and he had been there.

He was still there. She could feel it.

The next day, her Sunday routine would overtake her again. Church with the community, dinner with Stephen, false smiles and gracious gestures. Monday afternoon, she would give her final party of the year, and people would come from miles around to bask in the radiance of the grand Lady Hartley. But tonight . . . tonight the memories hung too close, making her ache, making her wish, making her want what it would be madness to have.

She took a sharp breath, as though with that physical movement she could plant herself firmly back in the real world. She would not stay in the empty house tonight. And suddenly she knew where she could go.

The Ladies Society for the Betterment of Our Tragic Poor had been meeting at Widow Brogan's house every Saturday night for the past three years. Anne had always been a generous supporter but rarely made an appearance, preferring, as she did, to keep her Saturday evenings to herself. Tonight, however, she would break a tradition. She would be late, of course, but perhaps if she hurried, she would arrive before the husbands came to call for their wives and after, hopefully, Mrs. Brogan brought out her stale cinnamon cookies and insipid tea. At least that was one place of which she could be certain of her welcome, no matter how late she was.

Perhaps somewhere in the back of her mind Anne was

aware of the foolhardiness of a woman setting out alone at night across isolated country roads. But being accustomed to doing what she pleased when she pleased, she did not give the matter a moment's consideration. That night, in particular, she was in no mood to be wise.

She took the Daimler, freshly cleaned and restored after its encounter with the ditch, ostensibly because it would take too long to hook up the buggy. If she were perfectly honest with herself, however, she had to admit there was a certain feeling of invincibility in the big machine, and her self-confidence needed all the shoring up it could get.

She had not gone a mile before she realized two distinct disadvantages to the motorcar, however. The first was that it was cold. The night chill at ten miles an hour whipped through her driving cloak and lap robe most uncomfortably. The second was that the Daimler was not equipped with running lights, and although Anne's knowledge of the roads was infallible, there was something eerie about moving through a darkened landscape at this speed, without a horse's steady foot and sensitive nose for danger to guide her.

Under ordinary circumstances, the freedom of the night, combined with the surge of the powerful motorcar, would have exhilarated her. But her nerves were on edge and her mind was distracted, and once underway, the trip gradually began to lose its appeal.

The soft half-moon scuttled in and out of clouds. Anne thought that until this moment she had never really appreciated how deserted and still the ranch was at night, and how very lonely. The roar of the engine added a sense of isolation, as though she were being propelled through time and space without control or visible landmarks, and Anne found she did not quite like the feeling.

Once, when she rounded a corner, she was almost certain she saw a movement behind her, a form silhouetted for an instant by the moonlight. When she brought the motorcar straight again and turned to look, there was nothing behind her but empty road. She found herself straining for sight and sound as she progressed, and yes—wasn't that counterpoint to the engine's noise very much like the beat of horse's hooves? Once again she turned to look, and once again she saw nothing.

Her chest and stomach muscles began to tense. Someone was following her. She was certain of it. Then she chided herself for being a fool. No one was following her. And even if someone was behind her, it was no doubt some innocent traveler who happened to be going her way. The road that cut through Three Hills was of public access, after all. What had happened to her that she had allowed herself to turn into a fainting flower for no good reason at all?

This was absurd. Was she really going to travel eight miles in the dark just to spend an evening rolling bandages and gossiping with women she barely knew and hardly liked? She had let Josh Coleman drive her out of her own house, and now her overwrought imagination was seeing phantoms in the dark. A surge of anger and shame went through her, and when she saw a wide place in the road, she swerved the motorcar toward it, intending to turn around.

Perhaps emotion had impaired her judgment, or perhaps the dark had weakened her vision. At any rate, she should have known better. The shoulder was much too narrow to turn the vehicle, and before she knew it, the nose of the

Daimler was resting flat against an embankment, its back wheels sunk into a ditch.

"Oh, blast you!" she exclaimed out loud, giving a vicious thump to the steering column. "Bloody mechanical contrivance! You're far more trouble than you'll ever be worth."

She stood up in the car and looked impatiently around. She was a little more than two miles from the house, a long, uncomfortable walk home in the dark. Directly ahead of her, in the field about fifty yards away, was an abandoned derrick, and she knew that Chance and his men made their camp not too far beyond. Though she despised the thought of trekking across the stubbly field in her flimsy slippers, she saw no choice except to go to the camp and borrow a horse. With another muffled oath she climbed out of the motorcar.

As she moved away from the engine noise Anne was struck again by the powerful certainty that she was not alone. She could almost hear the rustle of footsteps matching her own, and above the sound of her own somewhat strained breathing she thought she heard the soft whinny of a horse. She stopped and started to call out, and then she saw the proof of her suspicions.

Beyond the derrick, perhaps a hundred yards away, there was a small flare of light against the shadows, very much like the striking of a match. It was such an ordinary thing, the flare of a match against the darkness. Chance or one of his men was doubtless casually lighting a cigarette, and all sinister implications immediately vanished. She called out in relief, "Hello! Who's there?" and started immediately across the field toward the derrick. "I've had a spot of trouble. I wonder if you could—"

"Anne, *stay back*!"

In her shock she did not recognize the voice. She whirled around, looking for its source, and suddenly rough hands grabbed her by the waist, dragging her back. She screamed and tried to strike out, struggling against the ruthless strength of a man's arms intent on crushing her. Suddenly she was flung to the ground with such force that her breath left her lungs in an agonizing vacuum; the heavy weight of her assailant threw itself upon her as the entire world exploded with a flash and a roar.

The night sky became day-bright, and the earth shook. Flaming bits of debris sailed into the air and rained down upon them in splinters and ashes. Screams echoed inside Anne's head, but her face was buried in a man's strong shoulder, and no sounds escaped.

It was Josh. His arms were wrapped around her, his body shielded her, and she could hear his voice, strained and hoarse and breathless, over and over in her ear, "Anne . . . dear God, Anne. . . ."

She uttered a sob of joy and blind relief and wrapped her arms around him, clinging to him. While the sky burned red and the world came to an end around them, she was safe in his arms. Josh—strong and solid and secure. Josh, who more than once had stood between her and disaster. Josh, who was always there when she needed him.

As the roaring in her ears faded and her vision gradually cleared, his face filled her eyes. It was white and streaked with fear, and he whispered, "Are you all right? Anne, tell me you're all right."

His large hands were unsteady as they pushed her hair away from her face, stroking her, soothing her. Anne's own fingers were shaking visibly as she touched his face, just needing to reassure herself that he was real, alive, and with her. She choked out, "Josh. Oh, Josh, thank God. . . ."

And then their arms were around each other again, crushing each other with the force of the embrace, their faces buried in each other's necks and tight with an explosive emotion that knew no release. It was stronger than a kiss, more intense than a vow. It was one endless moment of naked truth that neither could disguise nor deny; they clung to each other as though to life itself.

And then gradually his arms loosened and his weight eased. Josh pulled Anne to her feet and into the circle of his arms, gently holding and steadying her while their breath calmed and their muscles regained their strength. Anne had never felt more safe or more certain in her life than she did standing right there.

And then he stepped away a little, his hands holding her face. His own face was a mirror of raw concern, and he demanded hoarsely, "For God's sake, Anne, what were you doing out here in the dark all by yourself?"

Fractured bits of wood flamed and sizzled on the ground all around them; the air was acrid with the scent of smoke. In the distance there were shouts and hoofbeats as Chance and his crew rushed toward the scene of the disaster. Where once the oil derrick had stood there was nothing more than a few skeletal wood limbs linked together by flames.

Ann's ragged, indrawn breath felt like a sob as she looked wildly around. "My derrick!" She clung to Josh's arms, digging in her fingers. "Dear God, what happened? It just—exploded! How could this have happened?"

In the shadowed moonlight and firelight Josh's face seemed to grow grim, and he stepped slowly away from her. "Easy," he said.

He walked away from her and seemed to be searching the ground for something. Anne stood, helpless with shock and adrift with confusion, until he returned. In his open palm he held a bit of fuse and what might have been a blasting cap. "Dynamite," he said simply.

In a slow, cold wash of horror and incredulity, Anne took the bits of evidence from him. For a moment her head swam, and her words came from numbed lips. "Do you mean—someone did this on purpose?"

He did not answer.

The alarmed voices of Chance and his men were closer now. One fragment of exclamation rang clearly on the night air. "Goddammit, I knew it! I knew something like this would happen—"

Sometimes it starts with a hired gun. . . .

A shudder went through Anne, and she stared fixedly at the scraps of the crime left in her hand. The suspicion crept through, slow and hateful and utterly unpreventable, and she looked up at Josh. "What were you doing out here?" she asked carefully.

For a moment nothing registered on his face, and then slowly his eyes began to fill with contempt and disgust. Anne thought she had never seen anything more horrible in her life than the way Josh looked at her.

His face was as smooth as stone, and he responded coldly, "Blowing up your goddamn oil well, of course."

Then he turned and stalked away.

Chapter Sixteen

For as far back as anyone could remember, Three Hills had been the center of social life and hospitality in that corner of Texas. It had begun with Elizabeth Fielding, who had brought paintings and music and linen tablecloths to the frontier. People would travel for hundreds of miles to a Three Hills party back then, the ladies packing their ball gowns in their saddlebags and setting off with a shotgun across their pommels to attend the festivities, which sometimes lasted for weeks.

The annual Three Hills barbecue had become a tradition after the war, a home-style celebration where politics, good food, and boisterous camaraderie mixed in the energetic fashion of which Texans were so fond. There had been horse races, roping contests, speechmaking, and a general hell-raising good time. Nobody ever wanted to miss a Fielding barbecue back then.

Of course, things had changed a bit since Anne had taken over. Now there was a thing called the "social season," which began in the spring and ended in the fall. Of course, Texans, being the sociable folks that they were, had parties all year long, but it was an unspoken law that the "season" did not really begin until Anne gave her fancy dress ball in May, and no matter how grievously a hostess might try to make it otherwise, it was unmistakably over when Anne gave her garden party in September. And no one who was anyone dared miss either event.

Anne's parties were very refined affairs, with gentle conversation, the best musicians, and the most elegant atmosphere. The dress was always formal, and hard liquor was never served. The men grumbled that the world had come to a fine state when a man couldn't even have a good time at a party for choking on his collar, but the women always won out in the name of culture. Culture. It had begun with Elizabeth Fielding and her pianoforte, and it ended with pink punch and skinny sandwiches that wouldn't whet a hummingbird's appetite.

That day, over a hundred people wandered through Anne Edgecomb's formal back garden. In a well-screened corner a stringed quartet imported from Fort Worth played chamber music. A long buffet table was lined with white lace and spread with silver platters of scones and clotted cream, cucumber sandwiches, sugared almonds, and delicately iced petits fours. The centerpiece was a fountain of champagne punch that sparkled and tumbled gaily into a silver urn.

The garden was a palette of late summer colors—the brilliant yellow and white of chrysanthemum, beds of deep purple asters, flaming bronze borders of marigolds. The ladies, in their trailing silks and satins and flower-bedecked hats, rivaled nature's splendor; the gentlemen, in their afternoon coats and celluloid collars, looked like a flock of clipped pigeons strutting along behind their mates.

But today there was a new element to Anne's generally staid parties. An undercurrent of tension and the kind of excitement Texans love best ran through this elegant gathering as the most prominent society of the county descended upon Three Hills with dramatic expressions of sympathy and a vulturelike eagerness for details.

"Anne, dear, lovely affair, simply lovely, and after the shock you've been through—"

"Only imagine, a criminal like that running loose and you giving a garden party like you hadn't a care in the world!"

"Miss Anne, you've got more class than anybody I know."

"Lady Hartley is a woman of true courage and style. . . ."

And to all of this Anne bowed and smiled and welcomed her guests with all the grace and breeding six generations of the Hartley name could bestow. Occasionally she laughed and tossed off a light comment such as, "My goodness, it wasn't such a tragedy as all that! That old derrick wasn't even in operation, and in fact, I owe the saboteur a debt of thanks—he saved me the expense of tearing it down myself!" Anne wondered if the words sounded as hollow to others as they did to her.

Of course, the news had spread like wildfire. Although the attitude of most of her neighbors had been unsurprised—everyone knew, after all, that it was only a matter of time before she ruffled the wrong person's feathers—no one could help admiring the spunk with which she was standing up to the whole thing. Nothing, it was generally agreed, daunted Lady Hartley, and that was exactly the kind of backbone Texans had been bred to respect.

Amos Wright, all dressed up in a white shirt and string tie with his hair slicked down and jowls shaved, wandered around from group to group loudly proclaiming how this little setback was nothing, and how before the week was out he would be sinking a well that would bring in a gusher. Chance and his Yankee diggers stood off in a group by themselves, looking as though they had rather be anywhere else, and it was obvious their boss had dragged them there. With every ounce of defiance in her, Anne Edgecomb was making a statement, and there was no better place to do that than at her own party, with all the world to see.

The sheriff was of course invited, along with the doctor, the lawyer, the preacher, the undertaker, and everyone else of any importance in the town or surrounding county. Anne thought the sheriff's presence that day added just the right touch of drama, along with the definite reminder that no matter how her friends and neighbors might feel about the rightness or wrongness of the incident, she had been the victim of a crime. And the law existed for the punishment of crimes.

One of the unfortunate side effects to the sheriff's presence was, however, that he considered the party free license to continue, or at least give the impression of continuing, his investigation. In fact, considering the spotlight that Anne had unwittingly placed upon him, he obviously felt it was his duty.

He came up to her now. "Have you been able to come up with any ideas as to who might want to do such a thing, Miss Anne?"

Anne smiled and nodded to the doctor's wife across the buffet table, and her eyes happened to meet George Greenley's. Her smile did not falter. To the sheriff she said lightly, "Almost any man at this party, Sheriff Hawkins."

That was obviously not the answer he was hoping for, and Hawkins glanced uncomfortably down at his boots.

"What about your hands?" he asked. "Any of them got a gripe against you?"

She felt a sharp constriction in her throat, the same stab of fear she felt whenever she allowed herself to realize—to really and fully realize—that someone had actually brought physical violence to her property. Someone, possibly someone she knew, hated her that much.

Yes, she was frightened. And she was angry. And deep down inside she was sickened.

She chose her words carefully. "On a ranch this size there is always a certain amoung of . . . discontent. But I'm quite certain of the loyalty of my employees. None of them could have possibly done such a thing."

The sheriff's eyes were patently skeptical, and Anne quickly had to avert her own gaze so that he might not read the same thing in hers. She thought about Gil, who had lost his job. She thought about the anger in Big Jim's eyes when she had demoted him to the oil fields. She thought about Josh. . . .

She had told no one of Josh's fortuitous presence that night. By the time Chance and the others had arrived, he had gone, and there was no one to link him to the scene but Anne herself. And yet she had kept quiet. She hated herself for that but was powerless to change it.

Anne said with a smooth smile, "Do pardon me, Sheriff, but this is a party, after all. Perhaps all this could wait until another time? I must see to my guests."

And as quickly and gracefully as possible, she made her escape.

She had spoken to the minister's wife, offered her cheek for a kiss to several dowagers, and was just about to cross the lawn to Stephen, who had arrived late, when George Greenley caught her eye. Anne stood her ground.

"How kind of you to come, Mr. Greenley," she said, greeting him smoothly.

But he was not the kind of man to dance around with preliminaries. "I'm sorry for your trouble, Miss Anne," he said forthrightly. "But there's no sense in pretending I'm sorry for the cause of it."

Anne's smile remained invincible. "I quite understand. After all, you did warn me, didn't you?"

"I surely hope you're not implying something, ma'am," Greenley replied quietly. His expression was polite and mild—almost too mild to be the face of a man who was lying so unrepentently. "I've always dealt straight with you, Miss Anne, just like I would with any man in this county. I'm not going to deny that we've had our differences, but you should know by now that sneaking around in the dead of night is not my way."

Every muscle in Anne's body tightened, and she resisted the strong impulse to toss the glass of punch she held into his face. She managed to keep her expression pleasant and her voice smooth as she replied, "No, indeed. You prefer armed men with axes and hammers in broad daylight, don't you?"

She sipped her punch and was proud of the steadiness of her hand. But she could not quite keep the glitter out of her eyes, nor did she want to. "I feel it's only fair to warn you, Mr. Greenley, that strong-arm tactics will not frighten me away. I suggest you save your supply of munitions; they will only be wasted on me."

"Anne, I'm sorry to be late." Stephen touched her arm and smiled warmly into her eyes. He looked at George

Greenley, and Anne thought she detected a slight stiffness in his manner. "Good afternoon, George."

Greenley nodded to him briefly, then turned back to Anne. "Ma'am," he said by way of excusing himself, and walked away.

"That *odious* man," Anne ground out when he was gone. Now she had to hold the punch cup very tightly with both hands to keep from trembling with rage. "He dares to come to my home, look me in the eye, and pretend before all the world that he is innocent—"

"Darling." Stephen's hand was light upon her back, his voice soft and soothing. "You are indeed a grand lady. Simply going through with this party today took more courage than anyone here possesses, and they all know it. I'm so proud of you."

The reassurance of his smile was something of a sedative, and Anne tried to force herself to relax. "Nonsense, Stephen. It's always taken more courage for a Hartley to admit defeat than to go on fighting."

"So you've said. But the strain is beginning to show on you, honey. Let's go someplace and talk quietly. Let me take you to the gazebo—"

"No!" The violence of that exclamation, coupled as it was with a rush of searing memories, surprised even Anne. Quickly she gripped her emotions, fighting valiantly against the surge of color to her cheeks, and she added in a much more composed tone, "Don't be absurd, Stephen. It wouldn't be at all proper."

And all the while she was thinking distractedly, *Proper! A fine one you are to talk about proper. . . .* Would she never be able to go to the gazebo again without remembering?

Would she ever be able to look Stephen in the eye without the guilt and the shame . . . ?

But Stephen, perfect gentleman that he was, noticed nothing amiss. He tucked his arm through hers and answered, "Of course you're right. I'm sorry. Stroll with me, then. Just let me have you to myself for a few moments."

Anne smiled, generally grateful for his calming presence and, to her surprise, grateful for something else. Without the disaster that stood between the night in the gazebo and the meeting with Stephen, she doubted she would have been able to face him with such equanimity. Surely he would have read guilt in her eyes, seen the evidence of fornication on her face.

The previous day he had rushed over as soon as he'd heard the news, beside himself with outrage and concern. Anne could not help being moved by his display of genuine emotion, even though she found his protectiveness a bit overbearing. But at least his own distress had completely blinded him to any other undercurrent that might have existed. Now, if she seemed distracted and upset, he could attribute it to another cause altogether.

And much to Anne's confusion and shame, she did not feel nearly as guilty in Stephen's presence as she had expected to.

"Anne, when I think of it . . ." His voice went hoarse and his fingers tightened on her arm a fraction. "You could have been killed."

Anne made an obligatory bow to a group of ladies they passed. "I'm sure no one meant me any personal harm, Stephen."

"You can't be sure of that. At any rate, that's not the point. Anne, don't you see?" he insisted intently. "Can you imagine the kind of torment I've been through these past hours, thinking of you out here by yourself? If we were married, Anne, I could be here to protect you. You wouldn't have to go through this alone.''

Totally against her will, the treacherous thought sprang forth. *Protect me? Where were you when I faced down George Greenley and his bunch on my front porch with a hunting rifle? Where were you when I was trapped in the midst of a stampede? Where were you when my derrick exploded and fiery splinters rained down all around me? Were you taking the force of the blows with your own body, were you risking your life for me, were you protecting me then?*

She hated the thought and was shocked by the truth it exposed, but she could not repress it. She did not need Stephen; she never had.

She needed Josh.

Instinctively Anne stiffened, and she felt something within her uncoil. ''Stephen, please, not now,'' she said a little hoarsely.

He seemed to fight a brief inner battle, and then resigned himself with a forced smile. He patted her arm reassuringly. ''All right, sugar. You're right, of course, this isn't the time. But you'll come to see I'm right. I'm confident of that.''

He changed the subject. ''Has the sheriff made any progress?''

''Of course not.'' Her voice was a little sharp. ''How could he when he would have to start by arresting the man who practically pays his salary out of his own pocket?'' She caught the rising tone of her voice and compressed her lips briefly. She released an apologetic sigh. ''The sheriff seems to think it was someone on the ranch. I just can't believe any of my own men would betray me that way."

"He may have a point." He stopped and looked down at her. His face was serious. "Anne, has it occurred to you that all this trouble started when you took on that Coleman fellow?"

Anne flinched inwardly. Had it occurred to her? She had thought of nothing else. But when Stephen said it, it sounded like a threat, made her angry and defensive, and it was all she could do to keep her voice polite. "I have observed a distressing tendency in you Texans," she said coolly, resuming her pace again, "for automatic antipathy and suspicion toward anyone you consider an outsider. I am an outsider, so my oil wells are blown up. Josh Coleman is an outsider, so he gets blamed for it. It's really quite pathetic when you consider it."

Stephen drew himself up. "Anne, that's not fair."

"Perhaps not, but it appears to be the case."

"I was only suggesting that since we know nothing about him, he seems a logical choice for questioning."

"That sounds like something the sheriff should decide, not you."

Stephen looked at her closely. "You're awfully defensive on the subject of Josh Coleman."

"Not at all," she said somewhat brittlely. "I merely think we should leave the matters in the hands of the authorities. I have ultimate faith in the process of your judiciary system, after all."

She turned with what she hoped was not obvious relief to Amos Wright, who was passing by. "Are you enjoying yourself, Mr. Wright?"

He beamed at her. "Never better, Miz Edgecomb, never better. You sure know how to put on a spread."

Since Mr. Wright had apparently forsaken solid refreshments in favor of the champagne punch, Anne supposed that was a compliment. "I'm so glad. Do have a good time."

"Yes, ma'am. And don't you worry, I'm gonna have them maps up to your place next week just like I promised. We're gonna be rich, you and me. That I can guaran-damntee you."

Anne felt her first genuine laugh of the day surface, but Stephen was less than pleased as they turned away. "Anne, I can't believe you invited a man like that here," he said in an undertone. "He's making a spectacle of himself, you know."

"I should certainly hope so! He's my star attraction."

Stephen frowned. "You don't really believe that malarkey he's spreading around about having found oil, do you?"

"He believes it," she returned. "And with any luck at all, he'll have everybody at this party believing it too. I will *not* let them think I've surrendered."

And then she looked at him, letting a small glimmer of hope filter through. "Stephen, he claims this entire corner of Texas is sitting on a lake of oil. And with my owning the mineral rights to most of the county, all I have to do is pick a spot—"

Stephen's eyes went quick with alarm. "Anne, hold on just a minute. If you think you've got trouble now, just wait until you try to sink a well on one of these rancher's land!"

"No." Anne dropped his arm and turned to him, her eyes flashing. "No, they're the ones who are going to have trouble." Her voice was low and fierce. "If I have to arm every man on this place with a double-barreled shotgun and post a twenty-four-hour guard, I *will* sink my well! And anyone who tries to stop me had better be prepared for more trouble than he's ever seen before.''

''Oh, Anne.'' Stephen's expression softened with understanding and concern. He slipped his arm through hers again and squeezed it affectionately. ''You are an incredible, wonderful, spirited woman. And you know I'll stand behind you one hundred percent, whatever it is you decide to do. If you want me to hold a shotgun to George Greenley's head while you dig an oil well on his land, I'll do it. If you want me to cover every derrick you raise with barbed wire and sit on top of it every day and night, I'll do that too. I'm going to take care of you, honey. But . . .'' And his expression sobered. ''I've got to ask you, Anne—how much longer can you possibly keep this up?''

Anne was more irritated than she liked to admit by his reference to taking care of her, and perhaps for that reason her smile was a little wan. ''Not much longer, Stephen,'' she confessed. ''I can only afford to sink one more well, right? Hopefully Amos Wright will tell me which one.''

And then, because all of the attention Stephen insisted upon lavishing upon her was becoming a bit claustrophobic, Anne said quickly, ''My guests are going to think me the most outrageous boor who ever lived. I must move around. Please escort me while I make everyone welcome.''

Josh stood at the edge of the crowd, watching Anne. She looked like something off the front of a fancy ladies' magazine in a black-and-white-striped tea gown and a big white picture hat with clusters of roses and trailing black ribbons. Her head was held high, her smile gracious, and her posture regal. Just watching her, Josh felt an uncontrollable swell of pride, for he had never seen anything more beautiful in his life than Anne Edgecomb serving punch and cookies to the men who were trying to cut her throat and smiling while she did it.

He ached for her, and he resented the ache. He wanted her and he was angry with her, and everything about her made him want to grab her hard and shake some sense into her, but there she was, and there was nothing he could do about any of it.

Why had he stayed?

"Because you're worth saving, Duchess," he murmured out loud, and a wry, self-reproachful smile tucked one corner of his lips downward as he moved through the crowd. A wise man would have left well enough alone. But if Josh had had any sense at all, he would have ridden off the place long ago.

He stopped at the buffet table and helped himself to a small crystal glass of punch. He grimaced after one sip and put it down. "Lemonade?" he said speculatively to the rotund, bespectacled man beside him.

The man laughed heartily. "Know what you mean. Here, try the other one. It's got champagne in it, not half bad."

"Think I'll pass. Where does she keep the good stuff?"

"Not at this party, that's for sure!" The man thrust out his hand. "Doc Leeman at your service, sir."

Josh grinned and shook his hand. "Thanks all the same, but I hope I won't be needing your service. Josh Coleman. I'm the new foreman here."

The doctor lifted his brows. "That right?" Then he frowned a little. "Coleman. . . . Name sounds familiar."

Josh changed the subject before the doctor could remember that Coleman was the name of the man who had sent him his last patient, Gil. "She sure doesn't know much about giving a party, does she? Looks more like a funeral."

Leeman chuckled. "Well, these things are never much fun, I grant you that. But the wife thinks they're the finest thing since high-buttoned shoes, and what can a man do?" Then he sighed. "With all Miss Anne's troubles, I'm surprised she didn't call it off. Wish she had."

"Well, she does her best," Josh said, pretending to commiserate with him. "She just don't know much about Texas-style parties, is all." His eyes moved over the crowd until he found Anne again, standing with Stephen Brady and an older couple. "Who's that she's talking to?"

The doctor followed his gaze. "That's Brady, the banker, and Preacher Kirk and his wife."

Josh grinned. "Why don't I just see what I can do about livening up this shindig?"

He left the doctor with a friendly slap on the shoulder, and pausing just once to speak to the orchestra leader, he made his way over to Anne.

"Well, now, Duchess, you surely do look a lot better than you did the last time I saw you."

The sound of his voice went through Anne like an electric jolt. She whirled, almost spilling the cup of punch in her hand, and Stephen quickly stepped forward to take it from her. Josh stood before her as clear-eyed and relaxed as though he were the guest of honor rather than an intruder, and Anne could do nothing but stare at him.

Josh looked at Stephen. "Hello there, Steve. Nice to see you again." He turned to the older gentleman and lady with whom Anne had been speaking. "I hear you're the preacher around these parts."

The older gentleman regarded him curiously. Noticing the

expression on both Anne's and Stephen's faces, his tone wasn't particularly friendly. "I don't believe I've had the pleasure, sir."

"Name's Josh Coleman," he replied, promptly extending his hand. "And I'm the man who's going to marry Miss Anne."

The silence was absolute. The older couple's eyes went round with a shock that was almost comical; several heads outside their group turned to stare. Anne's head reeled.

And then Stephen, with a rush of color darkening his face, stepped forward. "Sir, you have overstepped yourself. I think you'd better leave."

In the background yet another bizarre element was added to Anne's already downward-spiraling impression of the events of the past moments. The orchestra, so highly praised for their delicate treatment of Mozart and Handel, suddenly sprang into a lively rendition of "The Yellow Rose of Texas."

Josh grinned at Stephen. "Not until I've had my dance."

And before Anne could even fathom his intention, he had swept her into his arms.

The next few instants were a blur of cheering voices, raucous music, and laughing faces as Josh swept her down the lawn to the steps of a reel. Her guests, galvanized as though by magic at the frst strains of the familiar tune, abandoned all pretext of decorum and swept off their hats, picked up their skirts, and joined the dance with untrammeled enthusiasm. Half a stanza had passed before Anne regained her senses—and her breath.

"How *dare* you!" The words were choked and furious. With a futile rush of defiant strength she tried to twist away. "Unhand me, you oaf, this very moment!"

"Now, Anne," he said, remonstrating her smoothly, "people are staring."

"How dare you say—how dare you imply—"

"Calm down, Duchess. You're going to make a scene. Now, we sure couldn't have that, could we? People might talk."

She had one glimpse of the cold sarcasm in his eyes, and then his hand tightened on her waist and he whirled her around. Her skirts whipped around her calves and her hat flew off; Anne's hand left his shoulder to grope at her tumbled hair, and she almost lost her balance. Josh caught her without missing a step.

All around her, couples were whirling and laughing in the carefree abandon of the dance. The orchestra gamely increased the tempo, and Anne had never felt so humiliated, or so helpless, in her life. And then Josh said, "Funny thing. The sheriff hasn't said a word to me about what happened the other night. I wonder how that could be?"

Anne stared at him. His face was smooth, his expression pleasant, but his eyes were hard and mirthless. The outrage and indignation inside her stilled for a new, much more uncomfortable emotion.

"Could be," Josh speculated, "that he just naturally knows I wouldn't have had anything to do with it, being the fine, upstanding character I am. Or it could be that nobody bothered to tell him I was there."

Anne drew in a breath, but his hand tightened on her fingers sharply, almost painfully, and the words died in her throat. "Anyhow," he continued, "if he was to ask, do you know what I'd tell him? I'd tell him that I saw the lady boss get in her car and set off after dark, and being the only man on the place, I didn't see as how I could just let her take off like that by herself. So I decided to ride along with her, staying out of sight because I knew she wouldn't appreciate my being there, just in case she had any trouble. And sure enough, she did.

"I'd tell him that when her car got stuck, I called out to her, but she didn't hear for the infernal noise that machine makes. Then I'd tell him how when she took off across the field, I saw a man, laying in wait, like. So naturally I went to investigate. And I saw a lit fuse. Maybe you can pick it up from there, Duchess."

Anne's eyes locked with his, and what she felt then was less like relief and more like certainty. God, how she wanted to believe him! How desperately she wanted to believe him. And yet hadn't she known it all along? Hadn't she, deep down in her heart, believed him before he even spoke? Or was that, too, only blind hope against stark evidence?

Josh said quietly, "Why didn't you tell the sheriff, Anne?"

But no. That was too much. She jerked her eyes away and said sharply, "That is quite beside the point—"

"Is it?" he demanded softly. His steps slowed, and his eyes seemed to pierce right through her soul, pinioning and demanding. "Is it, really?"

Anne's throat went dry, her heartbeat slowed, and she could not seem to break his gaze. She might have answered him, for it seemed the truth was but an inevitable breath away and there was no point in fighting it, none at all—but suddenly a hand grasped Josh's shoulder and Anne was jerked away.

Stephen stood there, his face livid. His grip was so tight on Anne's hand that the diamond he wore on his small finger dug painfully into her skin. Anne winced and wrenched her hand away.

Stephen spoke harshly to Josh. "All right, mister, you've gone far enough. Why don't you just leave quietly before I throw you out?"

Anne's hand flew to her throat. "Stephen!"

Stephen turned to her briefly, his eyes churning. "I'm sorry, Anne, but if you don't have the courage to get rid of this ruffian, I will!"

Anne's eyes widened, and furious color rushed to her cheeks. Except for the closest dancers, no one had noticed the encounter, but Stephen was dangerously close to making fools of them all. "Stephen," she said low, "leave this to me."

But Stephen was beyond the point of reason. He snapped his head back toward Josh. "Are you going to leave?" he demanded.

Josh looked only amused and mildly bored. "First would you mind telling me what I've done that's set your back up so?"

"You've insulted this lady, humiliated her in front of all her friends and neighbors, ruined her party. . ."

Josh looked around with unconcerned interest. "Well, now, I don't see that her party's ruined. Looks to me like these folks are putting up a pretty good show of enjoying themselves. And if there was any humiliating to be done, you've pretty well taken care of that."

Stephen's fists clenched, but Josh continued mildly, "And as for insulting her, how, exactly, did I do that?"

"You know perfectly well," Stephen said tightly.

Josh smiled. "Oh, you mean when I said I was going to marry her? Why, I was just making it easy on the lady. She's kinda shy, and I knew it would be hard for her to tell you herself."

Anne could feel the current of violence between the two men as though it were a physical thing poised on the edge of eruption. Anne could not believe it was Stephen acting in such an abominable fashion, she couldn't believe Josh was taking it so calmly, and she knew she was only moments from disaster.

Stephen's jaw clenched, his skin darkened another shade, and his eyes locked with Josh's as though in mortal combat. He said lowly, "You're lucky I'm not carrying a gun, mister."

Josh merely smiled, though his eyes were like steel. "No," he answered. "*You're* lucky. Because I *am* carrying one."

Stephen made an incredible, furious lurch toward him, and Anne could take no more. She stepped quickly before Josh, her eyes blazing, her hands turned out as though to ward him off, and she hissed furiously, "Stephen Brady, are you out of your mind? Stop this this minute! I'm ashamed of you!"

"Anne, stay out of this—"

"No, *you* stay out of it!" And before Anne could stop herself or even register what she had said, she stepped forward and grabbed Stephen's arm, turning him forcefully away. "I'm tired of your interference in my affairs under the guise of 'protecting' me," she hissed. "I don't need your protection or your interference, and I won't stand for it a moment longer! You're the one who's ruining my party, Stephen, and humiliating me! I would have expected more from you—at least you've always pretended to be a gentleman!"

Stephen stared at her as though slapped. "Anne, I can't believe you mean—"

But Anne had taken too much for one day; she was far

beyond the point of controlling her outburst or even wanting to. "You had better believe it," she returned angrily, "because I've never meant anything more in my life. And unless you cease and desist this outrageous behavior this moment, I'm going to be forced to ask you to leave."

Stephen stiffened. His eyes went to Josh, then back to Anne. She could not be certain what she saw in his gaze then, but she was certain that nothing between them would ever be the same again. And, strangely, she was not sorry.

"I can tell you are not yourself," Stephen said formally. His expression was controlled. "Perhaps it would be best if I left, after all."

"Perhaps it would," Anne snapped.

He bowed to her and walked away.

He had gone half a dozen steps before he turned and looked back at Josh. The look in his eyes would have shocked and frightened Anne had she seen it, and would have made everything that had gone before seem petty in comparison. It was cold, calculating, and unmistakably murderous.

But neither Anne nor Josh saw, and after moment Stephen turned and walked away, his face once more the bland mask that was customary of Stephen Brady.

Anne stood there a moment longer, her head reeling with the implication of what she had done, fury churning with Josh and with Stephen. She started to whirl on Josh, but just then another hand caught her arm.

"Miss Anne," said Dr. Leeman boisterously, "might I have the honor?"

She allowed herself to be swept across the lawn in the steps of another rousing dance, twisting her head around for some glimpse of the man who had started all this.

The last she saw of Josh, he was waltzing enthusiastically with the doctor's plump wife and having the time of his life.

The sun set slowly over the aftermath of the party, its fiery rays painting an unrelenting portrait of destruction. The usually meticulous lawn looked as though it had been trampled by a calvary unit: bits of turf were torn and scattered; gallant chrysanthemum blossoms had been ground into the dirt; crushed petits fours littered the grass. The damask tablecloth was irreparably stained, no less than three crystal glasses had been broken, the silver urn now adorned a topiary bush like a cocky top hat. In the background the servants quickly and furtively went about the business of cleaning up, disguising their amusement with quick, anxious glaces toward Anne, ever wary of their mistress's fulminating temper.

In the center of it all stood Anne. The last of her guests had just driven away, enthusiastically praising her for the most enjoyable time they'd ever had. Her hair was disheveled, her demi-train torn, and her emotions, so long repressed in the name of hospitality, were churning. Then she spotted Josh, complacently lounging in a brocaded matron's chair that was tilted back on two spindly legs and about to crack beneath his weight. That was all it took to bring Anne to the breaking point.

She picked up her skirt and strode across the lawn, her slippers squishing on the abandoned remnants of sandwiches and cakes. Just as Josh glanced up at her, she drew back and kicked the chair out from under him.

Josh leapt to his feet in time to keep from tumbling to the ground, and she faced him with eyes blazing. "How dare you!" Her foot throbbed from the violent contact with the chair, but it was a small price to pay for the surge of vindication she felt. ''Is there no end to your uncivilized behavior? You storm into a private party uninvited, you embarrass me within an inch of my life, you make outrageous statements to my friends, you turn my entire party into a circus—how could you? Why would it ever enter your head to do such a thing?''

Josh endured her tirade with amused patience and restraint. ''Well,'' he answered easily when it appeared she had run out of breath, ''if you're asking why...'' He cocked an eyebrow. ''That is what you're asking, isn't it? I just figured you deserved a second chance, that's all.'' And as she drew in a furious breath to challenge him, he continued, ''One of your problems—and only one of them, mind you—is that you don't know a thing about giving a Texas shindig. I just thought I'd help out a little, that's all. And just tell the truth—did you ever see a bunch of folks have a better time?''

Anne stiffened, for she had no argument to that, and he knew it. The mocking gleam of truth was in his eyes.

Anne turned away sharply. ''That is not the point.'' She took a deep breath, pressing her hands together before her. ''You came here today because you wanted to make a fool of me,'' she said firmly, without looking at him. ''You were angry with me because—because you thought I accused you of something the other night, and this was your method of getting even.''

Josh inquired mildly, ''Are you saying you didn't accuse me of anything?''

Anne turned. Her shoulders were straight, her head held high, her voice even. As much as better judgment clamored against it, there was no way in the world she could have prevented what she said next. "Why didn't you tell the sheriff what you saw that night?" she inquired calmly.

She waited, breath suspended, for some answer, even a silent one. His face was implacable.

Some wicked, prodding demon urged her on. "Maybe because you didn't see another man at all," she suggested. "Maybe because you were already there, lighting the fuse yourself. You despise my oil venture; you've said so. You also have . . . personal reasons for retaliation against me. This would have been a perfect revenge, wouldn't it?"

His eyes was blank. "So naturally I saved your life."

Anne swallowed hard. She knew she had gone too far, but there was no way to retreat now. "I'm sure . . . personal injury would not have been in your plans. No one could have known I would be there when the derrick exploded."

For a moment there was absolutely no reaction. Anne's words hung between them like poisonous spores, and nothing would take them back now. Did she believe any of what she had said? How could she believe it? Then why had she said it?

And then Josh released a slow breath that could have been formed around a dry, mirthless laugh. He cast his eyes away, as though seeking guidance, and shook his head sadly. When he looked back at Anne, his eyes were humorless, touched with frustration, and laced with pity.

"You are," he said softly, "the damnedest woman I've ever met. You'll look for any excuse to convince yourself I'm not for you, and when you can't find one, you make one up. Now I'm a criminal. It's perfect. How could the grand Lady Hartley possibly want a man who's a criminal?"

And then his eyes hardened; he took a step toward her. "Well, let me tell you something, Duchess. You're wasting your time, because the excuses don't work anymore. I don't mind you lying to me, or the rest of the world, but when you start lying to yourself, something's got to be done. And *that*'s why I came here today.''

He was less than two feet from her, his rangy form radiating certainty, his tone stern with quiet authority. Anne felt her skin prickle with his closeness, her heartbeat grow shallow and rapid just as it always did when he was near. She did not want to hear what he said next. Everything within her recoiled from what she sensed was coming.

The perception in his eyes frightened her as it always did. It left her vulnerable and exposed. But today, for the first time, he was looking into her and he was disappointed in, even contemptuous of, what he saw. That hurt her more than she ever would have thought possible. She wanted to hide from him, and then she wanted to shout at him, because he had no right to look at her and make her feel this way—

''You just ask yourself this,'' he demanded quietly. His eyes blazed with a low, subtle fire. ''What if it's true? What if I am a low-down horse thief and gunslinger that goes around tearing up toolsheds and terrorizing innocent women? Would that change what you feel inside? Would that make your heart stop beating fast whenever I touch you, and your eyes stop lighting up every time you see me? What if somebody came to you right now, today, and showed you warrants for my arrest from three different states—would you turn me in?''

His words rained down on her like blows, each one sending another crack through her armor. But she held firm. She did not flinch.

He took a short, disgusted breath. ''Don't bother. You'll

lie about that too. You'll lie out loud, maybe you'll lie to yourself, but that won't change the truth."

Anne couldn't just stand there and take it in silence. She couldn't face the contempt in his eyes without a defense. "I didn't tell the sheriff," she flung at him, her fists tightening. "I could have, but I didn't!"

"Well, I guess I ought to be real grateful for that, ma'am. Real grateful."

He started to turn away, and Anne surged toward him. She caught herself before reaching out to grab his arm. Her color was high and her eyes were blazing, but inside she felt as though she were breaking apart. "What do you want from me?" she demanded fiercely. It was all she could do to keep her voice from shaking. "What do you expect?"

The smile that traced Josh's lips was quiet and rather sad. "If I have to tell you that," he answered simply, "then it's not worth having."

He walked over to the buffet table, where, at some time during the past hours, his hat had landed. Anne watched him silently; aching, angry, and confused.

He pushed back his hair and put the hat on his head. His eyes were solemn. "It doesn't take courage to keep quiet, Duchess. It takes courage to tell the truth—even if it's only to yourself. When you think you're woman enough to do that, let me know."

He was almost around the corner when she opened her mouth to call him back. But at the last minute she stopped, biting her lip, and turned away. She realized she didn't have anything to say.

Chapter Seventeen

Late in the afternoon four days later, Josh was supervising the disposition of a string of mustangs that Anne had wanted brought in. Three Hills was of a size that allowed its horses to breed and graze in the wild; foals were branded whenever they were found, and when the ranch developed a need for fresh stock, the best of the bunch was rounded up, corraled, and broken. It had been an all-day job, and he was tired. That was probably why he was feeling a little sentimental.

October had come in crisp and clear, and the taste of winter was definitely in the air. The snows would have already started in Colorado. Josh wondered if Jake had gotten the herd to the lowlands in time without his help. It was always a mess this time of year, with the steers sluggish and recalcitrant, and the cowhands wanting to slow down their pace too. He wondered if Bethy and her new husband had gotten the roof on their barn. Josh had been working on it before the wedding and had hoped to have it secure long before winter.

His mother would be putting up preserves now, and the kitchen would be fragrant with the sweetness of autumn's last fruits. The girls would be chopping spices and boiling glass jars, trying to sneak a taste of the sugared fruit behind their mother's back. Then Jake would come in, brushing the snow off his hat, and Jessica's eyes would light up. . . .

A pain swept over him that was like having the very breath drained from his body, a longing so intense and so unexpected that he thought it would crush his chest. He had to stop and steel himself against it. For that single instant he wanted to be home more than he had ever wanted anything in his life, and he wanted everything to be the way it once had been. But he didn't have a home anymore, and all the things he treasured about that place might never have even existed. Love, family, pride, belonging . . . nothing more than a mirage.

He saw Anne come out, dressed in her riding skirt and boots, striding toward the corral. Her step was brisk, and her eyes were alive with interest as she looked over the new stock. Watching her only sharpened the pain in Josh's chest. Then she saw him; her eyes met his, and for a moment there was something. . . . But then it was gone. Anne quickly averted her gaze, and Josh fought back the bleakness that threatened to chill his soul. He turned back to work.

Anne strolled casually over to the corral, her heart racing and her skin tingling from that brief shared glance. After all that had happened between them, it was still like that every time she saw him. Perhaps it would always be.

They met every day, briefly, impersonally, on ranch business. Josh never overstepped the employer-employee boundary, and Anne did not give him an opportunity to do so. To herself she affirmed victory; this was what she had wanted. She and Josh were working together for the benefit of the ranch, nothing more and nothing less. But every encounter left Anne feeling empty and wounded inside, and she did not sleep well at night.

Five or six of the hands had gathered around to watch as the fruit of their labors were turned into the corral, bucking and kicking and racing around its perimeter wildly. The cowboys enjoyed the show, grinning over a job well done and speculating among themselves.

"That dun is going to break somebody's butt before he gets a saddle put on him."

"Keep your eye on that stallion. We're gonna end up shootin' him. Looks like he's been shot out of hell, a real killer."

"Misses his mama, that's all."

Anne sat on the fence post at the far side of the corral and watched with a mixture of admiration and remorse as these beautiful creatures from the wild tasted their first hours of captivity. She was particularly taken with a white-faced bay who pranced a bit away from the herd, the gleam in his eye promising a challenge to any who approached.

She glanced down at one of the men leaning on the post next to her. "How soon will you be able to start breaking them to the saddle?"

Dakota pushed back his hat. "Well, we'll let 'em get used to the corral first, ma'am. That'll take a few days."

Another volunteered with a grin, "You won't be riding any of them to preachin' next Sunday, anyway. It's gonna take a while to get these critters calmed down."

Anne returned a cool smile. "I'm quite aware of the procedure, thank you. Which of you will break the horses?"

Behind her, Josh said, "I will."

Anne turned. She hardly even regarded the extra beat her heart gave when she heard his voice, nor noticed the way her skin tightened all over when she looked at him. Such things had become customary.

She inquired, "Is it usual for the foreman to take on such a task? I don't believe Big Jim ever did."

Josh pulled on his gloves, his eyes squinting in the sun as he looked over the corral. Anne was struck unexpectedly, and just as powerfully as she had been the first day she had met him, by what a singular-looking man he was. Calmly alone, rugged and stalwart, yet as familiar to her as the view from her window on a still summer day. He was apart from everything, yet he belonged to this place; he was as much a part of it as she was herself. Perhaps even more.

He said, "That's the way it's done now. I won't send any man to do a job I can't do." He leaned a forearm on the top rail, close to her thigh. "You got any particular horse in mind?"

"The bay, I think."

He nodded. "He'll make a fine saddle horse."

It was a very ordinary conversation, businesslike and matter-of-fact. There was nothing within it to generate that tension in her stomach, the tightening of all her muscles as though for self-defense, the dryness in her throat that she could not control. As long as Josh was here, her life would never be her own again. Her days would be ruled by glimpses of him, her nights by thoughts of him, and she was wrong to think this could ever work. She was trapped in a cage of her own making, and there was nothing she could do about it, ever.

Josh said, watching the horses, "I always feel a little bit sorry for them when they first come in like this."

Anne saw the wild-eyed confusion in the animals' eyes, the futile rearing and pawing, the restless trotting around looking for escape, and she knew how they felt. Her reply was a little muffled. "Yes."

Josh looked at her, his sun-bright eyes calm with understanding, and Anne felt a catch in her chest with the familiar contact. There was a moment of expectation taut with unsaid words and filled with shared perception, as though the very nature of their relationship was poised on the brink of change. But perhaps Anne only imagined it, for his eyes moved casually over her shoulder, and he commented, "Company's coming."

Josh walked away as Anne turned, shading her eyes toward the two riders approaching. She climbed down from the fence as Sheriff Hawkins, accompanied by a grim-faced Stephen, stopped before her.

"Good afternoon, Sheriff," she said, and then glanced uncomfortably at Stephen. "Hello, Stephen."

She had not heard a word from Stephen since the afternoon of the party, and he did not look any too happy about whatever business had brought him here today. Considering the way Anne had treated him at the party, she could not blame him.

The two men returned her greeting and dismounted, holding their reins loosely in their hands. Anne inquired, "What brings you out this way, Sheriff?" But she knew the answer. Obviously he had news of the saboteur; news which to her could only be welcome. Then why was dread clenching at her stomach so? And why did Stephen look so grim?

Hawkins said, "We've got bad news for you, ma'am."

Anne's heart began to thud.

"You know a Mr. Amos Wright?"

"Of course." She looked at Stephen anxiously, but he wouldn't meet her eyes. "He works for me."

The sheriff's eyes traveled over the coral, and then back to her. "He died this morning, ma'am."

And even as a gasp was fighting its way through Anne's throat, Stephen corrected tightly, "He was murdered."

Anne's eyes flew to the sheriff.

"We figure it happened sometime last night," Hawkins explained. "He was camping on your land, wasn't he? He was seen leaving the saloon about midnight, and Duke Brody found him on the Three Hills Road about sunup. Somebody'd worked him over good with his fists and left him in the ditch. By the time Duke got him in to the Doc, he was about gone. He died a couple of hours ago."

Anne's fingers tightened on the fence post. She felt cold all over. Her voice was hoarse. "But . . . he was just a harmless old man. Who would do such a thing? Why?"

Stephen spoke up quietly. "His pockets had been turned out. Nothing of value was taken—his money, pocket watch, knife—all were still there. But there was a pile of ashes on the road nearby, as though someone had burned some papers."

"My maps," Anne whispered. "He was bringing my maps. . . ."

The sheriff nodded, glancing over the corral again. "That's what we figure, ma'am."

"Oh, dear God." Anne had to grip herself to stop the trembling, but her voice came out very weak. She felt sick inside. "If I hadn't made him come to the party and boast about his finds . . . Someone killed him because I—"

"No Anne, don't blame yourself," Stephen said quickly. He stepped forward and placed a hand lightly on her arm. "Everyone knew what he was up to, long before the party.

He hadn't been here a week before he was bragging in the saloon about putting up derricks all over the county.''

"That doesn't change the fact that he would be alive today if not for me."

Anne turned away, wrapping both hands tightly around the fence boards. The dusty autumn day had grown dim, shadowed with a faint overwash of bilious green. The men around her had grown silent, watching and listening. Every pair of eyes was like a pointing, accusing finger. Hostile neighbors, vandalism, violence . . . and now people were dying. How much more, Anne? How high does the price have to get before it ceases to be worth it?

The sheriff said, "Could be the killer never meant to kill. Maybe he just wanted to teach Wright a lesson or scare him off. But he was an old man and kinda puny. Not like Gil."

Anne turned, staring at the sheriff. Her voice was very stiff. "What are you implying?"

"I think that's obvious, Anne," Stephen said quietly.

The sheriff look around at the group of men who were gathered. "Can any of you boys swear in court where Coleman was after midnight last night?"

The men looked around, averted their eyes, mumbled to themselves. Anne demanded sharply, "Come along, gentlemen. You all share the bunkhouse, don't you?"

"We don't post guards, ma'am," someone explained patiently. "Mostly we're sleeping, and what a man does in his off time is his own business."

Stephen offered helpfully, "Then let me put it this way. Did any of you see him leave the bunkhouse last night?"

There were some uncomfortable looks and shrugs that were as damning as a confession. "Might have," somebody mumbled. "Sometimes he does. Can't rightly say."

Anne felt panic rising.

"I need to take Coleman into town, ma'am," the sheriff said.

"You're arresting him?"

"I don't have enough evidence to do that. I'm just going to ask a few questions."

Anne thought, *This is it, then. The solution to all your problems.* She had said nothing about her suspicions, she had not mentioned the stolen horse, and she had kept quiet about Josh's presence at the scene of the sabotage. She was guiltless; no one could ever accuse her of betraying him. Fate had stepped in, and it was out of her hands. The sheriff would take him away and do his duty, and Josh Coleman would no longer be her problem.

This was what she wanted.

Anne took very slow, deliberate breaths. She did not feel calmer, but she looked it. "Is it usual procedure to take a man to jail for questioning?"

"That was my idea, Anne," Stephen said. "It's for your own protection."

Anne did not even look at him. "You're taking orders from private citizens now, Sheriff?"

Hawkins was unmoved. "He's right, Miss Anne. I know how you hate folks messin' in your business. That's why I brought Brady along. Thought maybe he could make you see reason. I might not have hard evidence against Coleman, but I've got everything else. The man is dangerous, ma'am, and I wouldn't be doing my duty if I let him stay out here with you alone."

"And you think if you take him into town, you'll get a confession out of him?"

"I wouldn't be surprised."

Anne wondered briefly what methods would be employed to obtain that confession, then sternly averted her thoughts. Josh could take care of himself.

She took a deep breath. "And suppose he's not guilty?"

"Why don't you just let me worry about that," replied Sheriff Hawkins. His smile was faintly condescending. "Now, you want to tell me where to find him?"

"You looking for me, Sheriff?"

Josh came up behind him, his voice casual, his face impassive. The sheriff turned and looked him over thoughtfully.

"Yessir," he drawled after a moment. "That I am. A man by the name of Amos Wright was beaten to death last night. You know him?"

Josh pushed back his hat. "To speak to."

Stephen said, "He was here the day Mr. Wright first got to Three Hills. He knew him as well as any man in these parts."

Anne's heart was beating very fast. This was it. They were going to take him away; it would all be over. She would have nothing to worry about anymore.

Hawkins said, "I think you'd better come on into town with me, mister. I've got a few questions to ask you, and maybe on the way in, you can think up some good answers. Like where you were last night between midnight and sunup, and why you'd want to beat up an old man like Amos Wright and leave him for dead."

The Sheriff fastened his hand on Josh's arm, and Josh didn't protest. Anne took a quick step forward. "Sheriff—"

Stephen touched her arm. "Anne, let the man do his job."

Anne pulled away. For a moment her heart raced so fast, she could barely hear herself think. And then she looked at

Josh, and suddenly she was very calm. "Sheriff," she said distinctly. "Let him go. This is absurd. Mr. Coleman can't possibly be the man you're looking for. He was nowhere near the Three Hills road last night."

The sheriff regarded her patiently. "Now, Miss Anne, how can you know that?"

All eyes were on her. Stephen, the sheriff, a half dozen of her employees, all waiting for what she would say next. And in the end it wasn't very hard at all. Because Josh was watching too.

She swallowed hard and lifted her chin. "Because," she said simply, "he was with me."

Chapter Eighteen

Anne tried to remember when she had last cried. When she was eight, she had taken a fall from her pony and snapped a bone in her arm. The pain had been excruciating, but her father had looked at her with stern, dark eyes and told her firmly that Hartleys did not cry. Anne had bitten her lip and suffered the surgeon to set the bone without a whimper or a tear. Afterward her father had brought her blancmange and called her his little soldier, and she had felt warm and proud and secure.

When Marc died, she had been in something of a state of shock. She remembered standing beside the open grave while the wind tugged at her dark veil and cloak and gray clouds scuttled overhead, lost and alone in this foreign land surrounded by strangers, not knowing what she was to do or where she was to go. But she had bitten down hard on her lip and resolved she would not cry in front of these people; she would hold her head high and act like a Hartley. She hadn't shed a tear.

Now she sat in the twilight shadows of the gazebo all alone while tears, silent and sluggish, coursed down her cheeks. She could not stop them, and she did not even try.

On every level the fabric of her life was unraveling. How clear it all had been when she had come to Texas. There had been Marc—and so many dreams. They were going to build the empire her grandfather had foreseen sixty years ago and rule over it indomitably. They were going to claim the frontier in the name of progress and build a dynasty.

Then Anne was alone, and the dream required some rearranging. She had held fast and made a place for herself in this land. She had seen the future and had taken hold of it, and never once had she doubted she would succeed.

Now everything was out of control. There were enemies on every side. Her neighbors were out to destroy her. Her own employees despised her. She pushed away the one true and loyal friend she had ever had in this country, Stephen. Today a man had died because of her, and for the first time she saw the dream begin to waver and slip away. She was tired and hurting and afraid, and she cried.

She heard a footstep, and the shadows stirred. Josh sat down beside her, and she made no effort to avert her face or wipe her eyes. He closed his hand about hers and said nothing, and the tears flowed faster. She leaned her head against his shoulder and closed her eyes, letting the tears come.

Josh sat with her silently, offering her what comfort he could. He knew what pain was like and how it was to meet it alone. He did not need to know why she cried. He just needed to be with her. *I hurt, too, Anne*, he thought. *The nights are long and filled with too many memories, and I want . . . so much*. But being with her, lending her his strength in whatever small way, made his own sorrows easier to bear. It was better not to be alone.

The day died around them. The sounds from the bunkhouse grew more muted, the horses shuffled in the corral, and the birds chirped out their last, melodious notes as they settled into their nests. The last rays of the sun painted silver-blue shadows across the landscape, still and lovely. As Josh took her hand in his, the sharing between them was silent and rich.

After a time her tears expended themselves, and Anne straightened up, blotting her face with the back of her hand. "You must think I'm quite foolish," she said shakily.

"Oh, I don't know." Josh's smile was indulgent. He reached into his pocket and presented her with a folded handkerchief. "They say General Lee used to go on a crying jag before every battle, and Teddy Roosevelt just broke down and sobbed after the charge up San Juan Hill."

Anne pressed his handkerchief against her eyes, muffling a weak, unsteady laugh. "I don't know your General Lee, but I suspect you are lying about Mr. Roosevelt."

"Hell, you're not even American," he said, gently scoffing. "What do you know?"

Silence fell, but it was easy and comfortable. Josh's hand was warm around hers, his presence beside her intimate and soothing.

After a while he said, "Speaking of damn fool things . . ."

"Were we?"

He looked at her. "What you did this afternoon wasn't real smart, Duchess."

This time Anne's laugh was a bit more natural, though still husky and choked. "How comforting to know some things will never change. You are as ungallant as ever, Mr. Coleman, and always know precisely the wrong thing to say."

He turned her hand over in his, lightly stroking the

underside of her thumb with his forefinger. She found the caress calming, as welcome as a mother's kiss. "You didn't have to do it, you know."

Anne thought, *Didn't I?* But she didn't say it out loud. She placed Josh's handkerchief on her skirt and began to press out the wrinkles with her fingers.

"Then why did you?" he persisted.

Anne remembered the look on the sheriff's face when she had told him that Josh spent the night with her. She remembered the cowhands shuffling and avoiding her eyes and trying to hide their grins. But mostly she remembered the shock and hurt in Stephen's eyes, the accusation, and—yes—the repulsion.

She had stood there in front of what had seemed at the moment to be half the world and confessed to illicit behavior with one of her cowhands. She could hardly believe it. A week ago that had been a scene from one of her nightmares. But somehow, sometime, something had changed within her. She could not say how or when, nor even precisely why; she only knew that she would have done nothing differently if given the moment to live over again.

Anne smiled a little dryly. "Perhaps you've noticed I have a tendency to act before I think."

"Yeah." His voice held a rueful note that reflected her own. "I've been accused of doing that myself, once or twice." And then he added, "I warned you it would get you in trouble someday."

She looked at him. "Yes," she said softly, "you did."

His eyes were filled in that moment with a combination of things—tenderness, respect, gentle surprise, and perhaps even a touch of uncertainty. She read each emotion as clearly as though it was her own. And then, as though somewhat taken aback by his own vulnerability, he lowered his eyes. "I hope," he said a little gruffly, "that's not what you were crying about."

Anne sighed. As easy as it was to talk to him, this was difficult to put into words. She wondered if even he, who knew her so well, would understand. "It's only that I get . . . so tired sometimes."

He understood. He glanced at her soberly. "Wondering whether this whole oil thing is worth it?"

After a moment she nodded, reluctantly. Josh opened her hand and laid it flat on his thigh. He seemed greatly preoccupied with tracing the shape and ridges of her fingers. Anne loved the feel of his rough-textured fingers against her skin.

He said quietly, "Thinking about giving up?"

Anne took a breath. "I can't," she said tightly. Her fingers curled a little against his thigh. "This is my last chance. The ranch has been steadily losing money for the past eight years. When Marc and I took over, no one thought it could be saved. Everything I have is mortgaged now, and there is no place left to borrow. If I don't strike oil, I'll lose the ranch, and I can't let that happen. I just *can't*," she repeated with an intensity that closed her fingers tightly around Josh's.

The return embrace of his hand was warm and encouraging. "Anne," he said firmly, "that's just what I've been telling you. There's another way. You don't have to sit around waiting for miracles. You've got a fortune here already. All you have to do is let it pay off. We can make this ranch what it used to be, using just what it's got—land and cattle. We're not going to lose this place, Anne," he said lowly, and the grip of his fingers tightened. "I promise you that."

She wanted to believe him. How desperately she wanted to believe him. But her eyes were filled with despair as she said, "Oh, Josh, don't you see? Even if this ranch were operating at peak efficiency, we would only be breaking even. The cattle boom is over—it began with the Blizzard of 1891—and it has been going steadily downhill since. The entire industry is feeling it, but it's the big ranches, like Three Hills, that are suffering the most."

She shook her head slowly, trying to explain. She could feel Josh's eyes on her, and the intensity of his attention. "It has been the same throughout history. Those who try to hold on to the past always lose. It's only the ones who can see the future who make a difference."

"Sometimes," Josh said quietly, "when the past is all you've got, that's what you hold on to."

"But it *isn't* all we've got," Anne insisted. "When this country's frontier was settled, everyone believed the future would be in agriculture. But a few men of vision imagined a whole new industry built on cattle—that's how Three Hills came into being. Now it's those who have their money in cattle who are going to lose, because the times have changed around them without their noticing."

Her voice became taut with certainty. "Oil is the way of the future, don't you see that? Look around you. We are living on the threshold of a grand new age—the age of machines. The cities are run by them; households are being changed by them; the newspapers are full of them. And what is going to power all those machines except oil? Oh, perhaps not today, perhaps not even tomorrow. . . but *soon*. The only way to survive is to look ahead."

Josh smiled. "The only trouble with looking ahead is, sometimes you miss what you've already got."

He leaned back with his shoulders against the lattice support, her hand wrapped in the gentle, supporting strength of both of his. His face was in the shadows now, and she could not see his expression, but he had never felt so real to her, so close and solid and alive. His voice was softened with rumination but rich with a vibrancy that came from deep within him. When he spoke, Anne felt as though she were receiving a treasured gift.

"A long time ago," he said, "there was wilderness. The forests were like churches, the rivers went on forever. There were so many buffalo that a single herd covered three whole states, and when they moved, the earth shook for hundreds of miles around. There were eagles in the mountaintops and such plentiful game in the valleys that a man could live out a lifetime without ever having to hunt. Even a hundred years ago a man could ride for days in any direction from where we sit without ever coming upon a white man's tracks."

He spoke, and Anne could see it, as though he were painting pictures inside her head. Within him she could feel a change, a reverence and a conviction for a past he had never witnessed but of which he was as much a part as the buffalo and the eagle of which he spoke. The mere sound of his voice held her mesmerized.

"And then folks tore down the trees to build their houses, they dug up the land to plant crops," he went on quietly. "The game scattered, the rivers dried up, the buffalo were slaughtered. The railroads came, scarring the land. Towns grew up, miners wiped out whole mountains and left a pile of rubble behind. There's hardly anyplace you can go nowadays where somebody hasn't left their trash behind. There's hardly anything worth saving anymore."

And he looked at her. "Folks have been busy looking at the future for a long time now. Seems to me somebody ought to stop and take account of what it's gotten them. What you've got here, Anne—your land, your streams, your meadows—that's eternal. It's served a lot of generations well. And it's not going to stop serving until we forget what it's there for. It's worth saving."

She closed her eyes, a sad and poignant smile touching the corners of her lips. "The buffalo will never come back," she said softly, "or the Indians. The land my grandfather saw will never be the same again, but I don't think he would want it to be."

And she turned to him, taking his other hand in hers, holding both of them tightly. Her voice grew tight with conviction, her eyes bright with the effort to make him share her vision, just as she had shared his. "We're living in the twilight of that age, don't you see? The cowboy, the prairie, the open range—they are all fading away, even as we speak. But there's a new day on the horizon, a bright, exciting future, and we can be a part of it—all of us. It's worth waiting for, it's worth fighting for. It's worth everything."

Josh looked at her. Her eyes were glowing, her face flushed with the passion of her speech. He was swept up by an emotion so intense and so unexpected that it took his breath away. How had it happened, this deep and powerful need of her that filled his pores and swelled inside his head? For it was more than just physical. It was all of Anne he needed—her strength, her conviction, her anger, and her tears—the parts of her that were wrong and the parts of her that were right, he needed them all.

Yet how could it not have happened? She was as wrong for him as he was for her, but she was in his blood, as far apart from him as twilight was to dawn but just as necessary to the continued order of the universe. He had never meant it to happen, but he could not stop it now.

He reached up his hand and lightly touched her hair. She had become part of his dream. "Do you think," he said huskily, "that there might be a place for two people like us in this bright new world of yours?"

Anne's eyes were clear. She could feel her own heartbeat, steady and sure. The tenderness in his eyes made her ache inside. "I don't know," she whispered.

Josh's finger touched her forehead and lightly glided over the shape of her eyebrow. His gaze was gentle and quiet, filled with nothing but the simple truth. He said, "There's room for us in my world. There always has been. And I think you know that too."

Anne dropped her eyes. For a long, slow moment there was nothing but the sound of their soft breathing, the muted symphony of night frogs, the spicy scents of the late fall garden, and the warmth they shared. Then she looked up at him and lightly touched his shoulder.

"Let's go inside," she said.

A grainy light in tones of violet and gray was all that remained of the day, casting only shadows in Anne's bedroom. The fireplace grate was cold, and the servants had not yet been in to light the lamps. At the threshold of the room Josh released Anne's hand and turned to close the door, turning the key in the lock.

Perhaps it was the click of the lock—so definite, so final—or the absence of his strong, supporting hand, but

Anne was suddenly seized with an attack of nervousness. It was more than nervousness. It felt like the first threads of an insidious panic, and all she could think was, *Dear God, what am I doing?*

Before, there had been the magic of the night, the heat of passion, a flirtatious game that had gotten out of hand and propelled her onto a course she could not control. It had been blind, swift, and intense.

This was different. She had brought a man who was not her husband to her bedchamber. The door was locked behind them and they were alone. He stood in the center of her frilly, feminine room, filling it with his alien presence, and what had seemed so sure and right a moment ago was suddenly awkward, and she was afraid.

This time she could not pretend it was an accident. After tonight she could not pretend anything anymore.

Quickly she crossed the room to the night table, fumbling for matches. She found the tin of matches, but her clumsy fingers opened it too hastily, and most of them spilled on the floor. She tried to strike a match but it broke, and then Josh's hand closed calmly over hers.

"It's all right," he said gently. "Don't bother with the lamp."

"Of course," she murmured, and everything inside her felt tight, as though muscles of which she was not even aware were struggling to keep from quaking. "Silly of me. One hardly needs a lamp to . . . I mean, such things are best done in the dark, aren't they?" And heat flamed to her face; she was wretched.

Josh placed a finger under her chin, turning her to look at him. In this light his eyes were dark and quiet, the planes of his face softened in definition. He looked at her soberly, and she wanted to hide. Miserable embarrassment burned her skin, and uncertainty twisted in her stomach.

"Anne," he inquired softly, "are you sorry?" His eyes probed hers. "I don't want you to be sorry."

She had to turn away, wrapping her arms about herself. Her heart was pounding strongly against her ribs. She didn't want to be sorry, either. She wasn't sorry. She was Anne Edgecomb, a grown woman and a widow of some years; she was acting like a skittish virgin upon her first bedding, and she felt like a fool.

"I'm not very good at playing the femme fatale, I'm afraid." She tried to make her voice light, but it came out rather shaky. She hugged her elbows more tightly and took a breath, trying to still the trembling. "Perhaps you're the one who will be sorry."

He asked quietly, "Do you want me to leave?"

Her heart lurched in alarm. *No*. No, she did not want him to leave her, not now, not ever.

She swallowed hard and spoke to the empty fireplace. "I'm . . . not terribly experienced at this sort of thing." The words came slowly and with difficulty. "I . . . Marc and I always had separate bedrooms, and I . . . was brought up to believe that was the proper way." She drew a deep breath, and the exhalation was unsteady and shallow. "I . . ." She made herself turn then, looking at him, pleading with him, and knowing nothing else to say except the truth. "I just need someone to hold me tonight," she whispered.

Josh looked at her, so brave, yet unsure, and he understood. His heart filled to breaking with understanding. And all he could say was, "Yes."

He walked forward and took her gently in his arms. He lowered his face to her hair and simply held her.

Josh didn't want to frighten her, nor shame her. All he wanted to do was make things right for her. He had taken her before in mindless passion, without care or consideration for the fragile creature she was inside. He had wanted her then, with the careless, consuming greed of primitive needs; he had known it was wrong, and he had not cared for the consequences. Later he had regretted it. He did not want either of them to regret this night. Whatever happened, *he* did not want to regret it.

And so, though his muscles were aching to crush her to him, to hold her tight and never let her go, he kept his embrace light, his arms a shelter but not a prison. He would protect her but never bind her. And he wanted her to know that.

Anne laid her head against his chest, her hands against his strong shoulders. She felt the beat of his heart and the warmth of his skin beneath the soft fabric. His breath stirred her hair, and his fingers gently stroked her shoulder blade. In his arms she felt secure, and the panic of uncertainty began to fade. She wanted to stay like this, quiet in his arms forever. *Oh Josh*, she thought. *Please let it be right. Let me believe, just for tonight, that things can be right between us. . . .*

She needed him, and perhaps that was what frightened her the most. She had never needed anyone before.

"Anne," he said softly. He touched her hair, and she slowly lifted her face. There was something in his eyes she had never seen before—an openness—and he spoke as though the words were difficult for him to say. "I never meant for you to think . . . I never meant to make light of you. I've always wanted to make love to you, because when a man sees a beautiful woman, that's what he wants. But it was more than that with you."

He lowered his eyes, as though searching for the words, and when he looked back at her, Anne knew she was seeing a part of Josh he did not reveal easily. It was simple and unvarnished and sincere, the part of him she had always sensed instinctively but which he had never allowed her to touch before. It was as though she were seeing him for the first time, knowing him for the first time. The wonder of that knowledge moved her, and frightened her a little.

"What happened between us before..." he said. "I never intended it to be that way. I didn't plan it. I could have stopped it, and I should have, but I wanted you so much, and sometimes I only do what's right for myself. So I ended up embarrassing you and hurting you. I'm not proud of that, and that's why if you want me to leave now, I will. I don't want it to be like that again. Making love shouldn't be something you're ashamed of."

She looked at him, her eyes wide and still and heart-rendingly vulnerable. For a moment Josh almost hoped she would say no, would ask him to leave. She deserved better than him. The responsibility of loving her was almost more than he could bear.

"I'm not ashamed," she whispered.

Josh took a slow breath. How could he tell her how precious she was to him, how badly he wanted to make this night perfect for her. *Let it be slow*, he thought. *Let it be beautiful, let it be a beginning for us.* All the rest of his life hung in the balance against what he could create with her tonight.

He leaned forward and kissed her forehead softly, lingeringly. Her scent filled him like the taste of innocence. "Let me show you, Anne," he said huskily. "Let me show you what we were meant to be."

His lips sent a shiver of heat through her, a quiver of expectancy and yearning. A tiny breath caught in her throat. She wasn't afraid of him. She wasn't afraid of the scorn of society or the damage to her reputation or the flouting of moral conventions. She was afraid of the passions Josh evoked in her and of the knowledge that after tonight nothing about her would ever be the same. This she did of her own free will. She had never suspected that the most courageous act of her life would be to love a man.

She looked at him, and Anne knew there would be no turning back. She touched his lips lightly with her forefinger, tracing their softness and their shape for a trembling moment. She whispered, "Yes."

Josh drew her slowly against him, closing his eyes, and he had to part his lips for breath. Her arms went around him, and he felt her slim muscles tightening with the intensity of an embrace. The emotion that swelled up inside him left him momentarily dizzy. He turned his lips to hers.

He kissed her with a gentle, exploratory care that was like caressing the petals of a blossom to full bloom. Anne could feel herself opening to him, layer by layer. She felt the warmth that spread through her skin and seeped deeper into her veins, her arteries, her muscles, her very bones. She felt the weakening, flowing softness that caused her body to form to his without her conscious thought. She felt the tiny fibers of awareness begin to grow, expand, and fill with him. And as passion began to flutter its wings inside her, he drew slowly away, leaving her with the taste of something sweet, longing for more.

He was smiling, a vague, pleasure-dazed smile that seemed

not to come from his lips or his eyes but, in fact, from his whole being. That smile was a reflection of the way she felt inside. His hands touched her hair very lightly, and drifted down the planes of her face, a feather touch that seemed hardly to touch at all but rather to trace her shape in the air. She could feel the fine, invisible hairs on her skin prickling in response, as though stirred by the mystical essence of him rather than by the physical touch itself. Her breath was still in her throat.

He lifted his hands to her hair again and tugged loose the pins that bound it, one by one. He threaded his fingers through her hair and let it fall about her shoulders, his eyes brightening as he said, "You are so lovely."

Anne rested her hands upon Josh's arms, wanting to do more, yet too uncertain to be bold. She felt the texture of the soft, much-washed fabric, and beneath it the ropy firmness of his strength. When he lifted his arm to stroke her hair, a muscle flexed, and the simple movement seemed to contain the very miracle of life. Josh. Strong, solid, present. Hers.

He brought his lips to her hair. She felt the deep expansion of his chest, the long, warm whisper of his exhalation. "Anne," he said softly, "I don't want to frighten you. I don't want to hurt you. Tell me what you want . . . please."

Anne's eyes closed with an intensity of emotion she could barely contain; she closed her arms around him and pressed herself close. Need rose up in her like the pressure of tears, and she held him tightly. *I want*, she thought, *to believe in you, just a little while longer. . . .*

But of course she could not say that. So she did the only thing she could: She turned her mouth to his for a kiss.

This time the kiss was long, and passion strained to the

end of its tether. When they parted, both were flushed, their breathing unsteady; Josh's eyes, as he scanned Anne's face, were as bright as jewels. His voice was part whisper as he said, "Do you mind . . . would you let me undress you?"

Anne's heart lurched, and something that felt like alarm flared to her skin. Alarm . . . or excitement. But shyness was out of place, and it was too late to hold back. In a moment she managed a small shake of her head, and then, lowering her eyes, she took a modest step backward.

She was wearing a slim ribbon around the high neck of her shirt; Josh's fingers felt twice their normal size as he untied it and let it fall away. He began to work the tiny pearl buttons. To his clumsy fingers the process seemed to take forever. His heartbeat was like an anvil in his chest, and with every button he released, his skin seemed to grow tighter. She stood before him with her head lowered and her hair shielding her face like a silvery veil, and whenever his fingers brushed her skin, heat branded him.

He slipped the shirt off her slim white shoulders and unfastened the tab on her skirt. It was difficult to draw a breath. A satin corset bound her torso, her breasts covered by a filmy chemise, and a single muslin petticoat outlined the shape of her hips and legs. His loins were full and aching for her, and the sensation penetrated every cell of his body. Even his heart seemed swollen, barely able to beat with the weight of his need.

Josh tugged at the knot that fastened her corset with awkward movements. Carefully he removed the heavy garment, and then released the ties of her petticoat. Lightly, reverently, he ran his hands down the length of her naked arms and felt her trembling. And he felt her heat.

He pulled the tiny ribbon bow that fastened her chemise

and slipped the straps of the garment over her shoulders, down to her waist. Her breasts were bared before him, roses and cream, like the rest of her. Lightly he touched one pink nipple and felt it swell and harden with his caress. He caught his breath.

He unfastened the ties of her pantalets, and he felt her stiffen. With ultimate care, trying hard to restrain the trembling of his own hands, he gathered the material and slipped chemise and pantalets over her hips. He knelt and tugged down one gartered stocking, and then the other, supporting her foot in his hand as he removed each garment. Then he stood, and for a moment he could only look at her.

She was a slender vision of alabaster femininity in the wash of filtering twilight; too lovely, too perfect even to touch. He filled his eyes with her. Her firm, perfectly rounded breasts, her spare waist, the small convexity of her abdomen and fluted hipbones. The neat, light triangle of downy hair between her thighs, the silky length of her legs . . . Anne, all of her, naked and revealed and his. He could simply look at her forever.

He saw her fingers start to close at her sides, as though she were fighting the impulse to cover herself, and he went to her, wrapping his arms around her, covering her with his own body. He took a long breath to draw air into his tight, aching chest. It was like an intoxicant—her softness against his hardness, her pliancy against his rigidity, smooth, warm skin against his aching fingers. He was filled with her.

"Anne," he whispered hoarsely, and though his mind was bursting with things to say, the words wouldn't come. He wanted to show her every pleasure that had ever been between a man and a woman. He wanted to give to her all it was possible to give and more.

Anne was dizzy with the sensation of his embrace; the strangeness of his clothing against her naked, sensitized skin, the power of his muscles against the weakness of her own. His leather belt was cool against her abdomen, and his jeans brushed roughly against her thighs. A collage of conflicting emotions assaulted her: She felt shy but she felt bold; she felt wicked but she felt free. In his arms she was alive.

Josh's hands caressed her back, tracing the shape of her spine, and drifted lower to cup her buttocks. No one had ever done that before. Anne felt his chest expand for breath, and the pressure made her breasts ache suddenly. Electric quivers closed up her throat while he touched his lips to her neck; then he lifted his head and moved away a little.

She arched her neck as his lips met and lightly closed around her nipple. A touch of moisture and warmth rushed to her head. His hand spread across her abdomen, and she held on to his arms for support. She felt the touch of his lips, the caress of his tongue, on her other nipple, and then his hand slipped between her legs. She gasped, and a liquid warmth expanded to the place his hand cupped, sending a rush of dizziness to her head. His arm came down beneath her hips, sweeping her off her feet to carry her the few steps to the bed.

He kissed her with an intensity that left her aching and weak, burning with the imprint of him, dazed with the flood of anticipation. Her breasts ached, her skin tingled, and the sensation between her legs was so intense that she had to press her thighs tightly together to ease it.

Anne could feel the dampness of Josh's face as he bent over her. She wanted to draw him back to her so that she might taste him and hold him. Her hands tightened on his shoulders as he started to move away. But he touched her face and straightened up, sitting on the edge of the bed to remove his boots.

She had never watched a man undress before. Josh did it quickly and without grace, tugging off his bandanna, stripping off his shirt, then stepping out of his pants. Yet the mere watching made her stomach tighten and her breath grow shallow in her throat, as though with the discovery of a great secret or the receipt of an unexpected gift.

He came back to her, sitting beside her on the bed, easy in his nakedness and intense in his beauty. He took her hand and brought it slowly to his lips, kissing each finger separately, then taking the fingers, moist with the touch of his mouth, and placing them against the side of his face. He closed his eyes with the pleasure of her touch. "Oh, Anne," he said softly, "I want to touch you, to know you . . . every part of you. And I want you to know me."

Yes, she thought. To know him, to belong to him, to claim him for her own. She let her hand drift down over his neck, savoring the smooth, hot texture of his skin, spreading her fingers over his shoulders, discovering bone and sinew. She watched his eyes as her hands moved, and the pleasure she saw reflected there thrilled her with power. "No more secrets between us," she whispered.

She saw the convulsive movement of his throat as he swallowed, and the brief lowering of his eyes. "No," he answered thickly. "No more secrets."

Her hands moved downward, brushing through the silky swatch of hair on his chest to muscles and ribs and the taut musculature of his waist. Boldly she moved even lower and saw his eyes grow dark, then bright, with surprise and pleasure as she touched the shape of the most intensely private part of him.

She felt shy and brazen as her fingers explored the hardness of him, the length of him, the power and fragility that was exclusively his own. As she watched his face she saw his breath quicken and his eyes half close with the intensity of sensation. His pleasure was her own because she had given it to him, and the thrill of knowledge was heady.

She brought her hands back to his waist. She explored the length of his back, the heat of his scalp, and the feathery texture of his eyelashes. She took his fingers into her mouth and knew the shape and texture of each one. She felt his heart race beneath her hand and the perspiration gather on his brow. He was giving himself to her completely.

Josh laced his fingers through hers, stretching her arms out to the length of his on either side of her. His chest brushed her straining breasts as he leaned over her, and with his lips he caressed each of her outstretched arms in turn from shoulder to wrist, touching the downy sprinkling of hair beneath her arms, drawing against the throbbing pulse inside her elbow, teasing the tender underside of her wrist.

His weight barely covered her now. The hairs of his chest tingled against her swollen nipples, and the power of his manhood brushed her abdomen. His heat, his scent, his presence, engulfed her. His hands cupped her breasts, and his mouth caressed them. Pleasure rose on waves and tightened in spirals; the ache of need knotted in her womb and spread lower. Anne moved restlessly against it, tightening her thighs to contain it.

His hands moved beneath her and around her, stretching to caress her legs and drifting upward to stroke her thighs.

His hands moved in gentle, insistent, hypnotic rhythms until her legs parted helplessly for him.

She gasped when she felt his hand there, gently stroking and separating the folds of her flesh. His slender fingers gently probed and withdrew, they sought deeper, bringing her to the brink of madness. Never had she guessed how intense wanting could be, how completely sensation could consume. And when Anne thought she would cry out from wanting him, his hands slipped beneath her knees, lifting them and positioning them on either side of him. He pressed himself into her.

It was a long, slow moment in which every sensation was vividly magnified. She felt the heat of him inside her, his slow, filling length; her muscles tensing and then relaxing as her body molded itself to the shape of him. She saw his face above her, the blur of his eyes, hazy with intensity and brilliant with awareness. The beat of his heart was strong against hers. She felt the stillness of her breath in her throat and the slow, sliding pressure of his entry, opening her, filling her, making every cell of her body throb with the awareness of him inside her, and the emptiness that was no longer there.

She could feel the trembling in the muscles of his arms as he held himself for a long, intense moment, still inside her, and the whisper of his breath across her damp and heated face as he touched a kiss to her cheek. "Anne," he said huskily. "Remember this and how it is between us now. I want you to feel like this always. I want always to be a part of you."

Anne closed her eyes against a rush of joy, of sheer and simple beauty, so strong that tears flooded her throat. She wrapped her arms around him and drew him close, for she could never have enough of him, and she thought, Yes. Always . . .

Josh kissed her mouth and throat. His hands stroked her hair, tracing her lips and the shape of her eyes and her ears, first with his fingers, then with his lips. He began to move inside her with slow, caressing strokes. She was drawn into his rhythms and into the promise he brought, into the simple beauty of the harmony they shared. And then the ache that surrounded the place where he was began to grow, each of his thrusts coaxing it into new intensity, building an urgency that could not be contained.

She clutched at him, straining. His need was a powerful hunger that fueled her own, and together they strove, merged, and were swept up and out of themselves. The first ripples of pleasure built into a cascade of fulfillment that grew and doubled upon itself; physical sensation faded away and was consumed by something greater and more enduring, until at last it seemed their very souls stretched and shattered and slowly reformed, blending together into one. Anne, holding Josh tightly, squeezing her eyes closed to contain the wonder, thought, *This is love. I never knew before* . . . .

A long time afterward, Josh lay in the dark holding her, touched by something deep inside him that felt almost like reverence. Anne's body was smooth and soft against his, her fragrance sweet and warm and musky. Her breasts fit perfectly against the curve of his chest. Even her legs fit his, a smooth and silky encasement of his own.

He turned his head on the pillow, filling his eyes with her. Her face was gentle in repose, her lashes forming drowsy half-circles against her cheeks. Her hair was tousled and a little damp; it fell over her naked shoulders and shadowed her face like flax. Josh's heart swelled.

Anne . . . he thought. So many words, none of them adequate. He would never be able to say to her all he wanted to say that night.

Gently he lifted a strand of hair from her face and tucked it behind her ear, smoothing it with his fingers. "Anne," he said softly, "you never asked me."

She lifted her eyes to him sleepily. "Asked you what?"

He turned his head toward the ceiling, and then, slowly, back to her. "About Wright. Whether or not I was guilty."

Her eyes were moon-soft and quiet. They seemed to read into his soul. "No," she answered softly, after a moment. "I didn't."

She curled her hand into the hollow of his shoulder and closed her eyes. In a moment she was asleep.

Chapter Nineteen

The moon had set; the sun was not yet up. The subtle changes now occurring in the character of the dark were visible only to one whose eyes had grown accustomed to them, and Josh had been awake for hours, watching Anne sleep.

Josh, who had always considered himself knowledgeable in the ways of men and women, had never known anything like this—the simple contentment of watching a woman sleep in his arms and knowing that he wanted it to be like this forever. He was absorbed in her. The velvety texture of her skin, the delicate structure of her bones, the gold tips of her eyelashes which he had never noticed before, the way each eyebrow traced a perfect arc over the bones. He memorized each plane and shadow on her face and found renewed beauty in every curve. He watched the gentle, sleeping movements of her eyes behind lids that were as delicate as a child's, and he wondered if she was dreaming of him.

This, he thought, was what it must feel like after years of marriage—the sense of permanency and rightness, tinged with a trace of excitement that promised no new day would ever be faced alone. Josh had never expected to know this feeling himself. He had never even imagined it.

Yet behind his barely contained flood of joy there was anxiety, for it was all too new. Too much still stood between them, and the dawn was coming too soon.

As though touched by the very nature of his thoughts, Anne stirred and opened her eyes. Her smile was drowsy, her eyes the color of morning mist rising from a still lake. She whispered, "Hello."

Josh placed a lingering kiss on her forehead. "I have to go soon."

Her arms only tightened around him, and she nestled her head in the hollow of his shoulder. "I wish we could stay like this forever," she murmured, still half asleep. "I feel so strong when you're here."

Josh smiled. "You don't need me to make you strong."

Anne drew the flat of her palm across his chest, exploring the musculature and the silky pattern of hair that textured his skin. And for a moment she was so filled with quiet adoration that words choked in her throat.

No one else had ever said that to her: Stephen, who protected her; Marc who was amused by her; her father, who commanded her . . . none of the men in her life had ever allowed her the freedom to be strong in her own right. But from Josh it was a gift given naturally, without question or constraint, as easily as he gave all other parts of himself.

This was what love was, two people who were stronger together than they could ever be apart.

She turned on her back so that her head was even with his on the pillow. Suddenly she was filled with a flood of things she wanted to say to him. She threaded her fingers through his hair and caressed his face.

"I've spent a lifetime trying to be brave," she said softly. "I was only pretending. You always knew that. I was afraid because I was alone, and I never trusted anyone enough to give up being alone. I never believed in anyone but myself, and I was afraid. I'm not afraid anymore," she said simply, and it was as though with the words a lifetime's burden had fallen away. It was true. Of all the gifts he had given her, that was but one.

Josh felt his throat grow tight, and looking at her made his eyes ache. He said hoarsely, "Do you believe in me, Anne?"

She laced her fingers through his and brought their joined hands to rest atop his chest. "Yes," she said softly. She fixed her eyes upon their entwined fingers, studying the pattern of light upon dark, softness interwoven with strength. "I don't know that I should. I'm not sure it's right. I'm not sure it matters." And she looked at him. "But I do."

A twist of guilt went through Josh, and he thought, *Tell her.* The time for secrets between them was past. He wanted to give her all of him, but he had not even told her his name. He wanted to offer her a lifetime, but so far all he had offered was lies. He had to tell her.

Would she hate him when she knew? He could not bear it if she hated him.

Her hand drifted across his face, playing over his throat, his shoulders, stirring quiescent needs to life again. Her eyes were wide and a little uncertain, and she whispered, "Don't leave me yet. Could we make love one more time?"

She was so lovely. He needed her so much.

Tell her, Josh. The voice was clamoring at him, but he looked into her eyes and could say nothing. Not now, when she looked so innocent and content, when her trust of him was so new and tentative a thing.

He knew his identity would give Anne the strongest reason of all to distrust him. And he couldn't tell her yet. He was glad his grandfather couldn't see him now. From Jed Fielding to an outlaw to Josh—more than the times had changed. The men who had lived to carry on the Fielding name had changed, too, he reflected soberly.

The right time will come, Anne, he thought. *For now, just let me love you. . . .*

And helplessly, inexorably, he was drawn to her.

Her hair was spread across the pillow like an aura, shimmering with particles of muted light. Josh lifted a strand and drew it across his chest, where it glimmered with a soft brilliance against the darkness of his skin. He brought the strand to his face and inhaled its sweet, soft scent, then let it drift through his fingers like mercury.

He was filled with visions of her: Anne astride a blooded horse, calmly looking over her domain; Anne when the sun turned her face to translucent porcelain and her eyes to silver; Anne absently pushing back a straying tendril of hair; Anne with mischief in her eyes as she brought a cigarette to her lips; Anne throwing back a curtain to confront him in the bath; Anne in an elegant tea gown smiling to her guests; Anne, proud and defiant, Anne with fire in her eyes, Anne laughing and Anne weeping . . . Anne. Everything else faded away, and nothing mattered but Anne.

He touched his lips to the hollow between her shoulder and her neck, breathing deeply of the rich, exquisite fragrance of her. She touched his hair, and the thrill of her caress went right through his soul.

"Anne," he whispered huskily, "it was always meant to be like this."

Her breath floated across his cheek. "I know."

Anne brought her lips to his, very lightly, tasting him with the delicate care of a bee gathering pollen. His eyes drifted closed in sweet, suspended rapture at her touch, arcing shadows upon his cheeks. She let her hands explore the long, clean planes of his back, the firmness of his buttocks, the shape of his ribs, and the lean musculature of his arms. There was no shyness, no awkwardness, and urgency was poised against the exquisite beauty of this moment. She touched him, she knew him, and she claimed him. Joy swelled inside her with every caress.

His hands drifted over her body. With his fingers and his lips he offered himself to her. Her skin tingled, her fever grew, and the emptiness inside her expanded and ached for him. But the ache was sweet, because she knew that he, and only he, would fill it.

The need for each other flowed between them like a river seeking its source. Each new discovery brought Anne more pleasure, more delight, than did the last, so that at times she thought that if there was no more than this, she would be content. Soon she would die of happiness.

She knew the curve of his earlobe and the secret hollow at the angle of his jaw where a single curl nestled. She knew the smooth texture of his teeth and the slight unevenness at his wrist, where a bone had once been broken. She knew the taut, smooth flesh that stretched over his ankle and the warm indentation behind his knee; the silky hair on his legs; and the flat, hard texture of his nipples. She thought dizzily that God was quite right to forbid such pleasures between men and women, for soon humans would lose all interest in heaven.

She lovingly committed each part of him to memory, so that at last his very cells seemed to belong to her, sealed inside the essence of who she was and who she had always been. For this was much more than physical pleasure. What she shared with him now was all of her; what she took from Josh was all of him. They explored, discovered, and blended.

When at last he paused above her, his face was flushed and damp with pleasure, his eyes so brilliant that she could see their color even in the dark. He whispered, "Anne, I need to be inside you. Let me be a part of you."

She touched his face with a trembling hand, stroking it. And she answered, "You already are."

He slid into her slowly, filling her. The sensation was so exquisite that she gasped. Josh gathered her close and held himself still and deep inside her for an endless moment. It seemed so right and good, as if all of her life before this had been nothing but a shadow of living.

He began to move inside her, drawing her toward him, releasing her, bringing her back. She strained for him, her very soul stretching to its thinnest extension, then blossoming toward contentment. It was slow and sweet, shaking her to the very core of her being. Before he had taught her passion; now he was teaching her love. And the beauty of it was so intense that tears came to her eyes.

Like opposite magnetic poles, they sought each other. Their breath, their heartbeats, their minds began to move as one. Together they spiraled upward and lost themselves; and the power of their final joining was so intense, it left them blinded and weak, lost in each other. Neither would ever be separate again.

That was all that mattered.

They lay wrapped in each other's arms while dawn gently filtered through the window in shades of pink and gray, a silent intruder into the beauty of the night. Josh didn't want to leave, but he knew he had to.

Anne, sensing his thoughts, looked up at him. "Will you come back tonight?"

Tonight. He would tell her tonight. The smile he gave was meant to be indulgent, but it felt tight. He leaned down to kiss her forehead. "Like you think I wouldn't," he answered.

He gathered his strength to leave her, and it felt like tearing away a part of his own flesh. He couldn't leave her yet. He had to ask her. He had to hear her say the words.

"Anne," he inquired quietly. "Yesterday... you never told me. Why did you lie for me?"

She smiled, a shy, secretive smile that seemed as uncertain as it was brave. She threaded her fingers through his and spent a moment stroking the outline of his knuckles with her other hand. Then she said softly, "I know some Scripture too. Do you know the one, 'Faith is the substance of things hoped for'?"

"The evidence of things unseen," Josh finished for her a little thickly.

She glanced at him and then quickly back down at his hand. "When hope is all one has," she said so very softly that he had to strain to hear the words, "a leap of faith doesn't seem much of a risk at all." And she looked back at him, her eyes quiet and certain with a simple truth. "Sometimes, in fact, it's necessary. So, you see, I really had no choice. Do you understand?"

Josh closed his eyes slowly. A breath of tenderness and

sadness and enormous remorse momentarily stifled the words in his throat. *I'll make it up to you, Anne*, he thought.

He kissed her softly on the lips. "I do," he assured her somewhat huskily. "I do understand."

She whispered, looking into his eyes. "I think you do."

He left her slowly and reached for his clothes. He dressed quickly and hesitated, unable to leave, unable to stay. *Don't be sorry, Anne*, he thought. *Please don't ever let me make you sorry. . . .*

He rested one knee on the bed and kissed her. He kissed her like a husband departing for the day, and like a lover anxious to return. He felt both of those things and more. He felt so much more that he was afraid to hold her too long, and he pulled himself away.

She whispered, "I wish you didn't have to go."

He looked at her for a long time. "Yeah," he answered at last. "I wish so too." But then he made himself smile, and he touched her cheek lightly before he got to his feet. "I'll be back," he promised, and he quietly left the room.

Eddie Baker had the two indispensable traits of a survivor: optimism and pragmatism. And he knew the most important tool of a professional gambler—the ability to play a fine-line game, to lose just enough to make one's opponents reckless and then pull out the stops. In order to do that, one's confidence in oneself must be impenetrable. By the same token, one could not live outside the law for as long as Eddie had without a supreme conviction that it was simply impossible for him to be caught. Guilt had a way of setting its own trap, and so did anxiety.

But it was equally important to know when one had

played out one's hand. The ability to fold his cards and walk away had saved Eddie's life on more than one occasion.

Fifteen years ago he had been one of the shrewdest operators in the West. He had made a very successful living selling stocks in phony mines, banks, and railroads, always one step ahead of the law and not afraid to kill when the distance between himself and discovery started closing in. His youth and his apparent naïveté had been the rook, his skill had won the game, his coldhearted ruthlessness had kept him alive. Ten years ago he had folded his hand and walked away from that part of his life, but he was still a gambler. And he was still a survivor.

So far the game seemed to be going against him, but he wasn't worried. The odds were in his favor, and the risk was worth it.

He was just finishing breakfast when an unexpected visitor rode up. He remained where he was, sipping his coffee, and when George Greenley strode into the dining room, Eddie's face reflected nothing but genial welcome.

"Well, George"—Eddie half rose, gesturing with his cup—"have a seat and pour yourself some coffee. Had breakfast?"

George Greenley stopped a few feet before him, shaggy eyebrows drawn together in a dark expression. He stared at Eddie's hands. "So," he said at last, "you're hiring your work out nowadays. I didn't think it was much like you to meet a man head-on with your fists. A bullet in the back's more your style."

Eddie got up and went to the sideboard, taking down another cup. "I can't imagine what you're talking about, George."

"A man's dead, Eddie," George said lowly. "That wasn't part of the deal."

"Oh?" Eddie turned with a smile, handing George a cup of coffee. "What was the deal, exactly?"

"You know damn well." George set the cup on the table with a force that spilled half its contents onto the mat. "You've got the money, you've got the influence. All you had to do was persuade her—"

"If all it took was persuading," replied Eddie calmly, "you wouldn't have needed me." He resumed his seat and sipped his coffee, holding George's eyes mildly. "You always knew that, didn't you, Mr. President of the Cattleman's Association?"

George's face went florid. "Damn it, you almost killed her with that dynamite scheme!"

"Regrettable," Eddie admitted with a shrug. "Fortunately *almost* is the operative word."

"I thought you had changed," George said quietly. "I thought ten years of going straight might've got to be a habit. But you're slipping back into your old ways, aren't you, Eddie?"

He smiled. "I confess, there's an excitement to it all I've missed. Maybe some habits are harder to break than others."

George held his gaze for a moment, then turned and stalked to the window. He spent a long time staring out.

Things had gotten out of hand. It was supposed to be a simple matter of economics, of triumph of the mightiest. It should have been a simple thing. She was only a woman with a harebrained scheme—a stubborn woman, granted— but a lone woman who needed to depend on men to show her what was right. All it should have taken was a little pressure, a little guidance. Nobody was supposed to get hurt. When it was all over, nobody could accuse George Greenley of anything but power brokering. But things had gotten out of control.

"It's got to stop, Eddie," George said flatly to the window. "I'm calling it off."

Eddie laughed softly. "Oh, you are, are you? Well, maybe it doesn't suit me to call it off."

George turned sharply. "Is it going to suit you when the sheriff comes knocking on your door with a murder charge?"

Eddie feigned surprise. "Is that what's worrying you?" And he shook his head, chuckling softly. "George, George. The trouble with you is you have absolutely no imagination. Human nature, George, that's what you've got to understand," Eddie explained patiently. "In my line of work, knowing human nature is a tool of the trade. And the fact of the matter is, it's human nature to look for the obvious. Nobody's going to suspect a fine, upstanding citizen like you or me of a thing like murder, not when there's a mean, no-account drifter on the loose looking for trouble."

"You think your hired gun won't turn you in? There's only so much loyalty money can buy!"

"They won't even have to look that far. We've got somebody all lined up to take the fall, and the beauty of it is, we hardly had to lift a finger. He's digging his own grave, nice and neat. It's like that sometimes. You think you're losing, and then Lady Luck steps in and turns the game around. That's why it's always important to play out your hand."

George didn't understand much of what Eddie was saying, and it didn't much matter. All that mattered was that Eddie had gotten out of control, and he had to be stopped.

"You've overplayed yours, Eddie," he said coldly. "It's time to cut your losses and run."

"Oh, I see." Eddie shook his head sympathetically. "You're still under the misapprehension that you're calling the shots. Well, as fate would have it . . ." He smiled, and it was a cold, mirthless smile that went right through to the bones. "You're not."

His eyes were as flat as a dead man's, his face contained and unreadable. "You see, George, your first mistake was getting into this thing without knowing what the stakes were. For you it was just a matter of a pesky little woman and a few oil wells. For me it was a whole lifetime."

He leaned back in his chair, withdrawing a long cheeroot from his pocket and lighting it leisurely. "You see"—he took a few puffs, checked the ember, and brought the cheeroot back to his mouth—"I've kind of gotten to like being respectable. It's an easy life. Money, nice little house, people looking up to you. Yeah, it's nice. And I've got every intention to making it better. I've been waiting a long time for a chance to make it better. And how much do you think a sealed letter in a safe-deposit box is going to mean to me when I'm the owner of the biggest ranch in this county? Why, this time next year I might have your job, Mr. President of the Cattleman's Association, and do you really think anybody's going to care too much about looking into my past? Do you think I'm going to let them?"

He laughed again, quietly, and shook his head. "No, George. I went along with you because it suited my purposes, not the other way around. There comes a time when you've got to lay down everything you have, and that's what I've done. It's the only way to win."

"It's also the best way to lose."

"I rarely do."

For a moment George Greenley stood there, looking at the other man, studying him, slowly resolving what he thought he knew with what he saw now. He watched the balance of power shift, his own control slip. And there was nothing he could do but watch.

He said at last, quietly, "You're a dangerous man, Eddie."

And Eddie only smiled. "You always knew that, George."

For a long time after George had gone, Eddie sat there smoking, staring absently out the window, thinking. He wasn't worried about Greenley; he had been prepared for this moment since the day they'd set the bargain. But it was apparent things were coming to a head, and he hadn't made as much progress as he would have liked. It was time to speed things up a little.

He thought he'd better have another meeting with the cowboy.

Chapter Twenty

There were comments in the chow line.

"Good thing the sheriff ain't asking for alibis today. I sure couldn't swear to what time Coleman came to bed last night. You see him come in, Ribs?"

"Nah, not me. Bunk didn't even look slept in."

"He was probably out beatin' up folks."

"Or gettin' hisself another alibi."

Josh didn't reply. He hardly even heard. His senses were filled with Anne, his head reeling with conflicting thoughts and emotions. His body was on automatic. *Anne*. Finding her was like being blind for a lifetime and suddenly seeing colors. The touch and taste and scent of her still clung to him. She was the missing part of him, and now he was whole and it felt like a miracle.

That was what frightened him. He was too close to lose her now.

God, how could he have been such a fool? How could he have ever thought he would get away with this? He should have told Anne the truth from the beginning, or if not from the beginning at least before now. Why had he let it go this far?

And the answer was quite simple: because he had never expected it to matter. He hadn't planned on loving her.

But it wasn't too late. They had too many things working against them already, and Josh was not going to be the cause of hurting her. He was going to see to it that nothing ever hurt her again. He might not have much to offer her *except* his name, but he could at least offer her that. Tonight he would come to her with a clean slate, and they would start over. If she would have him.

And if she wouldn't—well, he wouldn't give up, that was all. He would fight for her to prove to her that he was no longer the same man who had ridden in a month ago with all those glib lies. He would do whatever he had to do, because Anne was the only thing that mattered now. She was the only thing that had ever mattered.

He would make things right for her. Whatever he had to do, he would make things right.

He gave terse, almost distracted orders for the day's work, and then he and Dakota rode north. Josh kept the house in sight as long as he could, hoping for a glimpse of Anne, imagining her in his mind. In a few hours he would see her again, and until that moment his whole life seemed to be teetering on the brink. Suddenly he wished he had kissed her just one more time.

He usually rode with Dakota because he was easy company and because he was the only one of the hands Josh knew well enough to trust. Dakota had one more asset to recommend him, which today was particularly valuable: He wasn't afraid to pull his gun. And where they were going, Josh thought it best to be prepared.

But Josh had never mistaken Dakota for a saint, and after a mile of hilly country he wasn't surprised when Dakota cast a sly glance his way. "Well, hell, man, you gonna keep it to yourself all day? I thought we were pardners."

Josh didn't reply, and Dakota chuckled, shaking his head. "Who'd've ever thought she'd go for a scrawny thing like you? Now you take Johnson, there, or even Shep—big, strapping bulls, both of 'em, and not bad-lookin' if you catch them with a shave—"

Josh said curtly, "Shut up."

Dakota looked surprised, then peered at Josh more closely beneath the brim of his hat. "It's like that, is it?" he said after a moment, softly. "Well, that *is* something."

He seemed to contemplate this, then said quietly, "I had me a woman one time. Prettiest little thing you ever did see. A shop girl, decent family. Damn near broke my heart. Guess I know how you feel."

They rode in silence for a while, but it was an easy silence. For more reasons than one, Josh was glad he had chosen Dakota.

They had crossed through the woods and were out in the open again when Dakota said, "Listen . . . I don't want to make you mad or anything, but I gotta know. It's driving me crazy."

Josh turned a glance his way, waiting. Dakota met his gaze with sun-narrowed eyes. "Did you have something going with that creek fellow?" he asked plainly. "Now, you know I got no stake in this, and just between you and me, there's talk. It looks kind of bad for you."

Josh half smiled and shook his head. "No, it wasn't me." The smile turned grim. "But I know how it looks, and that's just what we're going to fix."

Puzzlement shadowed Dakota's face, but he didn't question Josh. He just turned his horse to follow Josh's lead.

They skirted the two derricks that were still standing, and Josh examined each site closely, stopping to speak briefly with the diggers. Then they headed toward the line shack where Big Jim and his crew were camped.

Bacon was sizzling on the fire outside the camp, and four men, bleary-eyed and half dressed, huddled near it cradling tin cups of coffee. They looked up suspiciously at the sound of hoofbeats and grew more wary when Josh and Dakota grew close enough to be identified. A couple of them got to their feet.

Josh reined his horse but did not dismount. He pushed his hat back and looked over the group. "Morning, boys," he said. "Your boss around?"

Big Jim came to the door of the shack, leaning against the frame. His pants looked as though they had been slept in more than once, his flannel undershirt was stained and filthy, and he hadn't bothered to pull up his suspenders. There was a week's bristle on his face, and his eyes showed signs of a hangover of long duration. He scowled at Josh. "You got business with me, pretty boy?"

Josh did not bother to disguise the contempt in his eyes, but he kept his voice mild. "I've been riding around the drill sites. Maybe I'm getting nearsighted, but I didn't see too many fences being strung."

Big Jim spat on the ground. "She put me in charge, not you. It'll get done when it gets done."

Josh let his eyes roam easily over the camp and to the hills beyond. "Yeah, well, I guess there're just so many hours in a day. I can see where you might not find the time to do your job. . . ." And now he brought his eyes back to Big Jim. "What with blowing up oil wells and dry-gulching old men."

All the men at the fire were on their feet now, and Josh noticed in passing that none of them wore guns. He was almost sorry.

Big Jim took a step forward. His bloodshot eyes were mean and narrow. "What the hell are you trying to say, boy?"

Josh rested his forearms on the pommel. "I've never met a man who had more trouble understanding plain English," he commented. "You got problems with your hearing, Big Jim? Maybe next time you set off dynamite, you ought not to stand so close to the charge."

Big Jim's face went dark, and Josh abandoned the pretense at friendliness. His eyes were hard, his words distinct. "Now let me tell you the way it is, mister. Somebody's trying to put Miss Anne out of business. He broke into her storage shed and wrecked equipment, blew up an oil derrick and damn near got her killed, and put the man she hired to find her oil out of the way for good. I think that somebody was you. You're close enough to do it; way out here by yourself it's not likely you'd get caught, and nobody I know has better reason.

"You blame oil for putting you in this no-account job, you want to get even with Miss Anne, and it wouldn't hurt your feelings none if I was to just disappear and leave your old job open, would it?"

Big Jim looked contemptuous. "You're out of your mind, boy."

And someone else added angrily, "Everybody knows none of this started until you rode up."

"You're just trying to cover your own tracks by settin' blame on Big Jim, you lying sidewinder..."

Josh ignored them, his eyes fastened on Big Jim. "You

want to tell me where you were night before last when Amos Wright was killed?''

Big Jim spat again, his small, dark eyes never leaving Josh's. ''Somewheres else,'' he said flatly.

One of the men spoke up curtly. ''Who appointed you sheriff, Coleman? If you ask me, you're the one that ought to be behind bars, not out here messin' with honest folk.''

Josh said quietly, ''I'm only going to say this once, Big Jim. This little war you got going on out here is going to stop. Right now. Today. Because if one more thing happens to Miss Anne's oil wells—just one—you'll answer to me, personally. And by the time the sheriff gets here, it'll be too late.''

He turned his horse and left the camp.

They had ridden about five hundred yards before Dakota spoke up. ''You didn't really expect him to just up and confess, did you?''

Josh's features were shuttered. ''Nope. He just needed to know somebody's watching him, that's all.''

''Think it'll do any good?''

''No. Common sense hardly ever works with men like Big Jim.''

Dakota glanced at him beneath the brim of his hat. ''Or you.''

''Maybe.''

''Do you really think it was him, or are you just trying to put a burr under his saddle?''

Josh was thoughtful for a while. ''Maybe it *was* him. Seems likely. But if it wasn't, you can be damn sure I'm going to find out who it was.''

Dakota shook his head slowly. ''It just don't make any sense. You were as much against them oil rigs as Big Jim was—might even say that's the only thing you two had in common. Everybody heard you arguing with Miss Anne about it the day of the cattle stampede. I'd've thought you'd be the first one to want to see the wells pulled down.''

Josh's expression was thoughtful and unreadable, and his gaze moved quietly over the landscape. "Hell," he said tiredly. "I don't know who's right or wrong anymore. I'm not even sure it matters. I just know violence isn't the way to get things done."

Dakota chuckled. "You sure had a change of heart. That's what a woman will do for you, I reckon."

Josh shrugged. "I don't know. Maybe she's right—times are changing. There's no point in fighting that."

He glanced at Dakota. "Remember the big cattle wars? That's the way men used to get things done out here—they saw what they wanted, they hired a couple of gunslingers, they rode in and took over. But it's just not that easy anymore. They call it civilization. The outlaws, the hired guns, the cattle barons—maybe even the cowboys, like you and me—there just doesn't seem to be much place for them anymore.

"I guess what it boils down to," he added with a strange, abstract expression on his face, "is that you just can't go around changing the world with a gun anymore. All you can do is change yourself to live in the world we've already got."

Dakota didn't answer, and his expression was thoughtful and disturbed as they rode back to the ranch.

Chapter Twenty-one

Anne had two things to do that day. Neither one was easy, and both had to be done while she was still full of courage and determination. She would have had neither had it not been for Josh.

In the morning she met with Chance.

"I thought you'd be giving up," he drawled laconically, squinting into the sun. "I know you was depending an awful lot on that creekologist to tell you where to dig."

Anne said firmly, "That's exactly why I can't give up. If I do, his murderers will have won."

Chance thought that over. "We ain't got much left to go on but common sense. So far that hasn't brought in too many gushers."

Anne took a breath. "I'll be frank with you, Chance. I only have enough money left to sink one more well. I want you to use your best judgment as to where it should be."

"I can't give you any guarantees, ma'am, but if you want my opinion, we've been digging too far out all along. Now, I can understand you wanting to keep all the racket and mess out in the middle of a cow pasture—being a woman and all, you like things neat. But it seems to me the best place to dig is right up where your house is sitting. Only reason I didn't mention it before is 'cause I knew you wouldn't want to go along with it, and we had a few other good shots. But seeing as how this is your last chance..."

She stared at him. "Near the house? How close?"

"Well, that whole two acres there looks good. At least we know we won't be hitting bedrock."

Anne found the entire concept aethestically unappealing, of course, and Chance was right—if he had brought up the idea sooner, she would have rejected it. But at this point her back garden seemed a small sacrifice indeed, and there were very few options left.

She took a breath. "I'd like you to start right away, then." She started to go, then turned back with a wan smile. "One consolation, at least. If the derrick is close to the house, it will be much easier to guard."

The second thing she had to do was much harder. She was going to go to George Greenley and inform him of her plans. She wanted him to know he had a murder on his conscience for nothing, and she wanted to look into his eyes when she told him. It had become a game of chess between them with human lives as pawns, and she had made her move. The next one would be his, and she would be ready for it.

Since Greenley was a working rancher, Anne waited until late afternoon, when the chances were good of finding him at home. The days were growing shorter, which meant she would probably be returning in the dark, and for a moment Anne thought of asking one of the cowhands to ride with her... even Josh. But no. This was between herself and George Greenley and an old man who had died because of both of them. There were some things she still had to face on her own.

Remembering what had happened the last time she had driven the Daimler after dark, she saddled her horse and rode cross-country. Even then she found she had arrived too early. George Greenley had not yet come home.

The housekeeper showed her into the parlor and, by the time she returned with Anne's tea, informed her cheerfully that Mr. George had just ridden up. He would be in shortly, she went on chattily, but Mr. Greenley liked to take care of his horses himself and always gave them a good rubdown and a bag of oats at the end of the day, so it might take some time. But if Miss Anne wanted, she would be glad to run out to the stables and tell him to hurry, though he wouldn't much like it, and the way he had ridden in here, he didn't seem to be in a very good temper, anyway—

Anne cut off the monologue with a kind smile and informed the woman there was no need to bother Mr. Greenley. She would be glad to wait.

George Greenley's home was what Anne thought of as typically American. There were shutters instead of curtains on the windows to keep out the harsh Texas sun, the oak floors were covered with washable rugs instead of carpets, a breezeway and dark-paneled walls provided relief from the summer's heat. The parlor was furnished with a mismatch of styles—colorful rag rugs, chintz chairs, a big leather sofa, and sturdy Colonial tables. The remnants of his wife's feminine influence were visible in crocheted doilies and painted lamp globes—and the portrait of Elizabeth Fielding over the fireplace.

Anne had coveted that portrait from the moment she first saw it, and many times over the years she had tried to purchase it from George Greenley to return it to Three Hills where it belonged. His refusal to sell was only another one of his power plays, his subtle way of reminding Anne Edgecomb that she was still an outsider and that no amount of money or good intentions could ever purchase a heritage that was strictly Texan.

Anne went over to the fireplace now and stood looking up at the portrait of the young girl with dark hair and laughing eyes, trying, once again, to take courage from she who had gone before her. Elizabeth, the first of the Fielding wives. Elizabeth had never held the fascination for Anne that Jessica did, but hers, too, was a story worth remembering.

She had come to Texas as a young bride from an aristocratic family, much like Anne had. She had built the house in which Anne now lived and had laid the foundation of the garden Anne had completed. She, without a doubt, had had a much harder life here than Anne had, but what Elizabeth had brought to Texas lasted until this day. Some people still spoke of her as a legend.

Today the portrait captivated Anne in a way it had never done before. She was a beautiful girl, and even on canvas a certain inner strength came through. The spirited green eyes, the confident tilt of her head, the slightly impish smile . . . they all seemed familiar to Anne somehow, as though a distant memory were nudging her, trying to tell her something. It was strange. She must have seen the portrait a dozen times, but it had never seemed so vital to her, so compelling. Anne took a step closer to study it.

She *had* forgotten. Her eyes were glued to the newly shined name plaque underneath. It read, "Elizabeth Coleman."

A sound from the open window distracted her, and curiously she went to look out. The rider drew up to the hitching post just as she arrived, and her eyes went wide with surprise. It was Josh.

Quickly she put down her teacup and started for the door. But the sound of George's Greenley's voice halted her, and the words he said made her heart stop beating.

George Greenley was on the porch when he saw the rider round the bend beneath the arched Double G gate. He had never used his gun against a man before, but instinctively he slipped the leather thong off the revolver at his side and stood waiting. That was the state of mind he had been in since his conversation with Eddie Baker that morning. It never hurt to be prepared.

He had seen the Three Hills horse in the stable and by the saddle could tell that his visitor was Anne Edgecomb. As this new rider grew close enough to identify, George was at first puzzled, then slowly—far too slowly for a man as generally astute as he was—everything began to come together. He had been right. Eddie had sent his hired gun, just like George had expected him to.

He was willing to bet everything that the man on the roan didn't have any idea his boss was inside. As a matter of fact, George was betting everything. It was a long shot, but in the past few hours George Greenley had become a desperate man.

Josh drew up to the hitching post but didn't dismount immediately. As George Greenley stood waiting for him on the porch, Josh's eyes were quick to notice the gun loosened in his holster.

Greenley smiled and drawled, "Well, well, Mr. Fielding, I wondered how long it would take you to come to me."

For a moment Josh felt absolutely nothing—not shock,

not alarm, not even danger. It all seemed somehow quietly inevitable, and he felt nothing at all.

In the end he said only, "How did you know?"

Greenley chuckled. "I didn't, until this minute."

George Greenley walked down the steps, and with every step his certainty grew, a swift and rapid volley of information and ideas that gradually began to form a clear picture. Oh, yes, he had known. He hadn't given it a whole lot of thought because he had had too much else on his mind these past weeks and had not, until this moment, seen a way to use his information to his advantage. Now it was clear. Beautifully clear.

He had to give Eddie credit. A drifting gunslinger was undependable and dangerous, likely to cut and run at the most inconvenient time. But Josh Fielding, a man who had a stake in this, a man who could be bought, perhaps, with more than money... No wonder Eddie wasn't worried.

"Oh, I had my suspicions," he went on conversationally, "about who you might be. The first time I saw you, when you drew a gun on me, you put me in mind of old Jake Fielding so much, I swear that a goose walked over my grave. The stories I could tell you about Jake Fielding..."

He paused and smiled reminiscently. Then he continued, "Of course, Jessica was married to Senator Daniel first—I guess you knew that. I'll never forget that wedding as long as I live. Everybody all dolled up, laughing and dancing. One thing about Daniel, he sure knew how to throw a party. Then in rides the bride's crazy father, shoots Daniel in the shoulder, and flings Miss Jessica across his saddle, kicking and screaming. Lord, what a mess. I thought for sure Jake was gonna kill somebody then—he was that hotheaded. But with Daniel laid up and all, it was Jake that ended up going after Miss Jessica, and I really didn't think we'd ever see either one of them again.

"But sure enough, a few months later they showed up here, Jake with a price on his head. I don't guess we'll ever know the truth about *that* story, but I'll tell you one thing—I wasn't a bit surprised when Jake and Jessica ended up together all those years later." He cast Josh a sly glance. "I think it all started between them on that trip back."

Josh's head was reeling and he said nothing. He simply listened, harder than he had ever listened in his life.

George Greenley patted the roan on the rump and smiled. "Jake's still running the Clover Three brand, I see. Not a very good job with the running iron, boy. Good thing the sheriff never got a close look at this, him being suspicious by nature and all."

He straightened up. " 'Course, you went about this whole thing right sloppy, if you ask me. Not too many people around these parts remember the name Coleman, it's true, but I got a picture of your grandma hanging right on my wall, with the little gold plate saying Elizabeth Coleman as plain as day. It was painted before she married, you know. You're the spitting image of her, too—have been ever since you were a calf. Come on in the house, I'll show you."

Josh's mind was racing now, assimilating and assessing and rearranging his plans with every word Greenley spoke. He knew the man was up to something; he didn't know what. All Josh could do was play along and learn what he could. So he kept his face expressionless, and his movements were easy and relaxed as he dismounted and followed George Greenley up the steps.

"So how come you never said anything?" Josh asked casually.

Greenley shrugged. "Why should I? It was nothing to me. And like I said, I wasn't one hundred percent sure. You were named for her, weren't you? Joshua for your granddad, Coleman for your grandma?"

"That's right."

George chuckled, pleased with himself. "I guess the old memory box ain't as bad off as I thought. Then again, it's kind of a hobby of mine, remembering things."

In the parlor, Anne turned slowly back to the portrait. There was a peculiar coldness in her muscles, and the taste of ashes in her mouth. The room itself seemed foggy and far away, the floor beneath her feet taking on a springy, sucking texture. But the portrait was very clear.

Elizabeth Coleman. She had seen that face a dozen times. She had seen it again in Josh's smile, Josh's eyes. An elusive memory, something she could not quite grasp. And it had been here all along.

Josh Fielding. Jessica's son. She felt, rather hysterically, as though she should laugh.

George opened the door and gestured Josh inside. The door to the parlor was open, and he took his time moving down the breezeway. Eddie Baker had been right about one thing. Sometimes, just when it looked like you were on a losing streak, Lady Luck dumped a mother lode in your lap. But he hadn't won yet. He made sure that Josh walked in front of him, and he chose his words carefully.

"I should've seen this coming, I guess," he said. "You Fieldings would do just about anything for that land. Lie, cheat, steal, murder—and you have, down through the years. I should've figured you'd be turning up sooner or later. Nothing ever stopped a Fielding.''

"I reckon that's right.''

George glanced at him shrewdly. "I've got to say, it had me stumped for a while. But who else would take on the great Lady Hartley? You folks have been feuding for generations. You damn sure wouldn't be above blowing up a few oil wells to get that land back.''

Josh agreed mildly, playing out his lead. "Nope. I reckon I wouldn't. For a spread like Three Hills, a man would do just about anything. And like you said, there's no love lost between us and the Hartleys.''

An instant before Josh stepped into the parlor, he knew he was being set up. He didn't know how or why; he just suddenly *knew*. But that instinctive warning came an instant too late.

He stepped over the threshold, and everything was starkly clear, a vignette frozen in time. George Greenley stood at his elbow, still, alert, and strangely satisfied. The last rays of a dying sun cast a dimly filtered light across the room, gleaming on tabletops, fading into shadows. Above the fireplace was an ornately framed portrait of Elizabeth Coleman Fielding. Below the portrait stood Anne. Her face was white, her eyes enormous, dark, and as still as a frozen mountain pool.

For a long time nothing moved. It almost seemed as though no one even drew a breath. And then Anne moved toward him.

She stopped no more than an arm's reach from him. In her eyes there was nothing but hate, and her voice was cold and flat and completely without emotion. It had the power to freeze his very soul.

She said quietly, "You bastard."

Then she walked past him without looking back.

Josh listened to the sound of her boots clicking on the floor, the banging of the door, her progress down the steps. And then, a long time later, hoofbeats moving away. He stood still.

George Greenley cleared his throat. "Well, that's a pity."

Josh turned slowly. "You knew she was here." Not a question, not a challenge, just a quiet, deadly statement of fact. "Why?"

Perhaps George caught the gleam of something dangerous in Josh's eyes; perhaps he remembered Jake Fielding. Perhaps he simply realized that further evasions would be pointless now. At any rate, he did not argue. He moved into the room, crossed to a table containing a collection of bottles, and poured himself a drink. Only then did he turn.

He said, "I thought it might not be a bad idea to have somebody else hear your confession, if it came to gunplay between us."

Still Josh's voice held no emotion. "You were figuring on me shooting you?"

Greenley's eyes were steady. "Or me shooting you." He took a sip from the glass, never letting his eyes flicker, keeping his free hand by his gun. "You see, I knew somebody would be coming after me. The only thing I didn't figure on—at least not until you rode up—was it being you. That kind of worked in my favor, you see. A man with a secret is a lot easier to deal with."

Of it all, only one thing stood clear in Josh's mind. "Why?" he demanded quietly. "Why should anybody be coming after you?"

Greenley answered mildly, "Because I'm the only man who can stop him."

"Stop who? The same man that's been after Anne?"

Greenley only stared at him, and Josh took a swift, violent step forward. "Who, goddammit!" he shouted.

The moment was explosive, and George Greenley's face reflected the sharpness of it—swift startlement, instinctive alarm, and then simple incredulity. In that volatile instant his fingers might even have flexed for his gun, but they never completed the motion. He stared at Josh.

"You don't know," he said slowly. "You really don't know."

With an almost physical effort Josh pushed back the wild rush of fury, grasped the hungry surge of raging energy, and subdued it. Slowly the red veil that hazed his vision receded; forcefully he calmed the pound of his pulse. He made his hands unclench. Over, he thought. The worst was over. But he still had business to take care of that night.

He said, very distinctly, "No. I don't know. But you're damn well going to tell me who it is."

George Greenley merely shook his head, like a man slowly awakening from a bad dream and not fully able to believe it's over. Suddenly he no longer looked like a big man, or even a powerful one. He looked only tired. "If it's not you, then I don't know who . . ." And he let his voice trail off.

Josh said softly, "Shit."

He drew in a slow breath through his teeth. For this, Anne, he thought. For this . . .

He had been so close. George Greenley, talking the way he had been, sounding like he had all the answers. Josh had seen his chance and taken it. He had been certain that any minute Greenley was going to put a stick of dynamite in his hand and point him to the nearest oil well. Then he would have had proof.

But it had all been for nothing. If Greenley believed—and he had genuinely believed—that Josh was the saboteur and responsible for Amos Wright's death, then it proved only one thing. That George Greenley was innocent.

Josh was no further ahead than when he had started this morning. He had nothing to bring Anne, and the chances were that he had lost her forever.

George drew himself up with an effort, and his eyes sharpened. "If it's not you, then what the hell are you doing here? What do you want?"

"Nothing," Josh answered. He was bone-weary. "I came here to find out if you're the one that's behind all this. I guess I got my answer."

Slowly George Greenley relaxed. He turned back to the table and poured another drink. He crossed the room and handed it to Josh, and Josh took it without looking at it.

"Well, son," Greenley said at last, thoughtfully. "Look like you and me are in the same boat. We both look guilty as hell, and there's not much way we can prove otherwise. What are you going to do?"

Josh looked at the portrait. His grandmother. His eyes, his dark hair, his smile. Elizabeth Fielding. He should have felt moved, even awed. He felt only empty. *Anne*, he thought, *I'm sorry*.

Josh lifted the glass to his lips but barely tasted its contents. "You seem to know so much about me. What do you think I ought to do?"

Greenley smiled, glancing at the contents of his glass. "Depends on who you take after, I guess—your uncle or your father. Old Daniel would have been calm and reasonable and found a way to think it through. He would have been right. Your Uncle Jake would have opened fire on everything in sight and probably gotten his fool self killed. And he would have been right." He shrugged. "Depends."

Josh moved his eyes away from the portrait and down to the glass. Soberly, abstractedly, he studied the play of pinkish sunlight in the amber liquid. "Maybe," he answered at last, "I don't take after anybody but myself."

Greenley nodded thoughtfully, looking him over. "Maybe you don't," he agreed, and lifted his glass in a silent salute.

Josh rode back to the ranch, but he did not go to the house. He spent hours riding along the perimeter, moving through still forests and across streams, walking his horse over open meadows, speaking softly to the cattle who were bedded down in flocks in the winter pasture. It was dark and he couldn't see much, but he knew by feel and scent, by shadow and curve, every trail he took. How familiar this place had become to him in such a short time. How familiar—and how precious.

The moon rose, and he made his way toward the field where Anne had planted her last two derricks. He rested his horse atop the rise and sat looking down over them for a long time, trying to think. If he had made up his mind to put Anne Edgecomb out of the oil business, what would he be planning now? If he was the saboteur, what would his next move be?

The only remaining possibility seemed to be Big Jim. If Josh were hiring men for a job like that, he would try to get someone on the ranch, someone whose presence would not be noticed if he were found in odd places at odd times, someone who was close enough to the goings-on here to keep up with them, someone who had access to a ranch horse that would leave no distinguishing tracks. That was obviously the thinking of the sheriff, too—and Greenley and just about everybody else in the county. They all thought it was Josh, and all things considered, Josh couldn't blame them.

Josh didn't think Big Jim was the type to hire out his gun. He might act on his own behalf out of spite or revenge, but a man like Big Jim had been on his own too long ever to take orders from somebody else. So who did that leave? Almost any man on this place, Josh realized, and a hundred others he didn't even know.

One thing seemed sure. Nothing was going to happen that night. It was too soon after that Amos Wright business; whoever it was would be lying low for a while. There was no point in sitting here watching. He turned his horse away and slowly began to weave a path through the woods.

God, how had everything gotten so messed up? All he had ever wanted was a little piece of his own past, something to hold on to, to take pride in, something to look back on and to say firmly, *This was mine. This is who I am and where I came from.* For Jed Fielding and Elizabeth, for the father he had never known . . . he wanted them to be proud of him.

He had brought trouble, unrest, and enmity to everyone he touched. Now he had hurt the only woman he would ever love, and he had no one to blame but himself. He wondered if the price was really worth it.

He released a long breath through parted lips. *What are you going to do, son?*

"Pa," he whispered out loud. "What would you do?"

And then his throat convulsed, and he had to close his eyes, because when he said the word *Pa*, he was thinking of Jake Fielding, the outlaw.

Maybe there was nothing he could do. Maybe it was in his blood. Or maybe he now could begin to try to change the past.

He jerked the reins sharply and turned toward the house—and Anne.

Josh Fielding had been gone some hours before it finally came to George what Eddie was planning. He had been right to think Eddie would want to be rid of him. He had been wrong to think it would be this soon.

Eddie Baker was a man who hadn't forgotten how to get what he wanted. George was only now beginning to realize how much Eddie wanted, and how badly. Once he had Three Hills Ranch, nothing could threaten him. If he could put George Greenley out of the way, he would have no trouble at all disposing of a secret letter in a safe-deposit box. And no blame would ever be directed toward Eddie, not for any of it. Because Josh Coleman made a perfect fall guy.

In a way George had to admire Eddie's ingenuity. A nameless drifter and a troublemaker, a suspicious stranger to conveniently take the fall. . . . It would have been perfect.

It would have been perfect if Josh Coleman were a drifter, a stranger, a nobody. But he was a Fielding: Senator Dan Fielding's son; Jake Fielding's nephew and adopted son. There would be an investigation that reached from here to California, and everything would come out. Everything. But that was only one of George's problems that night.

Eddie had always been a ruthless man, but now he was

only one step from being invincible. And George Greenley was the only person who could stop him.

George took out his revolver, checked the chamber, and holstered it again. Then he pulled on his coat and went out into the night to saddle his horse.

This had gone too far.

Chapter Twenty-two

In the parlor a single lamp was lit, its low flame casting a small circle of yellow light over one corner, leaving the rest of the room in shadows. Anne, wrapped in a floor-length shawl, sat in a small sewing chair near the fireplace, her head high and her shoulders straight, staring ahead. Nothing remained of the fire except an occasional lone spark drawn upward through the chimney, for the log had burned down some hours ago. The room was cold, but Anne hardly noticed it. The cold that was inside her was the kind neither a fire nor a shawl could warm.

Her mind was a blank, gray screen across which a random demon would scamper now and then, playing out its taunting, cavorting dance before it faded away. Her emotions were frozen solid deep inside. Occasionally something would struggle to the surface—a phrase, a flash of memory, a scrap of cognizance—and agony would flower and twist and threaten to spread throughout her body, then it, too, would slowly die and leave her numb again. Even the energy it took to feel pain was too much for her.

Stephen's voice: "Did it ever occur to you, Anne, that all

this trouble began the minute that Coleman fellow rode up?"

Big Jim: "He's a hothead and a troublemaker...."

Sheriff Hawkins: "He was an old man and kinda puny, not like Gil...."

George Greenley: "You Fieldings would do just about anything for this land."

Yep, I reckon we would.

Jed Fielding, who had killed Anne's grandfather and left him in an unmarked grave. Jake Fielding, who had stolen his brother's wife. Josh Fielding, who had returned to claim what was his.

Josh, standing against a background of flaming debris and drifting ashes, holding a blasting cap in his hand. A horse bearing the long forgotten Clover Three Brand. A familiar smile, dancing green eyes. It was all so clear, so logical, so beautifully simple. She had known. From the beginning she must have known. She had simply chosen not to believe.

She had dreamed too high and risked too much. Now she must pay the price.

She heard the footfall on the floor with little surprise. She turned and he was there.

The circle of lamplight cast gentle, subdued shadows on his face, softening it into sober planes and lines. His face, so beautiful, so familiar, so strong. His eyes, looking at her, touching her, quiet and waiting.

Slowly, without warning or expectation, the pain began to stretch on tentacled fingers to every fiber of her being. Josh. He had done this. He had lied, used her, even murdered. Hate rose up in her like bile and then began to disperse into despair. She didn't want to feel it. She didn't want to feel anything. But he was here, and she felt everything.

She got slowly to her feet. "What did you come back for? What more can you do?" Her voice was very steady, almost calm. "You've blown up my oil well, you've even killed a man. But now it's over. I know who you are. What are you going to do—kill me too?"

He didn't move. He said quietly, "Do you really believe that?"

A spasm of pain tightened, and Anne jerked her chin up in defense of it. "What do you expect?"

"I never meant to lie to you, Anne."

An ugly, bitter smile twisted her lips. She hated it but she couldn't stop it. "That's right, I'm sure. After all, you did tell me, didn't you, that you came here to swindle me out of my fortune and take my virtue? Congratulations on a job well done."

She saw then a flash of pain in his eyes, and her own body reacted to it, like fiery fingers winding around her heart. She stiffened every muscle in her body against it.

"Anne, I should have told you who I was." His voice sounded heavy and tired. "I never should have let it go on this long. I can't blame you for hating me for that."

Now the agony was like a blanket enfolding and suffocating her. Her chest was hot with it. She took a breath through parted lips and met his eyes with the last of her strength. "Oh, no, Josh Fielding," she said softly. "That wasn't the worst thing you did."

Her hands tightened against a sudden attack of tremors that she refused to let penetrate her voice. "You made me love you," she said very steadily, very quietly. "I've never loved anyone before, and you made me love me. I can never forgive you for that."

She picked up her skirts and swept past him. In a moment

Josh heard her swift footsteps on the stairs, and the slamming of a door.

Josh made himself stand very still. He fought down the anger, he fought down the pain, he fought down the slow, rising flooding of emptiness that was sweeping his very soul. *Go*, a firm, commanding voice told him. *Let her go, leave it alone, you've done enough to her. . . .*

But he couldn't go. Not now, not tonight, not with her thinking what she did. Not after coming so close. Not without telling her . . .

And then it was no use fighting anything. His heart was beating hard, his muscles were aching, and he couldn't stay still. Not with all they had to lose.

He turned and took the stairs two at a time.

"Anne!" He knocked on the door to her room, hard. "Anne, let me in."

No response. He tried the doorknob, and it rattled against the bolt. "Anne, listen to me. You have to listen to me."

Silence.

A surge of desperation and fear rushed in him and swelled in his temper, and he brought his fist against the door again, harder. "Damn it, Anne, I'm not going to let you do this! Open this door!"

He rattled the doorknob, furiously this time. He was beyond anger. He was on the brink of desperation. "Damn you, Anne," he said tightly, releasing the doorknob with a jerk. "You're not going to lock me out—not tonight!"

He took a step backward and delivered a single hard kick to the center of the lock. The bolt splintered and the door flew open, bouncing on its hinges. Josh strode in.

Anne stood against the far wall. Her face was white and strained, her eyes brilliant with a high, wild emotion, her lips tightly compressed. Her hands were wrapped around the butt of a pearl-handled revolver, and she was pointing it at him.

Josh stood still. His heartbeat slowed to become heavy and ponderous. He felt the blood drain slowly from the pulsing vesicles of his skin, leaving him with a cold, seeping emptiness that withered through every cell. And not because of the gun. Because of the way she was looking at him.

"Don't come any closer," she said lowly. She moved both forefingers inside the trigger guard, and the gun did not waver.

He could see her chest rise and fall in slow, steady beats. The taut skin across her cheekbones reflected the subtle gleam of the lamp, and a few pale tendrils of hair curled against her neck. Her shoulders were square, her arms straight. And in her eyes was more than hate. Hate, he could have borne. What he saw in her eyes was betrayal and pain, and a desperate defense against both. But beyond all that and deep beneath the surface was fear, and that was what he couldn't bear. That was what took his heart and slowly twisted it in two.

He took a step toward her. "If you really believe I'm the man who dynamited your well and killed Amos Wright," he said quietly, "then go ahead and shoot. No one would blame you."

Anne's breath moved in and out in great, surging waves, and each wave gathered a new peak of raw, wild energy. Every sense was alert, every nerve singing with awareness. He moved closer.

"Before God," she breathed, "I'll shoot." Her voice was shaking now but not with fear. Everything she had ever been, or ever known, was concentrated into this single vivid moment, and she knew without a doubt that she would do it. She was backed into a corner, and there was no place left to run.

"I wouldn't even blame you, Anne." He kept coming. "If I've done all the things you say, I deserve to die. And if you believe them, then I guess I'd rather."

"I mean it, Josh!" Her voice was shrill, and now even her muscles were trembling. She was a woman defending herself in the only way she knew how, this time against more than a physical threat. Much more. Anne's hysteria swelled and grew, pushing against the fragile bars of its cage, and she did not know how much longer she could keep it at bay.

"I'll do it," she warned tightly. "If I have to, by God, I'll shoot."

The expression that flickered across his face seemed vaguely sad. "I know you will," he answered simply. "But at this point it doesn't seem to matter much."

Anne pulled back the hammer with both thumbs. The click it made locking into place echoed loudly.

He was less than four steps away from her now. The distance seemed immense, the time it took to span it infinite. She could hear her heart beating and the rustle of her breath. He fastened his eyes onto hers as he kept walking toward her. She couldn't take her eyes off his. Her fingers tightened on the trigger.

And then he filled up her vision—his eyes, deep and quiet and searching, his face still and intense, his lips taut.

The gun wavered and fell to her side limply. Anne dropped her head on a stifled sob that only began to describe the awful flood of emptiness and defeat that consumed her. Slowly she released the hammer. It was over. He had won.

She felt the long release of his breath cascade over her cheek, the tension that rippled through his muscles and stirred the air of the few inches between them. "All right, Anne," he said, and the words were like a whisper, little more than a heavy breath. "All right. Now you'll listen to me."

He took her shoulders in a grip that was hard but not cruel; he pulled her toward them so that she had to lift her head to look at him. His eyes were dark and intense; his face torn with a raw and agonizing emotion that reflected her own. His voice was tight.

"This is what I'm guilty of," he said low. "I came here under a false name. All I wanted was to find out the truth about my past, and I thought it would be easier if nobody knew who I was. Then I saw this ranch and I wanted more. I saw you and it looked easy. I'm not proud of it and I'm not making any excuses. I lied to you, I used you—and then I fell in love with you. And whatever else I might have done, neither one of us will ever know because after you, nothing else mattered."

He took a breath, his eyes probing into hers, fierce and determined. "I know how it looks. I can't make you believe me. I can't even ask you to. But I didn't sabotage your well. I didn't kill that old man. And God knows I wish I could take back everything else I have done . . . but I can't."

She felt the despair in him; she saw it in his blazing, searching eyes—eyes that seemed to want to peel back the layers of her soul and force his truth inside and knowing, even as he spoke, the hopelessness of it all. And then he whispered savagely, "Anne!"

Josh pulled her against him, crushing her mouth with his kiss. It was fierce and hungry and wild. It blotted out everything and left within Anne but a swirling, aching yearning that could not be filled. It was powerful and powerless, despairing and determined, savage and sorrowful, and it was final. When she pulled away, it was like tearing out part of her own soul.

She brought the back of her hand to her trembling lips, tasting him, feeling him, consumed by him. "No," she said shakily. "You're not going to do this again." Her voice caught on a fierce, determined breath, and she raised eyes to him that were wide with pleading, dark and glittering with anguish. "I'm not going to let you do this to me again."

Josh let his hands drop; he took a step away. There was such bleakness in his face that Anne wanted to sob out loud with it; with the last of her courage she held herself straight and still.

"All right," he said quietly. "Believe what you have to. But I'm innocent, Anne. And I love you. That's all I wanted you to know."

He turned and left the room.

The door closed behind him with a soft and final click, and Anne was alone. She closed her eyes and tried to draw a breath. Her trembling knees sagged beneath her weight as she sank slowly to the floor, leaning her head back weakly against the wall. And she cried.

Josh crossed the moonlit lawn toward the bunkhouse without feeling his feet touch the ground, or the chill night air on his face. All he could feel was an emptiness inside him as vast as all eternity. All he could see was the torment in Anne's eyes as she faced him across the length of a revolver.

Vaguely he looked over the still landscape—the rolling hills in the distance, the flat silhouettes of cottonwood and pine, the scrubby fields and pastureland that stretched toward the woods. He thought absently about the winter shelters that were only half completed and the grain still stacked in the fields. He had made some headway in the last month, but there still was a lot that needed to be done. Strange, how little it seemed to matter now.

All his hopes and plans had turned to ashes in his hands. Josh had thought he had come here looking for his past, but maybe what he'd really been doing was running from it. And now it had caught up with him. The lies, the anger, the bitterness—it was a simple matter of reaping what he had sown.

He had come full circle. It had begun with a betrayal that led to his pulling a gun on the only father he had ever known, and had ended with a betrayal that had put Josh on the other end of that gun. His punishment would be to live with the look in Anne's eyes for the rest of his life.

There was nothing left for him here. The only thing he could do for Anne now was to get out of her life, and maybe in time she would forget and heal. He never would.

It was after midnight, and the bunkhouse was dark, filled with the snores and shuffling bed sounds of a dozen sleeping cowhands. Josh sat on the edge of his bunk and reached for his saddlebags, careful not to disturb Dakota in the bunk next to his.

And then he noticed that Dakota's bunk was empty.

At first the significance didn't register. His mind was too dull, his senses too numb, to make much sense of anything.

Absently he looked around at the other sleeping forms, thinking about the weeks he had spent here, the men he had gotten to know. There was nobody he wanted to say good-bye to, nobody who would be sorry to see him go—except, perhaps, Dakota.

Dakota.

He looked around again, swiftly. All the bunks were filled, except Dakota's. He hadn't assigned any night duty. He couldn't think of a single reason for anybody to leave the bunkhouse at this time of night . . . except one.

He whispered fiercely, "*Damn.*" He rose swiftly from the bunk and strode, half running, from the room.

Big Jim was worried. More than that, he was angry. Since that little visit from Coleman that morning he had been slowly seething, considering and rejecting a dozen schemes for revenge, and being forced, at last, to face the truth.

Coleman was right. Big Jim did look guilty. He had made no secret about how he felt about Miss Anne, or her oil wells, or the fancy-pants foreman she had brought in to take his place. And here he was, stuck out in the middle of an oil field with every opportunity and every reason to get even. It looked bad. Real bad. If Josh Coleman himself had set this up, he couldn't have done a better job.

Big Jim knew that since he had come to Three Hills he hadn't done much to be proud of. The men liked him because he didn't much give a damn what they did, but being liked wasn't part of a foreman's job. He had let Miss Anne's place go to hell. Since she had banished him to the oil fields, he hadn't done a blessed thing but lean back and collect wages, and that was his method of revenge. He had set himself up for something like this. He hadn't even thought about fighting back.

Over the years he had lost his wife, his family, and his ranch. And along with that had gone his will to fight. About the only thing he had left was his good name, and now that was on the line.

He knew Coleman was behind all this. Everybody knew it; the trouble was that nobody had taken the trouble to try to prove it. Well, by damn, Big Jim was going to prove it, even if it meant posting a twenty-four-hour guard around every blasted oil well on the place. Even if it meant Big Jim had to do the guarding himself.

At nightfall he left the line shack and walked the few hundred yards to the derrick site. He settled himself behind a bush where he could keep both derricks in sight and began to wait.

He hadn't lost his touch. His eyes were as clear as when they'd scanned the horizon for Yankee soldiers, his ears as sharp as when they'd listened for moccasin steps on the sand. And, shortly after midnight, his vigilance was rewarded.

A shadow moved close to the ground in direct line between the two derricks. The moonlight caught the gleam of a belt buckle. Energy began to pump through Big Jim's veins. He could taste the excitement of the chase in his mouth. His nerves were steady, his senses alert. The figure moved toward the nearest derrick, carefully laying out something on the ground.

Silently Big Jim slid his revolver from the holster and began to move closer. For the first time in many years, he felt like a man.

* * *

Dakota had a bad feeling about this job. It was too close to the old man's death, for one thing. Folks were pretty stirred up about that, and Dakota couldn't blame them. It wasn't that he felt remorse, exactly, but he hadn't planned on killing the old fool—just teaching him a lesson. Things had just gotten a little bit out of hand.

And for another thing, he had always been careful to do his work on Saturday nights, when all the hands were in town and nobody's presence was expected to be accounted for. It was too risky, leaving the bunkhouse like this—and with Big Jim and his crew sleeping in the shack less than shouting distance away.

But the most unsettling thing had been the ride with Coleman earlier that day. That was one man who didn't miss much, and now he was riled up. He damn sure wasn't going to let this one pass. Now was the time for a smart man to be lying low, not running unnecessary risks.

He had explained all this to the boss man, but he had only tucked five hundred dollars into Dakota's pocket and told him to do his job. Dakota was used to doing his job.

But what Coleman had said that afternoon had stayed with him. He was right. Dakota had known that for some time now, maybe even since he'd started this job; he just hadn't wanted to admit it. Times were changing, men were changing, and things just weren't as easy as they used to be. Dakota had been born out of his time, and time was catching up with him. He knew this would be his last job.

But for five hundred cash dollars it was worth taking one more risk. Coleman wouldn't be back at the bunkhouse that night—with a sweet little thing like Miss Anne waiting for him, why should he?—and Dakota had made sure nobody else had seen him leave. Tonight the last two wells would go up, and Dakota would be out of here. It wouldn't matter who remembered he wasn't in his bunk when the explosion hit, for Dakota would be far down the trail. Moving on was something of a special talent of his, and he hadn't been caught yet. He could make it work one more time. After that he'd start giving some real thought to settling down.

He had only unwound half the fuse when he heard a step behind him. A voice said quietly, "Hold it right there, mister."

Dakota turned.

He saw the glint of the pistol barrel, the surprise on Big Jim's face, heard the startled exclamation, "You!"

But Dakota's gun was already swinging from its holster, his finger squeezing the trigger, and Big Jim never had a chance. The big man fell backward in a thunder of gunfire, and Dakota had only the chance to think, *I knew it was a bad risk*, before all hell broke loose.

Josh saw Dakota's horse and knew his guess had been right. Josh left his own mount tied to a tree and made his way silently across the field, his gun in hand, keeping to cover and out of the moonlight. He came upon the scene an instant too late.

He saw Big Jim fall beneath Dakota's bullet, and almost simultaneously Josh fired. Dakota was in the shadows, illuminated only for a split second by the flare of his own pistol muzzle, and Josh could not tell whether he had made a hit or not. He left cover and raced a few steps closer. He thought he saw a movement, but it was too quick and vague for Josh to take aim, and then it didn't matter.

Dakota was nowhere in sight. The men at the line shack had been roused by the gunfire, and the sounds of their

shouts and running footsteps obscured all hints of whatever
direction Dakota might have taken. Quickly Josh started
back toward his own horse, hoping to pick up a trail, but he
had to stop and check on Big Jim.

Bit Jim lay where he had fallen, his eyes still wide with
shock, a neat, round puncture wound in the center of his
forehead. Blood from the exit wound had already soaked the
grass black.

Josh knelt and closed the big man's eyes, swallowing back a
wave of bitterness and remorse. "Damn it, old man," he
whispered huskily, "what the hell were you doing out here?"

But Josh thought he knew. If it hadn't been for Josh's
visit that morning, Big Jim wouldn't be out here keeping
watch. He had died trying to defend himself against a false
accusation, and Josh was responsible.

Josh straightened up, his face grim, his hand tightening
on the handle of his pistol. He turned, but it was too late.

Three men were upon him. Their guns were drawn, their
faces dark. They saw Big Jim, lying dead on the ground;
they saw the gun in Josh's hand.

One of them said, "You dirty bastard. I ought to shoot
you down where you stand."

Another man, breathing hard, eyes blazing: "Don't be a
fool, Johnson. We've got him now. We've damn well got
him. Shootin' is too easy for the likes of him."

Protest rose swiftly and angrily to Josh's throat, flared for
less than an instant, and died. Damn Dakota, who was at
this minute getting away, his escape covered by angry voices
and running feet. Their two shots had sounded like one; now
Big Jim was dead and the barrel of Josh's pistol was still
warm. Not a person in the county would believe his
story. . . not even Anne. Josh saw his fate march by in a

series of seconds and strangely felt no surprise. It almost seemed inevitable.

Josh's gun was jerked from his fingers, and a rough arm clamped around his throat, dragging him off. Josh put up very little fight at all.

Anne felt the echoes of disaster before she heard or saw anything. She was standing at the window, staring blankly out at the empty night landscape with the memory of Josh's face imbedded in her mind. Suddenly she was shaken by a shudder so intense that she had to grip her arms to contain it; it was as though an icy wind had blown right through her soul. Grief-deadened nerve endings flared to life, her eyes grew sharp, her muscles tensed as though for flight.

And that was why, a few seconds later, when the rider came flying across the yard, his hat bouncing against his shoulders and his horse skidding into the turn, she didn't hesitate. There was no curiosity, no surprise, no idle puzzlement. She *knew*. She picked up her skirts and ran from the room.

Lights were on in the bunkhouse by the time she arrived, gasping and stumbling. Men were spilling out of the door, pulling on hats and coats and fastening gun belts. Voices were shouting, and a riotous, disorganized tension clogged the air.

Anne grabbed the first arm she could. "What happened?" she demanded. "What's going on?"

The cowhand turned to her distractedly, his lips tight and his eyes churning. "Big Jim's been shot. Murdered. And they've got the man that did it. They're holding him out at the north line shack."

He started to pull away, but Anne's fingers dug into his

arm. "Who?" She barely had the breath to form the word. The coldness was back in her veins again.

"Your foreman." He spat out the word as though it were poison. "Coleman."

For a moment the night sounds and night sights faded away; the angry voices, the furious activity, the rampaging excitement of a dozen roused men receded to the impact of a muffled heartbeat and she thought, No. Not this, Josh, it's too much. . . .

And then with a jolt that snatched her breath away and galvanized strength into an explosive rush, reality locked into place again. Somebody brushed past her, and she grabbed him. "Saddle my horse," she ordered.

The man looked at her impatiently, so charged with energy that he barely seemed to recognize her. "Woman, we've got a murderer out there! I ain't got time—"

"Saddle my horse, goddamn you!" Her eyes were burning and her voice was a furious shout, and after a moment the man went to do as he was told.

She remembered nothing about the flight across the darkened countryside. She had no coat and the wind cut through the thin material of her dress, her skirts were hitched up to her knees and billowing over the back of the saddle, the reins cut into her ungloved hands, and her hair was tugged loose from its pins, but she felt none of it. The first and only thing she felt was a choking sense of horror as she came upon the scene of the crime.

She jerked her horse to a stop that caused his back legs to skid, and slid out of the saddle. A crowd had already gathered, and the peaceful night landscape was torn by the eerie orange shadows of waving torches and the sounds of gathering violence. The men who had ridden up with Anne leapt from their saddles and rushed toward the crowd, shouldering their way through, shouting, "Where the hell is he?"

"Let me get a look at the son of a bitch!"

"I knew it from the minute I laid eyes on him—hanging's too good for him!"

But Anne did not have to hear the words or look at the faces to know that what was happening here was hovering on the brink of being out of control. There were too many men, too much anger, and madness crackled in the air. She had for a moment a weird sense of being out of time and place—standing at the edge of the circle while cavemen threw stones at an intruder, watching the mob push a witch toward the flames, listening to the slide and crack of the guillotine against a nobleman's neck. It was primitive, barbarous, and timeless. Watching, Anne felt the grip of a sick paralysis creep over her; for what seemed like an endless moment she couldn't even move.

Then a gulp of cold air rushed into her lungs; she strode forward, pushing through the sea of shoulders and chests and raging voices. Someone shoved her sharply, and she struck out with her fist; the man she had struck didn't even notice. Someone else tried to pull her back, shouting at her; she neither heard the words nor heeded the hands. And then she saw Josh.

They had tied him to a tree at the edge of the mud hole that surrounded the derrick. His hands were bound behind him, his feet lashed together, and his body sagged against the rope around his chest. One side of his face was a swollen mass of purplish-red bruises, his mouth was cut and bleeding, and a dark stain matted his hair. Anne's hand went to her throat and all she could think was, Josh . . . no . . .

Then, as she watched, someone lunged forward and kicked him hard in the ribs. She saw his face contort, heard the sickening rush of breath leaving his lungs, and she let out a low roar of primal rage, rushing toward him. "Are you mad?" she screamed. "Stop it!"

The man who had kicked Josh grabbed her arm; she twisted away. "Has every one of you lost your bloody minds?" She whirled on the crowd. "Go home, all of you! Get away from here, I say!"

The clamor died, but it gave way to something even uglier. The glow of the torches, caught by the wind, cast ragged, weaving shadows over the crowd, painting lines of mutiny on their faces and the gleam of hatred in their eyes. She knew in that moment that nothing was beyond them. Something wild and savage was singing through the air and catching in their blood, and there was nothing she could do.

Someone stepped forward—a tall, somber-faced man whose name she could not remember. He said quietly, "Maybe you're the one that should go home, Miss Anne. This is no business for a woman."

Someone else spoke up furiously, "We caught him red-handed! Standing over Big Jim with the gun still smoking in his hand!"

"Then take him into town!" Anne cried. "Get the sheriff! What are you all standing around for?"

"Oh, the sheriff can have him," the somber-faced man said grimly. "When we're done with him."

Another voice spat bitterly, "If there's anything left."

From the edge of the crowd Chance stepped forward, tossing something at her. "And here's something else for you, ma'am!" A length of fuse struck her skirt, and Anne made no effort to catch it. "He was laying this between the derricks when Big Jim must've caught him. There's your proof, Miss Anne—here's your saboteur.''

Anne stared at him. She was breathing very hard. ''Chance,'' she commanded firmly. ''I want you to ride into town right now and get the sheriff out here. Right now!''

Chance didn't move. ''We're camped less than five hundred yards from here,'' he said. ''It could be me or any one of my men who caught him out here tonight. It could be one of us lying under that blanket.''

Anne saw, only a short distance away, a shadowed form hastily covered by a horse blanket. A boot and one hand were visible. For a moment she swayed on her feet. *God*, she thought, *don't let me faint now. Not now. . . .*

She caught her breath; she turned back to the crowd. She raised her voice, high and clear. ''Every one of you, get back to the bunkhouse. You've got no business here. I'll take care of this—''

A man at the front of the crowd spoke up sharply. ''Meaning no disrespect, ma'am, but we've seen how you take care of things. You've been *taking care* of that no-good saddle tramp since he rode up, and maybe Big Jim would be alive today if you hadn't took such damn good care of things!''

A murmur swelled and seemed to grow, and the somber-faced man closed his hand around her elbow. ''Get on out of here, Miss Anne. There ain't a damn thing you can do here. We all know how you think about Coleman, but Big Jim was one of us and he ain't gonna get away with murder. Now get on back before you get hurt.''

Anne looked around the crowd wildly. She was afraid—for herself, for Josh, for the madness that swelled through the night and turned a group of ordinary men into a mob eager for the taste of blood. She pulled away from the hand that gripped her arm; she took a halting, frantic step toward Josh.

His head was against the tree trunk, blood dripped from his mouth, and the wavering orange light magnified the bruises on his face into hideous deformities. His eyes were closed. She whispered, "Josh . . ." but the sound was choked in her throat. He did not look at her.

She whirled on the crowd. "I'm going for the sheriff," she said low. Her voice was shaking. "If there's a man among you, you'll ride with me."

No one moved. The hatred that radiated from them was fierce and savage and barely contained.

"You will not take justice into your own hands!" she shouted at them. "We're not animals! Do you hear me? You can't do this thing!"

There was nothing in the eyes that looked back at her, nothing but the gleam of torchlight and the surging impatience of defiance. There was nothing she could do. She couldn't reason with them or control them; it had all gotten out of hand. . . .

With a sudden, swift, strangulated breath she pushed through the crowd. Someone grabbed her arm, and someone else said, "Let her go. She can't do nothing, anyway." Then she was running, lifting her skirts and swinging into the saddle. Even as the horse reared and took off at a furious gallop across the night, she was afraid it was too late.

Chapter Twenty-three

Stephen Brady had worked quite late at the bank, then spent several hours at the saloon making certain he was seen and recognized. These days, Stephen made certain his whereabouts at any given time could be attested to by several unimpeachable witnesses. Not, of course, that he ever expected to need the alibis, but it never hurt to be prepared. And he was too close now to let outside chances stand in his way.

He let himself into his small ranch house and paused to light the lamp on the table by the door. The sound of a hammer being drawn back clicked softly in the dimly lit room, and he stood still.

"Hello, Eddie," said George Greenley.

Stephen Brady turned. His face registered no surprise, no anger. His lips curved into the mildest of welcoming smiles. "Well, George, to what do I owe this unexpected pleasure?"

George Greenley was sitting comfortably in an overstuffed chair beside the fireplace. He held the Colt in a relaxed, almost casual fashion, but there was no mistaking his aim.

George smiled. "Here's the thing, Eddie. That derringer of yours is a sweet little gun, and probably real good for wounding rats and cockroaches. You'll likely get off the first shot, and you might even hit me. But at this distance a Colt .45 will put a hole in you that'll blow you to kingdom come, and all I'll have is a tear in my jacket. So, because I'm right partial to this jacket and I really don't want to clean up the mess you're gonna leave on the floor, why don't you just hand over the derringer?"

Stephen slowly opened the palm that concealed the derringer, his smile never wavering. George crossed the room, took the gun from him, and tucked it into his coat pocket. Stephen crossed his arms casually and leaned back against the door. "So, is that all you wanted?"

George gestured with his gun toward the nearest chair. "Have a seat, Eddie," he invited pleasantly. "We've got us a little talking to do."

Anne knew she wasn't going to make it. Her lungs were burning, her side was aching, and perspiration ran down her face in rivulets that blurred her vision. Even in daylight the rocky road to town was over an hour's ride, and by the time she returned with the sheriff, dawn would be near and who knew what the angry mob would have done? It was a foolish idea, a desperate, insane chance, but what more could she have done? What choice did she have?

Oh, Josh, she thought, fiercely, hopelessly. Don't let it end like this. Please don't let it end. . . .

Her horse was lathered and wheezing, but she drove him mercilessly, regardless of the hazards of the dark, uneven road. Even if she made it to town, she would have to take time to change horses. . . .

Without warning her mount slipped on a loose stone and went down. Only Anne's excellent horsemanship—and her desperate determination that nothing could stop her now—prevented her from taking a fall herself. But when her horse staggered to its front legs again, he was limping badly, and Anne felt the panic of despair flooding her. She had to have help. She had to have a fresh horse, and she had to send help back to Josh. And she had to do it quickly, quickly—

There was only one house between here and town. She started toward it unerringly, leading her crippled horse.

"So," Stephen said, leaning back in the chair. "What's this all about?"

George Greenley stood over him, resting his hip on the table by the door, the gun still held in precise position. "Just a little follow-up on this morning's visit. You see, I don't think you quite got my point. In fact, I think you might even be considering getting rid of me."

Stephen shrugged. "It crossed my mind. But I don't think it'll really be necessary. After tonight, George, we'll both have what we want. The oil wells will be down, Anne will be out of money—neither one of us will have any room for complaint. Why break up a partnership that's going so well?"

"Because it's not going as well as you think," George returned calmly. "Because Josh Coleman isn't going to stand trial for any of this. Anne Edgecomb isn't going to marry you. Because, Eddie, old friend, you are losing your touch."

Stephen was unimpressed. "Well, it seems what we have here is just a simple difference of opinion. It doesn't really matter who stands trial, as long as it's not me or you—but I happen to think it will be Coleman. That alibi Anne gave the sheriff the other day won't hold water; I know her and she was lying. After tonight's work I don't think she'll be inclined to lie for that smooth-talking saddle tramp anymore.

"As for Three Hills—well, I admit marriage was my first choice, and it's still not entirely out of the question. Women are odd creatures—betrayed by one man, they invariably turn to another for comfort, and I intend to make myself very available. But"—he shrugged—"I've never been one to rest my fate in the hands of a fickle woman, and it doesn't really matter in the long run where Lady Hartley chooses to bestow her affections. The mortgage on Three Hills comes due in another eight weeks, and one way or another I'll be living in the ranch house by the end of the year."

Greenley nodded. "Sounds good. Real logical. But you left out one thing. Me."

"I can't think of a single reason why you'd want to stand in the way, George. Not with all you've got to lose."

"You know, Eddie," Greenley said thoughtfully, "time was when 'kill or be killed' was the only way to survive in this country. When a man would shoot another man as quick as he'd shoot a snake, because this was a growing land, a hard land, there wasn't room for sidewinding outlaws who got in the way of the good things we were trying to do here.

"But it's not like that anymore. If it was, I'd be pulling the trigger right now, instead of sitting here talking to you. I told you this morning I wasn't going to be part of murder. That's why I sent one of my men on ahead to bring the sheriff back here. He can't be more than half an hour behind me. I figure you've got just about that long to pack your duds and get out of town.''

Stephen smiled. ''Remember what I was telling you about human nature? You're a selfish man, George. You bring the law into this and it's all going to come down on you. You don't want to do that.''

''That's right, I don't. That's why I'm giving you a chance to get out. It would be real embarrassing for me if the folks around here find out what I've done—making an outlaw head of the bank, conspiring with him to put a widow woman out of business, staying quiet while he hired a gunman to destroy her property and kill a man. But I've thought about it a lot, Eddie, and when it all gets down to dirt, I decided I'd rather be embarrassed than dead.''

Stephen smiled. ''You might end up being both. Things usually have a way of working out for me.''

George looked at the clock over the mantel. ''Twenty minutes, Eddie.''

''You're bluffing.''

George settled more of his weight against the table, resting his gun hand on his forearm. ''Well, I guess we'll just see, won't we?''

Anne dropped the reins of her horse and ran, stumbling, the last few dozen yards to Stephen's gate. Every gasp for breath was a painful sob, and sparks of dizziness flashed before her eyes. Her stays squeezed against the beat of her heart, and with every step she was certain she couldn't take another. But she had seen a horse, riderless and saddled, lazily cropping grass by the side of Stephen's drive, and she didn't wonder at the providence that had placed it there, she didn't question why or how, she simply ran toward it. And all the while some detached and fuzzy part of her brain was convinced that this was just another part of the nightmare, a trick to taunt and tease her, and that as soon as she reached the horse, it would disappear.

She stumbled over a shadowed form in the drive and almost fell. The gasp that was torn from her as she stared down at the body at her feet would have been a scream, but the sound never made it past her throat.

Dakota's face was white and shiny, his hand pressed limply to a spreading stain on his coat. As Anne dropped to her knees beside him, his dull, glassy eyes gradually seemed to focus.

"Ma'am . . ." he whispered, and tried to smile. "Didn't expect—to see you here."

"Dear . . . God." Her struggle for breath ceased; she barely felt the pounding of her heart anymore. No more, she thought desperately. Please, God, no more. . . .

She cast a frantic glance toward the house, where a single yellow glow from the window testified that Stephen was at home and awake. She tried to raise her voice to call out but couldn't. "We've got to get you in the house," she said quickly. Her skirts, where she knelt on the ground, were already wet with his blood. "Stephen—will help. Please— you'll be fine, I'll get—"

"No." He grasped weakly for her hand as she started to get up. His grip was slippery and left red streaks on her fingers. "I thought I could make it, but I can't. In my line of work I guess you don't expect to live forever."

"No. You're bleeding. . . ." Panic rose in a hot flood to her throat, and Anne searched Dakota's pockets for a bandanna, a handkerchief, anything to stanch the flow of blood. She found a balled-up bandanna, but it was already soaked, and when she pulled it out, the edges fell back to reveal a wad of money wrapped inside.

Dakota smiled weakly. "Might as well keep it. Don't have much use for it now, and I guess you deserve—" He broke off with a sharp, strangled sound in his throat, and then his eyes sharpened. He plucked at her hand. "I didn't plan—to kill him. He never done nothing to me. Tell them that—will you?"

Anne's head was spinning, his words incoherent. She tried to press her hands against the wound, but there was so much blood.... "Who?" she whispered. "Who did you kill?"

"Big Jim. He shouldn't've been there. Didn't plan on it. And Coleman ... must've followed me. Didn't—plan on that, either." A grimace crossed his face that might have been another attempt to smile. "Should've known better."

The strength left Anne's arms; a breeze chilled the perspiration on her face. She could hear her own breathing now, a high, shallow whistling sound in her ears. Her lips barely formed the word. "You?"

"Tell him—" His face contorted once more with pain, and Anne moved quickly.

"Hush. It doesn't matter now. Let me get help—"

"Tell Coleman," Dakota insisted, and now his grip on her hand was fierce, strong, and terrifyingly cold. "It wasn't nothing personal. I was just doing my job."

And then his grip relaxed; his head sagged. He was dead.

Anne moved slowly away, every muscle straining with the effort as though moving under water. She stared down at the empty body, and the back of her hand went to her face to stifle a scream that wouldn't come. The wad of bills she was still gripping in her hand left a bloody smear across her cheek.

And then, with a low, shuddering sound that was less than a moan, she picked up her skirts and ran toward the house.

Stephen chuckled, standing gracefully. "You must think I'm a fool. You couldn't make up a story convincing enough to get the sheriff out of bed to arrest the local banker at this hour of the morning. And you're certainly not going to shoot me. You just got finished saying you don't want to be a part of murder. How long are we going to play this game, George? It's late."

"We'll play as long as you're feeling lucky. Because if you make one more move away from that chair, I am gonna shoot you, and it'll be self-defense. That would solve all our problems, wouldn't it, Eddie?"

It all happened in a rush. The door flew open; and Anne burst in, blood on her hand and her skirts, and mingling with the tears that streaked her face. She cried, "Stephen!" Greenley whirled toward the door; and Stephen lunged at Greenley. Greenley fell back against the wall, and the gun was in Stephen's hand.

Anne took in the scene wildly, only another part of the nightmare with a cruel thread of reason running through it. Greenley was here, his cohort was dead at the gate, and now he was preparing to kill Stephen. It happened in an instant; she understood it in a fraction of the time. Then Stephen, holding the pistol firmly on Greenley, reached into George's pocket and removed the derringer, backing a few steps away.

Stephen smiled. "I told you, didn't I, George, that things usually work out my way? Lady Luck."

Anne sobbed and took a stumbling step toward Stephen. "Stephen, thank God—"

Greenley said sharply, "Miss Anne, stay away from him!"

Stephen didn't take his eyes off Greenley. There was an odd, cold smile on his face that distantly penetrated Anne's consciousness—something strange and unfamiliar. But none of it mattered, not Greenley, not the dead man outside, not Stephen's near escape, because there was Josh, and already it might be too late.

"Stephen, you've got to come—the ranch . . . you must help me! Big Jim has been killed—"

His eyes cut toward her sharply and then calmed. "It's all right, Anne." He extended his hand to her, keeping the gun pointed firmly at Greenley. "Come over here to me."

"No, you don't understand!" Hysteria was rising and falling in waves, and nothing about this bizarre scene made sense: Stephen's quiet, calm face; Greenley's tense posture behind her; the gun; the dead man at the gate. But it didn't matter; none of it mattered.

She cried, "I've got to get the sheriff! The men—they're crazy, they've got Josh and they think he did it, but he didn't! The man who killed Big Jim is outside—he's dead, Stephen, and he told me . . . Stephen, you've got to help!"

She saw Stephen's face go tight, and a muscle clenched near his jaw. Greenley said softly, "Well, now, maybe things aren't going your way, after all. A dead body on your doorstep might not be so easy to cover up."

But Stephen answered smoothly, "You're such a pessimist, George. Dead bodies, however inconvenient they may be, do have a certain advantage—they hardly ever talk."

"You're not going to get away with this, Eddie."

Anne was halfway to Stephen, her hand outstretched in a plea, her head roaring and her heart pounding and a dozen things racing through her mind. It might have been the sound of George Greenley's voice so calmly addressing Stephen by a name Anne did not know; or the feel of the bloody wad of bills clenched in her fist and the memory of Dakota's dying words; or it might have been that for just the moment, she looked at Stephen's face and saw a killer there.

She let her hand fall and stared at Stephen.

George Greenley said quietly, "Maybe I should introduce you, Miss Anne. This is Eddie Baker. He used to make his living in the mine camps and settlements of the territories, selling phony stocks, playing crooked cards, setting up bank runs and land panics. One of the best in the business, too, until about ten years ago, when he killed a man for the papers in his pocket and came here to play another kind of game."

Anne said nothing. Distantly, almost as an afterthought whose significance was all but lost, the irony occurred to her. Josh, whose secret past had so tormented her; Stephen, whose dark and murderous secrets she had never even suspected. Stephen, whom she had trusted. And Josh, who would pay for Stephen's crimes.

Why wasn't she angry? Why didn't she feel betrayed, devastated, shocked? She looked at Stephen, and she felt nothing at all—not even surprise. She should have felt something, and yet . . . the answer occurred to her slowly, with simple inevitability. She had never felt anything for Stephen. Nothing he could do or say would ever matter to her. The only thing that mattered was that she was trapped here with him, while the life of the man she loved was in danger and seconds were ticking by—

Stephen glanced briefly at Anne. His eyes were cool, faintly sardonic. "I'm sorry about you, Anne. I really liked you; we would've made quite a team." He shrugged. "But there are other towns, other women. I've started over before. And I wouldn't worry too much about that cowboy of yours. You're better off without him."

He turned back to Greenley. "Well, now, George, I'll have to hand it to you. Looks like you've won this hand." He gave a small, deprecating lift of the pistol but never lost his target. "My only problem now is what to do with the two of you. I think I'll take you up on your advice, maybe try my luck back East. But it's a lot harder for a man to disappear than it used to be, especially when there are two people who know the story."

Anne thought simply, clearly, No. In her mind was a picture of Josh, his face bleeding, his hands bound, at the mercy of an angry mob. Before her eyes stood Stephen, a gun in his hand. And she knew with a plain and certain determination that he was not going to kill her. Not now, not when Josh needed her, not after she had come this far. She was not going to let him do this thing. She refused to let this happen—

With a low cry of rage Anne threw back her hand and lunged at Stephen. The bloodstained bills she had been clutching scattered through the air, and Stephen, startled for a moment, stumbled backward. George Greenley flung himself at Stephen, and the gun exploded.

Faintly Anne heard the pounding of hooves on the dirt outside, but her eyes were fixed on the two men before her, locked in a death struggle. Greenley's powerful hands were locked around Stephen's wrist, trying to wrest the pistol from him; Greenley lost his grip. Stephen levered the gun into position.

Anne turned wildly toward the door, and Sheriff Hawkins burst in, his gun drawn, followed closely by two deputies.

"All right, gentlemen. What's going on here?"

Chapter Twenty-four

"We've waited long enough. Let's get it done."

"She said she was bringing back the sheriff—"

"The hell with the sheriff! He don't care nothing about us. If he did, he'd'a caught this bastard before now!"

"You know damn well what's gonna happen once the sheriff gets into this! Who do you think elected him, anyway? Folks with money, that's who, and ain't nobody got no more money than Lady Anne Hartley!"

"Are we gonna let Big Jim's murderer go loose on account of some rich woman's itchy pants? You know damn well she'll buy off every—"

"Big Jim weren't nothing but a poor old cowpoke like us. How much do you think that's gonna weigh with the rich ranchers around here that probably *paid* this son of a bitch to kill him?"

The voices rushed in and out like a distant roar, a wave of violence washing over Josh and then receding. He struggled to focus, but strangely, the words had little meaning for him.

One of his eyes was swollen shut, and the vision in the other was badly blurred from blood and sweat that he couldn't wipe away. At least two ribs were broken, and every breath he took felt like the dull edge of a knife slicing at his lungs. His head was fuzzy, swathed in a thundercloud of dull, swelling pain; sometimes the pain seemed the focus of all he knew, sometimes he hardly noticed it at all. He knew he was about to die. That fact had seemed inevitable from the beginning and concerned him very little now. What mattered was that Anne would be alone and he wouldn't be able to do anything to help her. She didn't even know what she was up against.

Josh was jerked to his feet. A red haze of pain flared from a bruised thighbone upward to his head and burst there, leaving him gasping and momentarily weak. When the night swam into focus again, a familiar face was before him, a hand hard on his bound arm, a harsh voice commanding, "Move, damn it! You walk or we'll tie a rope around you and drag you."

Josh concentrated on the face. "Shep," he managed at last. He struggled to form the words through swollen lips. "Listen to me."

His voice was raspy, punctuated by painful drags of air, but there was an intensity to his tone that must have caught Shep's curiosity. He paused, just for a moment.

"You're going to kill me," Josh said. "I know that. There's nothing I can do about it. I've got no cause to lie to you. But listen to me."

His voice went tight with the desperate effort to make the other man hear, and even his muscles, throbbing as they were, strained to add emphasis to his words. "The man who shot Big Jim—the man who's been terrorizing this ranch— got away. He was paid by somebody to do what he did. And killing me is not going to end it. Whoever paid him to do this is still going to be here, and more people are going to be killed. It's not going to stop. You can't—''

Blood exploded behind his eyes with the force of a fist; his head snapped back. A surge of fierce intensity was his only hold on consciousness, and he cried, "Damm it, Shep—all of you! This ranch is your responsibility now! Somebody's out to ruin it, and you've got to fight for the brand! You can't—''

"Shut up, you lying son of a bitch!"

"It was Dakota!" Josh shouted at them. "Look around—where is he? Find the man that paid him—''

"I said *shut up*, goddamm it!"

Another explosion in his head, and the last thing Josh thought as consciousness reeled and faded away was, *Anne, I'm sorry, I tried. . . . Dammit, I tried. . . .*

The first gray fingers of dawn were pushing away at the horizon when Josh, jolted and shoved, struggled his way back to consciousness. Not really dawn, he noticed absently, no genuine hint of light in the sky, just a flat, gray darkness that somehow seemed more dull, more empty and lifeless, than the blackest midnight. It looked as though the sun would never rise again.

He turned his head and saw the clear silhouette of a noose hanging from the support beams of the nearby derrick. He thought, So that's the way it's going to be, then.

The unfairness of it all struck him. Not that he was about to hang for another man's crimes, nor that he was only twenty-two years old and was not ready to die. But that he was going to die without ever seeing Anne again, without having a chance to tell her. . . .

He felt the ropes being cut from his feet. Rough hands

half dragged, half carried him to his horse and flung him
into the saddle. He hardly saw the movements or heard the
harsh clamor of hate-thickened voices. But his mind was
very clear, and that seemed only right. A man shouldn't die
without knowing what he was leaving behind.

By the time Jed Fielding was twenty-two, he had fought
to free a nation, carved paths through the wilderness, and
begun to build a legacy that would endure for generations.
The lives of all who came after were changed because of
him.

When Jake Fielding was twenty-two, he had been running
the biggest outfit in Texas, pushing huge herds up the
Chisholm Trail to supply the hungry markets of the north,
developing new and hardier strains of cattle whose descen-
dants still populated the fields and pastures of this part of
Texas. What remained of Three Hills today was due to Jake
Fielding.

Neither Jake nor Josh were great men, nor perfect men.
They had done what they had to do to tame a hard
land, and they had left something of themselves behind
for those who came after. No one could ask much more
than that.

But Josh had nothing to leave behind. He had deserted his
family in pain and bitterness; he had crossed two states to
lay claim to something that had never belonged to him and
had left a trail of blood and lies to mark his passing. Josh
Fielding, at age twenty-two, had nothing to show for his life
except that once he had loved a woman and taught her to
hate him.

They pulled his horse over to the derrick, its hooves
sucking in the mud, its ears pricking back with the unfamiliar treatment. Josh's heart beat slow and steady, and he sat

up tall in the saddle. The only thing left for him to do was die, and that, at least, he would do well.

"Come on, boys, let's get this over with. We wasted enough time on this piece of scum."

Someone climbed up on the scaffolding and slipped the noose over his head. The rough hemp bit into his throat as the knot was tightened.

The horizon was just beginning to streak with yellow now. Josh's last sight would be of the sun coming up over Three Hills. He filled his eyes with it.

"Stop fooling with that goddamn rope, Johnson! Let's get it done."

The rope dug sharply into his windpipe, crushing off breath. It would be quick, then. That was good.

Josh tried to pray. His mother would have wanted him to pray. Strangely, for all his sins, he could not form a single prayer.

"Shit! Somebody's coming! Get down from there, Johnson— hit that horse!"

"You do and you're a dead man."

George Greenley pushed his horse through the mob, his rifle cocked and pointed, his face as hard as stone. He had brought a deputy with him, and for a moment murmurings ceased; the angry vigilantism of the mob wavered on the edge of uncertainty.

Anne slid out of the saddle, her feet sinking deep into the sucking gumbo. She stumbled and almost fell, but she kept her eyes on Josh. Josh, above the swaying heads of the crowd, his hands bound behind him and his eyes straight ahead, a noose around his neck. She began to struggle through the mob, her skirts dragging with every step, and it seemed to take a lifetime to reach him. . . . Her lifetime and Josh's lifetime.

Then somebody shouted, "This ain't no business of yours, Greenley! Get the hell out of here. We take care of our own."

"Since when do you take up for a no-good murdering saddle tramp, Greenley? We don't need his kind around here, and by God, this is one night we're gonna do something about it!"

The crowd surged forward, and Greenley lifted his rifle, keeping his horse between Josh and the crowd. The deputy moved around and pulled the noose over Josh's head, then cut the ropes that bound his wrists.

Greenley said, "The sheriff wants you to know he would've been here himself, but he was kinda busy with the man that really killed Big Jim."

"What the hell are you talking about? We got the man that killed him, and you're turning him loose!"

Somebody drew a pistol, and Greenley swung his rifle sharply toward the sound. The deputy's pistol left its holster, and for a moment the tension that crackled through the air was sharp enough to taste.

Then, slowly, George Greenley lowered his rifle. As he swept the crowd his eyes were filled with contempt and laced with sorrow. "You fools," he said quietly. "Not one of you is even worth shooting."

Anne made her way to the edge of the crowd, and then she could go no further. Josh stood beside his horse, absently rubbing his wrists. His clothes were torn, his face battered, and there was an angry red ring on his throat. Anne's heart stopped, twisted, and wanted to cry out to him. But she couldn't move.

George Greenley's voice was weary, yet it rang clearly in the dawn stillness. "Look at you," he said. "Look at every one of you. You take care of your own, all right. You're so busy taking care of your own that you let the real killer get away while you hang an innocent man. And you hang him for nothing more than being a stranger that got on your bad side by trying to put this ranch back on its feet.

"Well, let me tell you something, boys. This stranger has got more right to be here than any one of you. His name's Josh Fielding, and his grandfather built this ranch. But I don't reckon that means much to you. Too many things don't mean much anymore."

There were some uneasy shufflings and murmurings among the crowd. Greenley went on quietly. "But I tell you one thing. Too many men have spilled too much blood on this land trying to civilize it for me to sit by and watch something like this happen without feeling sick to my gut. This ain't the way, boys. And I'm just as guilty as any one of you."

Greenley's face was sad, his eyes bleak. "It's got to stop sometime," he said quietly. "And as far as I'm concerned, the time is now. I used to be proud of being a rancher, a Greenley, and a Texan. But I tell you what, boys . . ." His eyes swept the crowd one more time, soberly. "Right now I'm not proud of much at all."

He turned his horse and walked it over to Josh. The eyes of the two men met, but Greenley said nothing. After a moment he joined the deputy, and the two of them moved slowly away.

The crowd began to disperse. Their gaits were shuffling and uncomfortable, their faces ashamed. Nobody spoke.

Torches were extinguished in the mud, horses were mounted. Josh watched each of them pass, but no one would look
at him.

And then only Anne was left.

She was standing only a few feet away from him, her
dress splattered with mud, her hair limp and tangled around
her shoulders, her face white and strained and streaked with
the grime of the night. He thought, Oh, Anne...and
though the single thought was torn from the core of him,
there was nothing more. Nothing he could say or do.
Nothing he could offer her to give back what he had taken
from her.

She started toward him, haltingly. He noticed that the
stains on her face and her dress were partially dried blood.
He said hoarsely, "Are you all right?"

Something clenched in Anne's chest at the sound of his
voice. She whispered, "Yes." Then, more strongly,
"Dakota...is dead. It was...was Stephen who paid
him."

Josh nodded slowly. "I should have known."

None of this was what she wanted to say. None of it had
any relevance to them; none of it mattered. Nothing mattered
except Josh, whose face was bruised and torn, whose wrists
were bleeding, whose eyes were tired and old. Josh, who
was alive and here, yet so far away. Terrifyingly far away.

She took another step toward him. "The sheriff...has
him in custody. It's over now, Josh."

Anne's heart was beating, fast and loud. There were so
many things she wanted to say to him, to explain, yet the
words locked in her throat and died there. There was
nothing she could say that would take back the horror of that

night, nothing she could do that would take away the ache from inside her or fill the emptiness in his eyes.

She half lifted a hand, as though to touch his swollen, discolored face, then let it fall. She had done this. She had turned her back when he had asked her to believe in him. Her faith had been shallow and her will weak, and she had been unable to give the one thing he had asked of her. She could not ask him to forgive her for that. She could not even forgive herself.

She tried to force strength into her voice. "Come . . . back to the house. Let me—"

He shook his head slowly. He did not have to say anything. She saw the answer in his eyes.

"No. I'm all right. I've caused you enough trouble. I guess . . ." The next words were the hardest he had ever had to say. "I'd better be moving on."

It was over. Josh waited for the relief, the lightness, the simple joy of being alive. He looked at Anne, and all he felt was a bleakness, a dull, empty yearning. It wasn't over. It would never be over.

He wanted to reach for her but he couldn't. Too much guilt, too much pain, too many lies lay between them. He couldn't erase the past. He could only somehow try to find a way to live with it.

Anne felt the life drain out of her. Her voice was very small. "Where . . . will you go?"

His eyes moved slowly over the horizon, where pink streaks of dawn were lacing their way across the east, and then back toward the west, where the sky was still gray with the remnants of night. Where would he go? Two thousand miles away was a family he had never known, a past better forgotten. Here in Texas was a home that no longer welcomed him and a woman he had almost destroyed.

"I don't know," he said slowly. "There's a lot of country I've never seen. I guess maybe someplace there might be room for a cowboy who doesn't know how to be anything else."

His eyes wandered once again over the sprawling fields and dimly silhouetted hills that lay beyond. His eyes were vague with sorrow. "It's funny. I came here to find out the truth, and I ended up tripping over my own lies. I thought something had been stolen from me—a family legacy, a pride in who I was, something. I thought I could make up for that somehow, by making the ranch what it used to be, and the Fielding name what it used to be . . . but it hardly even matters anymore. I guess the only thing that matters is what a man can make of himself, and it's time I found out what that is for me."

He looked at her solemnly. "I think maybe you were right—about what you said the other night. Times are changing, and there's no point in looking back. What you're trying to do here is right, Anne. Don't you let anybody tell you different."

The flood of tightness that closed around Anne's throat almost subdued her breath. *Don't* . . . she wanted to cry. *Don't do this thing.* . . . But she could say nothing. She only nodded.

Josh looked at her, aching and empty. He wished things could be different. He wished he could be different. He wished he could take the past few weeks and with a single sweep of his hand wipe away all the hurt and struggle and deception and be worthy of loving her. But he couldn't.

"I can't change, Anne," he said simply. "And I don't belong here. I never did."

Anne watched him reach for the reins of his horse. Her heart was breaking, the emptiness swelling and consuming her and leaving nothing but helplessness in its wake. He was right. There was nothing left for him here, nothing left for the two of them. Nothing but unspoken promises and shattered dreams and an ocean of hurt and betrayal. It was better this way. Neither of them would ever change, and there was nothing they could do now.

He hesitated and turned back. For a moment hope flickered, then died. He looked over her shoulder. "There's still a lot that needs to be done before winter." His voice was strained, as though the words were difficult. "The herd needs to be culled, and the calves brought down from the woods. . . . You'll need the market price they bring, come spring. The best thing to do is find a good foreman to get you through the winter."

Anne's chin went up, her shoulders squared. So, then. That was it. She said, "I don't need one. I know what needs to be done now. I can take care of it myself."

For a moment it seemed he almost smiled. "Yeah," he said softly. "I guess you can."

Then he turned and grasped the pommel. Pain twisted in him as he mounted, but it was more than the pain of bruises and broken ribs. He tightened his muscles against it and didn't look back.

Anne stood there, her head held high, her arms stiff at her sides, and watched him guide his horse slowly away. It was better this way. He never should have come here, and she never should have let him stay. There had been nothing but tragedy and mistakes between them from the beginning, and today he had almost died. The only thing left to do was to start over and try to forget.

She would never forget, and there was nothing worth starting over for. But perhaps the only true test of courage was the courage it took to admit defeat.

Anne did not have that kind of courage.

A burst of anger, defiance, and determination surged up within her, and she whirled, her eyes glittering, her color surging. "Go ahead!" she shouted at him. "Turn your back, ride away!" She took a few running steps and then stopped, her fists clenched against her sides, her chest heaving. "But it's not going to do you a scrap of good, Joshua Coleman Fielding! You're not going to be rid of me that easily."

Josh stopped. He sat as though frozen, his shoulders square, his arms still, his back to her. Anne took another step toward him, and slowly he turned his horse.

Anne could feel her blood soaring, her heart expanding with every beat, but inside her was a calm, a low and peaceful certainty that spread through her like liquid light. And she stood still, watching him. Everything within her gentled and spread toward him as she met his eyes. "I'll be in the air you breathe and the sun on your face and the ache you feel in the dark when you're all alone," she said softly. He did not move, and she held his eyes. "I'll be the name you cry out in the middle of the night when nobody answers. I'll be the fever in your blood, the hunger you can't fill. I'll haunt you, Joshua Coleman Fielding, every minute of every day for the rest of your life. You'll never be rid of me."

The words hung between them like a captured echo suspended on the morning air. Nothing stirred, nor even breathed, and it seemed even the sun arrested its ascent in the sky, waiting. And then, slowly, Josh dismounted.

He took a step toward her, then another. With a muffled cry Anne closed the remaining distance. Their arms wound around each other, their breath and their heartbeats mingled, and they held each other tightly, fiercely, while the sun climbed slowly in the sky and the morning came to life.

Epilogue

January 1, 1900

The parlor, dining room, and entrance hall of Three Hills
had been cleared of furniture and lined with rows of straight
chairs, each row swagged with satin ribbons and garlands of
seasonal greenery. The rows were filled with elaborately
dressed guests representing the most prominent citizens of
the county. The stringed quartet, having exhausted their
repertoire, began Beethoven's Prelude for the fifth time, and
the room was filled with the curious murmurings and
shufflings of concerned guests.

At the back of the room stood the cowhands, uncomfortable in their Sunday best but aware of the honor that had
been bestowed upon them with the invitation—yet uneasy
for more than one reason.

"It's a quarter past three," somebody mumbled, pulling at
his string tie. "What time was this shindig supposed to
start, anyway?"

"You don't reckon he's run out on her, do you?"

"Hell, if anybody's run out, it ain't him. Fancy lady like
Miss Anne—she'll never go through with it."

"I don't know about you boys, but I feel right peculiar
being here."

"I feel peculiar every time I look him in the eye,"

354

somebody else said softly, and there was an uncomfortable silence.

"Well," another put forth after a moment, studying his words, "whatever else you say, you've gotta admire the boy. If it'd been me, after what happened, I woulda hightailed it out of here a long time ago. But he's treated us just like decent folks, like it never happened. He's a good man, and I ain't gonna be ashamed to be riding for his brand."

There were subdued murmurings and nods of consent, for it was still difficult for the men to talk about what had happened that torchlit night three months ago, even among themselves. As though to avoid the awkward turn of the conversation, someone craned his head toward the staircase and, turning back with a sigh, asked again, "What time was this thing supposed to start, anyway?"

In the rows of seated guests marked by bonneted heads and celluloid collars, the subdued murmurs of speculation were much more lively.

"I wonder if anything is wrong?"

"Perhaps someone should go and check."

"She doesn't have anyone standing up for her, does she?"

"You know Miss Anne. Never one to do anything in the ordinary way."

"Do you believe this? Lady Hartley marrying one of her own hired hands!"

"Nothing that woman does surprises me."

"Good heavens, Julia, he's not exactly just *any* hired hand. . . ."

"Funny thing, Jake and Jessica didn't make it out here for the wedding. You'd think they would try—"

"I heard there was some kind of quarrel—"

There was a stirring at the back of the room, and everyone turned.

"Well, looky there. If it's not George Greenley."

"Prancing in here just like he was the father of the bride...."

George Greenley made his way to the very front row, nodding and smiling benificently, causing several people to stand and move over in their seats to accommodate him in the center. After that was done, the guests turned back to their gossip.

"Do you know what I heard? He gave Miss Anne that portrait they've been fighting over for so long as a wedding present. You know, the one of Elizabeth Fielding that he was always bragging about...?"

"Yeah, he and Miss Anne are really tight now."

"Well, it was his testimony that put Stephen Brady behind bars."

"I still can't believe it about old Stephen. He left such a trail of warrants behind him that it'll be a long time before he sees the light of day again."

"Sometimes you just can't tell about people. All these years the president of the bank, and every one of us trusting him with our money." A sigh and a shake of the head. "Stephen Brady turns out to be a crook, and Josh Coleman a Fielding. You just can't tell."

"It'll be something, having Fieldings back at Three Hills."

"Lady Anne Hartley and a Fielding?" There was a muffled snort and a shake of the head. "I give this marriage six months."

"If it ever gets started."

* * *

Upstairs in her bedchamber, Anne smoothed her skirt for the dozenth time, straightened the bodice, and adjusted the lace at her throat. The skirt was of cream-colored peau de soie, molded tightly around the waist and hips and falling into full, graceful lines in back, trimmed at the seams with ecru embroidery. The bodice, of the same cream color, was fashioned with long, narrow sleeves and decorated with ecru lace at the neck and wrists. Anne wore a small cameo at her throat, and a spray of net atop her upswept hair. She carried a small bouquet of yellow hothouse roses imported from Fort Worth, and the effect was simple, elegant, and understated, just as she had planned for it to be. Everything was as she had planned . . . except for one thing.

She went anxiously to the window once again and peered out. It was a dreary, misty winter day, gray and cold. The yard was filled with the carriages and buckboards of waiting guests, but the drive was empty. Already she had delayed forty-five minutes. She couldn't wait any longer.

The door opened, and a breathless Lizabelle rushed in. "Miss Anne, the preacher wants to know if you're about ready. Folks is gettin' mighty restless, and the fiddlers done run outa music and—"

"Yes, yes." Anne glanced once more toward the window. "Has everyone arrived? Have there been any messages?"

Lizabelle puckered her small brow. "Yes'm. No'm. Mist' Greenley, he just walked in, and the house is full and ain't nobody sent regrets."

Anne muffled a sigh. So, then, they weren't coming. Perhaps it was for the best. She had been uncertain even until the moment she had sent the telegram, for she and Josh had argued about the matter before. Perhaps he was right. It was best to put the past behind them—all of the past—and let life begin anew for them on this day. But she had wanted to give him a gift, something no one else could give, a gift of healing and forgiveness. She had been so certain that if only she could bring the family together, everything would be all right.

She couldn't help being disappointed. She had wanted this day to be perfect for both of them, a beginning for their life together that could wash away all the hurt from the past. And now something was missing.

There was a soft knock on the half-open door, and Josh stepped in. He looked magnificent in his dark suit and tie, and just the sight of him made Anne's heart skip a beat. No, she was wrong. Nothing was missing from this day. Not as long as Josh was here.

He smiled at her. "Having second thoughts?" Behind the lightness of his words Anne could see real anxiety in his eyes, and she went toward him quickly, clasping his hands.

"Many," she assured him, squeezing his fingers. "All good."

He searched her eyes, even as the corners of his mouth turned up indulgently. "Last chance to change your mind."

"Oh, no," she answered softly. Her eyes were bright and full of him. "My last chance was over the minute you rode up to my door. What about you?"

She felt the subtle undercurrent of tension within him relax, and he lightly brushed her cheek with the tip of his finger. "I like my mind just the way it is. And after three months of sleeping in the bunkhouse, I'd kind of like to make this thing legal."

She chuckled throatily. "Sleeping in the bunkhouse was your idea."

"I didn't want any gossip," he told her firmly. "I wanted everything to be perfect for you."

She was filled with so much happiness then that she could barely contain it. "It is," she whispered, and wrapped her arm around his. Her face was radiant. "It is."

The ceremony was still and hushed and reverent, a quiet recitation of words that only confirmed the entwining of two hearts and souls and minds that had begun months ago. Anne held Josh's hand throughout so that she could feel the strong, steady beat of his pulse. The sense of rightness between them was a solid, powerful thing, the inevitable conclusion to destiny's plan.

Just before the preacher asked them to repeat their vows, there was a slight draft from the door being opened and closed, a stirring in the congregation. Anne's heart leapt and began to race. Her hand tightened on Josh's, and briefly she closed her eyes in a prayer of thanks. Her voice was trembling with excitement as she promised to love, honor, and obey this man for the rest of her life.

Josh slipped upon her finger a simple gold band, and his kiss was poignant but all too brief. For then the crowd was around them, urging their congratulations, slapping Josh on the back, seeking Anne's cheek for a kiss.

Breathless and laughing, Anne allowed herself to be passed from one embrace to the other. She returned the greetings of her friends and neighbors almost distractedly as she searched the crowd, and then she saw them. She would have known them anywhere.

The woman was lovely. She was shorter than Anne, with a soft, rounded figure and the most beautiful, serene blue eyes Anne had ever seen. She was wearing a lavender wool suit and a small hat and veil atop her hair, which was dark and thick with curls, lightly peppered with gray. She was everything Anne had imagined.

The man who held his wife's elbow protectively as they moved through the crowd had Josh's green eyes and tall, lithe build. There were arrows of gray at his temples, and his face was sun-darkened and weathered. Anne looked at him and could almost see Josh in twenty years. He was a striking figure, distinctive in any crowd, and it was only a moment before the excited murmurs began.

"Jake—"

"Jake Fielding, is that you?"

"By God, it is!"

The crowd parted at the couple's approach, and Anne caught a glimpse of Josh's still, shocked face. Quickly she went forward.

"Jessica!" she exclaimed softly, clasping the other woman's hands. Her own excitement colored her face and sparkled in her eyes, and her words came out in a rush of joy. "I'm so glad you came! The weather has been so foul, and I was so afraid—but you're here, and that's all that matters. Oh, Jessica, I've been so looking forward to meeting you. I feel as though I know you already—" And then she caught herself, blushing a shade deeper. "But listen to me. You must think I'm terribly forward. Do you mind greatly if I call you Jessica?"

Jessica's eyes danced with delight, and she responded, "As a matter of fact, I'd like it much better if you called me Mother." And the two women embraced.

Jessica turned to her husband, her face glowing. "Oh, Jake, look!" she exclaimed softly. "Isn't she lovely?"

Jake smiled and cupped Anne's chin lightly in his hand.

"She looks," he answered, "like a Fielding bride. And that's more beautiful than any woman has a right to be." He leaned forward and kissed Anne's cheek. "Welcome."

He straightened up, and his eyes met Josh's.

There was a stillness, a moment of awkwardness and even dread that pricked at the pit of Anne's stomach as she looked anxiously from her new husband to her parents-in-law. And then Josh said simply, emotionlessly, "What are you doing here?"

Jake met his son's gaze quietly. "You're my only son," he answered. "Did you really think I'd miss your wedding day?"

Anne could see the strain on Josh's face, and her heart ached for him—for all of them. Josh answered, with difficulty, "You don't have to pretend anymore; I know the truth. I'm not your son."

Jessica wound her arm through Jake's, her huge eyes dark with pain. "Yes," she said softly. "You are."

For a moment a flicker of confusion—or perhaps it was anger—crossed Josh's face, and Anne went to him quickly. "Josh, please take your parents into the library where it's quiet. You have a great deal to discuss."

She could feel his pain, and it became her own. He said slowly, "No, I don't think so." With an effort he turned his eyes away from his parents and back to Anne. "I asked you not to do this," he said quietly.

All Anne wanted to do was to take that haunted look from his eyes, to bring back the joy that had been there a moment ago. He had been through so much; must she ask him to endure this too? Had she made a mistake?

But the very stubbornness that had enabled her to endure the ordeals of the autumn would not desert her now, and she lifted her chin. "But I did it," she responded evenly. "They're here, and you must talk to them."

She clasped his arm as he started to turn away. "Josh, please," she whispered, searching his tight and stricken face. "Do this one thing for me. Let's not let anything unfinished from the past spoil this day."

She saw the uncertainty in his eyes. She knew she was hurting him. And she knew he would do this too. Josh turned back to his parents and silently led the way to the library.

Anne watched until the door closed behind the three of them; then she closed her eyes and prayed she had not been wrong.

The sounds of festivity were muted through the thick walls of the library. A cold mist congealed against the window, dripping and smearing the scene outside, and the constant thud and creak of Anne's newest drilling well could be heard far in background, for she kept it in operation even on her wedding day. A fire crackled in the grate, and above the mantelpiece Elizabeth Coleman, restored at last to her rightful home, smiled gently down upon the three who were gathered below.

Jake and Jessica sat close together on the small, high-backed divan, their hands entwined. Josh was opposite them in a brocade wing chair, his hands between his knees, his head bowed. In the room all was very still.

From the moment he had seen the two of them, Josh had been caught in a savage battleground of needs and emotions. There was shock and, for the briefest of moments, an instinctive flare of welcome and joy. They were only his parents, whom he loved. How could he not love the woman who had given him life and the man who had taught him all he knew about living?

The sight of them meant home, familiarity, all that was good about life. He wanted to embrace them and ask about the ranch and the girls, and how they had fared this Christmas without him. He was glad they were here. All that was in an instant, or even less.

Then there was the anger—at Anne, at his parents, and even at himself for feeling anger at all. He still felt hurt and shamed and tainted by what he felt sure was the truth. He had wanted only to forget. He was starting a new life, and they had no right to bring the ugliness of the past to this place. Their unexpected appearance had blotted what should have been the happiest day of his life and left him torn and miserable.

Now that he had heard their story, he did not know how to feel.

His voice was dull, and he could not lift his eyes. "All those stories you used to tell about Grandpa Jed and Elizabeth and Three Hills . . . You never told this one. You never even hinted. . . ."

Jake's voice, too, was heavy. "I wanted you to be proud of who you were and where you had come from. I wanted you to know the best things about being a Fielding."

At last Josh looked up at his father, his face ravaged by a score of emotions too complex to be defined. "But you never did anything wrong." His voice was hoarse. "You were just protecting Ma."

Jake's face was sober. "I spent three years on the run to protect your mother from a crime she committed in self-defense. And I've spent twenty years protecting you from a truth I knew would hurt you. I was wrong," he said simply.

Josh took a long, uneven breath. He focused on the portrait of his grandmother. "They said . . . I thought it was murder."

The brief stab of pain that crossed Jake's eyes tore at Josh's heart. "No, son," he said quietly. "Your mother could no more have murdered that man than I could've killed my own brother. What happened—" His hand tightened on Jessica's. "What happened was a nightmare we tried so much to forget that I guess—I guess maybe we did forget, in a way."

Outside the room there was a burst of laughter, and the booming voice of George Greenley raised above the crowd in some kind of toast. The orchestra struck up a lively tune, and they heard the scuffing sounds of furniture being cleared for dancing. Almost, Josh smiled. Anne had finally learned how to give a party.

"Anne," he said, and once again he had to clear his throat. "She always said there had to be more to it than I knew. I guess she knew my own folks better than I did." He glanced at his mother. "She's a real big admirer of yours, Ma. I think you're going to like her." He tried to smile, but the effort fell short. He was battered inside with all he had learned—the sufferings of his parents that made his own seem petty in comparison.

Jessica did smile, but it was a brave gesture, dredged up through sorrow. Her lashes were damp with tears she had not shed, and she tucked her free hand through Jake's arm, both giving and receiving comfort. "Joshua," she said softly, "I never meant to hurt you. Neither your father nor I ever wanted that."

She lifted her chin in a determined manner that Josh recognized with a start as reminiscent of Anne's. She went on in a stronger voice, "I was married to Daniel Fielding and I had his brother's child. That is my shame. But we've paid for the sins of the past, Joshua. We paid all those years Jake was on the run for a crime he didn't commit, never even knowing he had a son. We paid when Daniel died, struck down by a bullet that was meant for Jake. We paid in all these years of secrecy and deceit. . . . I told myself I was protecting *you*, but I was really only protecting myself. Because *I* was ashamed."

She took a breath, her eyes glittering. "Well, I'm not ashamed anymore, Joshua," she said. "Maybe, through all of this, that's the one good thing that has happened. Because when you left . . . when I saw the look in your eyes that day you left, I had to look back and face it all. And what I found was that it was long past time I stopped being ashamed of the most precious thing in my life. I'm proud of your father, Joshua, and of myself, and of what we built together. You should be proud too."

Jake looked at his wife, his eyes a soft glow of love and tenderness, then he looked back at his son. "I want you to tell this story to your children, Josh," he said soberly. "Don't let them grow up thinking the world is an easy place and that all the heroes wear gold armor. Tell them about their great-grandfathers, Hartley and Fielding, who went to war for this land in the days when people made their own rules. Tell them about your mother and me, and their great-uncle Daniel. None of us were perfect, but we did what we had to do, and we did it for love. Tell them about the only things that last and the only things that matter— family and loving. Don't let them grow up without knowing what it means to be a Fielding."

Josh looked at them, and the room suddenly seemed filled

with the presence of spirits past—Jed and Elizabeth, Anne's Grandfather Hartley, Daniel Fielding—all of them weaving their own threads into the tapestry of his life, marking the map that brought him to this place today. Good and bad, right and wrong, and sometimes a mixture of both, they were an inextricable part of this land and of him. They had brought him Anne, and they had brought him home.

Peace swelled inside him like a tangible thing, along with a mixture of pride and certainty. And love. It was all right. For the first time in his life everything was right.

He got up and crossed the room, bending to embrace his mother. "I'll tell them," he said. His voice broke with emotion, and his mother tightened her arms around him on the whisper of a sob. "I'll tell them," he promised.

Then, with his free arm, he embraced his father, and the three of them held one another tightly for a long time.

Late in the afternoon Jessica once again found Jake in the library. They had danced and visited with old friends, and in a few short hours they had gotten to know—and to love— their new daughter-in-law. Jessica knew her husband would eventually return to this room.

He was standing with a pensive look on his face beside one of the book-lined shelves, an open volume in his hand. Jessica, after so many years of marriage, need not ask what he was thinking. So much had happened in this room. She had married Daniel Fielding in this room, beneath the portrait of his mother above the fireplace. She and Jake had first been introduced in this room. Jake had spent hours at his father's knee here, listening, much as Josh had listened to Jake, to the stories of the past. Of all of Three Hills, this room held the most memories.

Jessica softly closed the door on the continuing celebration outside, and Jake glanced up with a smile. She came toward him, caressing his arm affectionately. "Are you sorry?" she asked softly.

Jake closed the book and returned it to the shelf. "Of course I am. I miss this place, I wish things could have been different. But I can't change the past, and . . ." He looked down at her with the warmth of a smile in his eyes that still had the power to speed her heart. "I wouldn't trade our years together for any of it. We made a good life together, Jessica." He lifted his hand and caressed the back of her neck, toying with the few curls that escaped there. "It wasn't always easy, but it's the hard times that make the good times worth it."

Jessica nodded. "I think our son has learned that too."

"I wouldn't doubt but that you're right." Jake was thoughtful. "You know, when he left us this summer, he was a spoiled, hot-tempered kid. My fault as much as yours, I guess. But when I looked at him today, do you know what I saw?"

"A man," Jessica answered for him, and they smiled at each other.

They slipped their arms around each other's waists and walked to the window. The mist had not let up, and the landscape looked barren and chill. The wooden derrick and drill, less than two hundred yards away, was particularly ugly. But as they watched, two figures crossed the lawn. Anne, a cloak hastily thrown over her wedding dress, and Josh, hatless and still in his wedding suit. They walked with their arms around each other, heads close together, laughing and talking, oblivious to the damp and cold.

Jessica could not help laughing softly with sheer contentment. "Look at them."

"I think he's finally met his match." Jake squeezed her
shoulders, his eyes crinkling with an affectionate grin. "Just
like I did in you."

Jessica rested her head against his shoulder. "I'm glad we
decided to give them the money."

"He'd earned it. Besides, it was selfish on my part, you
know. I want my grandchildren to grow up here the way I
did."

"Well, maybe not exactly the way you did. Times have
changed, Jake."

He kissed her forehead. "For the better, as far as I'm
concerned."

Jessica leaned back against his shoulder again with a
happy sigh, and for a time they simply stood there looking
out the window at the landscape that was so familiar yet
so different, watching the young people with a parental
pride.

Then Jake mused, "Who ever would have thought the
Fieldings would end up here again?"

Jessica chuckled softly. "Who ever would've thought the
Hartleys and the Fieldings would end up here together?"

"It's about time." And he smiled, an absent, far-reaching
smile that seemed to see into the future as well as into the
past. "You know," he said thoughtfully, "I think Pa would
be real proud to see this day."

Jessica turned to him, her eyes glowing with love and
contentment. "I think so too."

Their arms tightened around each other, and they came
together in a kiss.

* * *

Anne tightened her arm around Josh's waist. The cold, gray mist gathered on her face and melted the creases in her gown, but she hardly felt the damp for Josh's warmth. "I'm so glad you're not angry with me," she said.

"I should be." He tried to keep a formidable expression but couldn't manage it. He squeezed her waist briefly, a faint measure of the love and joy that filled him to overflowing. "But it's hard to be mad at a woman who's right. Are you always right?"

"Not at all," she admitted. "Just stubborn." Her eyes sparkled as she looked up at him. "Just like you."

"You should've told me that before I married you."

She struck out at him playfully, but he was prepared. He caught her hands in one of his, and her face in the other, then leaned forward to kiss her on the lips. It was a light kiss, gentle and far too short, for the currents of passion that surged between them were too powerful to be controlled for long.

Josh's eyes were dark and full as he looked down at her; hers were as bright as diamonds. He traced her parted lips and the shades of pink color in her cheeks with an unsteady forefinger. "Anne," he said huskily, "after such a bad beginning . . . can there be a chance for us?"

"I think," she answered softly, "that we both always knew the only chance we had was together."

Josh closed his eyes and took a breath. Every time he was near her, he lost more of himself to her. "I feel," he said slowly, "like you are so much more than I deserve."

Anne laid her forehead lightly against his shoulder, curling her fingers into his lapels. Her own voice was unsteady with emotion. "Perhaps we are both . . . more than either of us deserves. I love you, Josh."

"So much," he added hoarsely, and he could say no

more. He held her tightly, and she held him, until both knew that in only a matter of moments it would be impossible to break away.

They turned once again, their arms entwined, to walk. Anne could feel a slight tremor to Josh's muscles, and her own breath was unsteady. But they had the rest of their lives together. The thought was almost too magnificent for comprehension. The rest of their lives.

Aimlessly, without any real purpose, they were walking toward the derrick. Chance saw them and lifted his arm in greeting. Both returned the wave.

Then Josh said, "Pa wanted me to have my inheritance now. He wants to save the land for the girls and thought I'd have more use for the money."

Anne glanced at him. "They've done well, then."

Josh nodded. "I didn't know how well until I looked at this bank draft." He reached into his pocket and took out a folded paper. "I want you to have this and put it into the oil business."

Anne shrank away. "Oh, no, I couldn't—"

"Listen," he insisted firmly. "I've looked at your books. You've got too much tied up in this scheme to back down now. We've got to try to get back some of what you put in, and the only way to do that is to hire a real geologist and put in some more wells."

Anne shook her head, that stubborn look coming into her eyes. "No, Josh, you were right. The only way to keep this ranch going is to start putting money in it. Cattle are our cash crop, and the proceeds from that are what will finance the rest of the operation. You know about cattle; take the money and put it in breeding stock."

A trace of impatience crossed Josh's eyes. "Cattle won't make the kind of money we need."

"I've squandered too much on pipe dreams already—"

"Confound it, woman, you'll be arguing about something to your dying day! I'm trying to tell you—"

"You're supposed to be so levelheaded!" Her eyes were flashing. "From the moment you got here you've been trying to tell me how to run this ranch, and now you've changed your mind. This is a *cattle* ranch! Are you going to manage it or not?"

The annoyance in Josh's eyes faded to amusement with the lift of her chin, the spark in her eyes. He said, "First maybe I'd better learn how to manage my wife."

"Good luck on that, sir!" she retorted with a toss of her head, and he suddenly drew her into his arms and kissed her.

"I think you may be learning," she murmured a little shakily when at last they parted.

Josh smiled at her, his color high, his eyes bright. "Half oil, half cattle?" he suggested.

Anne, somewhat dazzled, nodded, and went into his arms again.

There was a distant roar of thunder, and suddenly the very ground beneath their feet began to shake. They whirled around, and the rumbling grew louder. Chance shouted something and started to run, just before the derrick less than fifty feet in front of them began to sway.

Josh grabbed Anne's waist and tried to drag her away, but she stood rooted to the spot. In a single, magnificent instant the ground beneath the derrick erupted with a roar into a geyser of mud and gumbo. Pipes snapped and creaked, debris scattered through the air. Josh shouted at her, grab-

bing her waist, but Anne stood on that spot, staring.
Another explosion erupted, mightier than the first, and a
huge spout of green-black liquid shot from the ground high
over the derrick.

The sky began to rain dark slush; it spattered Anne's dress,
matted her hair, streaked across her face, and blurred her
eyes. She tasted it and opened her fingers to it as she stood
transfixed in a cloudburst of thick green slime, laughing and
weeping and crying, "Oil! Josh, it's oil!"

Josh's face and hands were smeared with the rich, dark
stuff. He clutched Anne's waist and looked at her, his eyes
stunned and disbelieving, then turned toward the derrick.
His face was brilliant with incredulous joy, and he shouted,
"It is! By God, I think it is!"

She heard Chance's voice yelling instructions. People
were pouring from the house, their expressions frightened
and alarmed, shouting and questioning and staring at the
sky. Josh and Anne stood in the center of it all, their hands
upheld to the sky, laughing senselessly.

Jake and Jessica reached them first. "Mother Fielding!"
Anne cried, grabbing her hand in a slippery, oil-smeared
grip. "It's oil! It is! It finally happened—it's oil!"

"Damn it, it is!" Jake exclaimed, and pounded his son
on the back. "I've never seen anything like this—Jessica,
look at this!"

Jessica said, "Is it worth anything?"

Then everyone began to laugh; Anne hugged Jessica and
Josh hugged Jake, and oil poured down in a great, thundering deluge on all of them. And then Anne found herself in
Josh's arms again, and the shouting, shoving, running
people, the mineral cloudburst around them, all faded away,

and there was nothing but the two of them as she looked into his eyes.

"Happy new year, darling," he said softly.

Anne ran a hand through his oil-slick curls. Her eyes were brilliant beacons from the midst of her own glistening, sooty mask, and she replied, "Welcome to the twentieth century."

And their mouths met in a single long, triumphant kiss.

On a nearby hillside the mist rolled away, and just for a moment the summer sun shone brightly. The breeze was warm and fragrant, and the barren January ground was carpeted in daisies.

Looking down at the scene below stood a tall blond giant of a man in buckskins and a dark-haired woman with laughing green eyes dressed in the fashions of fifty years before. Their hands touched, their eyes smiled, and their gazes moved from the scene below and toward each other.

It lasted for only an instant, and then they turned and slowly walked away, their figures growing dimmer and dimmer until they were swallowed again by the mist.

Author's Note

Although oil had been drilled sporadically in Texas since the early part of the nineteenth century, few people at that time thought of oil as one of Texas's chief commodities. Even after the Blizzard of 1891, which began the decline of the great cattle empires of the American West, only a few men and women of vision recognized the value of the mineral resources that lay beneath the Texas ground. It would be the early part of the twentieth century before their visions were fully realized.

The Corsicana strike of 1894 was one of the first profitable oil fields in Texas, and one of the first to compete with oil fields in the East by building its own refinery. On January 10, 1901, the Spindletop gusher was brought in at Beaumont, Texas, and ushered in the beginning of a new empire in Texas: one built on oil.

About the Author

Leigh Bristol is a pseudonym for Donna Ball and Shannon Harper, who have written some fifty novels under various pen names, including Rebecca Flanders.